The Eridanos Library

Gabriele D'Annunzio

THE FLAME

Translated from the Italian by
SUSAN BASSNETT

The Eridanos Library
MARSILIO PUBLISHERS

Original Italian Title
Il fuoco (1900)

Published in the USA
by arrangement with Quartet Books, London,
by Marsilio Publishers
853 Broadway, Suite 600
New York, NY 10003

Distributed in the USA by
Consortium Book Sales and Distribution
1045 Westgate Drive
St. Paul, MN 55114

ISBN 0-941419-89-4

PRINTED IN ITALY

CONTENTS

INTRODUCTION

Il fuoco was first published in 1900 and caused an immediate scandal. A French translation came out within weeks, followed by an English edition entitled *The Flame of Life*, and critics throughout Europe expressed their outrage, one even calling it 'the most swinish novel ever written', and when the great actress Sarah Bernhardt was sent a copy by the author, she returned it unread.

Like Byron before him, D'Annunzio lived in the public eye. His earlier novels, such as *Il piacere*, *L'innocente* and *Il trionfo della morte* were all considered shocking on account of their voluptuous sensuality and their preoccupation with death and morbid relationships. D'Annunzio's private life was no less sensational: he eloped with a Roman aristocrat when he was barely twenty and subsequently, while the marriage continued in name only, became involved with a series of wealthy, often married women, many of whom lost their reputations and their fortunes when the love affair came to an end.

His declared ambition was to find a unity of life and art, and he romanticized himself as a dangerous, almost diabolical man, a great lover, the finest writer of his day, a poet with a mission to revitalize Italian literature and create a new aesthetic for a new age. The speech that Stelio Effrena gives to the Venetian nobility in the first part of *Il fuoco* is based on a speech D'Annunzio himself gave in 1895, in which he expressed his beliefs about the relationship of beauty and sensuality to art.

D'Annunzio was born in 1863 into a middle-class family in the coastal town of Pescara. While still at school in Florence, he published his first collection of poems; even at that time his flair for self-dramatization was apparent, as was his belief that poetry should disturb and should celebrate the sensual. Influenced by Baudelaire and the French decadents, D'Annunzio is nevertheless different from other writers of his day. He saw himself as a man of action, a contemporary Renaissance hero, and rejected the image of the poet as a contemplative. Born too late to take a part in the unification of Italy or to have fought alongside Garibaldi, he yearned for a similar moment of history in which to prove his mettle. Much later on, at the age of fifty-six, in protest against the drawing of Italian boundaries under the treaty of Versailles, he crossed the Adriatic in 1919 with two thousand 'legionaries' – deserters from the Italian army – and took Fiume, becoming *comandante* of the city for fifteen months. His outrageous gesture was repudiated by the government of the day, and D'Annunzio and his men were forced to withdraw, but by many he was acclaimed a national hero, and photographs of the artist turned man-of-action in military uniform were widely admired. From this time until his death in 1938 he lived in a luxurious villa on the shores of Lake Garda, surrounded by acolytes.

However, at the time he wrote *Il fuoco*, D'Annunzio's military career was a long way off. Well established as a poet and novelist, he was intent on developing his career as a playwright, and it seemed at last that he was finding a way to integrate his personal life with his work. In 1894, in Venice which provides the setting for *Il fuoco*, he began a relationship with Eleanora Duse which lasted until 1904. At that time La Duse, unquestionably the greatest actress of her day, was at the height of her career. In the early stages of their passionate affair, they shared a belief in the need for a new Italian poetic drama and dreamed of establishing a huge open-air theatre in the Alban hills outside Rome, similar to that imagined by Foscarina, Stelio and his friends in the novel: 'Let us have a marble theatre on a Roman hill!' Like D'Annunzio, Stelio sees himself as bearing a torch of artistic vision, which he received from the 'creative barbarian', the dying Wagner. D'Annunzio wanted his work to be performed to the masses in great arenas by the greatest performers. La Duse, for her part, was in search of more demanding roles, and she was constantly looking for plays which would revolutionize the conventional repertoire of the day. She was drawn to writers, and before D'Annunzio had been involved for many years with Verdi's librettist Arrigo Boito, who had written several pieces for her.

The idyll did not last very long. Quite apart from D'Annunzio's inability to remain faithful, he was also immensely ambitious. He wrote a play for her, *La città morta (The Dead City)*, in 1895, with the same plot as the play Stelio is writing for Foscarina, and then gave it to La Duse's greatest rival, Sarah Bernhardt, instead, an act of betrayal that La Duse found difficult to endure. Two years later La Duse appeared in his next play, *Il sogno d'un mattino di primavera (Dream of a Spring Morning)*, but it was not a success. Indeed, on the whole D'Annunzio's plays were not popular, and although La Duse insisted on touring in them, she consistently lost money, especially outside Italy. Ironically, his one great success in the theatre, *La figlia di Iorio (Iorio's Daughter)*, starred Irma Gramatica in the title role, when La Duse was taken ill and unable to perform and D'Annunzio refused to delay the opening. The success of that play, which she had been denied, was probably the final straw in their troubled partnership, and a few months later La Duse left him for good.

Il fuoco aroused such a storm because it is a *roman à clef*; its details suggest that D'Annunzio must have kept notes of La Duse's most intimate confessions. She is depicted as an ageing heroine, 'the woman who is no longer young', contrasted with her lover, 'the young man' (although at thirty-one, D'Annunzio was only four years younger than La Duse). Her rival in the novel is a singer, the 'slender youthful virgin', a second muse for the perfection of the hero's art.

Critics were also shocked by Stelio's confession that his desire for Foscarina is fuelled by his fantasy of her being possessed by many other men. That image is twofold: as an older woman she has enjoyed many intimate experiences, as an actress he sees her as being forever possessed by her audiences. He experiences 'an envy which turned his desire to madness', and his feelings are shaped by 'cruelty, bitterness, poetry and pride'.

Somehow D'Annunzio managed to convince La Duse that his writing of *Il fuoco* was indispensable to great art. La Duse knew he was writing it; he even read passages to her and to Antongini, his private secretary and later biographer, who claimed he saw her on several occasions correcting fragments of the manuscript. Even as early as 1898, her impresario Schurmann had questioned the wisdom of allowing him to use their love affair as material for a novel, and she had explained in a brief note that she was willing to allow publication because 'my suffering, however great, is of no account when it is a question of enriching Italian literature with yet another masterpiece'. She later confessed, 'I am a forty-one-year-old woman in love', though when at last she broke with D'Annunzio her bitterness at what she called 'that Book, that perverse Book' finally emerged.

Though D'Annunzio claimed to adore his mother and to love a great many women, he portrayed his heroines suffering mental torture and physical pain and disability; when passion dies their role is to serve. D'Annunzio's heroes on the other hand are powerful, and always excessive in their passions, behaviour and aspirations. Ultimately the man rejects the woman; in *Il fuoco*, Stelio is aroused sexually and inspired creatively by women, but he is also repelled by them, finding true freedom only when he is absent from them – out at sea, riding with his hounds or expounding his theories to faithful male followers. D'Annunzio's brilliant portrayal of the heroine's passion and vulnerability contains deliberate cruelty, and there is no hint of a resolution of the author's ambiguous feelings towards women in *Il fuoco*.

After the Second World War came the reconstruction of Italy as a nation and fascism was firmly rejected by mainstream opinion. D'Annunzio's *fin-de-siécle*-style nationalism had led him to make links with Mussolini in the 1920s and his remarkable mystique had faded. As an artist too he lost popularity; the excesses of both his style and his ideas had gone out of fashion. Although his lyric poetry continued to be read, his plays and novels were forgotten and he came to be considered a parody of the decadent aesthete.

But there are signs now, in the 1990s, of renewed interest in D'Annunzio's work. There have been several films based on his writings, notably Visconti's *L'innocente* (*The Intruder*, 1976); his novels have been republished and his contribution to Italian literature and to the question of the power struggle between men and women, is being reassessed. For his works are more than idiosyncratic autobiographical tracts; he wrote with energy and commitment and addresses themes shared by such diverse fellow modernists as Artaud, Jarry and D. H. Lawrence. Though D'Annunzio's writings are megalomanic, they are nevertheless innovative and original; he tried to link the modern world with the greatness of the Italian literary tradition and the mythological past of the Graeco-Roman world.

Il fuoco has been forgotten for the best part of a century. It deserves to be reread for its remarkable linguistic power, and as a novel about the processes of creation and the renewal of life, in which two gifted artists engage in a passionate struggle for their love and their work. It is an example of literature that bridges symbolism and modernism, and the nineteenth and twentieth centuries. Part autobiography, part fiction, *Il fuoco* is about a real passion for the past and an exalted hope for the future: 'The heartbeat of the crowd and the poet's role give life back to the age-old walls . . . the people see the world with new eyes, feel, think and dream with new souls.'

Susan Bassnett

. . . fa come natura face in foco

(. . . do as Nature does in fire)

Dante Alighieri

I

THE EPIPHANY OF FIRE

'Stelio, isn't your heart beating fast for the first time?' asked Foscarina, with a slight smile, touching the hand of her silent lover, sitting next to her. 'You seem to me to be preoccupied and rather pale. This is such a wonderful, triumphal evening for a great poet!'

Her gaze brought all the extended beauty of that late September twilight perfectly into her knowing eyes, so that in those dark, living orbits the garlands of light which the oar formed in the water close at hand clasped the shining angels that gleamed down from the bell-towers of San Marco and San Giorgio Maggiore.

'As always happens,' she added in her softest voice, 'as always happens, everything is in your favour. On such an evening as this, what soul could shut out the dreams that you so love to summon up with words? Don't you already feel how eager the people are to hear what you are going to reveal?'

She went on soothing her lover gently in this way, wrapping him in an endless web of flattery, praising him continuously.

'One couldn't imagine a more splendid, more exceptional occasion that might bring a lofty poet like yourself down from his ivory tower. This special pleasure was reserved for you alone; only you are able to talk to the people for the first time in such a regal place as the Sala del Maggior

Consiglio, standing on the very balcony where the Doge used to address the gathering of patricians, with Tintoretto's *Paradise* behind you and Veronese's *Gloria* above your head.'

Stelio Effrena looked into her eyes. 'Are you trying to intoxicate me?' he asked, with a sudden burst of gaiety. 'This is the chalice that one offers to a man about to face his own death. But, yes, my dearest, I have to confess that my heart is beating a little faster.'

The sound of applause rose from the San Gregorio ferry and echoed along the Grand Canal, reflected back from the precious discs of porphyry and serpentine that are studded along the house of the Darios, bent over beneath the weight of its own ornament like an aged courtesan.

The royal barge went past. 'There is the woman who will be among your audience and who the occasion demands must be singled out for special attention from the beginning,' said the flattering woman, referring to the Queen. 'In one of your first books, I think I recall you admitting how much you respected and loved ceremonial occasions. One of your most extraordinary creations is your imagined day in the life of Charles II of Spain.'

The barge sailed close to the gondola, and the couple bowed as it passed. As she recognized the author of *Persephone* and the great tragic actress, the Queen turned round spontaneously out of curiosity, blonde and rosy-cheeked, her face alight with the freshness of her smile that never seemed to fade and shone out from the pale wreaths of Buranese lace around her. Beside her was the lady of Burano, Andriana Duodo, who cultivated a garden of web-like lace on the busy little island where antique flowers were gloriously restored.

'Don't you think that those two ladies have twin smiles, Stelio?' said Foscarina, watching the rush of water in the wake of the vanishing stern, where the reflection of that double sweetness seemed to linger on.

'The countess has a marvellously open heart, she is one of those rare Venetian souls who has stayed as vibrant as an image from an ancient painting,' said Stelio thankfully. 'I adore her sensitive hands from the bottom of my heart. They are hands that quiver with pleasure when they touch beautiful lace or velvet, and linger over the touching with a grace that is almost ashamed of its own softness. One day, as I was walking through the halls of the Academy with her, she paused before the *Massacre of the Innocents* by Boniface the Elder (you must remember that shade of green in the robes of the woman who has been thrown to the ground and is about to be butchered by one of Herod's soldiers, it is quite unforgettable!). She stood there a long time, and a sense of fullness and perfection emanated from her whole being, then she said: "Take me away, Effrena. I must leave my eyes here on that garment, I cannot bear to see anything else . . ." Oh, my dearest, don't laugh! She was so sincere and naïve when she said that; she really had left her eyes there on that scrap of canvas which art with just a little hint of colour had turned into the centre of infinitely joyous mystery. And I really was accompanying a blind woman, and I felt such reverence for her privileged soul where the magic of a colour had been able to produce such an impact that she actually forgot all about everyday life for a while and was unable to communicate at all. How would you describe such a thing? It seems to me that it fills one's cup to overflowing. And that is what I would like to do tonight if I did not feel so downhearted.'

Another, even louder burst of applause that lasted a while longer came from the two tutelary pillars of granite as the barge drew near to the crowded piazza. The densely packed, dark crowd swayed, the rooms of the Doge's Palace were filled with a confused roar like the imaginary sound that stirs in the curves of seashells. All of a sudden a shout rose up in the clear air and shattered against the slender marble forest, then leaped over the brows of the tall statues right up to the pinnacles and crosses and was finally lost in twilight and distance. Undisturbed by the agitation from below, the variegated harmony of sacred and profane buildings flowed on, while the Ionic modulations of the Biblioteca

5

rippled like a melody and the tip of the naked tower reared up like a mystic cry. And that silent music of immobile lines was so powerful that it created the almost visible phantom of a fuller, richer life in contrast to the sight of the agitated crowd. That crowd also seemed to sense the holiness of the moment; and by hailing the new image of royalty, the lovely blonde queen with her inextinguishable smile, as she drew up to the ancient landing stage, perhaps they were expressing some vague desire to transcend the narrowness of ordinary vulgar life and to harvest the gifts that eternal poetry cast upon the stones and on the water. The strong, covetous souls of their forefathers who used to applaud the triumphal mariners on their return from the sea began to reawaken in those men who were oppressed by boredom and the ᴊil of long days of mediocrity. They seemed to recall how great battle flags had stirred the air and then folded themselves like the wings of Victory after flight, or how the implacable sound of those flags had shamed vanquished enemy fleets.

'Perdita,' asked Stelio abruptly, 'do you know any other place in the world like Venice that sometimes has the power to stir great forces in human life and arouse desires to fever pitch? Have you ever encountered a more devastating temptress?'

The woman he called Perdita did not reply, though her face was wrapt in concentration and she felt the indefinable shudder right through her body that her young lover's voice always produced when he suddenly opened up his tumultuous, passionate soul, to which she was drawn by boundless love but also by utter terror.

'Peace! Oblivion! Do you ever find such things down there, at the end of your deserted canal, when you go home drained and exhausted after absorbing all the applause from audiences you drive wild with a single gesture? For my part, whenever I find myself floating on these dead waters, I feel that my life is expanding at tremendous speed, and sometimes it feels as though my thoughts were actually on fire, as though I were about to become delirious.'

6

'You have such strength and fire in you, Stelio,' said the woman almost humbly, without raising her eyes. He was silent, intent. Impetuous images and sounds were taking place within him, as though some mysterious process of fertilization were going on, and he rejoiced in that unexpected flood of richness.

It was still evening, the time that he had described in one of his books as Titian's hour, because everything seemed to be gleaming with its own rich inner glow, like that painter's naked bodies, almost lighting up the sky rather than taking light from it. The octagonal temple of the Salute, designed by Baldassare Longhena from the Dream of Polifilus, rose up out of its own glassy reflection, with its dome, its scrolls, its statues, its columns, and its balustrades, as rich and strange as one of Neptune's buildings with its tortuous sea-shapes, glistening with mother-of-pearl. Salt and damp had spread over it, and seemed to have left something fresh, silvery and jewel-like in the hollows of the stones that gave the vague impression of open oystershells lying in their pearly bed.

'Perdita,' said the poet, feeling a sense of intellectual joy run through him as he saw his imaginings taking shape around him, 'don't you feel we are part of Summer's own funeral procession? There she lies, in her funeral barge, dressed in gold like the wife of a Doge, like a Loredana or a Morosina or a Soranza from the glorious past. The cortège sails out towards the island of Murano where a master of glass-making, a Lord of Fire, seals her into a crystal coffin, and then when her body sinks into the lagoon she will stare out through her diaphanous eyelids and watch the swirling play of seaweed and believe that it is her own richly flowing hair waving around her body as she waits for the time when she will be born again.'

A spontaneous smile spread across Foscarina's face, starting in her eyes which really seemed to have seen the beautiful image. His unexpected story had indeed caught the feeling that was present in their surroundings, both in its rhythm and its imagery. Just as the milky blue of an opal

7

is filled with hidden sparks, so the still, pale waters of the great lagoon mirrored a deceptive splendour that was stirred by the movement of the oars. Beyond the stiff forest of ships at anchor, San Giorgio Maggiore emerged like a great rose-pink galley, its prow turned towards Fortune who called to it from the top of her gilded sphere. In the centre was the expanse of the Giudecca canal, like a placid estuary where the heavily laden ships that had come downriver brought with their cargoes of hewn logs the very spirit of the woods that bend over distant running waters. And from the quay, where the red and white wall over the double row of porticos open to popular acclaim ran down to embrace the greatest of dominating wills, the Riva stretched out in a gentle curve towards the shadowy Gardens, towards the fertile islands, as though it were leading natural forms of thought inspired by the blazing symbols of art to a place of rest. As though celebrating the summoning of autumn, a row of barges sailed past, piled high with fruit, like great floating baskets, spreading the scent of island orchards over the water in which the leafy pattern of cusps and capitols were forever reflected.

'Perdita,' said Stelio again, watching with obvious plea-sure as the barges sailed past, piled high from stem to stern with golden grapes and violet figs in an arrangement that was not unharmonious, 'have you ever heard one especially charming story about the Doges of old? The Doge's wife had certain privileges deriving from a tax on fruit that enabled her to defray the cost of her state robes. Don't you find that amusing, Perdita? Fruit from the islands dressed her in gold and hung pearls round her neck. The goddess Pomona granting Arachne her due: now there is an allegory that Veronese might have painted on the ceiling of the Robing Chamber. I feel such delight when I imagine that stately woman with the high jewel-encrusted heels on her shoes, and I think that she had something fresh and natural concealed in the folds of those heavy garments – the great gift of fruit. Her richness takes on such flavour! Now, my dearest, imagine that these grapes and these figs belonging to today's autumn will provide the price of a golden gown covering the body of our dead summer.'

'What a charming thought, Stelio,' said Foscarina, suddenly recovering her own youthfulness as she smiled in wonder like a little girl who has just been shown a picture-book. 'Who was it who once described you as the Great Image-maker?'

'Images,' exclaimed the poet, as a fertile glow raced through him. 'When one is in Venice, one cannot feel except through music or think except through images. They come from everywhere in such profusion, endlessly, they are more real and alive than the people who jostle us in a narrow street. We can bend down and gaze into the depths of their devoted eyes and divine the words they will say to us by the sinuous way their eloquent lips move. Some images are tyrannical, like overbearing lovers, and hold us beneath the yoke of their power for far too long. Others appear wreathed in veils like virgins, or tightly swaddled like infants, and only one who knows how to tear those coverings away can raise them up and transform them into perfect life. Today when I awoke my soul was already filled with such images, it was like a great tree laden with chrysalises.'

He paused and laughed. 'If all those chrysalises open tonight,' he said, 'then I shall be saved. But if they stay closed, I shall be lost.'

'Lost?' said Foscarina, looking into his face with eyes so brimming with confidence that he felt a deep sense of gratitude. 'You could never be lost, Stelio. You are always so sure of yourself. You hold your destiny in your own hands. I think your mother must never ever have worried about you, not even at the worst of times. Isn't that right? The only thing that makes your heart uneasy is pride . . .'

'Oh, my dearest, I love you so and I am so thankful to you for this!' Stelio confessed openly, taking her hand. 'You keep feeding that pride of mine and you make me believe that I really have reached the heights that I aspire to all the time. I sometimes feel that you have the power to bestow some kind of divine quality on the things that are made in my heart, so that they even seem worthy of adoration in my eyes. Sometimes you arouse in me a sense of holy fervour, like the sculptor who took the images he had made of the gods into the temple one night, when they were still warm from the pressure of his hands, still marked by the touch of his shaping fingers, and then next morning he saw them standing on their pedestals, wreathed in a cloud of incense, breathing godliness from every pore through the dull clay out of which his mortal hands had made them. My dearest, every time you touch my soul you perform a similar miracle. That is why, whenever fate allows me to spend some time with you, you become essential to my life. Even through those long – too long – periods when we are apart, I can still live and you can live too because we both know what marvels can arise out of the perfect union of our two lives. So while I know what it is that you give to me and, moreover, what you could give to me, I feel that you are lost to me, and when I call you by that special name that I so love to use I am trying to express my awareness and my infinite regret that . . .' He broke off, feeling the trembling of the hand he still held in his. 'When I call you Perdita,' he went on in a low voice after the pause, 'I feel that you ought to see my desire advancing towards you with a lethal weapon buried in its heaving side. Even if it managed to touch you, the tips of its rapacious fingers would already be turned to ice.'

A suffering that she knew well came over her, as she listened to the skilful, beautifully wrought words that came from her lover's lips with a readiness that proved he was sincere. Once again she felt an uneasiness and a sense of fear that she could not explain. She seemed to lose touch with her own life and to be moved into a kind of intense, hallucinatory fictitious life where it was difficult even to breathe. She was compelled into that blazing environment as though into a forge, where she felt herself succumb to all the transfigurations that the creator imposed upon her to satisfy his constant need for beauty and for poetry. She felt that the manner in which her own image appeared in his poetic

10

spirit was not dissimilar in nature from that of dead Summer, enclosed in her crystal coffin, and yet still so clear as to appear tangible. She was assailed by an almost childish desire to look into his eyes, as though into a mirror, in search of herself, so as to see her real image reflected back at her. What made her suffering more serious was her recognition of a vague analogy between those agitated feelings and the anxiety that overcame her whenever she was about to create a sublime artistic role through the fiction of theatre. Was he not driving her to live in that same loftier realm of life, and was he not hiding her behind magnificent ghostly creations so that she could forget her own everyday being? But while she was not given to living at such a pitch of intensity without tremendous effort, she saw that he could sustain it as easily as if it were his natural way of life, and that he could rejoice in the miraculous world that he was constantly renewing through continuous creativity.

He had reached the point himself of being able to combine art and life intimately together and so find in the depths of his being an unending source of harmony. He had reached the point of being able to renew ceaselessly in his own spirit that mysterious state that results in the birth of works of great beauty, and he was able to transform all the fleeting characters of his own existence miraculously into ideal figures. He had referred to precisely this capacity of his when he had made one of his characters say: 'I saw within myself the constant process of genesis of a higher life-form in which all appearance was transfigured as though by the power of a magic mirror.' He had an extraordinary gift with words, and was able to translate instantly even the most complex aspects of his own sensitivity into his own language with such precision and such vivid detail that sometimes the moment they were uttered they seemed to belong to him no longer, and seemed to be made objective through the power to isolate that his style possessed. His clear, penetrating voice seemed to shape the clear outlines of the musicality of every word, and added emphasis to the singular quality of everything he said. So much so, that sometimes

11

when people heard him for the first time they felt an ambiguous mingling of admiration and revulsion, for he expressed himself in such strongly determined forms that appeared to derive from a constant desire to establish the profoundly unsurmountable distance between himself and others. But since his sensitivity was as great as his intellect, those who loved him and were close to him were easily able to catch the warmth of his passion and enthusiasm through the crystal clarity of his words. They knew the extent of his ability to feel and to dream, and they knew that out of that combination flowed the beautiful images into which he habitually transformed the substance of his own inner life.

The woman called Perdita knew that only too well. Like a pious woman waiting for the supernatural aid of her Lord in order to realize her own salvation, she seemed to be waiting for him to bring about in her the state of grace that would ensure her elevation into the same flame. She was driven towards that flame by a wild desire for immolation and destruction, desperate at having lost the last vestige of her youth and terrified of finding herself alone in a desert of ashes.

'Now it is you, Stelio,' she said with her slight, enigmatic smile, pulling her hand completely away from that of her lover, 'that is trying to intoxicate me. Look,' she exclaimed, to break the spell, pointing to a loaded barge coming slowly towards them, 'there are your pomegranates.' But her voice was unsteady.

In that dream-like evening, they watched the barge sail past over the water that was coloured with the delicate green and silver of new willow leaves, piled high with the symbolic fruits that stirred images of rich and secret things, and looked almost like red leather jewel-cases containing the crown of a beneficent king. Some of the fruits were closed, others lay half-open revealing the clusters of treasure within.

In a low voice, the woman repeated the words Hades addresses to Demeter's daughter Persephone in the sacred tale, when she tastes the fatal pomegranate:

'When you pluck the Colchian herb in flower on the soft
earthly meadow, close to your blue-robed mother,
– just as one day the lovely Oceanides will walk
beside you in that meadow – there will come into
   your immortal eyes
a sudden weariness, the weariness of daylight.
Your heart will tremble, Persephone, your great soul,
recalling its dark dream, Persephone, will mourn for
its dark kingdom. Then shall the blue-robed mother
see you weeping silently apart.
And you will say: Oh mother, Hades calls me from
his dark kingdom, Hades calls me back from daylight
to rule over Shadows; Hades calls me back alone,
back to his insatiable desire . . .'

'Oh, Perdita, how well you bring that darkness into your
voice,' the poet interrupted, feeling a sense of harmonious
night fall over the lines she was reciting. 'How skilfully you
can turn yourself from evening into night. Do you recall
the scene where Persephone is about to throw herself into
Erebus while the chorus of Oceanides are lamenting? Her
face is just like yours when the shadows pass across it. She
stands stiffly in her saffron robe, her crowned head thrown
back, and it is as though night itself were flowing through
her bloodless flesh, gathering there beneath her chin, in the
hollows of her eyes, around her nostrils, transforming her
into a darkly tragic mask. That is your mask, Perdita.
Remembering you helped me to summon up that divine
being as I was writing my Mystery. That narrow saffron
ribbon you almost always wear round your neck showed
me the colour that Persephone's robe should have. And one
evening in your house, as I was saying goodbye to you in
the doorway of a room where the lamps had not yet been
lit (you may remember, it was a stormy evening last
autumn), just one gesture of yours succeeded in bringing to
light in my mind the woman who was still waiting to be
unveiled. You never realized that you had brought about
such a birth, and you disappeared into the intimate darkness

13

of your own Erebus. I was so sure I could hear you sobbing, and yet there was a torrent of unstoppable joy racing through me. I have never told you this before, have I? I should dedicate my work to you, my ideal Lucina.'

She was suffering, as the creator looked at her, the mask on her face that he so admired made her suffer, and so did the joy that she could tell was always bubbling up inside him like a spring that would never run dry. Her whole being made her suffer, with the changes of expression that passed across her features, with the strange gift of acting that took over her facial muscles, with that involuntary skill that controlled the meaning of her gestures, with that shadowy expressiveness that she had so often known how to convey in her face in moments of expectant silence when she was on stage like a magnificent veil of anguish; that shadow made her suffer, which crept into the furrows that time had marked in her no longer youthful body. Cruelly, the hand that she adored made her suffer too, that noble, delicate hand that could still cause so much pain even with a gift or with a caress.

'Perdita,' said Stelio after a pause, during which he had followed the sharp curving path of his thoughts which left dark, isolated spaces in his mind where he knew that great riches would be found when the time was right, 'do you believe in the hidden power of signs? I don't mean horoscopes or astral powers. I mean that just as some people believe they are under the influence of a particular star, so we might be able to create some ideal correspondence between our own souls and some other earthly thing. Then that thing might gradually become steeped in our essences and become so huge in our minds that it might seem like the symbol of our very destiny and take on mysterious qualities at certain times in our lives. That's the secret of restoring some sense of primordial energy to our somewhat stultified souls. I know from experience how great a benefit we can derive from intense communication with some earthly thing. We have to transform our souls into something

14

other, so as to feel the vital energy of the living tree flowing through our veins, as wood-nymphs do.

'You must already have realized that when I talk like this I am referring to the words you spoke out there on the boat. You summed up all these feelings so succinctly when you said "There are your pomegranates!" You and everyone else who truly loves me know that they can never be anything but mine. For all of you, your idea of who I am is indissolubly bound up with the fruit that I have chosen as my personal symbol and which I have endowed with more ideal meanings than the seeds inside it. If I had lived in the days when men excavating Greek statues could still uncover the moist roots of ancient myths buried in the earth, then no painter would have been able to depict me on canvas without first giving me a pomegranate to hold in my hand. Trying to separate me from my symbol would have seemed to that naïve painter like cutting out a vital part of me, because in his pagan imagination the fruit would have seemed to be joined to the human arm as though to its natural branch. He would not have conceived an idea of me any different from his idea of Hyacinth or Narcissus or Ciparissus, who would all have appeared to him alternately as youthful figures or as symbolic plants. But even now there are a few skilful, colourful spirits who understand the full meaning and can really savour my imaginings. Perdita, even you enjoy growing that gorgeous pomegranate tree in your garden so as to see me blossom and bear fruit every summer, don't you? One of your letters, that really did come to me like a divine winged messenger, once told me about the special ceremony that you held when you decorated the tree with garlands on the day you received the first copy of *Persephone*. So you see, for you and those few who really do love me, I have truly brought an ancient myth to life again by turning myself in some profound, meaningful way into an aspect of eternal Nature. When I die (may Nature grant me fully to realize myself through my work before I die!) my disciples will worship me through the symbol of the pomegranate, and in the sharpness of its leaf

15

and the fiery colour of its blossom and the jewel-like quality of its fruits they will recognize some of the qualities of my work. By that leaf and that blossom and that fruit their minds will be led towards the flames and the riches within, as though their own dead master were speaking directly to them. You are only just finding out what the real benefits are, aren't you, Perdita? I have been led through some sense of affinity to develop my talents in accordance with the genius of the pomegranate, the tree that I so love to see as the symbol of my desire for a richer, more ardent life. I feel as though this tree, this vegetable effigy of myself, were able to reassure me that my strength will grow according to nature's plan and will lead to the result that is my destiny. *Natura cosí mi dispone** was Leonardo's epigraph that I wrote on the frontispiece of my first book. And the pomegranate that flowers and bears fruit keeps repeating that motto to me. We have to obey the laws inscribed in our own substance, that's how we stay whole amid so much fragmentation, bonded joyfully in unity and fullness. There is no discord between my life and my work.'

He was speaking quite freely and fluently, as though he could see the soul of the woman listening to him becoming concave, turning into a chalice to receive the flow of words and he wanted to fill that chalice to the brim. A sense of intellectual joy began to filter through him, growing stronger all the time, together with a vague awareness of the mysterious process that was taking place in his mind, preparing it for the next step. Now and then, as he leaned towards his lonely lover, listening to the sound of the oar measuring the deep silence of the immense estuary, he would see images flashing through his mind of a crowd of countless faces gathered in the great hall, and his heart would miss a beat.

'It is remarkable, Perdita,' he said, watching the pale, distant water-line, where low tide was starting to mark the shore with black patches, 'how easy it is for fate to help

* Nature so disposes towards me.

one's imagination in giving a certain quality of mysteriousness to things one sees in respect to things one imagines. I don't understand why poets today are so contemptuous about the vulgarity of the present and regret that they weren't born earlier or later. I believe every intelligent man can create his own happy ending in life, today or at any other time. All one has to do is to look at the whole confused maelstrom of life with the same sense of the fantastical that Leonardo advised his disciples to use when he told them to look at stained walls or at ashes in the fireplace, or to look at clouds or mud or in other places in search of "miraculous inventions" and "infinite things". Leonardo also said that in the same way you could find any name or word you wanted to imagine in the sound of bells. He knew very well that fate (as the sponge of Apelles points out) is always a friend of ingenuity. For my part, for example, I am always finding occasion to marvel at the ease and the grace with which fate helps my imagination to create in harmony. Don't you think that gloomy Hades must have made his bride eat the seven pomegranate seeds just to provide me with the material for a masterpiece?' He interrupted himself with a burst of the youthful laughter that showed so clearly the continuous, inborn joy within him.

'Look, Perdita,' he added, laughing, 'and tell me if I am being honest. Early in October last year, I was invited to Burano by Donna Andriana Duodo. We spent the morning in her web-of-lace garden, then in the afternoon we went out to visit Torcello. I had just started really to feel the story of Persephone coming alive in me, the work was taking shape inside my mind and I felt as though I were sailing over the waters of the Styx and crossing over into the Underworld. I have never had such a perfect, gentle idea of death, and that feeling gave me the sense of being so light that I could have walked through the fields of Asphodel without leaving footprints. The air felt damp, soft, greyish, the canals wound round like serpents through banks of fading flowers. (You probably only know Torcello in the sunshine.) But someone kept talking, arguing, making

17

speeches in Charon's boat, and as I regained consciousness I heard someone praising me. Francesco de Lizo was talking about me, and said that it was a pity such a magnificently sensual, princely writer (those were his words) should have to live in isolation, away from the stupid, uncaring throng, and celebrate the feast of "sounds, colours and shapes" in the palace of his own solitary dreaming. He became quite lyrical recalling the splendid, colourful lives of Venetian artists, and the way in which popular acclaim would raise them up to heights of glory like a whirlwind, and he talked of the beauty, and the power and the joyfulness that built up around them and was reflected in the countless images they painted on rounded ceilings and high walls. And then Donna Andriana said: "All right, I solemnly promise that Stelio Effrena will have his own triumphal occasion here in Venice." The Dogaressa had spoken. Just then I saw a pomegranate tree laden with fruit on a nearby grassy, green bank and it broke through the infinite dullness like some hallucinatory apparition. Donna Orsetta Contarini, who was sitting next to me, let out a cry of delight and reached out, greedily, impatient. There is nothing I like so much as the clear, strong expressing of desire. "I adore pomegranates," she said, as though she could already taste their sharpness on her tongue. She was as childlike about them as her foolish archaic name. I was moved, but Andrea Contarini appeared to disapprove wholeheartedly of his wife's lively behaviour. He is a Hades that has no faith, it seems, in the mnemonic powers of the seven seeds when applied to lawful marriage. But even the boatmen were touched and they steered towards the shore, where I was the first to jump out and pluck fruit from my blood brother, the tree. One simply had to repeat the words of the Last Supper with pagan lips: "Take and eat, this is my body that is given for you. Do this in remembrance of me." What are you thinking, Perdita? You don't believe I am inventing all this do you? It really did happen.'

She allowed herself to be carried away by the free, elegant game he was playing, in which he always seemed to be

18

trying out the quickness of his mind and the ease with which he could create images. There was something fluid in him, something voluble and powerful that stirred in her the twofold image of fire and of water.

'Now,' he said, 'Donna Andriana has kept her promise. Guided by the taste for ancient splendour which she has maintained so firmly, she has prepared a celebration fit for a Doge in the Doge's own palace, a copy of the ones that were held at the end of the fifteenth century. She wanted to rescue Benedetto Marcello's *Ariadne* from oblivion, and let her sigh out her desolation in the very place where Tintoretto painted the Minoidan woman in the act of receiving the crown of stars from Aphrodite. In the sheer beauty of that idea, can't you recognize the woman who left her beloved eyes on the ineffable green garment? Moreover, there is an ancient counterpart to the musical performance in the Sala del Gran Consiglio too. In that same hall, in 1573, a mythological composition by Cornelio Frangipani was performed, with music by Claudio Merulo, in honour of the most Christian Emperor Henry III. Perdita, admit you are astounded by the things I know! Oh, if you only knew how much I have learned about all this. I shall read you my lecture one day when you deserve to be punished.'

'Aren't you going to give that lecture tonight?' asked Foscarina, surprised and uneasy, afraid that he might have decided to disappoint the expectant audience, with his well-known lack of consideration for duty.

He understood her feelings of uneasiness and played upon them. 'Tonight,' he said calmly and deliberately, 'I shall come to have an ice in your garden and enjoy the sight of your bejewelled pomegranate tree, glistening under the stars.'

'Oh Stelio, how could you!' she cried, starting up. There was such a sharp reproach in her words and her movements, and at the same time there was such a strange reminder of the expectant crowd that he was disturbed. The image of the formidable monster with its countless human faces there in the gold and purple of the immense hall came back to him, and as she stared at him, breathing heavily, he felt a sense of foreboding. He abruptly sized up the danger that he had decided to face, relying only on the inspiration of the moment, and felt a sudden rush of horror at the thought of mental blackout, of unexpected vertigo.

'Don't worry,' he said. 'I was joking. I shall go and face the monster, and I'll go unarmed. Didn't you yourself see the sign appear again just now? Surely you don't think it can have reappeared without a purpose after the miracle at Torcello? Once again it has come to warn me that I must really be true to those talents that Nature has given to me. Now you know, my dearest, that I can only talk about myself. So when I am up there on the Doge's throne I shall have to speak out of my own heart, using some seductive allegory as a veil and casting spells with some delightful musical cadence. I shall improvise it all if the fiery spirit of Tintoretto sends me some feelings of fire and passion down from his Paradiso. I am so tempted by taking risks. But how I was deceiving myself, Perdita! When the Dogaressa first told me about the evening and invited me here as honorary guest, I started to compose a lavish speech, a really ceremonial piece of work, as huge and solemn as one of those purple vestments displayed in a case in the Correr Museum. I had a lengthy part in honour of the Queen at the start, and I had created a leafy garland of words for the lovely Andriana Duodo. For a few days I felt happy about living close to the soul of a sixteenth-century Venetian nobleman, someone of great literary distinction like Cardinal Bembo, a member of the Urania or the Adorni Academies, someone who went regularly to the gardens on Murano or the Asolo hills. I felt there was a closeness between the turn of my phrases and the great gold frames round the paintings on the ceiling of the council chamber. But when I came to Venice yesterday morning and sailed down the Grand Canal, I felt my tiredness soaking up the dark, transparent shadows where the night-time soul of marble was released, and I felt that my sheets of paper were worth less than the dead seaweed drifting in on the tide; my speech felt as alien to me as the *Triumphs of Celius Magnus* or the seafaring stories of Anton Maria Consalvi, works I had quoted from in composing it. I did not know what to do.'

He gazed round at the sky and the water, as though searching for an invisible presence, some newly arrived phantom. A yellowish gleam was spreading across towards the slender brushstrokes of the lonely shoreline that stood out against it like dark veining in agates. Behind, towards the Salute, the sky was flecked with light pink and violet clouds floating like sea-anemones in a light-blue ocean. The scent of vegetation steeped in light and heat drifted down from the nearby Gardens, heavy as perfumed oils that seemed to swirl in the bronze-coloured water.

'Can't you feel the autumn, Perdita?' he asked his lover, in a voice that roused her from her thoughts.

The vision of Summer lying dead, closed in her crystal coffin, sunk at the bottom of the weedy lagoon, came back to her. 'It has reached me already,' she replied with a sad little smile.

'Didn't you see it yesterday when it descended on the city? Where were you yesterday at sunset?'

'In a garden on the Giudecca.'

'I was out here, on the Riva. Don't you think that when human eyes see something so marvellously beautiful and joyous, their eyelids ought to close and stay sealed up forever? I'm going to talk about intimate things like this tonight, Perdita. I want to celebrate the marriage of Venice and Autumn in me, in the same way that Tintoretto painted the marriage of Ariadne and Bacchus in the hall of the Anticollegio, using shades of blue, purple and gold. Yesterday, all of a sudden I felt an ancient seed of poetry break open in my heart. I remembered a fragment of a poem I'd forgotten, that I started writing in *nona rima* here in Venice, when I sailed here for the first time some years ago, one September when I was very young. It was called 'The Allegory of Autumn' and it was about the god (he was no longer crowned with vine leaves, he was wearing a golden crown like one of Veronese's princes and his sensual body was throbbing with passion) who was about to migrate to the city of the ocean with its marble arms and thousand green garlands. At that time my idea still hadn't reached the right level of intensity for it to become a work of art, and I instinctively gave up trying to make it cohere. But no seed is ever really lost in an active mind which is like fertile soil, and now it is coming back to me at just the right moment demanding to be heard. What mysterious, fair-minded fates govern the world of the mind! I had to be able to respect that first seed in order now to feel it growing and developing in me. Leonardo da Vinci, who turned his attention to everything profound, was surely referring to the truth of this when he told the story of the grain of millet that said to the ant: "If you'll allow me the pleasure of bringing my desire into the world, then I'll grant you a hundred of me in return." Isn't that an admirable touch of grace in those fingers that could bend iron? He was such an incomparable master! How can I forget him and give myself up to the Venetians?'

The lively irony that he had been directing towards himself as he spoke suddenly vanished. He seemed totally absorbed in his own thoughts once more. His head was bent, his body shuddered convulsively in response to the extreme tension in his mind as he tried to uncover some of the hidden analogies which would bind together the rapid succession of different images that flashed across his soul like lightening. He was trying to work out the main lines that would shape his new work. He was so absorbed in this process that the muscles in his face quivered visibly, and as the woman watched him she felt pain reflected back at her, not unlike the pain she might have felt had he been straining every nerve to draw the string of a gigantic bow while she looked on. She knew that he was a long way away from her, he was a stranger, indifferent to anything that was not his own thought.

'It is late, it's already time, we must go back,' he said, shaking himself abruptly with a shudder, as though anxiety were pressing at him, because he had seen again the formidable monster with its countless human heads waiting there in the immensity of the great echoing hall. 'I must get back to the hotel in time to dress.' And as his youthful vanity flowed back into him, he thought about the eyes of all the unknown women who would be watching him for the first time that night.

'To the Hotel Danieli,' said La Foscarina to the oarsman.

The dentellated ironwork on the prow turned on the water with a slow movement as though it were alive, and both Stelio and La Foscarina felt a different but equally acute sense of anguish at having to leave behind them the infinite silence of the estuary that was already at the mercy of Shadow and of Death, at having to turn back to the magnificent temptress that was the city, whose canals, like the veins of a voluptuous woman, were already beginning to throb with the fever of night.

They were silent for a time, absorbed in their own inner tumult that whirled round within, penetrating the very roots of their being and threatening to tear them apart. Scents seeped down from the Gardens and swam like oil on the water where the shimmer of burned bronze flashed here and there in its furrows. A ghost of ancient pageants seemed to float in the air, which their eyes could distinguish in the same way that they had sensed the lost golden note in the harmony of enduring marble as they gazed at the palaces turned old by time. On that magical evening it seemed as though the breath of life of the far-off Orient which once stirred the concave sails and curved flanks of the galleys laden with rich spoils were being revived. Everything everywhere was celebrating the power of life in the man who wanted to lay claim to the entire universe so as not to die and the woman who wanted to throw her troubled soul on to a funeral pyre in order to die purely. A growing sense of anxiety pulsated in each of them, as they listened to time passing, as though the waters over which they were sailing might be flowing through a terrifying water-clock.

Both started at the sudden cannon-shot that hailed the lowering of the flag on a warship anchored close to the

Gardens. At the end of the dark jetty they saw the tri-coloured flag slip down its pole and sink into folds like the end of a noble dream. For a few seconds the silence seemed to deepen, while the gondola slid into darker shadows as it grazed the side of the great armed vessel.

'Perdita,' said Stelio Effrena unexpectedly, 'do you know Donatella Arvale, who is going to sing in *Ariadne*?' In that deeper shadow his voice took on a strange sound as it echoed against the metal hull.

'She is Lorenzo Arvale's daughter – the famous sculptor,' replied Foscarina after a brief pause. 'She is one of my dearest friends and she is also my guest. So you will meet her at my house after the festival.'

'Donna Andriana was talking about her so enthusiastically yesterday evening, saying she was quite brilliant. She told me that the idea of reviving this Ariadne from the grave came to her when she heard Donatella Arvale singing the aria "How can you bear . . . to see me weep . . ." so perfectly. We shall be hearing some wonderful music at your house, Perdita. Oh, I am so starved of music! When I was alone down there I never heard any music for months on end, except the terrifying voice of the sea.'

The bells of St Mark's rang out the Angelus, and their great peal rolled in long waves across the mirror of the bay, vibrated in the masts of ships and reached out to the infinite lagoon beyond. Other bronze voices answered, from San Giorgio Maggiore, San Giorgio dei Greci, San Giorgio degli Schiavoni, San Giovanni in Bragora, San Moisè, from the Salute, from the Church of the Redeemer, from the domain of the Evangelist, the distant towers of the Madonna dell'Orto, San Giobbe and Sant'Andrea, blending together in a vast single chorus that extended across the mute assembly of stones and water and formed a great invisible metal dome whose vibrations seemed to be communicating with the first glimmering stars. In the purity of the evening those sacred tones bestowed a gigantic ideal grandeur upon the City of Silence. From the summits of temples, from harsh cells open to the sea-winds, they passed on to troubled

24

mankind the message of countless immortal beings concealed in the shadows of long naves and made the glimmering votive lamps quiver mysteriously. To souls worn out by daily life they brought a message from the superhuman beings depicted on the walls of secluded chapels and in the niches of enclosed altars announcing a miracle, promising a whole world. All the images of Beauty the Consoler invoked by single-minded Prayer rose up in that great storm of sound and spoke in that aerial chorus, illuminating the face of the marvellous night.

'Are you still able to pray?' asked Stelio quietly, seeing that the woman had closed her eyes and clasped her hands on her knees while her whole being was absorbed in some inner process.

She did not reply, though she pressed her lips more tightly together. They both continued to listen, feeling the sense of anxiety overwhelming them once again, racing like a great river that has rushed on beyond the rapids. There was a grave, confused awareness in them both of the strange hiatus into which an unexpected new image had come into being between them and in which a new name had been spoken. The ghost of that unforeseen feeling that they had experienced as they sailed into the shadow of the great warship stayed with them like a separate burden, like an indefinable yet persistent point around which there was a kind of void that neither could explore. The sense of anxiety and of speed suddenly overcame them both again, and they flung themselves towards one another, united with such vehemence that they dared not look into each other's eyes for fear of seeing the brutality of desire.

'Shall we see each other tonight after the festival?' asked Foscarina, and there was a tremor in her faint voice. 'Are you free?' She was in a hurry now to hold on to him, to imprison him, as though he were about to slip away from her, as though she hoped to find some magic love-potion that very night which would bind him to her forever. And while she felt that the gift of her body had now become essential, nevertheless with the terrible clarity that blazed through the fire within her, she could see the inadequacy of that gift which had been so long denied. A painful feeling of shame mingled with fear and pride contracted her wilting body.

'I am free, I am yours,' the young man answered in a low voice, not looking at her. 'You know that nothing is so vital to me as that which you can give me.'

He too trembled within his secret heart, as he saw before him the two goals towards which the energy of his whole being was bending like a mighty bow – the city and the woman, both temptresses, both having unseen depths, both tired from having lived too long, weighed down with an excess of love, both exaggerated in their splendours by his imagination, and both destined to disappoint all his expectations.

For an instant his soul was overwhelmed by a violent surge of desire and regret. His pride, the intoxication of his long, arduous labours, his boundless ambition that had been forced into a field that was too narrow for him, his bitter intolerance of mediocre living, his aspirations to the privileges of aristocracy, his pretended enjoyment of the activity that was pushing him towards the crowds as though towards his chosen prey, his dreams of a greater, more majestic form of art that was in his hands at once a sign of illumination and an instrument of subjugation, all his proud, imperial thoughts, all his insatiable need for domination, for glory, for pleasure, all these rose up tumultuously, dazzling him and yet suffocating him with confusion. A heavy sense of sadness pushed him towards becoming the last great love of that lonely, nomadic woman, who seemed to carry with her in the folds of her silent garments memories of distant multitudes whose basic bestiality had been stirred to frenzy by the impact of her magnificent, divine artistic skills exemplified in a cry of rage, a shriek of agony or the silence of death itself. An obscure desire drew him towards that wise, desperate woman in whom he believed he could discern traces of every kind of voluptuousness and pain, towards that body which was no longer young, made soft by endless caresses yet still unknown to him.

'Is it a promise?' he asked, with his face lowered, holding himself tightly to control his agitation. 'At last!' She did not reply, but she looked at him with a desire on the verge of madness that he did not see.

They remained silent, while the bronze tolling passed over their heads so powerfully that they seemed to hear it in the very roots of their hair like a quiver of their own flesh.

'Goodbye,' she said, as they came to the quay. 'Let us meet at the second well as you come out of the courtyard, by the jetty.'

'Goodbye,' he said. 'Let me see you there in the audience when I am starting to speak.' A confused roar came from St Mark's above the sound of the bells, spreading across the Piazzetta out towards the Fortuna.

'May light shine upon you, Stelio!' said the woman, holding out her dry hands to him with passion.

As Stelio Effrena walked into the courtyard through the southern gateway, he saw the Giant's Staircase lit with the reddish glow of torches fixed in their iron holders and teeming with black and white faces. He experienced a sudden surge of revulsion that brought him to a halt in the passageway. He felt too strong a contrast between the invasion of those vulgar people and the sight of that extraordinary architecture which was made even more magnificent by the unusual nocturnal illumination and in which the strength and beauty of life in another age was so harmoniously depicted.

'Oh damnation!' he exclaimed, turning to the friends who were with him. 'How can I possibly find an image that will stir those thousands of starched shirt-collars in the Sala del Gran Consiglio from the Doge's throne. Let's go back. Let's go and soak up the atmosphere of the real masses. The Queen has still not left the palace, so we have time.'

'Until I actually see you up there on the platform,' laughed Francesco de Lizo, 'I shall not be sure that you are going to do it.'

'I think Stelio would rather be up on the balcony than on the platform. He would like to be up there haranguing a mutinous mob that was threatening to burn down the new law courts and the old Libreria,' said Piero Martello, trying to cheer the poet by appealing to his rebellious spirit and love of sedition, opinions that he also tried to imitate.

'Certainly,' said Stelio. 'Especially if my harangue, as you call it, were powerful enough either to prevent or cause something irreparable. I fully accept that the written word should be used to create a pure form of beauty that can be contained within the uncut pages of a book like a tabernacle that can only be opened after a deliberate decision has been taken to break the seal. But it seems to me that the spoken word which is directed at a mass of people should have but one aim, that of inspiring action, even violent action. Only on this condition can a noble mind communicate with the masses through voice and gesture without lowering itself. If it were otherwise, a speech would be nothing but histrionics. That is why I so bitterly regret having agreed to make a speech that is simply for entertainment. All of you will understand how humiliating it is for me to have been granted this great honour and how pointless my forthcoming speech is going to be. All these people that I do not know have been dragged away from their mediocre work or their favourite pastimes for the evening and have come to listen to me with the same stupid, pointless curiosity that they would show if they went to hear any other "famous name". The women in the audience will doubtless pay more attention to the way in which I have knotted my cravat than to the structure of my sentences. When it is over, the only thing that my speech will arouse will probably be a polite round of applause from all those gloved hands or a discreet murmur that I shall acknowledge with a polite bow. I am really about to touch the heights of achievement, aren't I?'

'You are wrong,' said Francesco de Lizo. 'You ought to be flattered that you have managed to infuse poetry into the life of this forgetful city even if only for a few hours and are going to show us the kind of beauty that could enrich our lives if Art and Life could be joined again in marriage. If the man who built the Festival theatre at Bayreuth were here, he would applaud you for bringing about the harmony that he predicted. But what is so admirable is that although you knew nothing about it and were not even here, the Festival seems to have been organized through your guidance, your inspiration, even your direction. That is the finest proof of the possibility of renewing good taste and making it more widely accepted despite current barbarity. Your influence today is much stronger than you realize. The lady who wanted to honour you, the lady you call the Dogaressa, has asked herself every time a new idea came to her: "But will Stelio Effrena approve?" If you only knew how many young people today ask themselves the same question when they consider their own innermost thoughts!'

'To whom should you be speaking, if not to these people?' asked Daniele Glauro, the fervent, ascetic lover of Beauty, in his gentle voice that seemed to express the white, inextinguishable flame within the heart that the poet loved best on account of its constancy. 'When you are there on the podium, look around and you will recognize your followers from the look in their eyes. There are a great many of them, and some have come a very long way. They are waiting for you with an anxiety that you perhaps don't understand. They are all the young people who have drunk in your poetry, who have breathed the fiery atmosphere of your dreams, who have felt the claws of your magic beasts. You have promised a better, stronger life to them, you have predicted that the world will be transformed through the miracle of new art-forms. There are so many of them, so many people who have been seduced by your feelings of hope and joy. Now they have heard that you are going to be speaking in Venice, in the Doge's Palace, in one of the most magnificent settings on earth! They are going to be able to see you and listen to you for the first time surrounded by all that splendour which seems an ideal frame for your character. The old Doge's Palace has been in darkness for such a long, long time and now it has suddenly come to life again and is lit up. You alone have had the power to light those torches. Now do you understand why they are so anxious? And don't you think that you simply must speak to them? You will be able to carry out the mission you set yourself in speaking to crowds. You will be able to stir their hearts so powerfully that they will be propelled towards the Ideal forever. Just think, Stelio, what an unforgettable night this will be for so many people here in Venice!'

Stelio put his hand on his friend's prematurely stooped shoulders and smilingly repeated Petrarch's words: *'Non ego loquar omnibus, sed tibi sed mihi et his . . .'** He felt the eyes of his unknown disciples shining within him, and now he could feel with perfect clarity the way in which he would begin his speech, how it would sound. 'Nevertheless,' he added cheerfully, turning to Piero Martello, 'the most jolly thing to do would be to raise a storm in that ocean of people.'

They were close to the corner column of the portico, next to the noisy, singleminded crowd that was gathering in the little square and which stretched out towards the Zecca, packed tightly by the Procuratorie, surrounding the clock tower and filling every inch of space like a formless wave, communicating its living warmth to the marble of the columns and walls against which it pressed violently in constant surges. From time to time a louder sound would be heard from the far end of the Piazza which would increase in volume until it exploded nearby like a clap of thunder and then faded away until it expired close by like a murmur. The line of the arches, the loggias, the spires and the domes

* 'I will not speak to everyone, but to you and to me and to them . . .'

30

of the golden basilica, the upper rooms of the Loggetta, the cornices of the Biblioteca were glimmering with innumerable tiny lights, and the great pyramid of the Campanile twinkled with silent constellations in the bosom of the night and reminded the crowd inebriated by noise of the immensity of the silence of the heavens. To the boatmen in the furthest part of the lagoon that light seemed like a new beacon, like the rhythm of a solitary oar stirring the reflection of the stars in the golden waters, a point of holy peace enclosed by the walls of an island convent.

'Tonight I want to be with the woman I desire for the first time, over beyond the Gardens, down towards the Lido, in a floating bed,' said the erotic poet Paris Eglano, a blond, beardless young man with a luscious red mouth that contrasted with the almost angelic delicacy of his features. 'In an hour's time Venice will offer some Nero-like lover nestling in the cabin of some gondola somewhere the Dionysiac sight of a city inflamed by its own passions.

Stelio smiled as he noticed the extent to which his companions had steeped themselves in his essences, and how profoundly the impact of his style had impressed itself upon their minds. The image of Foscarina had flashed into his desire, poisoned by art, weighted down with voluptuous knowledge, with the taste of maturity and the corruption of her eloquent mouth, with the dryness of a vain fever in those hands which had squeezed the juices of all deceitful fruits, with the traces of a hundred masks upon her face that had simulated the fury of all mortal passions. Thus he pictured her in his desire, and he breathed heavily when he thought that in just a little while he would see her coming out of the crowd as though emerging from something that held her enslaved and would give the necessary touch of intoxication to her features. 'Let's go,' he said to his friends, ready now. 'It's time.'

A cannon shot announced that the Queen had left the palace. A long tremor ran through the living throng, like something that precedes a storm out at sea. From the shore of San Giorgio Maggiore, a rocket shot upwards with a violent hiss. It flew straight into the air like the stem of a flower, exploding into a rose of sparks, then bent over, dwindled, dispersed in trembling sparks, expired with a dull crackle into the water. And the joyous acclamation that greeted the lovely woman in her crown – the name of the white starlike flower and of the pure pearl repeated in a unanimous shout of love that echoed against the marble – recalled the majesty of the ancient Promissione, the triumphal procession of art that accompanied the new Dogaressa to her palace, the immense wave of joy that swept the bejewelled Morosina Grimani to her throne while all the Arts laden with gifts bowed down before her.

'If the Queen truly admires your books,' said Francesco de Lizo, 'she will certainly be wearing her pearl necklace tonight. You will find yourself in a positive forest of gems; all the hereditary jewels of the Venetian aristocracy will be there.'

'Look, Stelio,' said Daniele Glauro, 'over there at the front of the staircase. There is a group of admirers waiting for you to pass.'

Stelio paused beside the well that Foscarina had told him about. He leaned over its bronze rim feeling the little carved figures against his knees and in that dark inner mirror he saw distant stars dimly reflected. For just a second he felt alone, he could no longer hear the noise around him, he felt himself sucked into the circle of darkness which gave off a slight chill, a sign of the silent presence of water. He felt exhausted by all the tension and by wanting to be somewhere else and by the vague need to go beyond even the ecstasy that he was promised that night. In the depths of his being his secret heart lay as still, as distant, as untouchable as that watery mirror.

'What can you see?' Piero Martello asked him, leaning over the edge that had been worn down by the ropes that for centuries had lowered buckets.

'The face of Truth,' replied the poet.

* * *

32

The rooms where the Doge had once lived, adjoining the Sala del Gran Consiglio, were now filled with pagan statues, the spoils of ancient wars. There Stelio Effrena waited for the master of ceremonies to give him the sign to go out on to the platform. He was smiling calmly enough at his friends as they chatted to him, but their words rang in his ears in broken fragments, with long pauses in between, like the sounds the wind brings from a distance. Every so often, as if he were moved by some powerful, involuntary force, he would go over to one of the statues and run his hands over it convulsively, as though he were searching for a weak point in order to destroy it; or he would lean intently over some medal as though he were trying to make out an indecipherable sign. But his eyes saw nothing, because they were looking inwards at the place where the accumulated strength of his will was summoning the silent shapes that his mellifluous voice would bring into being with the perfect music of words. His whole being was concentrated in the effort of representing the extraordinary feeling that possessed him with the greatest possibly intensity. Since he was only able to speak about himself and about his own world, he wanted at the very least to find an ideal image that would encapsulate the most perfect qualities of his art and would demonstrate visually to his disciples that unconquerable force and desire that impelled him through life. Once more he wanted to show them that in order to conquer both men and circumstance, it is essential to assert one's Self and to magnify one's dreams of beauty and of power. Leaning over a medal by Pisanello he could feel his very thoughts pulsating at incredible speed within his burning forehead.

'Stelio,' said Daniele Glauro, taking him aside and speaking in the reverential tones that he used whenever he spoke about his religion, 'do you see how the mysterious processes of artistic creation are working upon you, and how those thoughts of yours which are about to emerge into the light are being led by some infallible instinct that will enable you to choose the most perfect means of expression, a sign

33

of the most lofty style from the midst of so many different forms? Because you are having to work out your own ideas, you are drawn by some sense of affinity to a Pisanello medal. You are in touch with a sign left by a man who was one of the greatest artists the world has ever known; the man with the most purely Greek soul of the entire Renaissance. And straight away a sign of illumination has appeared on your brow.'

On the clear bronze was the form of a young man with beautiful wavy hair, an imperial profile and a neck like Apollo, a perfect type of elegance and strength. He was so perfect that the imagination could only picture him in life as free from all impurities, as timeless as the craftmanship that had enclosed him within the metal circle for all eternity. *'Dux equitum praestans Malatesta Novellus Cesenae dominus. Opus Pisani pictoris.'** Next to it lay another medal, a work by the same hand, on which was the form of young girl with a narrow bosom, a swan-like neck and hair pulled back into a heavy snood, with a high receding forehead that hinted already at the halo of the blessed. She seemed a vase of purity, hard, precise, clear as diamond and sealed forever, an adamantine pyx that enshrined a soul consecrated like the Host to sacrifice. *'Cicilia Virgo filia Iohannis Francisci primi Marchionis Mantuae.'***

'Look,' said the brilliant expert, pointing out the two unique impressions, 'see how Pisanello with that same marvellously gifted hand of his could pluck the proudest flower of life as well as the purest flower of death. Here you have the image of profane desire and the image of holy aspiration in the self-same bronze, both fixed by the same ideal quality of style. Can you recognize the analogies here between this work and your work? When your Persephone plucks the ripe fruit from the infernal pomegranate tree, there is something mystical in her great gesture of desire because as she tears

* 'The noble Knight Malatesta, young lord of Cesena, by the hand of Pisano, painter.'
** 'Cecilia, Virgin Daughter of John Francis, first Marquis of Mantua.'

34

the skin to eat its grains of flesh, that unconscious action will decide her fate. The shadow of the mysterious accompanied that sensual act. That was how you signified the character of all your work. No sensuality is more ardent than yours, but your senses are so sharp that even while they delight in appearances, they penetrate the very depths until they touch the heart of mystery which appals them. You have insights beyond the veil on which life has painted the voluptuous images that you enjoy so much. You bring together within yourself that which appears to be irreconcilable, you join two opposite poles without any apparent effort, consequently today you provide an example of a life that is complete and all-powerful. You must let the people who have come to hear you feel that, for it is that glorious combination in you that ought to be recognized above all else.'

He had celebrated the ideal marriage between proud Malatesta, leader of knights, and the holy Mantuan virgin Cecilia Gonzaga with the kind of faith an honest priest displays before the altar. Stelio loved him for that faith, and loved him too because he had never felt such deep, sincere belief in the reality of the world of poetry in any other man. He loved him too because of the frequent revealing insights he offered, because his comments often threw an unexpected new light on his own work.

'Here comes Foscarina with Donatella Arvale,' said Francesco de Lizo, who had been studying the crowd going up the Censor's Staircase and surging into the huge hall.

Then Stelio Effrena was once again seized by panic. He could hear the noise of the crowd blending in his eardrums with the blood pounding through his arteries from some vague distance, and above the roaring he heard Perdita's last words.

The rumbling sound grew louder, diminished, ceased altogether as he went up the steps to the platform, treading lightly but surely. As he turned to the crowd, his dazzled

35

eyes caught sight of the fearsome monster with its countless human faces between the gold and dark purple of the huge hall.

A sudden surge of pride helped him to control himself. He bowed to the Queen and to Donna Duodo, who returned the same twin smiles they had thrown him on the Grand Canal as their barge slipped past. He focused his gaze and saw Foscarina in the glitter of the front rows; he looked right across the audience to the very back that was no more than a dark area dotted with pale blurred spots. At that moment the silent, expectant crowd seemed to him like a gigantic creature with thousands of eyes, its bosom covered with shining scales that rippled out towards the darkness beneath the great scrolls of the heavy, rich sky that hung glittering above it.

The creature's breast was indeed splendid, sparkling with jewels that had once glittered beneath that self-same ceiling during some evening coronation ceremony. The Queen wore a diadem and long pearl necklaces, graduated clusters of light that made one think of the smile that was about to dawn on her lips. Andriana Duodo wore dark emeralds that had been torn from the hilt of some savage scimitar, Giustiniana Memo's rubies were fashioned into the shape of carnations by the inimitable craftsmanship of Vettor Camelio, while Lucrezia Priuli's sapphires had been taken from the high-heeled sandals that the Serenissima Zelia had worn on that triumphal day when she ascended the throne. Orsetta Contarini's beryls had been delicately set in opaque gold by the great Silvestro Grifo, Zenobia Corner's turquoises had turned strangely pale one night, when some mysterious affliction had touched them as they rested on Lusignana's damp bosom during the pleasures of Asolo. The most famous jewels that had adorned the age-old festivals of the city now gleamed with renewed fires on the creature's breast, and Stelio could feel the warm scent of female breath and skin. The rest of that shapeless, strangely spotted body stretched out almost in the shape of a tail, coiling between the two gigantic globes that reminded the Maker of Images

36

of the two bronze spheres on which the blindfolded monster rests its lion feet in Giambellino's allegory. The great animal life-form, blind to all thought, lay before the man who alone at that moment was to think on its behalf. It stayed motionless, compelling as an enigmatic idol, protected by its own silence as though by a shield able to meet and force back all vibration, and it waited for the first sound of the masterful word.

Stelio Effrena measured the silence into which his first utterance was about to fall. As his voice rose to his lips, led and sustained by an effort of will against his instinctive emotion, he caught sight of Foscarina standing close to the railing that surrounded the heavenly globe. The face of the great tragedienne was pale, her throat and the purity of her bare shoulders were unadorned, and she stood out against the sphere of signs of the zodiac. Stelio admired the technique behind her appearance. Focusing on those distant, adoring eyes, he began speaking very slowly, as though the rhythm of the oars were still in his ears.

'As I came back from the Gardens one afternoon just recently, along that warm bank of the Schiavoni which cannot but remind a wandering poet of some magical golden bridge reaching over the sea of light and silence towards a dream of infinite Beauty, into my thoughts came a picture of great intimacy, the nuptial alliance of Venice with Autumn under those skies.

'Everywhere there was a sense of the life-force, composed of passionate expectation and restrained ardour, and I was astonished at its vehemence. But it was not unknown to me, because I had already encountered it deep in the shadows during the almost mortal stillness of summer, and I had also felt it quiver sometimes in the strange, feverish scent of the waters, like a mysterious pulsation. So indeed, I thought, this pure City of Art truly aspires to a supreme condition of beauty, and for her it is an annual event, as it is for the meadow to produce flowers. She desires to reveal herself in complete harmony, as if she had within herself that strong conscious will to perfection which gave birth to

37

her and which has transformed her during the centuries into a divine being. Under the still fire of summer skies, she appears to have neither pulse nor breath, lying dead in her own green waters. But my feelings did not deceive me when I sensed that she was labouring in secret with a life force strong enough to renew the greatest of the ancient wonders.

'Such were my thoughts, as I watched the marvellous spectacle and through the gift of love and creativity that which my eyes drank in, my inner sight transformed into a deep, lasting impression. But how then to communicate my vision of beauty and joyousness to those of you here listening to me now? No dawn, no sunset can equal that special hour of light on stone and water. Not even the sudden appearance of a beloved woman in a forest in spring-time is as intoxicating as that unexpected daytime revel-ation of the noble, voluptuous City when she brought the richest dream of the Latin spirit to light and suffocated it in her marble arms.'

The voice of the speaker, clear, penetrating, icy cold at first, now seemed to be warmed by the invisible sparks that flew from his mind with the effort of combining improvis-ation and his acute, fastidious sense of hearing. As the words flowed without hesitation and the rhythmic shape of his sentences contained them like a freehand drawing fashioned in a single stroke, his listeners could feel the excessive tension troubling his mind beneath the harmony of his discourse, and they were fascinated by it, as though they were witnessing an ancient savage game in which the hercu-lean energies of an athlete made his tendons quiver and his arteries swell to bursting point. They could feel the warmth, the life, the immediacy in everything he said, and their enjoyment was all the greater because it was so unexpected, for everyone had thought that such a tireless perfectionist would have given a careful reading of a minutely prepared lecture. His disciples were deeply moved by his daring, feel-ing that they were privileged to see into the mysterious creative processes that had resulted in the works that had given them so much pleasure. And that first impulse of feeling spread like wildfire through the hall, until it rushed back at him in a solid wave and he was almost overcome by it.

It was the danger he had been expecting. He swayed under the shock, as though a mighty wave had hit him. For an instant his mind was seized by a mighty blackness; the light of his thoughts went out like a torch blown out by the unconquerable wind, his eyes clouded over as though he were about to faint. He could sense how great his shame would be if he gave in to that confusion. And his willpower created a new spark within the darkness, with a sudden rough movement, like steel striking a flint. With a look and a gesture he directed the attention of the crowd to the masterpiece that stretched across the ceiling of the hall in a blaze of radiance.

'I am certain,' he said, 'that the City must have appeared in the same guise to Paolo Veronese as he was searching in his own mind for an image of the Queen triumphant. Yes, I am certain that he too must have trembled within his very being, and knelt down in adoration like someone overwhelmed by a miracle. And when he tried to paint that marvel here on this ceiling to show other men he, the prodigal artist who appeared to embody all the wildest imaginings of the Orient, he, the poet whose soul was like that Lydian river which Greek lovers of harmony called Chrysorhoas, from whose springs filled with gold had descended a dynasty of kings rich beyond all others, he, the great Veronese, used an abundance of gold, jewels, rich stuffs, purple, ermine and every conceivable adornment but he had to paint her glorious face clouded in a shadowy halo. We should all join together in praising Veronese for the way he painted that shadow.

'All the mystery and fascination of Venice are contained in that palpitating, fluid shadow, so small and yet infinite, made up of living yet unknowable things, endowed with mighty virtues like the caves of legend where gems had eyes, and where one could encounter both freshness and passion at the same instant in a single profoundly ambiguous sensation. We should praise Veronese for this. When he depicted the all-powerful City in human form, he captured her essential spirit, which could only be symbolically an unquenchable flame seen through a veil of water. I know a man who steeped his soul in that sublime place for so long that when he withdrew it, he was charged with renewed power and able to take both his life and his work into his inspired hands.'

Was he not just such a one? By making that statement, he appeared to have discovered all his assurance and now he felt master of his thoughts and his words, well out of danger, intent on bringing the vast, many-eyed monster whose bosom sparkled with gleaming scales into the circles of his imagination, the ephemeral, elusive monster from whose side rose its daughter, the tragic muse, with her head raised among the stars.

Following his gesture, the countless faces turned to look up at the Apotheosis, their unveiled eyes gazed in astonishment at the marvel, as though they were seeing it for the first time or seeing it in a completely new way. The great bare back of the woman in the golden helmet gleamed out of the cloud with such a strong sense of muscular life that it was as tempting as earthly flesh. And that lively nakedness above them all, conqueror of Time that had darkened the heroic images of sieges and battles that lay below her, seemed to spread a sensuous enchantment fanned by the breezes of the autumn night floating in from the open balconies like a wave of scent around a perfumed rosebush, while the princesses of that lofty court leaned down from the balustrades between the two twisted columns, bending their burning faces and opulent bosoms over their most recent sisters in the world.

In that atmosphere of enchantment, the poet spoke his harmonious sentences like lyric verses.

'I felt just such a flame yesterday, I felt its power as it burned and endowed Venice and its beauty with a strength of expression that had never been seen before. I saw the entire City burning with desire before me, panting expectantly

40

in its thousand green girdles like a woman waiting for the time of her fulfilment. She was reaching out her marble arms to wild Autumn, whose damp, perfumed breath came to her out of the delicious death of distant fields. She was watching the light vapours that rose from the distant boundaries of the silent lagoon and which seemed to be coming closer like secret messages. She was listening intently to every slightest sound in the silence that she herself had created. The sound of the wind rustling through her own precious gardens had a musicality that extended beyond all confines. A kind of stupor built up around the solitary, imprisoned trees that were changing colour magnificently, like a burst of flame. The dead leaf that fell on to the worn stone of the quayside gleamed like a precious thing; above the wall studded with golden lichens the fruit of the pomegranate tree, swollen with ripeness, burst suddenly like a lovely mouth that opens in a surge of laughter. A barge went by, slowly, majestically, laden with grapes like a full wine-press, and it spread across the waters that were heavy with dead seaweed an intoxicating sense of harvest and a vision of solitary vineyards full of young people singing. Everything was profoundly eloquent, as though there were an invisible quality that was bound to the visible shape of things and as though thanks to some divine Hellenic privilege everything was alive in the superior truth of art. 'Surely then,' I thought, 'surely in this City of water and stone there is a spontaneous, constant desire for ideal harmony, as there is within the soul of a pure artist. A kind of rhythmic intelligence within the imagination takes over the process of image-making and shapes those images in accordance with some secret idea, pushing them towards some premeditated goal. This intelligence possesses hands that work wonders in shaping light and dark into a never-ending work of beauty, and her dreaming is incorporated into her work, while from that same dream, where all the inheritance of the past is transfigured, she draws the web of inimitable allegory that enfolds her. And since in the entire universe only poetry is truth, he who knows how to see poetry and bring her to him with the strength of his mind is close to understanding the secret of victory in life.'

His eyes sought those of Daniele Glauro as he spoke these last words, and he saw them shining with happiness beneath his great, thoughtful forehead that swelled out pregnant with an unborn world. The mystic was standing quite near, with his whole group of followers, some of those unknown disciples whom he had described to the poet, anxious and eager to hear more, filled to the brim with trust and expectation, desperate to break the bond of their daily servitude and discover the wild freedom of joy or pain. Stelio could see them all standing close together, like a nucleus of compressed energy, leaning against the great reddish-coloured chests in which countless volumes of forgotten, dead knowledge lay buried. He could make out their intent, animated faces, their long thick hair, their mouths that were either half-open in childlike wonder or clenched tight with violent sensitivity, their light or dark eyes across which lightness and shadows flickered as his words reached them, like a bed of delicate flowers stirred by the breeze. He thought he held their confused minds bunched in his hand like a banner, and that he could shake some or crush them or tear or burn them as he chose. Whilst his mind coiled and uncoiled so vigorously in that continuous rush of words, he still kept a strange capacity for observing what was going on around him that was almost a separate faculty of material observation. It appeared to be growing clearer and sharper as his speaking increased in speed and energy. He began to feel his effort becoming easier, and the effectiveness of his will was aided by a dark, free, instinctive energy that came from the depths of his own unknowing and functioned in some secret, inexplicable way. By way of analogy, he recalled extraordinary moments in the silence and intellectual warmth of his distant room, when his hand had written on the page an immortal line that did not appear to have come from his own mind at all, but seemed to have been dictated by an impetuous being which the unthinking hand had obeyed blindly. A similar miracle was taking place now

42

within him, as his ears caught with astonishment some unexpected sentence uttered by his lips. In the communion between his own soul and the soul of the crowd a mystery was happening, something that was almost divine. Something greater and stronger entered the feelings that he normally experienced. And it seemed to him that his very voice was gradually acquiring increased power.

At that moment he saw his ideal image complete and alive within himself, and he depicted it in the language of poetry, as those great masters of the visual who ruled in that place had done, with the luxuriance of Paolo Veronese and the passion of Tintoretto.

'The moment was fast approaching, the hour of the supreme Festival was at hand. A strange light was spreading across the sky over the distant horizon, as though the savage Bridegroom were riding by in his fiery chariot, his purple standard flying. The wind roused by his passage came laden with all the scents of the earth, and across the waters where delicate fronds of seaweed were drifting, there came to the waiting Bride the image of plump, white rosebushes that were slowly disintegrating like heaps of snow against the railings of the gardens overlooking the Brenta. The whole image of that distant land seemed to be reflected in the crystal air as though in some deceitful desert mirage, and that image of nature served to make the dream of art even more precious, since no autumnal display of orchards and gardens in the memory was comparable to the divine animation and transfiguration of the ancient stones.

'Surely some god is about to come down to the city as she offers herself to him? I said to myself, overcome by agitation and desire and the longing for joy that everything around me was expressing as though swept by some feverish, infinite passion. And I summoned up the greatest artist to depict for me that young, longed-for god in the most noble shape, with the most glorious colours.

'He was almost there! The inverted goblet of the sky was pouring a stream of glory over everything, a sight that was unbelievable to me at first, for it was richer than the richest inner light that ever inspired thoughts or dreams. The water seemed to be made of starry matter, of some unknown changeable nature in which were reflected the myriad images of an indefinable liquid world. It was trembling ceaselessly, and so wave after wave of stupendously simple destructions and creations swept across it, drawing in their wake a harmony that was forever renewed. Between these two marvels rose the multifaceted, many-souled stones like a forest and like a people, a silent vast mass from which the genius of Art extracted the hidden concepts of Nature, upon which Time had heaped up its mysteries and Glory had left its mark, through whose veins the human spirit rose up to the Ideal as sap flows up towards blossom along the very fibre of the tree. The multifaceted, many-souled stones constantly assumed expressions of life that were so intense and so new that the very property as stone was obliterated and its original immobility was illuminated by a marvellous sense of feeling.

'Each moment vibrated through matter like an unbearable flash of lightning. Everything glittered in a sublime jubilation of light, from the crosses erect on the top of domes swollen by prayer to the delicate salt-crystal droplets hanging beneath the bridges. Just as the look-out on the mast-top shouts aloud the anxiety that is stirring below him in the shape of a storm at sea, so the golden angel on the top of the highest tower burst into flame and announced the coming.

'And so he came! He came seated on a cloud like a chariot of fire, the hem of his purple garments trailing behind him. He was gentle yet strong. His lips, full of murmurings and woodland silences were half closed, and his hair flowed down over his strong neck like a mane. His broad manly chest was bare and the breath of forests throbbed within him. He turned his youthful face towards the City with her aura of unspeakable, inhuman fascination, an inexplicable cruel bestiality which contrasted with the profoundly knowing glances that flew from his sombre eyes. It was obvious that throughout his whole body the blood was boiling and

44

throbbing right down to his energetic feet and the extreme tips of his strong fingers. His being was filled with hidden things that seemed to conceal joy as grapes in blossom conceal the wine that is to come. All the mighty gold and purple that he brought with him were as clothing to his senses . . .

'Imagine the passion with which the City of Beauty in all her jewels, with her thousand green girdles, abandoned herself to that magnificent god!'

Raised up in the ascending spiral of words, the soul of the great crowd seemed suddenly to reach an experiencing of beauty, like a great peak hitherto never achieved, and it was astounded. The eloquence of the poet was echoed by everything around him, it was as though it took up and continued the rhythms obeyed by all that painted majesty and grace; it re-evoked the indefinable relationship that flowed between the forms created by human artistry and the qualities of nature in which those forms were preserved. This was why his voice had such power; this was why his gestures extended with such ease the outlines of images; this was why in every word he spoke the suggestive power of sound increased the literal meaning. There was, therefore, not only the usual effect of an electric communication between the speaker and his listeners, there was also a kind of enchantment that was contained in the very foundations of the mighty building and which became extraordinarily powerful as it came into unexpected contact with the beating heart of the assembled crowd. That heartbeat and the poet's voice appeared to give new life back to the age-old walls and restore to the cold museum its original spirit: a nucleus of powerful ideas made concrete and organic in the most durable of substances in order to proclaim the nobility of an entire race.

The splendour of divine youth fell upon the women as though they were in some sumptuous bedchamber, for each of them had experienced the anxiety of waiting and the voluptuousness of surrender, just like the lovely City. They were smiling langorously, almost overwhelmed by an excess

45

of feeling, their bare shoulders rising up out of their wreaths of gems. Andriana Duodo's emeralds, Giustiniana Memo's rubies, Lucrezia Priuli's sapphires, Orsetta Contarini's beryls, Zenobia Corner's turquoises, all that inheritance of jewels which sparkled with more than their intrinsic preciousness, just as there was more than the preciousness of art in the decoration of the great hall, seemed to arouse reflections of a joyous, shameless inner life in the pale faces of the patrician women. It was as if the souls of voluptuaries who had given their lovers bodies steeped in baths scented with myrrh, musk and amber and exposed their rouged breasts to public gaze had risen up in some secret way from out of the abyss to be revived within the women present in the hall.

Stelio saw the female breast of that great, many-eyed monster against which feathered fans were softly beating, and he felt a rush of overheated inebriation within his mind that disturbed him, for it suggested words of too carnal a nature, the living words of power that he used on women like caressing, arousing fingers. The enormous impact of the vibrations he had caused rushed through him, striking him with such force that he lost his sense of balance. He felt he was swaying over the crowd like a concave, sonorous object in which all sorts of resonances were being generated through some indefinable yet infallible will. During the pauses, he anxiously waited for the unforeseen manifestation of that will, while the inner echoes went on and on, as though a voice that was not his voice had spoken words expressing thoughts that were quite new to him. And the sky, the water, the stones, the Autumn that he described seemed to bear no relation to his own recent feelings but belonged instead to a world of dreams that he had glimpsed while he was speaking in a series of lightning flashes.

He was astounded at the unknown power which was building up within him destroying the boundaries of individuality and giving his lone voice the quality of an entire chorus. This was the mysterious pact that the revelation of Beauty could give to the daily life of the toiling masses.

46

This was the mysterious will that could possess a poet in the very act of replying to the multiform soul that questioned him about the value of life and longed to raise itself just once towards the eternal Ideal. At that moment he was simply the means through which Beauty transmitted the divine gift of oblivion to the people gathered in that place consecrated by centuries of human achievement. His task was to translate in the rhythms of his speech the visible language which ancient craftsmen had employed in the same place in order to depict the aspirations and longings of the human race. For the space of an hour people were able to see the world with new eyes, to feel, think and dream with new souls.

It was the greatest gift of Beauty made manifest. It was the victory of Art the Liberator over the poverty and anxiety and tedium of every day. It was a happy interval during which pain and need ceased to exist, when the clenched fists of Destiny seemed to be slowly prised open. His thought went beyond those walls that contained the heaving crowd in a sort of heroic cycle, a circle of red galleys and fortified towers and triumphant theories. The place now seemed too narrow for his sublime, new feelings, and once again the real crowd attracted him, the great unanimous crowd he had seen pouring past the marble courtyard, filling the starry night with a cry that intoxicated like blood or wine.

His thoughts did not only go out towards that crowd, but towards an infinite number of crowds. He imagined them in great theatres, ruled by some idea of truth and beauty, silent and intent as the great stage opened to reveal some marvellous transformation of life, or cheering wildly at the sudden glory of an immortal speech. The dream of the highest art of all rose up in him once again and showed him mankind overwhelmed once more with reverence for poets, for the chosen ones who are able to interrupt human suffering just for an instant, and assuage thirst and grant oblivion. The test he was undergoing now seemed too slight for him; stirred by the breath of the crowd, his soul felt able to create gigantic works of art. And the still unformed work he was nourishing within himself gave a proud shudder of life, as his eyes caught sight of the great actress standing against the globe of the constellations, the muse with the voice that knew how to reveal, she who seemed to bring the frenzy of distant crowds to him in the silent folds of her garments.

He was almost exhausted by the incredible intensity that he had experienced in the pause, but resumed speaking in quieter tones.

'In that image,' he said, 'that image which was so powerful and real to me then that I almost felt I could touch it, which of you is not able to see the connection that makes it the most extraordinary of all extraordinary things?

'The mutual passion of Venice and Autumn which raises both to the highest point of their sensuous beauty derives from a profound affinity between them, for the soul of Venice, that soul fashioned for the lovely City by ancient craftsmen, is autumnal.

'When I discovered the relationship between her inner and outer magnificence, I was overwhelmed with delight. The great assembly of everlasting shapes that comprise her churches and palaces responded from its very essence to the harmonies of daylight with such complete, powerful agreement that it swiftly assumed control. And because the light of the heavens alternates with shadow whilst the light of art remains unquenchable within the human soul, when the marvel of that hour was ended, my mind stayed in a state of solitary ecstasy surrounded by the glory of that ideal Autumn.

'So truly I perceive the creative process of art as consisting of the youth of a Giorgione and the age of a Tintoretto. It is clad in purple and gold, rich and expressive as is the majesty of earth beneath the last blaze of the sun. If I consider the wonderful creators of such powerful beauty, then the image that comes to mind derives from a fragment of Pindar: when the Centaurs understood the virtue of wine that was sweet as honey and could conquer men, they

48

swiftly banished pale milk from their tables and hastened to drink wine in silver horns . . . Nobody in the world knew or tasted the wine of life so well as they. They drank from it a kind of clear-thinking intoxication that increased their power and gave a fertile energy to their speech. In the most beautiful of their creations the violent throbbing of their veins persists across the centuries like the very rhythm of Venetian art itself.

'Think of St Ursula the Virgin in the pure, poetic sleep of her unstained bed! The kindest of all silences hovers in that solitary room where the sleeper's pious lips repeat her habitual prayers. The timid light of daybreak is creeping in through the doors and half-open windows, illuminating the word written on the corner of her pillow. CHILDHOOD is the simple word, that radiates morning freshness around the head of the sleeping saint: CHILDHOOD. The saint sleeps, she is already betrothed to the pagan prince and destined for martyrdom. Chaste, naïve, passionate, is she not surely the image of Art as the first artists saw it with their sincere, childish eyes? CHILDHOOD. The word summons long forgotten names to that bedside: Lorenzo Veneziano and Simone de Cusighe and Catarino and Iacobello and Master Paolo and Giambono and Semitecolo and Antonio and Andrea and Quirizio da Murano: all the family of craftsmen who made the tincture that perfectly reproduced the colour of flame out there on the island with its blazing furnaces.

'But surely even they would have cried out in amazement if they had seen the rush of blood that poured from the virgin's breast when the handsome pagan archer fired his bow? How could a young girl nurtured on "pale milk" produce blood of such brilliant scarlet? The killing becomes almost a celebration: the archers have brought their finest bows, they are wearing their most lavish garments, their movements are elegant, as though they were going to a festival. The golden-haired archer who strikes the saint with such grace and skill seems truly the young Eros, still in his chrysalis stage and wingless.

'This gracious murderer of innocence (or perhaps one of

his brothers) will then set down his bow, and tomorrow he will give himself up to the enchantment of music and dream a dream of endless pleasure.

'It was indeed Giorgione who gave him a new spirit and filled him to the brim with unquenchable desire. That magical music is not the melody that only yesterday angelic lutes were sounding down the curving arches reaching over radiant thrones or fading into the serene silence of distance, as envisioned by the third Bellini. It can still be summoned by holy hands from the heart of a clavichord, but the world that it awakens is full of joy and sadness in which sin lies concealed.

'Whoever has looked at the Concerto with the eyes of knowledge can recognize an extraordinary, unrepeatable moment of the Venetian spirit. Through the harmony of colours, whose power of meaning is as boundless as the mystery of sound, the artist shows us the first signs of longing in a spirit that has suddenly discovered the boundless possibilities of life.

'The monk seated at the clavichord and his elder companion bear no resemblance to the monks painted by Vettor Carpaccio as they flee from the wild beast tamed by St Jerome in the church of San Giorgio degli Schiavoni. They are of a stronger, nobler essence, the air they breathe is more refined and elevated, better suited to the birth of some great joy or great sadness or some superb dream. What are the notes that those beautiful, sensitive hands reveal as they move across the keys? They must be magic notes if they can create such a violent transformation in the musician himself. He is halfway through his earthly existence, he is already distanced from his own youth, on the verge of decay, yet now life appears to him as laden with good things as a forest is laden with dark fruits, fruits whose soft skins he has never touched, for his hands have always been engaged in other things. Because his sensuality is dulled, he does not fall under the sway of a single enticing image; instead he feels a sense of confused pain, where regret overwhelms desire, while through the web of harmony that he seeks to create, the vision of his own past appears like a magic tapestry, with all that might have been and all that never was. His companion, who is already standing on the threshold of peaceful old age, guesses at the storm raging within and lays his gentle, serious hand on the agitated man's shoulder in a calming gesture. But there is another man in the painting, emerging from the warm shadows like the personification of desire itself, a young man with unshorn hair and a feathered hat. He is the blazing flower of youth that Giorgione appears to have painted under the influence of that marvellous Greek myth which tells us of the ideal body of Hermaphrodite. So he is there, yet distanced and separated from the others, like someone who is only concerned about himself. The music exalts his unspeakable dreams and multiplies infinitely his power of enjoyment. He knows he is master of the life which is escaping from the other two, and the harmonies the musician is seeking are merely the prelude to his own celebration. He is looking intensely to one side, about to seduce something that attracts him. His closed mouth is heavy with kisses that have not yet been given, his forehead is so broad that the heaviest of crowns would sit lightly upon it, but when I imagine his hands, which are hidden from view, I see them about to pluck some laurel leaves with which to perfume his fingers.'

The hands of the speaker brought that lascivious gesture to life, as though he were really extracting the essence of a scented leaf. His tone of voice gave such substance to the image he had created that all the young men listening believed that they were seeing their own unspoken desire before them, seeing their own intimate dreams of boundless, endless pleasure. They were seized by feelings of agitation, a dark stirring of contained impulses, and they divined new possibilities, believing that at last what they had so vainly longed for might be close at hand. Stelio could see them throughout the hall, leaning against the great reddish chests in which the countless volumes of forgotten, dead knowledge lay buried. They were all standing, filling the

51

free spaces around the walls, right round the edges of the packed crowd like a brightly coloured border. They quivered in response to the breath of poetry, just as the extreme points of a banner floating in the wind flutter with the greatest liveliness.

Stelio recognized them; he could distinguish some by the particular way in which they were standing, by the excess of emotion revealed in the clenching of a jaw, the blinking of an eyelid or the colour of a cheek. The faces of some of them were turned towards the open balcony, and he could tell that they were enchanted by that autumn evening and delighted by the salt breeze blowing from the weedy lagoon. He followed the glances of some of them like a ray of love directed at a woman seated somewhere, engrossed in her own thoughts, made langorous by secret delights and softened in some impure way, with a snow-white face in which her mouth opened like a hive damp with honey.

There was a strange clarity in him that made him see everything in a heightened manner as though he were in the grip of a fever. Everything he could see was exaggeratedly alive. The portraits of the Doges that ran round the walls between the white tracings of the maps were breathing as truly as the bald old men at the far end of the hall who kept wiping their pale, sweaty foreheads with monotonous regularity. Nothing escaped his notice: he saw the steady drip of the torches hanging in the bronze baskets that were collecting the wax yellow as amber; he saw the delicacy with which a beringed hand pressed a handkerchief against sorrowful lips as though to soothe a burn; he saw the way in which a light scarf was wrapped around bare shoulders that had suddenly shivered at the night breeze sighing through the open balconies. And still, whilst he saw a thousand fleeting things, he held the overall image in his mind of the great many-eyed monster with its breast covered in gleaming scales, from whose side rose the tragic muse with her head against the globe of the constellations.

He kept turning back to the promised woman, who appeared to him like the living climax of a starry world. He was grateful to her for having chosen such a way of appearing to him in that act of first communion. He no longer saw in her the lover of a single night, her body ripe from many encounters, weighty with voluptuous awareness. He saw her now as the marvellous instrument for his new art, the woman who had made great poetry plain to him, the woman who would incarnate in her changeable being his future imaginings of beauty, the woman who would bear the word of enlightenment to the people in her unforgettable voice. He felt bound to her not with the promise of pleasure but with the promise of glory. And the unformed work that he was nourishing within himself gave another leap.

'Who among you,' he went on, 'cannot see the connection between these three symbolic figures by Giorgione and the three generations alive at the same time, who lit up the dawn of the new age? Venice, the triumphant city, appeared in their eyes like the great preparations for an excessive banquet at which all the wealth assembled through centuries of war and commerce was about to be spread out without restraint. There could be no richer source of voluptuousness to initiate life into insatiable desire. It was a time of heady turmoil, that in its fullness was as great as any heroic time. Laughter and seductive voices drift down from the hills of Asolo where the daughter of St Mark rules over pleasure, the Domina Aceli who found Aphrodite's girdle in the myrtle woods of Cyprus. Now the young man with his gorgeous white plumes is approaching the banquet like a leader of the dance followed by his wild train, and all fiercest desires are blazing like torches ceaselessly fanned by the restless wind.

'Such is the beginning of that divine Autumn of Art, and men will always look on its splendours with leaping hearts so long as there remains within the human spirit the desire to transcend the confines of everyday existence and live a fuller life or die a nobler death.

'I see Giorgione right there in that fantastic land, but I cannot make out his mortal shape. I have to search for it

53

in the fiery cloud that surrounds him. He is more of a myth than a man. No writer on earth can match his destiny. We know nothing, or almost nothing, about him, and some have even gone so far as to deny his very existence. His name does not appear on any work, and some claim that nothing can be attributed to him with any certainty. And yet all the art of Venice is fired by his revelations. The great Vecellio apparently took from him the secret of giving his creations luminous blood in their veins. In fact, what Giorgione represents in painting is the Epiphany of Fire. Like Prometheus, he deserves the title of "Bearer of Fire".

'When I consider the speed with which the sacred gift passed from artist to artist and the way in which colour took on greater hues of redness, I immediately think of those torchlight festivals when the Athenians celebrated the memory of the Titan son of Iapetus. On the day of the festival, a crowd of young Athenian knights rode out from Ceramicus towards Colonnus, and their leader carried a torch that had been lit at a sanctuary altar. Whenever the effort of the ride extinguished the torch, the leader would hand it over to his companion, who would relight it and go on riding. This would happen three, four times and so on until the last man laid it still burning on the altar of the Titan. This image, with all the energy that is contained in it, reminds me in some way of the festival of the great Venetian painters. Every one of them, even the least talented, held the sacred torch in his hand for an instant. Some of them, like the first Bonifacio who deserves our praise, seem even to have plucked the inner flower of fire with their own flameproof hands.'

He plucked that ideal flower from the air, from the invisible crest of the wave on which the seething spirit of the monster was rolling, towards the poet who had almost tamed it. His gaze turned towards the celestial globe, and he wanted to offer that fiery prize to the woman who was guarding the divine creatures of the Zodiac. 'For you, Perdita!' But the woman was smiling at someone far away, and her smile was a sign. As he followed that smile, he was drawn to an unknown person who was suddenly lit up against a dark background. Was it not that same musical being whose name had resounded against the armed ship in the silent shadows? She was like some interior image created unexpectedly in that part of his mind where the spirit of spontaneous feeling that he had experienced as they sailed into the shadows of the warship remained as an obscure, indistinct point. For an instant she was as beautiful as his own unexpressed thoughts within him.

'Today,' he went on, mounted lightly on the rising wave, 'a city endowed by its artists with such a powerful spirit is considered by most people to be merely a great, motionless shrine or a haven of peace and forgetfulness.

'But in truth, throughout the whole world I know of no other place than here on these sluggish waters, except perhaps Rome, where an alert, ambitious mind can activate the power of his intellect and direct all the energies of his being towards the supreme ideal. I do not know of any other mist that is able to arouse a hotter fever in human veins than the one we feel creeping towards us from the shadows of some silent canal. The man who spends his afternoons deep in the ripe fields of harvest-time in the extreme heat of summer does not feel a hotter rush of blood to his temples than that which sometimes clouds our eyes when we look too closely into the waters to see if we can discern an ancient sword or crown in the depths.

'And yet, fragile souls also come here, to a gentle place of refuge, together with those who are hiding a wound that cannot be spoken of, those who have made a final renunciation, those emasculated by some morbid love, those who are searching for the silence of their own dying. Perhaps to their lack-lustre eyes Venice seems like a kindly city of death clasped in the embrace of a somniferous pool. In truth, their presence weighs no more than the floating seaweed that laps against the stairways of marble palaces. They increase that particular scent of sickly things, that strange feverish scent that seems so sweet sometimes in the evenings, after a day's work, that we want to bask in the feeling of over-ripeness which, at times, is so akin to languour.

'Yet the ambiguous City does not always indulge the illusions of those who adore her as a bringer of peace. I know a man who started up in horror from his rest like someone who has been lying with the soft fingers of his beloved resting on his tired eyelids and hears the sudden hiss of serpents in her hair . . .

'If only I could tell you about the marvellous life that she possesses as she appears to me with her heart beating beneath her rich jewels and her thousand green girdles! She sucks out our souls every day, and then returns them pure and whole, refreshed with some completely original newness on which tomorrow the traces of things will be impressed with limpid clarity. She turns the soul into something cunning and voracious like a fire that destroys whatever it touches, and then sometimes in the evening we experience some extraordinary sublimation amid the ashes and the ruins. She convinces us each day to perform the act that generates our species: the effort of going further, unceasingly. She shows us the possibility of pain transformed into the most effective form of inspirational energy; she teaches us that pleasure is the most certain means of awareness that Nature offers us, and that a man who has suffered a great deal knows less than the man who has enjoyed a life of pleasure.'

A vague ripple of disagreement rustled through the hall at this remark which was deemed too outrageous. The Queen shook her head slightly in denial; some ladies exchanged glances of elegant horror. Then doubts were swept away by the youthful applause which rose up on all sides for the man who was teaching so clearly the art of ascending to superior forms of life through the power of joy.

Stelio smiled as he heard his disciples, for there were many of them. He smiled as he saw the results of his teaching which had already banished the dull mists of sadness from more than one mind and in still more had killed off the cowardice of useless tears, had instilled forever a scorn

56

for complaining about sorrow and for soft compassion. He rejoiced that he had finally put into words the principles of his belief, which came naturally from the very soul of art that he was glorifying. Those who had retreated to a hermit's cell, worshipping a dismal spectre that only existed in the dull mirror of their eyes, and those who had proclaimed themselves kings in a windowless palace, who had been waiting since time immemorial for a visitation, those who believed they could unearth the image of Beauty from under the ruins only to find it was just a corroded sphinx that tormented them with unresolvable riddles, those who stood on their doorsteps every evening to watch for the arrival of the mysterious stranger whose cloak was laden with gifts, pressing their ears to the ground, listening white-faced for the footsteps that seemed to come nearer and nearer and then faded away – in sum, all those who felt emasculated by the pain of resignation, or eaten away by desperate pride, all who had been hardened by pointless obstinacy or who spent sleepless nights of hopeless waiting, these were the people that he now wanted to call upon, so that they could recognize their disease in the splendour of that ancient yet ever-restorative soul.

'Truly,' he said, his voice rising in exultation, 'if everyone in Venice were to emigrate, abandoning their homes, drawn to other shores, just as the young men of the city were once tempted by the curve of the Bosphorus in the days of Doge Pietro Ziani, if the sound of prayers reverberating against the ringing gold bowls of her mosaics were no more, and if the rhythm of oars had ceased to mark the meditation of her silent stones, Venice would still always remain the City of Life. The ideal beings that shelter in her silence live wholly in the past and wholly in the future. We constantly discover in them links with the whole structure of the Universe, unexpected meetings with an idea that was born only yesterday, clear announcements of things within us that are still only premonitions, open answers to what we still do not dare to ask. They are simple and yet laden with boundless meaning. They are virginal, yet dressed in

luxurious garments. If we were to contemplate them indefinitely, they would never cease from pouring all kinds of
truth into our hearts. If we were to visit them every day,
they would appear to us each time in some new guise, of
the sea, the rivers, fields, woods or cliffs. Sometimes the
things they tell us do not reach our intellect, but they
emerge as a kind of happiness, in which our very essence
seems to quiver and dissolve. On a clear morning they can
show us the way to the distant forest where Beauty has been
waiting since time immemorial, wreathed in her mysterious
hair.

'How have they acquired such immense power?

'From the pure unknowingness of the creators who shaped
them.

'Those profound men did not realize the immensity of
the things they expressed. They were rooted thousandfold
in the soil of life, not like solitary trees but like great forests,
absorbing infinite elements and transforming and condensing them into ideal forms whose essence was unknown to
them, as the taste of apples is unknown to the branch which
bears them. The creators are the mysterious channels
through which Nature fulfills her eternal longing for things
that she cannot herself form from her own moulds. And
so, continuing the Divine Mother's work, their minds are
transformed into a likeness of the divine mind, as Leonardo
says. And since creative force flows constantly into their
fingertips like sap to the jewelled fruits of trees, they create
with joy.'

All the desire of the single-minded artist, desperately
trying to achieve the Olympian gift, all his envy of the great
masters of Beauty, who never flagged and never doubted, all
his thirst for happiness and glory could be heard in the tone
of his voice as he spoke those last words. Once again the
poet took the soul of the multitude in his hands without a
struggle, taut and quivering like a single thread made of a
thousand other threads upon which every sound was
immeasurably prolonged. There stirred again within him the
confused awareness of a truth that was hidden somewhere

in that crowd and which the poet was revealing to it all of a sudden in the form of a message that had never before been spoken. The crowd no longer felt ill at ease in that sacred place, where one of the greatest of human destinies had left such immense traces of glory; it could feel the ancient building coming alive all around it and beneath its feet, from the deepest foundations, as though memories were no longer fixed in the shadows of the past but were now flowing freely like breezes through a rustling forest. In the magical truce granted by the power of poetry and dream, it seemed that the people found the indestructible signs of primitive generations within themselves, almost a vague effigy of their distant ancestors, and were recognizing their right to an ancient inheritance from which they had been dispossessed, that inheritance which the messenger was telling them was still intact and could be recovered. As one, they felt the agitation of a man about to regain a lost treasure. And in the night that sparkled through the open balconies, as the red glow of the blaze that was about to enfold the harbour began to appear, there spread a sense of expectation of the return that had been foretold.

In the weight of that silence his solitary voice reached its climax. 'To create with joy! That is a sign of godliness! It is impossible to imagine a greater triumph for the human spirit. The very words expressing such a thought are as splendid as dawn itself.

'Those artists create in a way that is itself a joyous mystery: with colour, which is the ornament of the world; with colour, the manifestation of matter struggling to turn itself into light.

'The new musical sense of colour which they possess ensures that their creations go beyond the narrow limits of painted symbols and assume the power to reveal infinite harmony.

'Only when facing their great symphonic canvases do the words spoken by Leonardo da Vinci to whom Truth spoke one day and in a flash revealed its thousand secrets, appear clear to us: "Music cannot be described as anything other than the sister of painting." Their painting is not only silent poetry, it is also silent music. And so the most sophisticated seekers of rare symbols, those who were eager to impress the signs of an entire universe on the purity of a thoughtful forehead, seem almost barren to us compared with those great unconscious musicians.

'When Boniface in his *Parable of Rich Epulones* strikes a note of flame with the most powerful harmony of colour in which the essence of a proud, voluptuous soul has ever been portrayed, we do not question the blond youth listening to the music, sitting between the two magnificent courtesans whose faces shine like lamps of clearest amber. We go beyond the material symbol, tremulously we bow down to the evocative powers of the profound harmonies, in which our souls today find a foretaste of some mysterious evening heavy with autumnal gold and fatality beautified, in a harbour as still as a bowl of scented oils, where a galley fluttering with banners shall sail through a strange silence, like a butterfly at twilight in the veined chalice of some huge flower.

'Shall our mortal eyes not really see it some glorious evening as it draws near to the Doge's Palace?

'Does it not seem to have come from over a prophetic horizon in the *Allegory of Autumn* that Tintoretto offers us like a superior image created by our dreams of yesterday?

'Seated on the shore like a goddess, Venice receives the ring from the young god with his garland of vine-leaves who has descended into the waters, while Beauty flies freely into the air with a wreath of stars to crown their marvellous alliance.

'There is the distant ship! It seems to be bringing a message. Look at the thighs of the symbolic woman! They are powerful enough to bear the seed of an entire world!'

The great burst of applause was overwhelmed by the youthful roar that rose up in a vortex towards the man who had shown them a glimpse of great hopefulness, the man who had such powerful steady faith in the hidden genius of their race, in the lofty virtues of the ideals handed down by their forefathers, in the sovereign dignity of the spirit, in the indestructible power of Beauty, in all the great things that were despised by modern barbarians. His disciples reached out towards their master with a rush of recognition, a surge of love; for his fiery words had lit up their souls like torches, fanning their life-force to fever pitch. Giorgione's creation sprang to life in each one of them, the youth with the gorgeous white feathers reaching out for the great spoils he had gathered. It seemed as though their power of enjoyment had been infinitely extended.

The shout was so expressive of their inner turmoil that the poet shook inwardly, and a sudden wave of sadness rushed through him as he thought of the ashes of that fleeting fire and the cruel awakening for them on the following day. What bitter, wretched obstacles would their terrible desire to live encounter, their violent urge to shape the wings of Victory through their own efforts and to focus all their energies of being on the ultimate goal!

But night looked kindly on youthful delirium. All the dreams of power, voluptuousness and glory that Venice had aroused and then crushed to death in her marble arms rose up from the foundations of the palace, came in through the open windows, breathed like a people restored to life beneath the great curves of the ceiling that hung as rich and heavy as a treasure-hoard. The strength that swelled the muscles of gods, kings and heroes, the beauty of the naked goddesses, queens and harlots painted on the great vault and high walls, flowed like visible music; human strength and beauty transfigured by centuries of art came together in the harmony of a single image that the delirious followers believed was real and breathing before their very eyes, erected by the new poet.

They breathed out their delirium in the shout to the man who had raised a cup of his own wine to their parched lips. Now they could all see the unquenchable flame through the veil of water. Some even imagined they were about to pluck a laurel leaf to scent their fingers, and some had

61

already dreamed of finding the long-lost sword and ancient crown in the depths of a silent canal.

Now, in the rooms of the neighbouring museum, Stelio Effrena was alone with the statues, unable to bear any other kind of contact, for he needed to recover himself and to calm the unusual vibrations that seemed to have split his whole being into fragments and scattered them through the countless souls of the crowd. He could not remember anything of what he had just said, nor recall even a trace of his recent images. All that remained in his mind was 'the flower of flame' that he had conjured up when praising the first Boniface and which he had plucked with his own flame-proof fingers to offer to his promised woman. He recalled the way in which the woman had drawn back as he offered it to her, and how he had found a meaningful smile in place of her absent look. The cloud of exhilaration that had been about to dissolve seemed to form itself again within him, in the vague shape of that musical being who was holding the flower of fire in a triumphal pose. She appeared to his inner agitation like the ceaseless quivering of the sea in summer-time. As though to celebrate that image, the first notes of Benedetto Marcello's symphony came to him from the neighbouring hall, and the fugue showed straight away that it was a piece in the grand style. A sonorous, clear, strong idea like a living being grew as the music gathered strength. And in that music he recognized the power of the same principle around which he had wreathed the garlands of his poetry like vines around a Bacchic wand.

Then the name that had already echoed against the sides of the warship in the silence and the shadow, that name which had been lost like a sibylline leaf in the great wave of twilight bells, seemed to him to have given its syllables to the orchestra in the form of a new theme picked up by the strings. The violins, violas and cellos all repeated it in turn, the sudden peals of the trumpet exalted it, and finally the entire quartet flung it upwards with unanimous verve into the joyous heavens where later on the crown of stars offered to Ariadne by Aphrodite would be shining.

There was a pause, during which Stelio felt an extraordinary sense of bewilderment, almost a religious trance, before that annunciation. He understood what it meant for him to be alone with the white, silent images in that indescribably lyrical moment. He had brushed against the hem of that same mystery that he had touched beside the warship as against a fleeting veil, and it now seemed to hover on the threshold of that empty room which was yet so close to the human crowd. (Just as silent, on the shore close to the waves, lies the seashell.) He thought he could feel once again, as he had done at another extraordinary point in his journey, the presence of destiny that was about to give his being a new impulse, perhaps to arouse it to a marvellous act of will. And as he considered the mediocrity of the dozens of obscure destinies hanging over the heads of the crowd that was straining for a sight of ideal life, he was glad that he could stand apart from them and worship the joyful demonic being that had secretly come to visit him bringing an unexpected gift in the name of an unknown lover.

He started at the burst of human voices greeting the undefeated god with a triumphal acclamation:

Viva il forte, viva il grande . . .

The long hall resounded like an huge drum, and the sound extended down the Scala dei Censori and the Scala d'Oro, along the corridors, the courtyards, the vestibules, the loggias, as far as the wells, down into the foundations of the palace, like a peal of joyful thunder in the peaceful night.

Viva il forte, viva il grande
*Vincitor dell'Indie dome!**

The Chorus really seemed to be welcoming the magnificent

* Long live the strong, long live the great
  Conqueror of the vanished Indies!

god invoked by the poet over the City of the Sea. His purple garments seemed to quiver in the sound of those voices like flames in crystal holders. The living image hovered over the crowd that nourished it with dreams.

Viva il forte, viva il grande . . .

In the impetuous movement of the fugue, the basses, contraltos and sopranos repeated their wild greeting to the god of the thousand names and the thousand garlands, 'born on an ineffable bed', 'like a youth in the prime of life'. An ancient, Dionysian frenzy seemed to be returning to vigorous life, spread by that divine chorus. The fullness and freshness of life in the smile of Bacchus, he who frees the hearts of men from care, was expressed in that luminous burst of joy. The inextinguishable torches of the Bacchae flamed and crackled in it. As in the song of Opheus, his youthful brow crowned with heavenly locks was illuminated by reflected fire. 'When the splendour of fire invaded the whole earth, he alone chained up the strident whirlwinds of flame.' As in Homer, the sterile womb of the sea throbbed in it, and the measured beat of the countless oars driving the well-wrought ship towards unknown lands could be heard in it. The Blossoming One, the Fruit-bearer, the Remedy of Mortals made Visible, the Sacred Flower, the Friend of Pleasure, Dionysius the Liberator suddenly reappeared to the sight of men on the wings of song, crowning that evening hour with ecstasy, offering them once more all the good things of life from a brimming chalice.

The song grew louder, the voices fused together in the surge of sound. The hymn was celebrating the one who tamed tigers, panthers, lions, lynx. The Maenads seemed to be shrieking, their heads flung back, their hair wild, their clothing torn, beating the cymbals, shaking the tambourines – 'Evoe!'

Then out of that heroic sound there rose unexpectedly a deep pastoral rhythm which recalled the Theban Bacchus, he of the clear forehead girded with gentle thoughts:

Quel che all'olmo la vita in stretto nodo
Pronuba accoppia, e i pampini feconda . . . *

Two solo voices in a succession of sixths sang of the leafy
nuptials, the green wedding-feast, the supple bonding. The
image of the barge on the lagoon laden with bunches of
grapes like a vat in which the wine-pressing is about to
begin, that image which the poet had already created in
words passed once again before the eyes of the crowd. Once
again the song seemed to repeat the miracle that the careful
pilot Medeides had seen: 'And behold, sweet, fragrant wine
flowed through the swift, black ship . . . And behold, a vine
twisted itself around to the very top of the sail and countless
bunches of grapes hung from its length. And dark ivy coiled
around the mast, covered with flowers, and gorgeous fruits
grew from it, and garlands hung from every rowlock . . .'
   Then the spirit of the fugue entered the orchestra, and
eased itself in lovely waves of sound, while the voices beat
against the orchestral web in simultaneous percussion. Like
a delicate wand waved high above the Bacchic throng, a
single voice repeated the nuptial melody that held all the
smiling grace of a rural wedding:

> *Viva dall'olmo*
> *E della vite*
> *L'almo fecondo*
> *Sostenitor!* * *

The soloists created an image of the lofty Thiades, amid
the fumes of intoxication, slowly brandishing their wands
decorated with flowers and vine leaves, dressed in long
crocus-yellow garments, their faces flushed and breathing

---

* He who joins the vine to the elm in close
  bonds of wedlock, and makes the vine-leaves fruitful . . .
** Hail the sustaining one!
  He of the elm tree,
  He of the vine,
  Soul of fertility!

heavily, like the women depicted by Veronese, leaning over the lofty balustrades to drink in the music.

Then acclamation for the hero rose up once again with a final burst of strength. The face of the conquering god shone once more amid the wildly brandished torches. Voices and orchestra thundered in unison in a supreme impulse of rejoicing at the immense, many-eyed monster beneath the hanging treasure of the ceiling, in that circle of red galleys and fortified towers and triumphal processions.

> *Viva dell'India,*
> *Viva de' mari,*
> *Viva de' mostri*
> *Il domator!**

Stelio Effrena had gone through the doorway and stepped into the crowd that made room for him. He was standing close to the side of the platform occupied by the orchestra and the singers. His anxious eyes were searching for Foscarina over by the celestial globe, but he could not see her. The head of the tragic Muse no longer rose up above the constellations. Where could she be? Where had she gone? Could she still see him without his seeing her? He felt strangely disturbed, and the memory of what they had seen that evening out in the lagoon came back confusedly into his mind, along with the words of her final promise. He looked at the open balconies, and thought that she might perhaps have gone out into the night air and that she was leaning over the parapet, letting the waves of music flow over her icy neck, enjoying them as much as she would enjoy shivering beneath passionate kisses.

But the expectation of the prophetic voice overcame all his other concerns and drove all other worries from his mind. He suddenly realized that there was a profound

---

* Hail the conquering one!
  He of the Indies,
  He of the seas,
  Tamer of monsters!

66

silence in the hall, as had happened when he himself had opened his mouth to utter his first words. As had happened then, the elusive, changeable monster with the thousand human faces appeared to stretch itself silently and empty itself in order to receive a new soul.

He heard people around him whispering the name of Donatella Arvale. He turned to look at the platform, beyond the dark hedge of the cellos. The singer was invisible, hidden behind the delicate, trembling forest from which the painful harmony that accompanies Ariadne's lament was about to rise.

A prelude of violins sounded in the auspicious silence. The violas and cellos joined their deeper sighing to their beseeching plea. After the Phrygian flute and the Berecinthian tambourine, after the orgiastic instruments whose sound disturbs the reason and incites men to delirium, surely this was the noble, Doric lyric, the grave, sweet harmonious fulcrum of song. Such was the birth of Drama from the wild noise of the Dithyramb. The great metamorphosis of the Dionysiac ritual, the frenzy of the sacred festival become the creative enthusiasm of the tragedian, was depicted in that music. The fiery breath of the Thracian god had given life to a sublime form of Art. The crown and the tripod, decreed as victory prizes to the poet, had replaced the lascivious goat and the basket of Attic figs. Aeschylus, keeper of a vineyard, had been visited by the god who had inspired him with a spirit of flame. On the slopes of the Acropolis, near the sanctuary of Dionysus, a marble theatre had arisen fit for the chosen people.

Suddenly, in the inner world of the poet, the pathways of centuries opened up, stretching out through the distance of primitive mysteries. That form of art towards which he was now directing all his creative energies, drawn to it by the obscure desires of human multitudes, now appeared to him in the full sanctity of its origins. The divine grief of Ariadne, rising like a melodious shriek outside the raging Thiasus, made the unformed but living work within him leap once more. Again his eyes sought the Muse with the prophetic

67

voice against the globe of the constellations. As he could not see her, he turned to look at the forest of instruments from which the lament was rising.

Then, between the delicate bows that sparkled like long plectrums rising and falling over the strings with alternating movements, the singer emerged, straight as the stem of a flower, swaying slightly like a flower to the subdued melody. Her youthful, agile, strong body seemed to glow through the material of her dress like a flame through the thinness of polished ivory. Rising and falling around her white figure, the bows seemed to take their tone from the secret music within her. When she moved her lips, Stelio could feel the purity and strength of her voice before he heard it, as though he had before his eyes a crystal statue within which one could trace the rising of a living fountain:

> Come mai puoi
> Vedermi piangere . . .*

The melody of ancient love and ancient pain flowed from those lips with such pure, intense expression that it was instantly transformed into mysterious delight for the multiple soul of the audience. Surely this was the divine lament of the daughter of Minos as she held out her deluded arms in vain, on the desolate shores of Naxos, to the Flavian visitor? The story vanished, the age-old deception was annulled. The eternal love and eternal pain of gods and men was exhalted in that sovereign voice. The hopeless regret for joys lost, the last recalling of every fleeting happiness, the desperate imploring of every sail that disappeared out to sea, of every sun that sank behind the hills, and the implacable desire and the promise of death passed into that high, solitary song, which the power of art transformed into sublime essences that the soul could respond to without pain. Words themselves dissolved in it, meaning evaporated

* How can you bear
  To see me weep . .

68

and was changed into infinitely revealing notes of love and loss. Like a circle that is closed yet still dilates forever with the same rhythm of universal life, the melody enfolded the multiple soul that expanded with it into immense happiness. Through the open balconies, in the perfect calm of that autumn night, enchantment spread out over the sluggish waters, rose to the watchful stars, over the silent masts of ships, over the sacred towers inhabited by speechless bells. In the interludes, the singer would lower her youthful head, standing as still as any statue, a white figure in the forest of instruments amid the alternate motion of the long bows, perhaps unaware of the world that her singing had in an instant transformed.

Stelio Effrena had stolen down to the courtyard so as to avoid unwanted attention, and had taken refuge in a patch of shadow, from which he watched to see whether the two women, the actress and the singer who were to meet him beside the wall, would appear in the crowd at the top of the Scala dei Giganti.

He felt more and more disturbed by the waiting. Meanwhile, a great shout reached him, rising up around the outer walls of the palace to be lost in the sky that was reddened by a fiery glow. An almost terrible joy seemed to be spreading through the night over the City of the Sea. It seemed that a vehement breath had suddenly come to fill out confined chests, and an abundance of sensual life had come to extend the arteries of men. The reprise of the Bacchic chorus, celebrating the crown of stars which Aphrodite placed on the oblivious Ariadne's head, the great hymn of praise followed by the supreme orgiastic clamour of Thiasus had prompted the shout from the crowd packed tightly along the Molo beneath the open balconies. In the final elevation, when the chorus of Maenads, Satyrs and Egipans had sung 'Viva' in unison, the people's chorus in St Mark's harbour had replied like a gigantic echo. At that moment it seemed as though the Dionysian delirium, recollecting the burning of ancient

woods on sacred nights, had given the signal for the conflagration in which the beauty of Venice could be gloriously
resplendent.

Paris Eglano's dream flashed into Stelio's desire – the
image of symbolic flames offered to love upon a floating
bed. The image of Donatella Arvale lingered before his eyes:
her slender, youthful body, the powerful curve of her back
rising up out of the forest of sound amid the alternate movement of the bows that seemed to be drawing out the notes
of a secret music within her. And with a strange sense of
anguish through which almost a shudder of horror passed,
he summoned up the image of the other woman: poisoned
by art, weighed down by voluptuous knowledge, with the
taste of ripeness and corruption in her eloquent lips, with
the dryness of her vain feverish hands that had crushed the
juice from deceitful fruits, with the traces of a hundred
masks on her face that had imitated the wildness of all
mortal passions. Tonight at last, after the long intermittent
period of desire, he was to receive the gift of that body
which was no longer young, softened by so many embraces
and yet still unknown to him. How he had trembled and
shuddered a little while ago beside that silent woman as
they sailed towards the beautiful city across the waters that
had seemed to both of them to be flowing into an appalling
maelstrom! Oh, why was she now coming to meet him
with that other temptress by her side? Why was she joining
her despairing wisdom to the magnificent purity of youth?

He caught his breath as he saw in the light of the smoking
torches at the top of the marble staircase the figure of Foscarina, standing so close to Donatella Arvale in the crowd that
the two women were confused in a blur of whiteness. His
eyes followed them down the steps in suspense, as though
they were stepping on to the edge of an abyss with every
stair. In those few short hours the unknown woman had
already lived in his imagination so intensely that as he saw
her coming closer he felt as agitated as he would have felt
if he had suddenly seen the living incarnation of one of the
ideal creatures of his fantasy coming to life.

She came down slowly through the human sea that her singing had raised to the highest point of happiness for just a few seconds. Behind her, the Doge's Palace was criss-crossed with flashes of light and confused noise, creating the impression of one of those fairy-tale moments of awakening that suddenly transform inaccessible castles where some princess's long hair has grown through centuries of lonely silence, like an eternal willow tree over the river Lethe deep in the heart of the forest. The two custodial Giants turned red in the reddish light of the torches; the cusp of the Porta Dorata glittered with tiny flames; beyond the southern wing, the five domes of the Basilica rose majestically into the air like huge mitres studded with chrysolites. And the great noise kept rising, rising over the assembled marble, as lively as the roaring of the sea against the walls of Malamocco.

In that extraordinary festive tumult, in that contrast of unexpected images, Stelio Effrena saw the two temptresses appear to his desires, emerging from the crowd as if from the embrace of a monster. His desire roused bizarre promiscuities within him, which he felt he could make happen with the facility of dream and the solemnity of liturgical rites. He thought that Perdita was bringing that magnificent prize to him for some secret aim of beauty, some great vital labour that she herself wanted to shape with him. He thought how Perdita would say wonderful things to him during the night. His soul was assailed once more by that indefinable melancholy that he had experienced as he leaned over the bronze well and stared down at the stars reflected in the dark mirror of its depths. He was waiting for something to move in the deepest part of his being that secret soul which, like the unchanging mirror of water, was still, motionless, untouchable. By the wild speed of his thoughts he knew that he was in a state of grace, close to that holy delirium which only the power of the lagoon could give him. He stepped out of the shadows and went to meet the two women with a feeling of intoxicated presentiment.

'Oh, Effrena,' said Foscarina, as she reached the well. 'I didn't think I would still find you here. We are so very late, aren't we? I'm afraid we were caught up in the crowd, we simply couldn't get through . . .' Turning to her companion, she added with a smile: 'Donatella, here is the Lord of Fire.'

Donatella Arvale did not answer, but smiled in response to Stelio's low bow.

Foscarina added, taking her arm, 'We must go and find the gondola. It is waiting for us by the Ponte della Paglia. Will you come with us, Effrena? We must seize our opportunity. The crowd is surging towards the Piazzetta. The Queen will be leaving by the Porta della Carta.'

A long, joyful shout greeted the appearance of the golden-haired queen with her pearl necklaces at the top of the staircase where once the chosen Doge had received the ducal insignia in the presence of his people. Once again the name of the white star-shaped flower and the pure pearl was repeated and echoed by the marble walls. Flashes of joy burst in the sky. A thousand fiery pigeons flew from the pinnacles of St Mark's like the messengers of Flame.

'It is the Epiphany of Fire!' cried Foscarina, as she came out on to the Molo before the hallucinatory spectacle.

Beside her, Donatella Arvale and Stelio Effrena stopped in amazement and stared at one another, dazzled. Their faces were lit by the reflection, as though they were leaning over a furnace or the mouth of a crater.

Every conceivable aspect of volatile, multicoloured Fire was flashing across the sky, writhing in the water, coiling around the masts of ships, garlanding domes and towers, decorating cornices, wreathing statues, studding pillars with gems, enriching every line, transfiguring every detail of profane and sacred architecture within whose boundaries the deep harbour lay like an enchanted mirror that multiplied all those marvels. Their eyes were so dazzled that they could no longer distinguish the shape or quality of things, but saw an illusion of shifting measureless vision in which shapes lived a clear, fluid existence suspended in vibrant ether, so that the slender prows curving over the water and the dozens of gilded pigeons in the sky seemed to be vying with one another for lightness in their similar flights and to reach the heights of immaterial constructions.That which at twilight had appeared to be a silvery sea-god's palace, a structure of twisted sea-shapes, was now a temple built by the cunning genies of Fire. It was a gigantic version of one of those labyrinthine dwellings built on the iron of household shrines, at whose hundred doorways appear double-headed creatures that make ambiguous gestures at any virgin who notices them. It was a gigantic version of one of those fragile vermilion palaces at whose thousand windows salamander princesses peep out for an instant to laugh voluptuously at a contemplative poet. Rose-pink like a waning moon, the sphere of Fortuna carried on the shoulders of the Atlantides shone on the triple loggia near by and a cycle of satellites was generated by its reflection. From the Riva, from San Giorgio, from the Giudecca fiery bundles of stars converged in a continuous explosion in the air and burst into roses, lilies, palms, all the flowers of paradise making an aerial garden that kept dispersing and reforming with ever richer and stranger blossoms. It was like a rapid succession of heavenly springs and autumns. A great sparkling rain of petals and foliage fell out of that dissolving sky, covering everything in tremulous gold. Across the lagoon, through the spaces that appeared in that confused mass, a flotilla decorated with banners could be seen approaching, a fleet of galleys like the ones that sail through the dreams of a libertine sleeping his last sleep in a bed heavy with deadly perfumes. Like those dream-vessels, perhaps they too had ropes made of the plaited hair of slave-girls captured in foreign lands, still dripping with sweet oils; like them, perhaps their holds too were full of myrrh, spikenard, benzoin, Syrian balsam, cinnamon, myriad spices, and sandalwood, cedar, terebinth, all the scented woods piled up in layers. The indescribable colours of the fireworks that seemed to adorn them with banners were a reminder of perfumes and spices. Blue, green, turquoise, bright yellow, violet, indeterminate mixtures of colour, the fireworks seemed to be releasing themselves from an inner conflagration and take on the hues of unimagined sublimations. In the fury of ancient sieges, perhaps the reservoirs of essences destined for the baths of the wives of Syrian princes blazed in similar fashion. Now, over the waters covered with molten colour that glistened along their keels, the magnificent doomed fleet sailed slowly into the harbour, as though captained by intoxicated dreams that were leading it to sacrifice before the Lion on its column, like a gigantic votive pyre that would perfume and stupefy the soul of Venice for all eternity.

'The Epiphany of Fire! What an unexpected comment on your poetry, Effrena. The City of Life is replying to your adoration with a miracle. She is all on fire through her veil of water. Aren't you satisfied? Look there! There are millions of golden pomegranates hanging everywhere.'

The actress smiled, and the festival made her face shine. She seemed to be in the grip of a kind of happiness that Stelio knew well, that in a kind of dulled creaking way produced in him the image of an empty, boarded-up house where violent hands were suddenly tearing open all the doors and windows on their rusty hinges.

'We should thank Ariadne,' he said, 'for bringing the highest note of all to all this harmony.'

He had only said those words to make the singer say something, to hear what her voice would sound like when she descended from the heights of song. But his praise was lost in the repeated shouting of the crowd which had poured on to the Molo, making further delay impossible. He assisted the two friends into their gondola, then sat down beside them on the stool. And the long gleaming dentellated prow penetrated the enchantment.

'To the Rio Marin, along the Canalazzo,' Foscarina ordered the boatman. 'Effrena, do you know we shall have some of your closest friends to supper? Francesco de Lizo, Daniele Glauro, Prince Hoditz, Antimo della Bella, Fabio Molza, Baldassare Stampa . . .'

'It will be a veritable feast,' Stelio interrupted.

'But not, alas, the feast of Canaa!'

'Won't Lady Myrta and her Veronesean greyhounds be there?'

'Of course she will. Didn't you see her in the hall? She was in the front row, lost in adoration of you.'

As they spoke, they were looking into one another's eyes and both were overcome by sudden confusion. The memory of that wonderful hour at twilight that they had lived through on the same waters stirred by the same oar filled their hearts like a rush of torpid blood. They were overcome by a sudden return of the pain they had both felt as they left the silence of the estuary already in the power of darkness and death. Their lips rebelled against vain, deceitful words, and their souls shook off the effort of bending prudently towards the fleeting trappings of a life of pleasure, in which they could no longer discern any value, lost as they were in considering the strange shapes that rose up from their inner depths with forms of monstrous richness never before seen, like the mounds of treasure that shafts of light were uncovering in the night waters.

They both fell silent, as they had done when they sailed close to the vessel whose flag was being lowered, and in that silence they felt the presence of that musical being weigh more heavily upon them than she had done when they first heard the sound of her name. Little by little the weight became unbearable. Nevertheless, as Stelio sat beside her knee, she seemed as distant to him as she had appeared before in the forest of instruments, distant and unaware as she had been in the joyfulness of her singing. She still had not uttered a word!

Almost timidly, just to hear her speak, Stelio asked: 'Will you be staying long in Venice?'

He had been searching for the right words, but everything that he had been about to say had seemed to carry too many ambiguous meanings, to be too lively, or insidious, open to endless misinterpretation, like unknown seeds from which a thousand roots could grow. And he had not wanted

75

anything like that to be overheard by Perdita in case her love for him might be tinged with sadness.

Only when he had asked that simple, ordinary question did it occur to him that there might be a hidden import of desire and hope there too.

'I have to leave tomorrow,' replied Donatella Arvale. 'I shouldn't really be here now.'

The voice that was so clear and powerful in the heights of song was low and serious, with a slightly opaque quality, suggestive of precious metal encased in the most delicate velvet. Her short answer was a reminder of the place of suffering to which she was about to return, to undergo some familiar torture. A sorrowful strength of will, like iron tempered with tears, glistened through the veil of her youthful beauty.

'Tomorrow!' Stelio exclaimed, with genuine regret. 'Did you hear that, Signora?'

'I know,' said Foscarina gently, taking Donatella's hand. 'And I am truly sorry that she has to leave. But she cannot stay away from her father any longer. Perhaps you still do not know that . . .'

'What?' asked Stelio urgently. 'Is he ill? Is it true then that Lorenzo Arvale is ill?'

'No, he is simply exhausted,' replied Foscarina, touching her forehead with a gesture that was perhaps involuntary, but which reminded Stelio of the ghastly threat hanging over the genius of that great artist who had seemed as inspired and tireless as any of the old masters, such as della Robbia or Verrocchio. 'He is tired . . . just that . . . He needs rest and care; and his daughter's singing is the finest kind of care there is. Don't you believe in the healing powers of music, Effrena?'

'Of course I do,' he answered. 'Ariadne has a divine talent and so her powers can accomplish miracles.'

The name of Ariadne came spontaneously to his lips when referring to the singer as he perceived her. For he felt that he could not use the girl's real name and address her in the polite form as social convention demanded. He saw her as quite singular and self-contained, free from the petty constraints of habit, living her own separate life, like a great work upon which style had imprinted its indelible seal. He saw her set apart, like one of those figures that stand out against a clear, deep background, distanced from ordinary life, locked in her own secret thoughts. Before the intensity of that inner life he felt a kind of passionate impatience not unlike that of the man filled with curiosity who finds himself faced with something that tempts him, but which is hermetically sealed.

'Ariadne was granted the gift of forgetfulness for her suffering,' she said, 'but I am not.'

A bitterness that was perhaps unconscious coloured her words, and Stelio thought he saw in that the beginning of a desire for a life less oppressed by useless suffering. In a flash of intuition he saw in her a contempt for slavery, a horror of the sacrifice she was compelled to go on making, a wild desire to rise up towards glory, and he saw how she was poised like a sprung bow waiting for the masterful hand that would take hold of her for mighty conquest. He guessed that she had given up all hope of her father's recovery, and that it was painful to her to be no more than the guardian of a cold hearth, of ashes without a spark. The image of the great ravaged artist came to him, not as he was, since he had never met that decaying, ghostly figure, but as he had expressed his ideas of beauty through his craftsmanship in lasting marble and bronze. He stared at her, with a sense of icy terror more appalling than the worst aspects of death could arouse. All his strength, all his pride and all his desires seemed to jangle within him like a bundle of weapons scattered by a threatening hand, and every fibre in him trembled.

Then Foscarina lifted the funeral shroud that had suddenly transformed the gondola into a hearse amid the splendours of the festival.

'Look, Effrena,' she said, pointing to the balcony of Desdemona's house. 'There is pretty Nineta with her monkey and her little dog, receiving the honour of the serenade.'

'Ah, the fair Nineta!' cried Stelio, shaking off his sad thoughts and bowing to the laughing balcony, sending his own cheerful greeting to the tiny woman listening to the musicians by the light of two silver candelabra, on whose branches hung garlands of the last of the roses.

'I still hadn't seen her. She is the sweetest, loveliest creature I know. How lucky our dear Hoditz was when he found her behind the cover of a harpsichord as he was rummaging in a curiosity shop at San Samuele! He had two strokes of luck in one day: lovely Nineta and a cover painted by Pordenone. Since then his cup of joy has been full! How I wish you could go and see his little nest. You would really see a superb example of what I was telling you earlier today, at sunset. There is a man who followed his native taste for subtlety and has been able to make up his own minutely detailed fairy-tale, in which he lives as happily as his Moravian ancestors lived in the Arcadia of Rosswald. Oh, I know such marvellous things about him!'

A long barge hung with multi-coloured lanterns, laden with singers and musicians was moored beneath Desdemona's house. An old song about the brevity of youth and the passing of beauty rose up sweetly to the little woman who was listening, smiling her childlike smile between her monkey and her little dog, as though in a print by Pietro Longhi.

> *Do beni vu ghavé,*
> *Beleza e zoventú;*
> *Co i va no i torna piú,*
> *Nina, mia cara.**

'Don't you think that this is the true soul of Venice, and that the one you described to the audience was just in your mind, Effrena?' said Foscarina, nodding her head slightly to

* Two gifts you have,
  Beauty and youth;
  When they go, they'll never come back,
  Nineta, my darling!

the gentle rhythm that was floating along the Grand Canal and being taken up by other boats full of singers further away.

'No, this isn't it,' replied Stelio. 'Inside each one of us, like a butterfly fluttering over the surface of our profound hearts, there is a light, playful spirit that often carries us away and convinces us to indulge in bland, mediocre pleasures, in childish entertainments and simple music. This wavering uncertainty exists even in the most serious and most violent natures, like the idiot aspect of Othello's personality, and sometimes it can cloud our judgement. What you can hear now in the strumming of those guitars is the lightweight spirit of Venice. Her real soul can only be revealed in silence, and most impressively, you can rest assured, in midsummer at noon, just like great Pan. Though just now, when we were out there in the harbour of San Marco, I thought that you had felt it stir for an instant in the huge conflagration. You are forgetting Giorgione for Rosalba!'

Other boats were gathering round the singing barge, filled with languid women leaning towards the music with gestures of abandonment, as if they were about to sink into invisible arms. Around that sensual assembly, the lanterns reflected in the water trembled like a flowering of luminous, multi-coloured water-lilies.

> *Se lassaré passar*
> *La bela e fresca età,*
> *Un zorno i ve dirà*
> *Vechia maura;*
> *E bramaré, ma invan,*
> *Quel che ghavevi in man*
> *Co avé lassà scampar*
> *La congiontura.**

* If you let it go,
  Your sweet, fresh youth,
  One day it will call you

It was indeed the song of the last roses that were wilting around the branches of the candelabra. It aroused images in Perdita's heart of the procession for dead Summer, and the opalescent veil in which Stelio had wrapped the lovely corpse in its golden garments. She saw her own image in the glass coffin sealed by the Lord of Fire lying at the bottom of the lagoon in a seaweed meadow. A sudden chill ran through her limbs; again the horror and disgust of her own ageing body gripped her. She recalled her recent promise, thinking how her lover would ask her that very night to fulfil it, and once again a spasm of agonizing shamefulness mingled with pride and fear passed through her. Her experienced, desperate eyes examined the woman beside her, studied her, penetrated her, felt her hidden but certain strength, her untouched freshness, her pure health and that indefinable virtue of love which is given off like perfume from the chaste bodies of virgins when they have attained the perfection of their blossoming. She seemed to recognize the secret affinity between the girl and the poet; she seemed to divine the words he was addressing to her silently. A terrible, unbearable anguish seized her breast and her convulsed fingers clutched abruptly at the black rope of the handrail causing the little metal griffin that held it to rattle.

That movement did not escape Stelio who was watching her anxiously. He understood her terrible pain and for an instant he suffered acutely with her, but his feeling was mixed with a kind of angry impatience because, like a cry of destruction, she had cut into and disturbed a fiction of transcendent life that he had been composing in his mind so as to reconcile the contrast and overcome the new force that was presented to him like a bow ready to be drawn,

---

A wizened old pear!
You will hopelessly long
For all that you had,
And the chances you missed
That were once yours to share.

whilst still retaining the savour of maturity steeped in all the essences of life, and the blessing of her complete attention and her passionate faith in him, which sharpened his intellect like a flattering drug and fed his self-esteem with continuous praise. 'Oh, Perdita,' he thought, 'why has a pure super-human spirit of love never been released from the vortex of your countless human loves? Why did I want finally to overcome you with my desire even though I know it is too late, and why do you let me read in your eyes the certainty of the gift you are about to give adrift in a sea of doubts that will never be strong enough to reinstate the prohibition that has been set aside? Although we both knew that the very best of our long communication resided in that prohibition, we have not been able to maintain it. We are going to give in blindly at the very end and obey a sordid, nocturnal command. Yet just a little while ago when I saw your head rising out of the constellations I was not seeing my carnal mistress, I was looking at the prophetic muse of my work. All my soul's gratitude went out to you for that promise of glory, not for any promise of pleasure. You have always understood everything. With your fantastic imagination, you have always led my desire along the rainbow of your smile towards a special kind of glowing youthfulness that you have chosen and kept for me alone. When you came towards me down that staircase with her, you looked like someone bringing a gift or an unexpected message. No, perhaps not unexpected, Perdita, not unexpected; because I was waiting for your infinite wisdom to make something extraordinary happen . . .'

'Pretty Nineta is so happy there with her monkey and her little dog,' sighed the desperate woman, looking back at the light-hearted song and the laughing balcony.

> *La zoventú xe un fior*
> *Che apena nato el mor,*

E un zorno gnanca mi
*No sarò quela.**

Donatella Arvale turned to look back also, and Stelio Effrena with her. Without sinking, the light vessel carried the heavy destiny of those three faces over the water and the music.

E vegna quel che vol,
*Lassé che vaga!***

The melody about the transience of pleasure rippled along the Grand Canal, echoed by boat after boat into the distance. Entranced by the rhythm, even the servants of the oars joined their voices to the joyful chorus. That joy which had seemed so terrifying to the Creator when he first heard it in the shout of the crowd packed along the Molo was now much softer, more sensuous, had blossomed into grace and playfulness, had become gentler and indulgent. The playful soul of Venice was repeating the refrain about life's forgetfulness, plucking its guitar and dancing amid the festoons of lanterns.

E vegna quel che vol,
Lassé che vaga!

Suddenly, in front of the red palace of the Foscari where the canal curved, a great galleon flamed like a blazing tower. Another burst of lightning crackled in the sky. Another flock of fiery pigeons flew up from the quarter-deck, over the rooftops, skimming down over the marble, wings swishing over the water, and were multiplied into countless sparks that floated and steamed there. Along the parapets,

* Youth is a flower
  That dies at its birth,
  And the day will come
  When I change too!
** But come what may
  Let's still sail on!

the decks, the poop, the prow, a thousand fiery fountains burst and spread upwards simultaneously, poured into each other and lit up the canal from end to end, as far as San Vitale, as far as the Rialto. The galleon disappeared from view, transformed into a purplish cloud of thunder.

'Go down San Polo, down San Polo!' shouted Foscarina to the boatman, bending her head as though before a storm, shielding her ears from the thunder with the palms of her hands.

And Donatella Arvale and Stelio Effrena looked at each other again with dazzled eyes. Their faces were shining, illuminated by the reflection, as though they were leaning over a furnace or the mouth of a crater.

The gondola slipped into the shadows of the canal of San Polo. A sudden veil of ice fell upon its three silent occupants. Beneath the curve of the bridge their hearts could once more hear the sound of the oar, and the noise of the festival seemed infinitely remote. All the houses were dark, the bell-tower reared up dumbly and alone to the stars, the Campiello del Remer and the Campiello del Pistor were deserted and the grass could breathe there peacefully. The trees reaching over the walls of small gardens felt their leaves dying along the branches they were lifting up to the quiet sky.

'So at least for a few hours Venice felt the rhythm of art and the pulse of life beating together,' said Daniele Glauro, lifting a chalice that had no sacred paten over it from the table. 'Allow me to express, on behalf also of the many friends who cannot be present, our gratitude and enthusiasm that combine in one single glorious image the three persons to whom we owe the miracle: our gracious hostess, Lorenzo Arvale's daughter and the poet of Persephone.'

'Now why include the hostess, Glauro?' asked Foscarina, with a gracious smile of astonishment. 'Like you, I have received happiness, not created it. The laurels belong to Donatella and our poet. They deserve all the glory.'

'But your silent presence tonight in the Sala del Maggior Consiglio when you were standing beside the celestial globe was no less eloquent that Stelio's words, nor any less musical than Ariadne's singing,' answered the learned mystic. 'Once again you created a superb statue of yourself by silence, and that stays on in our memory along with the speech and the song.'

With a deep, hidden shiver Stelio Effrena saw once more the ephemeral, multi-faceted monster from whose side the tragic muse had emerged with her head outlined against the constellations.

'That's absolutely right,' exclaimed Francesco de Lizo. 'I thought so too. Anyone looking at you could see that you were the living core of the ideal world that each one of us – our group, I mean, the faithful – could feel starting to grow in our minds as we listened to the speech and the singing and the symphony.'

'We all felt that there was some strange, marvellous meaning in the way that you stood facing the poet and dominating the audience,' said Fabio Molza.

'It was as though you were the only person eligible to assist at the mysterious birth of a new idealism,' said Antimo della Bella.

'Everything there seemed to be preparing for the generation of that ideal which is going to be revealed to us, if having waited for it so faithfully means anything at all.'

With another shiver, the Creator felt the still unformed but vital work that he was nourishing within him stir again. His whole soul reached out impetuously as though propelled by the wind of lyricism to the power of fecundity and revelation that emanated from the Dionysian woman who was receiving the praise of his fervent followers.

She had suddenly become very beautiful, a night creature shaped by dreams and passions on a golden anvil, a living image of immortal fates and eternal riddles. Although she was quite still, although she was silent, her famous voice and her famous gestures seemed to live around her, vibrating indefinitely like melodies around the chords that repeat them or like rhymes around the closed book where love and sorrow go to search for them to find intoxication or comfort. The heroic fidelity of Antigone, the prophetic fury of Cassandra, the devouring fever of Phaedra, Medea's savagery, Iphigenia's sacrifice, Mirra before her father, Polyxenes and Alcestis before death, Cleopatra, changeable as wind and fire over the world, Lady Macbeth, the wakeful murderess with the tiny hands, and the great lilies pearled with dew and tears, Imogen, Juliet, Miranda, Rosalind, Jessica and Perdita, the sweetest souls of all and the most terrible ones and the most magnificent all inhabited her body, flashing in her eyes, breathing with her mouth that had tasted both honey and poison, the jewelled goblet and the cup of wormwood. Thus in unlimited space and endless time the shape of human age and substance seemed to widen and be extended, and infinite worlds of lasting beauty could be generated simply by the twitch of a muscle, by a sign, a gesture, a profile, a tremor of the eyelids, a slight change of colour, the faintest of frowns, a fleeting play of light and shadow, a flash of expressive power in that thin, frail flesh. The very guardian spirits of the places consecrated to poetry breathed over her and girded her round with changing visions. The dusty plain of Thebes, the thirsty Argolides, the burned myrtles of Trezene, the sacred olive groves of Colonnus, the triumphal Cydnus, the pale landscape of Dunsinane, Prospero's cave and the Forest of Arden, those lands furrowed with blood, laboured with pain, transfigured by dream or illuminated in an inextinguishable smile appeared, receded and melted away behind her head. And other distant lands, regions of mist, northern moorland, great continents across the oceans where she had passed, like an unknown force among the astonished crowds bringing words and fire with her, melted away behind her head, and with those crowds were mountains and rivers and bays, impure cities, ancient frozen races, strong peoples panting to rule the world, new people tearing the most secret energies from nature to serve in the all-powerful construction of buildings of iron and glass, colonies of bastard races fermenting and

85

turning rotten on virgin soil, all the crowds of barbarians to whom she had appeared like the sovereign revelation of Latin genius, all the ignorant throngs to whom she had spoken the sublime language of Dante, all the countless humanity that had aspired to Beauty, sending wave after wave of confused hopes and anxieties towards her. She was there, a creature of perishable flesh, at the mercy of the dismal laws of time, and a vast mass of real and ideal life weighed upon her, spread out around her, throbbed with the rhythm of her own breath. She had not only cried out in pain and stifled her sobs on a stage, she had done so in real life too. She had loved violently, fought and suffered in her very soul, in her very blood. What loves? What struggles? What wounds? From what depths of melancholy had she drawn the sublimation of her tragic power? From what springs of bitterness had her free genius drunk? She had certainly witnessed the most atrocious misery, the very darkest destruction. She had known heroic resistance, pity, horror, the boundaries of death. All her thirsts had kindled again in the delirium of Phaedra, and her tenderness had trembled again in Imogen's submission. Life and Art, irrevocable past and eternal present had made her profound, mysterious, many-souled; her ambiguous destiny had been magnified beyond ordinary human limits, she had become the equal of temples and forests.

She was there, breathing, before the eyes of poets who saw her as one woman and as many others.

'Oh, I will take you as though in a vast orgy, I will wield you like a bundle of wands, I will shake from your experienced body all those divine, monstrous things that weigh upon you and all those things that you have made and are growing in you as in a sacred place,' spoke the lyric demon of the Creator, recognizing in the mystery of that living woman the enduring power of primitive myth, a renewed initiation of the god who had combined all the energies of nature in a single ferment and who, by altering its rhythms, had raised human senses and the human spirit to the heights of joy and pain in enthusiastic worship of himself. 'It will be good, it will be good that I waited so long. The passing of years, the tumult of dreams, the throbbing of conflict, the speed of triumphs, the impurity of passions, the enchantment of poets, the acclamation of the crowd, the marvels of the earth, patience and fury, footsteps in the mud, blind flights, all the evil, all the good, everything I know and everything I do not know, everything you know and everything you do not know, all of this will make the fullness of my night . . .'

He turned pale and felt himself suffocating. Desire had seized him by the throat with a savage hand and he could not shake it off. His heart swelled with the same anxiety they had both felt at twilight sailing over the water that seemed to be pulling them into a terrifying water-clock.

The boundless vision of palaces and events vanished abruptly, and the creature of the night appeared again to be even more closely associated with the City with her great necklaces and her thousand green girdles. In both the woman and the city he could now see an expressive power that he had not seen before. Both blazed in the autumnal night and the same fever ran through the canals of the city as ran through the woman's veins.

Stars twinkled, trees swayed in the garden that stretched out behind Perdita's head. Breaths from heaven wafted in to the supper room through the open balconies, stirring candle flames and the chalices of flowers, making the curtains move, enlivening the old house of the Capellos where the last great daughter of San Marco whom the people had covered with glory and with gold had assembled her relics of the magnificent republic. Lamps taken from galleons, turquoise shields, leather quivers, bronze helmets, velvet scabbards adorned the rooms of the last descendant of the marvellous Cesare Darbes who had kept the *commedia dell'arte* alive in spite of Goldoni's reforms, and had changed the death-throes of the Serene Republic into a convulsion of laughter.

'All I ask is to serve that ideal with all humility,' said

Foscarina to Antimo della Bella, with a slight tremor in her voice as her eyes met Stelio's.

'Only you can make it triumphant,' said Francesco de Lizo. 'The soul of the crowd is in thrall to you forever.'

'Drama must be either a ritual or a message,' declared Daniele Glauro at that point. 'A performance should be as solemn as a ceremony, as it used to be, because it combines the two basic elements of any cult: the living being in whom the revelatory word is incarnated on stage as before an altar, and the silent presence of the crowd as in ancient temples . . .'

'Bayreuth!' interrupted Prince Hoditz.

'No, the Janiculum!' shouted Stelio Effrena, suddenly emerging from his heady silence. 'A Roman hillside! Not the wood and bricks of Upper Francony; let us have a marble theatre on a Roman hill.' The sudden opposition of his words seemed almost to have been provoked by a light-hearted contempt.

'Don't you admire Richard Wagner's work?' Donatella Arvale asked him, raising her eyebrows slightly in a movement that made her hermetic face seem almost hard.

He gazed into her eyes, feeling all that was faintly hostile in the young girl's manner, and experiencing slight hostility towards her himself. He saw her isolated still, living her own, circumscribed life, fixed in her own secret thoughts, distant and inviolable.

'Richard Wagner's work,' he answered, 'is based on the Germanic soul and its essence is entirely northern. His reforms are somewhat analogous to those attempted by Luther. His drama is the supreme flowering of his race, the extraordinary effective fusion of the aspirations that troubled the hearts of German composers and poets from Bach to Beethoven, from Wieland to Goethe. If you imagine his work on the shores of the Mediterranean, amid our bright olive-trees and our smooth laurel bushes, under the glory of our Latin sky, then it loses its colour and dissolves. According to his own opinion, the creator is able to see the future perfection of a world that is still unmade and is able to enjoy it prophetically in hope and in desire, and so I announce the advent of a new or renewed art-form that will continue and crown the huge ideal structure of our chosen race through the pure, strong simplicity of its lines, through its energetic gracefulness, through the enthusiasm of its contributors, through the pure potency of its harmonies. I rejoice in being part of the Latin race, and – please forgive me, Lady Myrta of dreams, and forgive me too, most sensitive Hoditz – I see a barbarian in any man of different blood from mine.'

'But Richard Wagner also developed his themes starting from the Greeks,' said Baldassare Stampa, who had just returned from Bayreuth and was still ecstatic about it.

'It's an uneven, confused line,' replied the poet. 'Nothing could be further from the *Oresteia* than the *Ring* cycle. The Florentines of the house of Bardi have penetrated far more deeply into the essence of Greek tragedy. Praise be to the Brotherhood of the Conte di Vernio!'

'I always thought the Brotherhood was a boring collection of academics and public speakers,' said Baldassare Stampa.

'Did you hear that, Daniele?' exclaimed Stelio, turning to the learned mystic. 'When did the world ever know a brighter intellectual fire? They were searching for the spirit of life in ancient Greece; they tried to develop the harmonious in all human energy, to show the complete human being with all the means of art. Giulio Caccini taught us that to be excellent a musician does not only need particular skills but also to feel the wholeness of things. The tawny hair of Jacopo Peri, the Zazzerino, flamed in song like that of Apollo. In the preface to his *Representation of Soul and Body*, Emilio del Cavaliere expounds the same ideas about new theatre that were put into practice at Bayreuth, including the precepts for perfect silence, the invisible orchestra and the importance of shadows. When he celebrates festival as spectacle, Marco da Gagliano praises all the arts involved, "in such a way that the intellect is praised along with all the most noble sentiments of the most delightful forms of art that the human mind has invented". Will that do for you?'

'Bernino,' said Francesco de Lizo, 'put on an opera in Rome, and he built the theatre himself, painted the sets, carved the ornamental statues, invented the machinery, wrote the text, composed the music, choreographed the dances, trained the actors, danced, sang and performed.'

'For heaven's sake, that's enough!' cried Prince Hoditz, laughing. 'The barbarian has been vanquished.'

'Not quite enough,' said Antimo della Bella. 'We should praise the greatest innovator of all, he who was consecrated a Venetian by his passion and his death, the man whose tomb is in the church of the Frari and is worthy of any pilgrimage – the divine Claudio Monteverdi.'

'Now there is the pure essence of a true Italian soul,' Daniele Glauro confirmed reverently.

'He carried out his work in the teeth of the storm. He suffered, loved and struggled alone with his faith, his passions and his genius,' said Foscarina, slowly, as though she were seeing that brave, painful life whose liver had nourished the creatures of his art with his own warm blood. 'Tell us about him, Effrena.'

Stelio quivered as though she had unexpectedly touched him. Once again the expressive power of her prophetic lips aroused an ideal image from some indefinable depths that rose up as though from a tomb before the poet's gaze, and took on the colour and breath of life. The old viola player, bereaved, sad and passionate as Orpheus in the story, appeared at the supper table.

It was an apparition of fire, bolder and more dazzling than that which had lit up the harbour of San Marco, a flaming life-force, flung from the deepest womb of nature towards the expectant throng, a vehement zone of light erupting from an inner sky to illuminate the most secret depths of human desire and human will, a word that had never been spoken, come from primeval silence to express all that is eternal and eternally unsayable in the heart of the world.

'Who would want to talk about him when he could speak

to us himself?' said the Creator, unable to contain the growing fullness within him that was rising like a tide of anguish. He looked at the singer, and saw her as she had appeared to him amid the forest of instruments, white and lifeless as a statue. But the spirit of beauty he had summoned had to manifest itself through her.

'Ariadne!' added Stelio quietly, as though to awaken her.

She stood up without a word, crossed over to the door and went into the next room. The rustle of her dress could be heard, and the light sound of her footsteps, then the sound of a harpsichord being opened. Everyone was silent, concentrating. A musical silence took over the empty place left at the table. A puff of wind bent the candle flames just once and stirred the flowers. Then everything seemed motionless, waiting anxiously.

*Lasciatemi morire!**

Suddenly their hearts were seized by a force like the eagle of lightning that snatched Dante in his dream up into the fire. They burned together in everlasting truth, they heard the melody of the world pass through their luminous ecstasy.

Lasciatemi morire!

Ariadne, was it still Ariadne weeping over some new pain? rising, still rising to new heights of martyrdom?

E che volete
Che mi conforte
In così dura sorte,

* Let me die!

91

In così gran martire?
Lasciatemi morire! *

The voice fell silent. The singer did not reappear. Claudio Monteverdi's aria was shaped in their memories like an unalterable line.

'Could any Greek marble reach such simple, secure stylistic perfection?' asked Daniele Glauro in a low voice, as though afraid to disturb the musical silence.

'What kind of grief ever wept like that in this world?' stammered Lady Myrta, her eyes overflowing with tears which were running down the furrows of her poor, pallid face, while her hands that were twisted with gout shook as she tried to wipe them away.

The austere intellect of the aesthete and the sweet, sensitive soul in the old, infirm body both testified to the same power. Nearly three centuries earlier at Mantua in the famous theatre, six thousand spectators had similarly been unable to contain their sobs, and poets had believed that the living presence of Apollo had appeared on the new stage.

'Now there is an artist of our own race. Baldassare,' said Stelio Effrena. 'He manages to reach the highest point of beauty with the simplest means, while the German only occasionally accomplished the same feat in his confused aspirations towards the land of Sophocles.'

'Don't you know the sick king's lament?' asked the young man who wore his flowing hair in the style of the Venetian Sappho, 'tall Gaspara', Collaltino's unhappy lover.

'All the anguish of Amfortas is contained in a motet that I know, *"Peccatem me quotidie"*, and its lyric impulse and powerful simplicity are extraordinary. I would almost say that all the power of tragedy is sublimated, like the instincts of a crowd are in the heart of a hero. Palestrina's language,

* For what
  Can comfort me
  In my harsh fate,
  In my great grief?
  Oh let me die!

92

which is even older, seems even more pure and more virile to me.'

'But what about the struggle between Kundry and Parsifal in the second act, the Herzeleide motif, the way he renders impetuousness and then renders pain out of the movement of the sacred banquet, the motif of Kundry's desiring, the prophetic promise theme, the kiss on the mad youth's lips, all that terrifying, wild contrast between desire and horror . . . "The wound! The wound! It is burning within me, it is bleeding within me!" And then above the temptress's wild desperation comes the melody of submission . . . "Let me weep on thy bosom! Let me join with thee for just one hour, and even though God repel me, I shall be saved and redeemed in thee!" And then Parsifal's answer when the motif of the Madman comes back in so grandly and solemnly, only now he has been transformed into the promised Hero . . . "Hell will hold us forever, if I let thee hold me in thy arms even for just an hour." And Kundry's savage ecstasy . . . "Because my kiss has made thee see, the full embrace of my love will make thee a god. One hour, one hour only with thee I shall be saved!" And the final effort of her diabolical will, the supreme moment of seduction, her imploration, her wild offer . . . "Only thy love can save me. Let me love thee. Be mine for just one hour! And for just one hour I shall be yours!" '

Lost, Perdita and Stelio gazed into each other's eyes. For a split second they came together, joined, knew pleasure and pain as though on a bed of voluptuousness and death.

Marangona, the largest bell of St Mark's, struck midnight. As had happened before, at twilight, they felt the echoing bronze down to the very roots of their hair, like a quiver through their flesh. They thought they could again feel the vast whirlwind of sound above their heads, through which they had suddenly seen the apparition of Beauty the peacemaker, summoned there by wholehearted Prayer. All the phantoms of the waters, the infinite waverings of dissembling desire, their anxiety, her promise, their leave-taking, the festival, the formidable monster with the countless human faces, the great starry globe, the applause, the symphony, the singing, the miracles of fire, the sail down the canal filled with music, the song of the brevity of youth, the battle and silent agony of the ship, the sudden shadow over their three destinies, the banquet illuminated by a gorgeous ideal, the toasts, the hopes, the pride, all the pulsations of life's vitality were renewed in their accord, moved even faster, were a thousand and yet were one. They thought they had lived beyond all human limits, and that in that instant there was an unknown vastness before them that they could absorb like drinking an ocean in a single gulp. For they had lived so much that they were empty; they had drunk so much, they were thirsty. A violent illusion has seized hold of the richness in their hearts, each thought they were growing immeasurably in the riches of the other. The virgin had disappeared. The eyes of the desperate, nomadic woman were saying over and over again: 'The full embrace of my love will make thee a god! One hour, one hour only with thee and I shall be saved! Be mine for just one hour, and for just one hour, I shall be yours!'

The enthusiastic speaker went on describing the outcome of the noble tragedy. Kundry, the wild seductress, the slave of desire, the Rose of Hell, the original Perdition, the cursed one, now reappeared at daybreak in spring. When she re-appeared she was pale and humbled, in the robes of a messenger, her head bent low, her gaze dim, her voice hoarse and broken as she spoke the words: 'Let me serve!'

The melody of loneliness, the melody of submission, the melody of purification were preparing for the enchantment of Good Friday around her humble state. Then came Parsifal in his black armour, his visor down and his spear lowered, wrapped in endless dreaming. 'I am come by dangerous ways, but perhaps this day I shall be saved for I can hear the rustle of the divine forest . . .' Hope, regret, remorse, memories, his vow, faith panting for salvation, mysterious sacred melodies seemed to be weaving a cloak of idealism to wrap around the Simpleton, the Pure One, the promised Hero sent to heal the uncurable wound. 'Will you lead me today to Amfortas?' He grew weak, his strength left him in the old man's arms. 'Let me serve! Let me serve!' The melody of the submission spread through the orchestra once again, replacing the lively, primitive line. 'Let me serve!' The faithful woman brought water, knelt down humbly and lovingly to wash the beloved feet. 'Let me serve!' The faithful woman took a vase of balsam from her bosom to anoint the beloved feet, then she dried them with her own flowing hair. 'Let me serve!' The Pure One bent over the sinner, he poured water over her wild head. 'Thus I fulfil my first task. Receive this baptism and believe in the Redeemer.' Kundry touched the ground with her forehead and burst into tears, freed from desire, freed from the curse. And then from the deep, final harmony of the prayer to the Redeemer came the melody of the flowering meadow, loosening itself and rising, extending outwards with superhuman sweetness. 'How beautiful is the meadow today. I was once drawn to gorgeous flowers, but no grass or petals were ever so scented as these . . .' Parsifal gazed ecstatically at the meadow and the wood, laughing through the dew of early morning.

'Who could ever forget that sublime moment?' cried the enthusiast, whose thin face seemed to shine with the reflection of that flash of joy. 'All of us in the dark theatre were sitting absolutely rigid, in one solid, compact mass. It felt as though the blood had stopped flowing through our veins to listen. The music was rising out of the Mystic Gulf like light, the notes were transformed into rays of spring sunshine and were coming to life with the same joy as the blades of grass, and the flowers that were opening and the budding branches and the insects spreading their new wings. All the innocence of things that were being born entered into us too. Our hearts relived a kind of dream of distant childhood . . . INFANTIA. Vettor Carpaccio's word, the word you repeated so rightly to us tonight, Stelio, confronting our old age. And how strongly you made us feel a sense of loss for all that we have lost, and gave us hope of recovering it, if art can once again be indissolubly linked to life.'

Stelio Effrena was silent, oppressed by the weight of the

gigantic opera constructed by the barbaric creator which Baldassare Stampa had so enthusiastically set against the blazing line of the composer of Ariadne and Orpheus. A kind of instinctive rancour, an obscure hostility that did not come from the mind, made him resent the tenacious German who had managed to inspire the world with his fire. To win a victory over men and things, he too had praised his own image and magnified his own dreams of conquering beauty. He too had gone to the crowd as his chosen prey. He too had set himself the task of relentlessly going beyond himself in his own work. And now he had a temple to his own religion on a Bavarian hillside.

'Only art can bring men together,' said Daniele Glauro. 'Let us honour the great master who has always borne witness to that belief. Although his Festival Theatre may be built out of wood and bricks and be less than perfect and too constrained, nevertheless it is sublimely important. For the work of art that is presented there appears like a religious act in a living form. His drama is a ritual.'

'Let us honour Richard Wagner,' said Antimo della Bella. 'But if this moment is to be memorable both for the announcement and for the promise that we are expecting from the man who showed the crowd that mysterious ship just a little while ago, then let us again call upon the heroic soul who spoke to us through the voice of Donatella Arvale as our patron. When he laid the first stone of his Festival Theatre, the author of Siegfried dedicated it to German hopes and German victories. The Theatre of Apollo which is being built with all speed on the Janiculum where eagles once flew bearing omens, will be the monumental revelation of the ideal towards which the genius of our own race is being led. We should reassert our privileged position, for nature has made our race uniquely great.'

Stelio Effrena was silent, overwhelmed by a vortex of feelings that stirred within him in a kind of blind fury, like the subterranean forces that burst out and transform volcanic landscapes, creating new mountains and new abysses. All the components of his inner life, overcome by the impact, seemed to be dissolving and yet at the same time increasing. Huge, terrifying images raced through that turmoil accompanied by storm-clouds of music. Thoughts concentrated and dispersed with extraordinary speed, rushing past like electric charges in a hurricane. Sometimes it was as though he could hear shouting and singing from behind a door that kept swinging open and then slamming shut again. It was as though the blasts were bringing him alternately the screaming from some massacre and a distant apotheosis. With the intensity of feverish vision, he suddenly saw the dry, fatal landscape where he wanted to place the characters of his tragedy, and he could feel the thirst of the place. He saw the mythical spring which broke through that dryness, and in the surge of water he saw the whiteness of the virgin who was to die there. He saw the mask of his heroine on Perdita's face, composed in all the beauty of an extraordinarily calm sorrow. Then the ancient dryness of the Plain of Argos turned to flame, the Perseian spring flowed like an ever-changing river. The fire and the water, those two primordial elements, passed over everything, cancelling out every sign, came together, wandered away, struggled, were victorious, talked, found words, acquired a language through which to express their most intimate being and to recount the innumerable myths born out of their eternal life. The symphony expressed the drama of two elemental Souls on the stage of the Universe, the pathetic struggle of two great living, moving Beings, two cosmic Wills, as the shepherd Arya imagined out on the high plains, gazing on the spectacle with the eyes of innocence. Then from the very centre of the musical mystery, from the deep abyss of the symphonic ocean, rose the Ode, brought by a human voice and soaring to the greatest heights. Beethoven's miracle was repeated. The winged Ode, the hymn, burst from the depths of the orchestra and emphatically, imperiously spoke of Man's joy and Man's pain. It was not the Chorus, as in the Ninth Symphony, but the lone, dominating Voice that was the interpreter and spoke for the multitude. 'Her voice! Her voice! She has disappeared! Her singing seemed to touch the heart of the world, and she was beyond the veil,' said the Creator, seeing in his mind once again the crystal statue through which he had seen melody flowing like blood. 'I shall look for you, I shall find you, I shall possess your secret. You will sing my hymns, raised up on the heights of my music.' He was free from all impure desires now, and in his mind the body of the virgin was just a receptacle that contained a divine gift.

He could hear the disembodied voice rising out of the depths of the orchestra to reveal the component of eternal truth that resides in ephemeral facts and fleeting events. The ode would crown the episode with light. Then, as if to lead the spirit, drawn away 'beyond the veil', back to the play of appearances, a dance motif shaped itself in the rhythm of the dying ode. A silent dancer entered between a parallelogram contained within the frame of the stage, as within the boundaries of the strophe, and with the line of her body that was redeemed for a short while from the dismal laws of gravity, she imitated fire and water and whirlpools and the making of the stars. 'La Tanagra, the flower of Syracuse, all made of wings like the petals of a flower.' That was how he thought of the Sicilian dancer who had become famous, and who had rediscovered the ancient Greek art of dance, as it had been in the days when Phrinicus could boast of having as many dance shapes within him as the waves in the sea on a stormy winter's night. The actress, the singer and the dancer, three Dionysian women, seemed to him to be the perfect, almost divine instruments for his creation. With incredible speed, his work took shape through words, song, gesture and the symphony and started to live its powerful life before the captive multitude.

He was silent, lost in that world of ideals, intent on calculating the effort needed to bring it into being. He could hear the voices of the people around him from a long way off.

'Richard Wagner says that the only creator of the work of art is the people,' Baldassare Stampa was saying, 'and all the artist has to do is to assemble and express the creative impulses of ignorant people . . .'

The extraordinary feeling that had astounded him before when he was addressing the crowd from the throne of the Doges, swept over him again. In the communication that had taken place between his soul and that of the crowd, something mysterious, almost holy, had happened. Something greater and stronger had been added to the feelings that he had about his habitual self. An unknown power had seemed to converge within him, destroying the boundaries of his individual personality and giving his lone voice the quality of a chorus. There really was beauty in the masses, and only a poet or a hero could draw out flashes of it. When that beauty was revealed by a sudden clamour in a theatre or in a public place or in a trench, then a torrent of joy would swell the heart of the man who had known how to provoke it with his poetry, or his speech or by brandishing his sword. So the words of a poet communicating with a crowd of people could be as powerful an action as a hero's deeds. It was an action that could create immediate beauty in the darkness of the manifold soul, just as a gifted sculptor can take a lump of clay and with just a touch of his talented hands turn it into a divine statue. Then the long silence, spread over the finished poem like a sacred veil, would cease. The substance of life would no longer be created by immaterial symbols, life would be depicted in its entirety by the poet, the word would become flesh, rhythm would quicken into a throbbing, breathing form, ideas would be uttered in all their fullness of strength and freedom.

'But does he – Richard Wagner – believe that the people consists of everybody who experiences some kind of common misery?' asked Fabio Molza, 'Some kind of common misery . . .'

'Towards Joy, towards eternal Joy,' thought Stelio Effrena. 'The people consists of everybody who feels some kind of obscure need to rise up through Art, out of the dungeon of their daily lives where they are confined and suffer.' Small city theatres in which actors prostituted themselves before

99

a gang of debauchees and harlots in suffocating heat and the stench of decay would disappear. On the steps of the new theatre he saw the true audience, the great single-minded audience which he had both smelled and heard a little while ago on the marble pavements beneath the stars. Even though they might not understand it, his art could deeply move rude, ignorant souls through the mysterious power of its rhythms, and make them feel like the prisoner who is about to be released from cruel bonds. The happiness of that freedom would gradually extend to even the most wretched beings; furrowed brows would clear, lips used to uttering vicious curses would fall open in wonder. And hands, those hard hands enslaved by instruments of toil, would join in unison and reach out to the heroine who expressed her immortal sorrow to the stars.

'In the existence of a people like ours,' Daniele Glauro was saying, 'a great artistic manifestation counts a lot more than a treaty or a tax law. Things which cannot die are worth more than things which decay. The cunning and bravery of Malatesta are sealed forever in a medal by Pisanello. And the only thing of Machiavelli's politics which survives is the strength of his prose . . .'

'That's right,' thought Stelio Effrena. 'The destiny of Italy cannot be separated from the fortunes of Beauty, for she is its mother.' That sovereign truth now appeared to him like the rising sun of the distant, sacred, ideal fatherland through which Dante had roamed. 'Italy! Italy!' The name that intoxicated the earth rang in his heart like a rallying cry. Surely a new kind of art was going to rise up, strong in root and branch, from the ruins steeped in so much heroic blood! Would it not bring together all the latent forces of the nation's heritage, would it not become a powerful determining factor in building a third Rome, would it not show those men in government what basic truths to apply in their new statutes? Faithful to the most ancient instincts of his own race, Richard Wagner had used his work to predict and support the aspirations of the German state to the heroic greatness of Empire. He had created the magnificent figure of Henry the Fowler waking up beneath the centuries-old oak tree: 'Let the warriors rise up from all the German lands!' The warriors had won at Sadowa and at Sedan. With the same impulse and the same tenacity, both the artist and the people had achieved their splendid goal. The same victory had crowned both the effort of iron and the effort of metre. Like a hero, the composer had carried out an act of liberation. Like the will of the Chancellor, like the soldiers' blood, his musical forms had contributed to the praise and continuity of the soul of his race.

'He came to stay here a few days ago, in the Vendramin-Calergi palace,' said Prince Hoditz.

Instantly the image of the barbarian composer came to mind, the lines of his face became visible, his blue eyes beneath his great forehead glittered, his lips closed tightly in sensuality, pride and contempt over his strong chin. His tiny body, bent with age and glory, straightened, became as huge as his works, assumed the shape of a god. His blood flowed like mountain torrents, his breathing sighed like the wind in a forest. Then suddenly all the youthfulness of Siegfried entered him, ran through him, shone out of him like dawn from behind a cloud. 'To follow the impulse of my heart, to obey my own instincts, to listen to the voice of nature within me: that is my one, supreme law!' The heroic words echoed through him, bursting from deep within, expressing the sound, young will that had triumphed over all obstacles and all evils, in harmony with the laws of the Universe. And then the flames that flared out from the rock-face at the stroke of Wotan's staff rose up in a circle. 'The way is open through the sea of flame! Oh joy, to fling myself on to the pyre! To find my bride in the flames! 'All the phantoms of myth gleamed, darkened. Brunhilda's winged helmet glittered in the sunlight. 'Glory to the sun! Glory to light! Glory to the radiant day! Long have I slept! Who has awakened me?' The phantoms rushed together, then vanished. Against a shadowy background the virgin of song, Donatella Arvale, suddenly reappeared, as he had first seen her against the background of purple and gold

101

in the great hall, holding the flower of fire in her enabling hands. 'Can you not see me? Are you not afraid of my gaze which is consuming you and the blood that boils within me? Do you too feel this savage burning?' Absent though she was, she took over the power of his dream. Infinite music was being generated by the silence that had occupied the empty place at the table. Her hermetic face concealed an inviolable secret. 'Do not touch me, do not disturb me, and I will reflect your luminous image forever. Love yourself, and renounce me!' Once again, as had happened out on the feverish waters, the poet was assailed by a kind of passionate impatience, and he saw once again the absent woman like a sprung bow waiting for the masterful hand that would take hold of her for mighty conquest. 'Awake, virgin, awake! Live and laugh! Be mine!'

His soul was being drawn violently into the orbit of the world created by the Germanic god. He was overwhelmed by visions and melodies, images from northern mythology took over the images created by his passion and his art and obscured them. His desires and his hopes were speaking the barbarian's language. 'I must love you in laughter. I must blind myself in laughter; and we must lose ourselves together in laughter. Oh radiant love, oh joyous death!' The warrior maiden's happiness on the cliffs within her circle of fire reached its highest point; her cry of sensuality and freedom rose up to strike the heart of the sun. What had that formidable manipulator of human souls not managed to express, what heights and depths had he not touched? What work could ever equal his? What eagle could ever hope to fly higher? His gigantic work was finished, the people had it already. The last chorus of the Grail, the thanksgiving hymn, was echoing around the world: 'Glory be to the miracle! Redemption to the Redeemer!'

'He is tired,' Prince Hoditz was saying, 'terribly tired and worn out. That is why we did not see him at the Doge's Palace. His heart, you know . . .'

The giant returned to being a man, his tiny body bent with age and glory, consumed by passions, dying. Stelio

Effrena heard once more the words Perdita had spoken that had turned the gondola into a hearse, those words referring to another great stricken artist, Donatella Arvale's father. 'The bow is named BIOS and death is its task.' The young man saw stretching out before him the pathway to victory, and though life is short, art is long-lived. 'Forward! Forward! Higher and higher!' He had to keep his eyes fixed on his goal every hour, every second, he had to focus all his energies without failing or giving up. He could feel that victory was as essential to him as breathing. A wild desire to fight stirred in his swift, Latin blood as he came into contact with the barbarian. 'Now everything is up to you!' the German had shouted from the stage of his new theatre at the inaugural performance. 'In the work of art of the future, the source of inspiration will never run dry.' Art was as endless as beauty in the world. There were no limits to strength or to desiring. Search, find, go further, keep going further. 'Forward! Forward!'

One great shapeless wave then took on all the aspirations and all the agonies of that delirium, rushed into a vortex, surged upwards in a maelstrom, seemed to become condensed and take on the quality of plastic matter, obeying the same untiring energy that shapes all beings and all things under the sun. An extraordinarily beautiful, pure form emerged from that effort, alive and shining with unbearable happiness. The poet saw it, his pure eyes received it, he felt it rooted in the core of his spirit. 'Oh to be able to express it, to show it to mankind, to fix it in its perfection for all eternity!' The sublime moment would never return. Everything vanished. Everyday life flowed on, fleeting words sounded around him, expectation throbbed, desire wore itself out.

He looked at the woman. Stars twinkled, trees swayed in the garden that stretched out behind Perdita's head. The woman's eyes kept saying: 'Let me serve! Let me serve!'

The guests had gone into the garden and had wandered off

along the walks and under the trellises. The night air was so warm and damp that they could feel it on their eyelashes like the approaching kiss of an advancing mouth. The hidden stars of jasmine flowers gave off their penetrating scent in the darkness, and the fruits were scented too, even more strongly than in gardens out on the islands. A powerful fertility came from that small patch of cultivated earth that was enclosed in a belt of water, which served to make its exile all the more poignant.

'Do you want me to stay? Do you want me to come back, when the others have gone? Tell me. It's getting late.'

'No, Stelio, please. It is late, it is too late. You said so yourself.'

There was mortal terror in the woman's voice. She was trembling in the darkness with her bare shoulders, her bare arms, and she wanted to be possessed and yet not to give herself, she wanted to die yet she wanted to be shaken by his masculine hands. She was trembling, her teeth trembled in her mouth. A glacial river flowed over her, submerged her, froze her from the roots of her hair to the tips of her fingers. Every joint in every limb was aching, and felt as if it was about to snap, while her jaw stiffened with terror and altered the sound of her voice. And she wanted to die, yet she wanted to be taken and conquered by the violence of his manhood. While all the time, over her terror and her iciness and her ageing flesh, hung the terrible words that her beloved had uttered and that she herself had repeated: 'It is late, it is too late!'

'Your promise, what about your promise? I will not wait any longer, I cannot wait, Perdita.'

The harbour, sensuous as a bare breast, the estuary lost in shadow and death, the City lit up with twilight feverishness, the water flowing through the invisible clock, the vibrating bronze in the sky, the suffocation of desire, her tightly closed lips, her lowered eyelids, her dry hands, everything returned in the recollection of the silent promise. He desired her profound flesh with savage passion.

'I will not wait any longer.'

His wild ardour came from a long way away, from the most distant origins, from the primitive bestiality of quick couplings, from the ancient mystery of sacred lust. Just as the throng possessed by the god had rushed down the mountain-side, tearing up trees, racing on with fury and becoming increasingly blind, gathering more and more frenzied beings within its number, spreading that frenzy wherever it went until it had become a huge, bestial yet human multitude, controlled by a monstrous will, so that crude instinct in him rushed to the fore, agitating and dragging with it all the images in his mind in the impetus with indescribable tumult. What he most desired in that desperate, knowing woman was the creature oppressed by the eternal servitude of her nature, the woman destined to succumb to the unexpected traumas of her sex, the woman who could soothe the high fever of the stage with dark, somnolent voluptuousness, the radiant actress who could pass from the frenzy of the masses to the power exerted by the male, the Dionysian being who crowned the mystic rite with an act of life like an Orgy.

His desire lost all proportion and turned to madness; it was filled with images of her trembling, captivated audiences, with the intoxication of her unknown lovers, with a vision of orgiastic sensuality; it was shaped by cruelty, bitterness, jealousy, poetry and pride. He was stung by regret at never having possessed the actress right after a successful performance, when she was still warm with the breath of the crowd, soaked in sweat, panting and exhausted, with the traces still on her body of the tragic soul that had cried and wept through her, with the tears of that intrusive being still wet on her tormented cheeks. He saw her in a sudden flash of lightning, desperate and filled with the power that had wrung a roar of approval from the monster, panting like a Maenad after the dance, parched and exhausted, yet needing to be taken, to be shaken, to be bent backwards in the final spasm, to receive his violent seed, to sink finally into a dreamless stupor. How many men had come out of the crowd to embrace her after having panted for her, lost in the human mass? Their desire was shaped by the desire of thousands, their powers were multiplied. Something of the drunken crowd, the fascinated monster, penetrated the actress's womb on those nights of passion.

'Don't be cruel, don't be cruel,' pleaded the woman, feeling all that savagery in his voice, reading it in his eyes. 'Oh, don't hurt me.'

Under the young man's hungry eyes her whole body clenched up again in the grip of a painful sense of shame. Desire for him tore at her like an open wound. She knew how much bitterness and impurity there was in his sudden excitement, and she knew how profoundly poisoned and corrupt he thought she was, weighted down by love, experienced in all pleasure, a wandering temptress who could never be satisfied. She sensed his resentment, his jealousy, the malign fever that suddenly burned in the old friend to whom she had for so long confided all that she held most precious and most true in herself, and for whom she had kept the goodness of all that was offered through constant refusals. Now everything was lost. Everything had suddenly been destroyed, like a fine kingdom that has fallen to rebellious, vindictive slaves. And as though she were on her death-bed, in her final moment of agony, she saw her whole sharp, stormy life pass before her, that life of pain and struggle, of loss and effort, passion and success. She felt the weight of it, the encumbrance of it. She remembered the ineffable feeling of joy, fear and liberation that she had experienced the first time she had given herself to the man who had deceived her a long time ago when she was young. And with a fearful stab, the image of the young girl who had left the room rushed into her heart, the girl who had disappeared, who was perhaps dreaming alone in her room upstairs, or weeping, or who had already promised herself and was lying enjoying the gift of that promise. 'It is late, it is too late!' The irrevocable words kept running across her brow, like the tolling of a bronze bell. And his desire hit her like a tearing wound.

'Oh, don't hurt me.'

She was pleading with him white and slight as the swans-down that rippled around her bare shoulders and her heaving breast. She seemed to be leaving all her power behind her, to be becoming light and weak, clad in a secret, gentle soulfulness, so easily broken, destroyed, sacrificed without spilling a drop of blood.

'No, Perdita, I shall not hurt you,' he stammered, shocked by the change in her voice and appearance, his bowels suddenly gripped by human pity that came from the same depths as that first, savage instinct. 'Forgive me, please forgive me.'

He wanted to take her in his arms and hold her, console her, let her cry, drink her tears. He felt he no longer knew her, the person before him was an unfamiliar being, infinitely humble and full of sorrow, with no strength at all. His pity and his remorse were like the feeling one has after having unwittingly hurt or offended a sick man or a child or some inoffensive, lonely little thing.

'Forgive me!'

He wanted to kneel down before her and kiss her feet in the grass or say something childish. He bent down and touched her hand. She shuddered from head to foot, stared at him with wide-open eyes, then looked down again and stood there motionless. Darkness gathered beneath the arch of her eyebrows and traced the curve of her cheeks. The icy river rushed over her once more.

They could hear the voices of some of the guests scattered through the garden. Then there was a great silence. An occasional footstep made the gravel rattle, then the great silence returned. Indistinct sounds came from the distant canals. Suddenly, the scent of jasmine seemed to grow much stronger, like a quickening heartbeat. The night was pregnant with wonder. Eternal forces were working in harmony between the earth and the stars.

'Forgive me! If my desire for you causes you pain, then I will go on smothering it. I can still give it up and do as you want. Perdita, oh Perdita, I will forgive everything that your eyes were saying to me in there, through all that useless talking . . . No embrace, no caress could ever join us more closely together. All the passion of this night has been pressing on us, throwing us into one another's arms . . . I have received you wholly into myself, like a wave . . . and now I feel that I can no longer get you out of my blood, and that you can no longer be distant from me, and we must set out together for the unknown dawn . . .' He was speaking quietly, putting his whole self into words, as though he had turned into a vibrant substance upon which all the changes of that nocturnal being could be impressed at every moment. He could no longer see a bodily form before him, the opaque, impenetrable flesh of the weighty human prison, but a soul that was exposed in a succession of appearances as expressive as melodies, a sensitivity that was both delicate and unimaginably powerful and which created in the frame of her body all the frailty of flowers, the resilience of marble, the force of flame, all that was shadow and all that was light.

'Stelio!'

She barely whispered his name, yet in the dying breath that came from her bloodless lips there was as great a wealth of exhaltation and wonder as in the loudest shriek. She had heard love in the man's voice: love, love! The woman who had so often listened to the beautiful, perfectly chosen words flowing in his clear voice and had suffered strangely from hearing them, as though she were being mocked or tortured, now saw her whole life and the life of the entire world suddenly transformed by the new tone in that voice. Her soul seemed to be turning upside down, the burden fell into unseen depths and vanished in endless darkness, while something light and luminous rose upwards, something free and unstained that spread outwards and curved like the heavens at daybreak. And just as a wave of light rises up from the horizon to the zenith in silent harmony, so the illusion of happiness rose to her lips. A great smile spread across her face, so vast that the lines of her lips trembled from it like leaves in the breeze, and her teeth gleamed like jasmine flowers in the starry brightness: the slenderest of shapes in elemental vastness.

'Everything has gone, everything has ended. I have never lived, I have never loved. I have never known pleasure, never known pain. I am completely new. All I know is this love I feel. I am quite pure. I want to die in the pleasure that you will give me. The years and all that has happened have passed over me without ever touching that part of my soul which I have been keeping just for you, that secret heaven which has now suddenly opened and has overcome all the shadows and is here only to hold the strength and sweetness of your name. Your love will save me, the full embrace of my love will make you a god . . .' Ecstatic words overflowed from her liberated heart, but her lips did not dare to utter them. She went on smiling, smiling her infinite, silent smile.

'It's true, isn't it? Say something, Perdita. Answer me! Haven't you also felt this need that has become strong by our very refusing, by our constancy in waiting for the right moment? I feel that all my hopes and all my presentiments would be worthless if this time had not come. Tell me that you too cannot reach tomorrow's dawn without me, as I cannot without you! Answer me!'

'Yes, yes . . .'

She was lost and surrendered in that faint syllable. Her smile faded, her mouth became heavier, and stood out in a line that was almost hard against the pallor of her face, as though thirst were swelling it, preparing it to attract, take and hold on insatiably. Her whole body that had become ethereal in her pain and terror now sprang back as though it had acquired a new bone structure, and took hold once more of its carnal power as a wave of impetuosity rushed through her. She became impure and desirable once more.

'We cannot delay any longer. It is getting late.'

He was trembling with impatience. The wildness seized hold of him again, desire gripped him by the throat with its feline claws.

'Yes,' said the woman again, but differently now, as her

eyes gazed into his eyes avidly, imperiously, as though she were now certain that she possessed the philtre that would finally bind him to her.

He felt the passions that dwelled in that profound flesh enter his heart. He looked at her and turned pale, as though his blood were being poured over the earth to soak the roots of trees in a dream, outside time, alone with that one woman.

She was standing under the tree laden with fruits that she had decorated with necklaces. Her body was as sharply bowed as her lips, and fever burned from her limbs like the breath that came from those lips. The sudden beauty made up of a thousand ideal forces that had shone from her during the dinner, now returned even more powerfully, burning with the flame that never fades, the energy that never diminishes. The magnificent fruit hung over her head, a supreme reminder of the crown of the kingly giver. The myth of the pomegranate lived again that night as it had done when the laden barge sailed over the twilight waters.

Who was she? Could she be Persephone, Lady of the Shadows? Had she dwelled in the place where all human troubles are but a game played by the wind in the dust of an endless road? Had she seen the world at its source, had she counted the roots of flowers, stiff as veins in a body turned to stone, down in that subterranean land? Was she exhausted or drunk with tears and laughter and human passions, or because she had touched every mortal thing in turn to make it blossom, to make it wither? Who was she? Had she beaten cities like a scourge? Had she closed forever with her kisses lips that had been singing, stopped the beating of a tyrant's heart, poisoned young men with her sweat that was salty as foam on the sea? Who was she? Who was she? What history had made her so pale, so ardent, so dangerous? Had she already spoken all her innermost secrets and given away all her gifts? Or could she still amaze her new lover, for whom life, desire and victory were one and the same, with some new things? Such thoughts, and more besides, were added to his imagination by the thin veins in her temples, the curve of her cheeks, the strength of her thighs, the bluish-green shadow, like the sea itself, in which her face dwelled, like an eye in its own moist bed.

'All evil, all good, all that I know and all that I do not know, all that you know and all that you do not know, all this has shaped the fullness of our night together.' Life and dreams had become a single thing. Their thoughts and senses were mingled like wine in the same cup. Their clothes, their naked faces, their hopes, the look in their eyes were like plants in that garden, like air, like stars, like silence. The hidden harmony in which nature had combined and concealed differences and diversities was revealed.

It was a sublime moment that could never return. Before his soul realized, his hands reached out desiringly and touched her flesh, pulled her to him, enjoying her delicious coolness.

As she felt the man's hands on her bare arms, the woman threw her head back as though she were going to fall. Through her dying eyelids, her dying lips, the white of her eyes and the white of her teeth gleamed like those things that glitter for the very last time. Then swiftly, her head came up again and revived, her mouth sought the mouth that was seeking hers. Lips were imprinted upon lips, and no seal had ever been stronger. Like the tree, love covered their mutual illusion.

They separated, they looked at each other without seeing. They could no longer see anything. They were blinded. They could hear a terrifying drumroll, as though the tolling of the bronze bell had penetrated their foreheads. And yet they were able to make out the dull thud of a pomegranate falling on to the grass, from the branch that they had shaken in their violent embrace. They shook themselves as though to throw off a burdensome cloak. They saw each other once more, now they were lucid again. They heard friendly voices through the garden and the faint, distant noise from the canals along which ancient retinues were perhaps sailing again.

'Well then?' the young man asked eagerly, burned to the very marrow by that kiss of flesh and soul.

The woman bent down to pick up the fallen pomegranate from the grass. It was ripe, it had burst open in the fall, spilling its bloody juices, which wet her dry hands and stained her white dress. The vision of the laden barge, the pale island, the flowery meadow returned to her loving spirit along with the Creator's words: 'This is my body . . . Take and eat . . .'

'Well?'

'Yes.'

She gripped the fruit in her hand with an instinctive gesture, as though she wanted to crush it. The juice ran down her wrist. Then her whole body contracted and trembled around a point of fire, craving submission. Again the river of ice overwhelmed her, flowed over her, freezing her from the roots of her hair to the tips of her fingers, but never extinguishing that fiery core.

'How? Tell me!' urged the young man, almost roughly, for he could feel his madness rising again and scent the Orgy returning from afar.

'Leave with the others, then come back . . . I shall be waiting for you by the gate of the Gradenigo Gardens.'

She was trembling with wretched, carnal shivers, in the grip of an unconquerable force. He saw the other aspect of her again in a sudden flash, soaked in sweat, panting like a Maenad after the dance. They looked at each other again, but they could not bear the animal gaze of their desiring. It wounded them. They moved apart.

She went towards the voices of the poets who had praised her idealized powers.

Lost, lost, henceforth she was completely lost! She was still alive, but defeated, humiliated, wounded, as though she had been beaten without mercy. She was still alive, and dawn was breaking and the days were beginning again and the fresh tide was flowing into *la Serenissima* and Donatella lay pure on her pillow. The hour that still seemed so close was already fading into infinite distance, the hour in which she had waited for her lover by the gate, had heard his footsteps in the almost funereal silence of the deserted pavement, had felt her knees give way as though she had been struck, while her head resounded with a terrible ringing. That hour was so far away already, and yet in her body, through the shuddering traces of pleasure, the sensation of waiting stayed strangely and intensely with her: she could feel the coldness of the iron against which she had rested her forehead, the overwhelming sourness rising from the grass as though from a macerating vat, the warm tongues of Myrta's greyhounds that had come up noiselessly to lick her hands.

'Goodbye. Goodbye.'

She was lost. He had risen from her bed as though from the bed of a courtesan, he had been almost a stranger, almost impatient, enticed by the freshness of dawn, by the freedom of morning.

'Goodbye.'

From her window she had seen him by the water, taking deep breaths of vivid air, then she had heard his clear, strong voice calling the boatman in the great calm.

'Zorzi.'

The man was asleep in the bottom of the motionless gondola, and his human sleep was like the sleep of the curved wood that obeyed him. When Stelio touched him with his foot, he awoke with a start, jumped into the stern and took hold of his oar. Man and wood, as united as a single body, were awake and ready to skim over the waters.

'At your service, sir,' said Zorzi with a pleasant smile, looking up at the brightening sky. 'Sit down, it's my turn to row now.' The door of a workshop opened across from the palace. It was a stone-cutter's workshop, where steps were made in the stone from Val di Sole.

'To climb up,' thought Stelio, and his superstitious heart was cheered by such a good omen. The name of the quarry seemed to shine out from the workshop sign. The image of a staircase signified his own progress upwards. He had already

113

seen it, in the abandoned garden on the Gradenigo coat of arms. 'Higher, ever higher!' Joy bubbled up from the depths. Morning stimulated human labour.

'What of Perdita? and Ariadne?' He saw them again at the top of the marble staircase in the light of the smoking torches, standing so closely together in the crowd that the two temptresses were confused in a blur of whiteness, both stepping out of the crowd as though from the embrace of a monster. 'What of Tanagra?' The woman from Syracuse with the long, goatish eyes appeared to him at rest, joined to Mother Earth, as a figure in a bas-relief emerges from the base on which it is carved. 'The Dionysian trinity!' He imagined them free from every kind of passion, beyond all evil, creatures of art. Swift, splendid images spread across the surface of his soul, like swelling sails on the sea. His heart grieved no longer. A sharp sense of the new was running through his whole being as the sky grew lighter. The heat of his night-time fever was being brushed away entirely by the breeze as the light mists evaporated. The same process that was happening around him, was happening within him too. He was being reborn with the morning.

'I don't need a light for you now,' muttered the boatman pointedly, extinguishing the lantern in the gondola.

'By San Giovanno Decollato to the Grand Canal,' cried Stelio, sitting down.

And as the dentellated prow turned down the side canal of San Giacomo dall'Orio, he turned to look back at the palace which was the colour of lead in the shadows. A single lighted window went dark, like an eye that is suddenly blinded. 'Goodbye, goodbye!' His heart gave a leap; pleasure surged again through his veins; images of pain and death flowed over all others. The woman who was no longer young was left alone in there, like a dying thing, while the reserved virgin was preparing to go back to her torture chamber. He did not know how to pity, he could only promise. He drew the illusion that he could change the destiny of those two women into his own happiness from the abundance of his strength. His heart grieved no longer. Concern

114

gave way to the simple pleasure his eyes derived from the sights of early morning. The branches that hung over garden walls with the twitter of wakening sparrows hid Perdita's pallid face from him. The singer's sinuous lips were lost in the swaying of the water. The same process that was happening around him, was happening within him too. The arching, echoing bridges, the floating seaweed, the moan of pigeons were like his very breathing, his confidence, his hunger.

'Stop in front of the Palazzo Vendramin-Calergi,' he commanded the boatman.

As he passed the wall of one of the gardens, he tore some slender flowering plants out of the gaps between the bricks that were the dark, rich colour of clotted blood. The flowers were violet, extraordinarily delicate, almost impalpable. He was reminded of the myrtles that grow round the gulf of Aegina, hard and proud like bushes of bronze. He thought of the dark little cypress trees that crown the stony tops of Tuscan hills, of the tall laurels that protect the statues in Roman villas. His thoughts increased the value of those autumn flowers that had been too slight for the One who had known how to give to his life the great victory he had promised it.

'Pull over to the shore.'

The canal, that ancient river of silence and poetry, was deserted. The green sky with its last dying stars was reflected in it. At first glance, the palace seemed airy, like a painted cloud resting on the water. The shadows that still enfolded it had the quality of velvet, the beauty of something soft and magnificent. And just as the eye can make out a pattern in thick velvet, so the architectural lines revealed themselves with their three Corinthian orders that rose up with grace and vitality to the pediment where eagles, warhorses and amphorae, emblems of noble life, were combined with the roses of Loredan. NON NOBIS DOMINE, NON NOBIS.*

* NOT UNTO US, OH LORD, NOT UNTO US.

115

The great sick heart was beating in there. The image of
the barbarian creator came back: his blue eyes shining under
his great forehead, his lips clenched and full of sensuality
over his strong chin. Was he asleep? Could he sleep? Or did
his glory keep him awake? The young man thought of all
the strange things he had heard tell about him. Was it true
that he could only sleep on his wife's heart, holding his
wife close, and that even in his old age he felt the need for
such loving contact? He thought of what Lady Myrta had
said, after she had visited him at Palermo in the Villa
d'Angri, where the cupboards in the rooms inhabited by
the old man were impregnated with such a strong scent of
essence of roses that she still felt dizzy. He saw the small,
tired body wrapped in sumptuous clothing, covered in
jewels, perfumed like a corpse ready for the pyre. Had
Venice given him, like Albrecht Dürer before him, a taste
for sensuality and luxury? On the very silence of the canals
he had heard the most fiery breath of his own music: the
mortal passion of Tristan and Isolde.

Now the great sick heart was beating in there; its formidable impulse was fading in there. The patrician palace,
with its eagles, its warhorses, its amphorae and its roses
was closed and silent as a great sepulchre. Above the marble
the breath of dawn was setting the sky on fire.

'Hail to you, Victorious One!' Stelio Effrena threw the
flowers down before the door. 'Move on! Move on!'

Spurred by that hidden impatience, the boatman bent
over the oar. The slender wooden vessel skimmed over the
water. A whole stretch of the canal was flooded with light.
A reddish sail passed noiselessly. The sea, the lively waves,
the laughter of the seagulls, the wind from the open water
all supported his desires.

'Row, Zorzi. Out to the Marina down the Rio dell'Olio,'
cried the young man.

The canal seemed too narrow for his soul to breathe in.
Victory was now as vital to him as breathing. Now that he
had emerged from his night-time delirium, he wanted to
experience the joyous part of his nature in the morning light

116

and the saltiness of the sea. He was not at all tired. He could feel a ring of freshness around his eyes, as though he had bathed them in dew. He did not feel any need to rest, and his hotel bed was as abhorrent to him as the vilest of resting places. 'The deck of a ship, the smell of tar and salt, the flapping of a red sail . . .'

'Row, Zorzi!'

The gondolier redoubled his efforts. The rowlock creaked occasionally with the pressure. The Fondaco dei Turchi melted into the distance in marvellously worn, faded ivory, like the surviving portico of a ruined mosque. They passed the Palazzo dei Cornaro and the Palazzo dei Pesaro, two opaque giants blackened with time as by the smoke of a great fire. The Ca' d'Oro passed them, a divine play of stone and air, and there was the Rialto bridge bending its great back, already filled with noisy everyday life, laden with its overflowing shops, smelling of vegetables and fish, like a vast horn of plenty emptying an abundance of the fruits of the earth and sea on either shore to nourish the all-powerful City.

'I'm hungry, Zorzi, terribly hungry,' said Stelio laughing.

'It's a good sign when the night makes you hungry,' said Zorzi. 'All it does for old men is make 'em fall asleep.'

'Pull over!'

He bought some grapes from Vignole from a barge, and some Malamocco figs piled on a plate of vine-leaves.

'Row!'

The gondola turned under the Fondaco dei Tedeschi, then slid down the narrow, dark canals toward the rio di Palazzo. The bells of San Giovanni Crisostomo, San Giovanni Elemosinario, San Cassiano, Santa Maria dei Miracoli, Santa Maria Formosa, San Lio rang out joyfully in the dawn. The bustle of the market with its smells of fish and vegetables and wine was lost in the salutation of the bells. Under a strip of sky, between the still sleeping walls of brick and marble, the strip of water was becoming ever brighter before the iron of the prow, as though their speed were lighting it up, and that increasing brightness gave Stelio the impression of flaming swiftness. He thought of ships being launched, and how sparks fly as they slide into the sea, how the water steams and the people shout and applaud . . .

'To the Ponte della Paglia!'

A thought that came as spontaneously as instinct swept him to the place of glory where traces of his lyrical words and echoes of the great Bacchic chorus still seemed to linger. '*Viva il forte . . .*' The gondola grazed the powerful side of the Doge's Palace, compact in a single mass shaped by chisels as skilled as musicians' bows in searching out harmonies. He embraced the building with all his reborn soul, he could hear the sound of his own voice once more and the burst of applause; he could see the great many-eyed monster with the glittering scales on its breast, its body coiling back into darkness under the great gilded scrolls, and he saw himself swaying over the crowd like a concave, sonorous thing possessed by a mysterious will. He was saying: 'To create with joy! That is a sign of godliness! It is impossible to imagine a greater triumph for the human spirit. The very words expressing such a thought are as splendid as dawn itself. . . .'

Out there in the open air, surrounded by water, by stone, by the ancient City, by the virgin dawn, he repeated to himself, 'To create with joy! To create with joy!' When the prow passed under a bridge and emerged into a mirror of light, the open space breathed into him all the beauty and all the strength of his past life, along with his hopes and his courage.

'Find me a boat, Zorzi, a boat going out to the open sea.' He needed yet more space, he needed wind, salt, spray, full sails, the bowsprit pointed towards the vast horizon. 'To the Veneta Marina, and find me a fishing boat, a *braghozzo* from Chioggia.' He caught sight of a big red and black sail that had just been hoisted and was flapping in the rising wind, proud as any ancient banner with the Lion and the Book of the republic. 'There's one! Catch up with it, Zorzi!' He waved impatiently to the boat, signalling to it to wait. 'Shout and tell the boat to wait for me.'

The man with the oar, red-faced and soaked in sweat, hailed the men in the boat. The gondola sped on like a punt in a regatta. The strong chest was panting loudly now.

'Well done, Zorzi!' But he was breathing heavily too, as if he were about to reach some place of happiness, meet his destiny, have the certainty of a kingdom.

'We've passed the finishing line,' said the boatman, rubbing his burning palms with an open laugh that seemed to refresh him completely. 'Lord, what folly!' His gesture, the tone of his voice, his ordinary remark, the astonished faces of the fishermen leaning over the side, the reflection of the sail turning the water blood-red, the inviting smell of bread coming from an oven, the smell of pitch starting to boil in a dockyard nearby, the noise of men in the arsenal going about their military tasks, the whole powerful impression of the shore where you could still smell the old rotten galleys of *La Serenissima* and where the hulls of Italian ships rang-out beneath hammer-blows: all those basic, healthy things aroused a great rush of happiness in the young man's heart that burst out through his mouth in laughter. He and the boatman both laughed, together, close to the patched, tarred side of the fishing boat which looked like a solid beast of burden, its skin rough with wrinkles, warts and scars.

'What do you want?' asked the oldest of the fishermen, turning to the sound of the laughter his bearded, weather-beaten face lightened only by his few white hairs and his grey eyes under eyelids forced upwards by salt winds. 'What's your business, sir?'

The mainsail flapped like a banner.

'The master wants to come aboard,' answered Zorzi.

The mast creaked from top to bottom, like a live thing.

'Let him come up, then. Is that all you want, sir?' asked the old man simply, and turned to fetch the hanging ladder. He fastened it along the stern. It consisted of a few worn-out pegs and a double width of frayed rope. But even that, like everything about the rough boat, seemed extra-ordinarily vital to Stelio. As he put his foot on it, he felt

119

ashamed of his elegant, polished shoes. The sailor's hard, rough hand tattooed with blue signs helped him, pulled him on board with a jerk.

'My grapes and figs, Zorzi.'

The boatman handed him the vineleaf platter from the gondola. 'That'll do you good!'

'Is there any bread?'

'We've got hot bread,' said another sailor, raising his handsome, sturdy blond body, 'It's just out of the oven.'

Hunger would certainly make it taste delicious, make him find all the bounty of wheat within it.

'At your service, sir,' shouted the boatman, waving. 'Let's hope you get a fair wind!'

'Luff!'

The Latin sail with the Lion and the Book swelled crimson. The boat tacked towards the open sea, turning its prow towards San Servolo. The shoreline seemed to arch itself to push. In its wake a greenish line and a pinkish one fused together in the water, making an opaline whirlpool, then changed, and all sorts of colours came and went, as though the wave at the prow were a liquid rainbow.

'Leeside!'

The boat veered violently. A miracle caught it. The first rays of the sun pierced through the heaving sail, glittered on the bold angles on the bell-towers of San Marco and San Giorgio Maggiore, turned the sphere of the Fortuna to flame, crowned the five mitres on the Basilica with lightning. The Sea-City was queen of the waters, and all her veils were torn.

'Hail to the Miracle!' A superhuman feeling of power and freedom swelled the young man's heart, as the wind swelled the sail that was transfigured for him. He stood in the crimson splendour of the sail and in the splendour of his own blood. It seemed to him that all the mystery of that beauty was demanding some triumphal action from him. He felt able to accomplish it. 'To create with joy!'

And the world was his!

II

THE EMPIRE OF SILENCE

'In time.' In a room in the Academy, Foscarina had paused in front of Francesco Torbido's *Old Woman*, that wrinkled, toothless, flabby, yellowish old woman who can no longer smile or weep, that species of human ruin that is worse than putrefaction, that earthly Fate who is not holding a spindle or a thread or scissors in her fingers, but rather a paper on which the warning is written.

'In time,' she repeated, in the open air, breaking the thoughtful silence during which she had felt her heart becoming heavier by degrees, and sinking like a stone into the depths of dark waters. 'Stelio, do you know the boarded-up house in the Calle Gambara?'

'No. Which is it?'

'The Countess of Glanegg's house.'

'No, I don't know it.'

'Do you know the story of the beautiful Austrian countess?'

'No, Fosca, I don't. Do tell me.'

'Shall we go down the Calle Gambara? It's really very close.'

'Yes, let's.'

They walked side by side towards the boarded-up house. Stelio held back slightly to watch the actress, to see her walking in that dead air. He embraced her whole person with his warm gaze: the gracious, noble line of her sloping shoulders, her free, flexible waist above her strong hips, her knees that moved lightly against the folds of her skirt, her pale, passionate face, her eloquent, thirsting mouth, her brow as strong and lovely as any man's, her eyes that lengthened into her lashes, as though moistened by a tear that kept forming and dissolving without being shed, her whole passionate face of light and shadow, love and pain, her feverish energy, her quivering life.

'I love you. I love you, only you, I love everything about you,' he said to her suddenly, very quietly, close to her cheek, embracing her as they walked, putting his arm under hers, unable to bear the thought that she was once more in the grip of that anguish, that she was suffering from the terrible warning.

She started, stopped, turned white and dropped her gaze. 'My dearest,' she said, in such a light voice that the two words seemed to have been spoken not by her lips but by the smile in her heart. All her sorrow had become fluid, transformed into one great wave of tenderness that poured over her lover with abandon. Infinite gratitude made her anxious to find some great gift for him.

'What can I do for you? What would you like? Tell me.'

She thought he might ask for some wonderful test, some wild, extraordinary proof of her love. 'Let me serve.' She wanted to own the world so as to give it to him.

'What would you like? Tell me. What can I do for you?'

'Just love me. Love me.'

'My love is sad, my poor darling.'

'It's perfect, it makes my life complete.'

'You are young . . .'

'I love you.'

'You should possess that which is strong like you . . .'

'You praise my strength and my hopes every day. My blood flows more strongly when I am near you and you are silent. That is when things happen in me that will astonish you in time. I need you.'

'Don't say that.'

'Every day you reassure me that all promises will be kept.'

'Yes, you will have a splendid destiny. I'm not afraid for you. You are sure. No danger can frighten you, no obstacle can block your path . . . Oh, if only I could love without being afraid! When one loves, one is afraid. I'm not afraid for you. You are invincible in my eyes. And I'm grateful to you for that, too.'

She was revealing her deep faith, boundless and clear as her passion for him. For a long time, during all that she had struggled for so intensely and all that had happened during her wanderings, she had kept her eyes fixed on his young, victorious life as though it were an ideal form born out of the purification of her own desire. More than once, in the sadness of fleeting loves and the nobility of what they had forbidden to themselves, she had thought: 'Oh, if only one day I could fashion wings for you for your highest flight of all, out of that strength of mine which has been tempered by storms, out of all the strong, clear things that pain and rebellion have revealed in the depths of my soul, from the very best of me!' More than once her melancholia had known the intoxication of an almost heroic presentiment. At such times she had subjected her soul by effort and by restraint, and at such times she had raised it up to the most glorious moral beauty, she had led it through deeds of pain and purity just in order to be deserving of what she had hoped and feared at the same time, just in order to feel worthy of offering her service to the one who was so impatient to be victorious.

And now a sudden, violent twist of fate had thrown her against him with her flesh quivering like that of a woman full of desire. She had united herself with him in all the salt of her blood. She had watched him on the same pillow, sleeping the heavy sleep of love's exertions; she had lain by his side and known the abruptness of waking troubled by cruel fears, known the impossibility of closing her tired eyelids in case he might look at her while she was asleep, searching her face for signs of age, in case he might feel disgust and pant for some fresh, unknown young being.

'Nothing else is worth what you give me,' said Stelio,

pressing her arm, his fingers searching for the bare wrist beneath her glove, with an almost insane need to feel the beating of that devoted life, the throbbing of that faithful heart in the desolate place where they were walking, in the dismal mist that encircled them, deadening the sound of their footsteps. 'Nothing is worth this certainty that I shall never be alone again until I die.'

'Oh, you feel it too then, you know that this is forever!' she cried with a sudden rush of joy as she felt her love triumphant. 'Forever, no matter what happens, no matter where your fate may lead you, no matter how you may want me to serve you, Stelio, be it close to you or far away . . .'

A confused monotonous sound that she knew well was spreading through the misty air. It was the chorus of sparrows in the Countess of Glanegg's garden, clustering in the great moribund trees. The words were silenced on her lips. She instinctively turned back, pulling her lover with her to go somewhere else.

'Where are we going?' he asked, startled by his companion's abrupt movement and by that sudden interruption which was like the end of a spell or a piece of music.

She stopped. She smiled her slight concealing smile. 'IN TIME.' 'I wanted to run away,' she said, 'but I can't.' She was there like a pale flame. 'I had forgotten that I was taking you to the boarded-up house, Stelio.' She was there in that ashen daylight, devoid of energy, lost as though in a desert. 'I thought we were going somewhere else. But we have come to the proper place. In time.'

Now she seemed to him as she had done on that unforgettable night when she had pleaded with him: 'Do not hurt me!' She was there, wearing her secret, tender soul, and it would have been so easy to kill her, destroy her, sacrifice her without spilling blood.

'Let's go,' he said, making as if to move her on, 'Let's go somewhere else.'

'We can't.'

'Let's go back to your house; we can light a fire, the

126

first fire of October. Let me spend the evening with you, Foscarina! It will rain soon. It will be so lovely to be in your room and talk and hold hands and be quiet . . . Come on! Let's go back!' He wanted to take her in his arms and hold her, console her, feel her weep, drink her tears. The very sound of his own comforting words increased his feelings of tenderness. Of all the things about his beloved, he desperately loved the delicate little lines that ran from the corners of her eyes to her temples and the little dark veins that made her eyelids look like violets, and the curve of her cheeks, and her tired chin and everything about her that was touched by the wasting sickness of Autumn, all that was shadow in her passionate face.

'Foscarina! Foscarina!'

Whenever he called her by her real name, her heart beat faster, as though something more profoundly human were entering their love, as though suddenly all the past had once more attached itself to that image which he was isolating in dreams and which countless threads were reattaching to all the fibres of remorseless life. 'Come on. Let's go back!'

She smiled piteously. 'Why should we, since the house is there? We can go down the Calle Gambara. Wouldn't you like to hear the story of the Countess of Glanegg? Look at it! It's like a monastery!'

The street was as lonely as a hermit's path, grey, damp, strewn with mouldering leaves. The north-east wind had created a slow, soft fog in the air that deadened all sounds. The confused monotonous noise vaguely resembled the creaking of wood or iron.

'Behind that wall a desolate heart has outlived the beauty of its own body,' said Foscarina softly. 'Look there! All the windows are closed, the blinds are nailed down, the doors are sealed. Just one door for the servants has been left open, and the dead woman's food is brought in there, as they used to do in Egyptian tombs. The servants are caring for a dead body.' The tops of the trees that were almost bare as they reared up over the surrounding wall seemed to be steaming, and the sparrows which were more in number than the sick leaves along the branches twittered and twittered without ceasing.

'Guess what her name is? It's a lovely, unusual name such as you yourself might have invented.'

'I can't imagine.'

'Radiana. The prisoner's name is Radiana.'

'Who is keeping her prisoner?'

'Time, Stelio. Time is guarding the doors with his scythe and his hour-glass, as in all those old prints . . .'

'Is this an allegory?'

A boy went past, whistling. When he saw the two people looking up at the closed windows he stopped to look as well, his eyes wide with astonishment and curiosity. They were silent. The constant twittering of the sparrows could not overcome the silence of the walls, the tree-trunks and the sky; for the monotonous sound echoed in their ears like the rumbling inside a seashell, and through it they could hear the silence of everything around them and an occasional distant voice. The hoarse wail of a siren faded out into the foggy distance becoming gradually softer like the sound of a flute. Then it ceased. The boy grew tired of looking. He could not see anything happening, the windows were not opening, everything was as motionless as ever. He set off at a run. They could hear the sound of his little bare feet running over the damp stones and mouldering leaves.

'Well?' asked Stelio. 'What does Radiana do? You still have not told me who she is and why she is kept a prisoner. Do tell me. I was thinking about Soranza Soranzo.'

'She is the Countess of Glanegg, one of the highest members of the Viennese aristocracy, and possible the most beautiful woman I have ever met in the world. Franz Lenbach painted her wearing armour like a Valkyrie, with a winged helmet. Do you know Franz Lenbach? Have you ever been to his red studio in the Palazzo Borghese?'

'No, never.'

'Do go some day. And ask him to show you that portrait. You will never again be able to erase Radiana's face from your memory. You will see it, as I see it now, unchanged

128

despite these walls. She wanted to stay unchanged in the memory of anyone who had seen her in all her glory. There came one excessively bright morning when she realized that the time had come for her to fade, so she decided to bid the world farewell and prevent men from witnessing her decay and the disintegration of her famous beauty. Perhaps what kept her in Venice was a sense of sympathy for things that fall apart and go to ruin. She gave a magnificent farewell banquet at which she appeared still supremely beautiful. Then she retired forever into this house that you are looking at, behind this walled garden, with her servants, to wait for the end. She has become a creature of legend. They say that there are no mirrors in the house and that she has forgotten what her own face looked like. She has even forbidden her dearest friends and her closest relatives from visiting. How does she live? What thoughts does she have for company? How does she while away the tedium of waiting? Is her soul in a state of grace, I wonder?'

Every pause in the veiled voice that queried the mystery was filled with such intense melancholy that it seemed almost palpable, almost measuring the sobbing rhythm of water being poured into an urn.

'Does she say her prayers? Does she meditate? Does she weep? Or perhaps she has become inert and no longer suffers, as a wrinkled old apple no longer suffers tucked away in the back of an old cupboard.'

The woman was silent. Her lips were turned down, as though the very words she spoke had withered them.

'What if she were suddenly to appear at that window right now?' said Stelio, whose ear had caught what seemed to be an actual sound of hinges creaking. They both peered at the gaps in the nailed shutters. 'She might be there watching us,' he added in a hushed voice. Each communicated their shudder to the other. They were right up against the facing wall and did not have the will to move a step. The inertia of everything was invading them, the damp greyish fog was wreathing itself more thickly around them, the confused monotonous noise was deafening them like a medicine that dulls the senses of fever victims. Sirens wailed in the distance. The harsh wailing gradually faded, turning sweet as the sound of flutes in the soft air, seeming to linger like the faded leaves which were abandoning their branches one by one without even a groan. How long it took for a leaf to detach itself and fall to earth! Everything was slow, was fog, desolation, waste, ashes.

'I must die, my dearest darling, I must die!' said the woman after a long silence, in a choking voice, raising her face from the pillow into which she had pressed to try and control the convulsion of lust and agony that his sudden, wild caresses had aroused in her.

She saw her beloved on the other divan, apart from her, over by the balcony. He seemed about to fall asleep, with his head thrown back, tinged with gold by the light of evening. She noticed a red mark like a tiny wound under his lip and his hair falling dishevelled over his forehead. She felt her desire feed on such things and flare up again. She felt her eyelids hurting her pupils the more she gazed on him, and she felt that gaze burning her eyelashes, as the incurable sickness entered her through her eyes and spread through her faded body. Lost, lost, she was lost now with no hope of salvation!

'Die?' said her lover weakly, without opening his eyes or moving, as though speaking from the depths of melancholy or drowsiness. She noticed how the tiny bleeding wound below his lip moved when he spoke.

'Before you come to hate me. . . .'

He opened his eyes, pulled himself up and stretched out a hand to her as though to prevent her from saying any more. 'Why do you torment yourself so?' He saw her looking ashen, her uncombed locks covering her cheeks, gnawed at by a kind of corrosive poison, bent double as though her soul had burst through her very flesh, terrible and wretched.

'What are you doing to me? What are we doing to each other?' said the woman in anguish.

They had fought together, breath against breath, heart against heart; they had joined together as though in combat, they had tasted blood in their saliva. They had given in suddenly to a surge of desire as though blinded by the urge to destroy. He had shaken her life as if he wanted to tear it up by its deepest roots. In the grip of desire they had felt the sharpness of teeth in their cruel kisses.

'I love you.'

'Not like this. I don't want it like this . . .'

'You disturb me. A wildness comes over me quite suddenly . . .'

'It is like hatred . . .'

'No, don't say that!'

'You shake me and crush me as though you wanted to kill me . . .'

'You blind me. Then I am not in control.'

'What disturbs you? What is it that you see in me?'

'I don't know.'

'I do.'

'Don't torment yourself! I love you. This is love . . .'

'And it has doomed me! I must die of it. Call me again by the name you used to call me.'

'You are mine! You belong to me! I shall never lose you!'

'You will lose me.'

'Why? I don't understand. What is this folly of yours? Does my desire offend you? And don't you desire me too? Aren't you overcome by the same madness to possess me and be possessed? Your teeth were chattering before I even touched you . . .' He was impatient now, and burned her even more within, opened her wound again. She covered her face with her hands. Her heart was beating like a hammer against her breast which had become quite rigid, and she felt the heavy blows reverberate against her skull. 'Look!' He touched his lips where it hurt him, pressing the tiny wound, then held out to the woman his fingers tinged with the drop of blood that had oozed out of it. 'You left your mark on me. You bit me like a wild animal . . .'

She stood up abruptly, twisting round as though he had

seared her with a red-hot brand. She opened her eyes wide at him, as though she would devour him with her gaze. Her nostrils flared. A terrifying force shuddered through her innards. She could feel her whole quivering body naked under her shift as though the material no longer covered it. The face that she raised out of her hands as out of a blind mask burned darkly like a fire without a glow. She was incredibly beautiful and terrible and wretched.

'Oh, Perdita, Perdita.'

The man will never, ever forget the step with which lust moved towards him, the way in which she drew near to him, the swift, silent wave that rushed at his breast, that wrapped herself around him, drank him in, gave him for an instant the pleasure and terror of being subject to divine violation and dissolving in a warm, lethal dampness, as though the woman's whole body had suddenly become a huge absorbing mouth that sucked him in entirely.

He closed his eyes, he forgot about the world and about success. A shadowy, sacred depth opened up within him like a temple. His spirit was opaque, motionless, but all his senses sought to transcend human limitations, sought the joy that is beyond all obstacles; they became sublime, able to penetrate the furthest mysteries of all, to discover the very darkest secrets, to derive pleasure from pleasure as one harmony follows another, they were instruments of miracle, infinitely powerful, as real as death itself. Everything was dissolving like mist. In the single union of the sexes all the energies and aspirations of the universe were being poured, it was being consecrated by heaven, made holy by shadow and the veil, accompanied by the roaring of death.

He opened his eyes. He saw the darkened room, and through the open balcony he saw the distant sky, the trees, the domes, the towers, the distant lagoon over which the face of twilight was bending, the blue, peaceful Euganean Hills like the folded wings of earth resting in the evening. He saw the shapes of silence and the silent shape of the woman clinging to him like the bark on a tree.

The woman was lying on him with all her weight, she

132

was holding him tightly, covering him, she was pressing her forehead against his shoulder suffocatingly, with her face quite hidden, in an embrace that did not loosen, was as unmovable as the arms of a corpse that stiffen around a living man. It seemed that she never wanted to let go, that she could only be prised off him by cutting off her arms at the elbow. He could feel the solidity and strength of her bones in that clasp, while he could also feel the softness of her flesh on his chest and along his legs, quivering every now and again like running water over gravel. Indefinable things flowed by in that quivering water, countless, continuous things, rising up from the depths, trickling down from far away, they kept flowing by, ever more thickly, darkly, impurely, a river of turgid life. Once again he knew that his sharp desire fed on that impurity, on that unknown burden, on the traces of lost loves, on that bodily sadness, on that unspeakable despair. Once again he knew that the phantoms of other gestures aroused the violence of his own gestures of desire for the nomadic woman. Now he was suffering for her, for himself, he felt her suffering, and he felt her belong to him as wood belongs to the flame that consumes it. Again he heard her unexpected words after their passion: 'I must die!'

He looked outside again. He saw the gardens fading into darkness, the houses being lit up, a star sparkling on the mourning dress of the sky, a long pale sword glittering in the depths of the lagoon, the hills blurring into the borders of night, distances stretching out towards lands rich with unknown treasure. There were deeds to be performed in the world, conquests to be made, dreams to be realized, mysteries to be solved, laurels to be gathered. There were mysterious paths down there full of unexpected meetings. Some veiled happiness might be passing by without anyone ever meeting or knowing it. Perhaps there was someone just like him out there in the world at that moment, a brother or a distant enemy, into whose mind the lightning bolt of inspiration that gives birth to an eternal work might be about to flash, after a long day's waiting. Someone might have just finished an important work or finally found a noble purpose in life. But he was there, in the prison of his own body, lying under the weight of a desperate woman. That marvellous destiny of pain and power, like a ship loaded with gold and iron, had crashed against him as though it had hit a rock. What was Donatella Arvale doing, what was she thinking in the evening, on her Tuscan hilltop, in her lonely house, with her mad father? Was she tempering her will for the struggle she was contemplating? Was she building up her secret knowledge? Was she a virgin?

He became inert beneath her clasp, he felt his arms blocked in by the rigid circle. Silently he lay without moving as revulsion flooded through his whole being. A melancholy as strong as any pain thickened around his heart. He thought that the silence was waiting for a scream. His veins throbbed painfully through his torpid limbs beneath her weight. Her clasp gradually slackened, as though life were failing her. The distressing words came back into his mind. He was assailed by a sudden terror, by the apparition of a funereal image. And yet he did not move, he did not speak, he did not attempt to dispel the cloud of anguish that was gathering over them both. He stayed quite still. He lost track of places, of the passing of time. He saw himself and the woman in the midst of a vast plain, with patches of dried-up grass, under a white sky. They were waiting, waiting for some voice to call them, for some voice to uplift them . . . A confused dream came into being in his lethargy, it fluctuated, changed, became sad in his nightmare. Now he thought he was climbing a steep slope with his companion, it was very difficult, and her more inhuman difficulty only made his own more disgusting . . . But he started and opened his eyes again at the sound of a bell. It was the bell of San Simeone Profeta, so close that it seemed to be ringing in that very room. Its metallic sound pierced his ears like a rapier.

'Were you dozing as well?' he asked the woman, feeling her as lifeless as if she had already died. He raised a hand and lightly stroked her hair, her cheek, her chin.

134

She burst into sobs, as though that hand were breaking her very heart. She sobbed and sobbed there, on his breast, but she did not die.

'I have a heart, Stelio,' said the woman looking into his eyes with a pitiful effort that made her lips tremble, as though she had had to overcome some primitive timidity before she could utter those words. 'I am troubled by a heart that is alive and, oh Stelio, so alive and hungry and tormented that you cannot imagine . . .'

She smiled her slight, concealing smile, hesitated, held out her hand towards a bunch of violets, took them and raised them to her nostrils. Her eyelids were cast down, her magnificently sad, beautiful brow was bare between her hair and the flowers.

'You hurt it sometimes,' she said softly, breathing into the violets, 'and sometimes you are cruel to it . . .' It was as though that humble, sweet-smelling thing helped her to admit her hurt, to conceal even more her timid reproof of her beloved. She was silent; he bowed his head. They could hear the crackling of logs in the fireplace, the even beat of the rain in the garden in mourning could be heard outside. 'Such a thirst for goodness, you cannot know how great that thirst is! . . . Goodness, my dearest, true, profound goodness that cannot speak but which understands, and knows how to bestow everything in a single glance, in one small gesture, yet is strong, secure, always upright against life that taints it and seduces it . . . Do you know what I mean?' Her voice was alternately steady and quavering, so warm with inner light, so full of the soul it revealed that the young man felt it pass right through his blood not as a sound but as a spiritual essence.

'In you, I recognize it!' He took her hands that were holding the violets on her knees. He kissed them both humbly, leaning over them. He stayed there at her feet, in a gesture of submissiveness. The delicate scent made his tenderness delicate too. In the pause, both the fire and the water spoke.

'Do you believe that I am sure of you?'

'Have you not watched me sleeping next to your heart?' he replied, with a change of tone, suddenly overcome by a new sensation, for he could see in that question her naked, proud soul offered to him, could feel her secret need to believe and to trust laid bare.

'Yes, but what does that matter? Youth sleeps soundly on any pillow. You are young . . .'

'I love you and I believe in you. I have given myself completely. You are my beloved. Your hand is whole.' He had discerned the familiar pain run through the lines of her beloved face, and his words had trembled with love.

'Goodness!' said the woman, stroking the hair on his temples with a light gesture. 'You know how to be good, you need to bring comfort, my dearest! But a mistake has been made, and we must atone for it. Before, I thought I would have been able to do the most lowly and the most exalted things for you; now I feel I can only do one thing: I can go away, disappear, leave you free with your own destiny . . .' He interrupted her, sitting up and taking her beloved face between his hands. 'I can do this, which love cannot do!' she said quietly, turning pale and looking at him as she had never done before.

He could feel a soul there in the hollow of his hands, an image of a living spring, infinitely precious and beautiful. 'Foscarina, Foscarina, my soul, my life, yes, I know you can give me even more than love, and nothing else is worth that gift which only you can give me, and no other offer could ever comfort me if I did not have you beside me on my journeying. Believe me! I have said this to you so many times, remember that! Even when you were not yet wholly mine, even when we were still separated by the prohibition . . .' Holding her in that position he bent down and kissed her passionately on the lips. She shuddered right through her bones; the icy river rushed over her, freezing her.

136

'No, no more!' she pleaded, white faced. She pushed her lover away from her. She could not control the heaving of her breast. She bent down as though in a dream and picked up the violets which she had dropped. 'The prohibition!' she said, after a silence. A dull roar came from a log that was resisting the bite of the flames; the rain rattled on stones and on branches. Occasionally the noise was like a stormy sea, recalling solitary hostile places, unfriendly distances, beings that wandered under savage skies. 'Why did we break it?'

Stelio was staring at the moving glory in the fireplace, but the amazing sensation still lingered in his open, upturned hands, a trace of something miraculous, a vestige of the human countenance through whose unhappy pallor the wave of sublime beauty had flowed.

'Why did we?' said the woman again, wretchedly. 'Admit that you too . . . that night, before we were swept away and overwhelmed by blind passion, admit that you felt that everything was about to be destroyed and lost. You knew that we should not give in to it if we wanted to save the good that had come to light within us, that strong, intoxicating feeling that I thought was the only precious thing in my life. Admit it, Stelio, tell the truth! I could almost remind you of the exact moment when the good voice first spoke to you. It was out on the water, wasn't it, as we were going home, when Donatella was with us?'

She had hesitated for a second before speaking that name, and afterwards she felt a bitterness that was almost physical which slid down inside her from her lips, as though its very syllables had become poisonous to her. She suffered as she waited for her lover to reply

'I cannot go back now, Foscarina,' he replied. 'Nor would I want to. I have not lost my goodness. I like your soul to have a sensuous mouth. I like the way the blood drains out of your face when I touch you and you feel that I desire you . . .'

'Be quiet,' she pleaded, 'do not keep distressing me so. Let me at least talk to you about my feelings of grief. Why won't you help me?' She sank back a little into the cushions on which she was sitting, tensing her body as though she were being violently attacked, staring fixedly into the fire so as not to look at her lover. 'More than once I have seen something in your eyes that has filled me with horror,' she managed to say finally with such an effort that her voice sounded hoarse. He started, but did not dare to contradict her. 'With horror!' she repeated more clearly, implacable with herself having overcome her fears by now and seized hold of her own courage.

They were both face to face with the truth, with their naked, throbbing hearts.

The woman spoke without a sign of weakness. 'The first time was down there in the garden that night . . . I know what you were seeing in me: all the mud through which I have walked, all the infamy that I have stepped in, all the impure things that have disgusted me . . . You would never have been able to admit the images that were arousing your fever! Your eyes were cruel and your mouth was twisted. When you realized you were hurting me, you were sorry . . . But then . . .' She was blushing and speaking rapidly, and her eyes were gleaming.

'To have nourished for years all that was best in me with a feeling of devotion and boundless admiration, near to you and away from you, in happiness and in sadness; to have received every gesture of comfort offered to mankind by your poetry with the purest act of gratitude, and to have waited anxiously for other even greater, more comforting gifts; to have believed in the great strength of your genius from its very dawn, and never to have ceased watching your rise or accompanying you with a vow that was my morning and evening prayer for years; to have silently, fervently gone on with the continual effort of giving some beauty, some harmony to my spirit so as to make it less unworthy of coming close to yours; to have shivered as I spoke immortal words out there on stage so many times, facing an enthusiastic audience and thinking about the words that you would one day give to the crowd through means of my voice; to have toiled ceaselessly, to have tried always to reach a simpler, more intense form of art, to have aspired constantly to perfection for fear of displeasing you, of seeming to be too unlike your dream; to have loved my fleeting glory only because one day it might serve yours; to have hastened on your latest revelations with the devotion of my absolute faith, so as to offer myself to you as an instrument of your success before I began to decline, and to have defended against everybody and everything this idealism hidden in my soul, against everybody, even against myself, in fact more fiercely and harshly against myself; to have made you my melancholy, my truest hope, my heroic test, the sign of everything that is best and strongest and most free, oh Stelio....' She paused for a moment, suffocated by it all, offended by the memory like some new shame. '... and then to come to that one daybreak and to see you leaving my house, in that atrocious dawn!' She turned white, the blood drained from her face. 'Do you remember?'

'But I was happy! I was happy!' he cried in a choking voice, disturbed to his very innards.

'No, no ... Don't you remember? You rose from my bed as though it were a courtesan's, you were satisfied with a few hours violent pleasure ...'

'You deceive yourself!'

'Admit it! Tell the truth! We can only save ourselves now with the truth.'

'I was happy, my heart was completely open, I was dreaming and hoping, I felt reborn ...'

'Yes, you were happy to breathe again and be free, to feel your own youth out there in the wind and the daylight. You mingled too many bitter things with your caresses, too much poison in your pleasure. What did you see in the woman who had suffered so much through her renunciation ... yes, you know that ... suffered rather than break the ban that was necessary for the dream she carried with her in her constant wanderings through the world to go on living. Tell me. What did you see other than a corrupted being, a lustful body, a leftover from occasional

139

passions, a vagabond actress who belongs to everyone and yet to no one in bed just as on stage . . .'

'Foscarina! Foscarina!' He threw himself upon her in agitation and upheaval, and closed her lips with a trembling hand. 'No, don't say that! Be quiet! You are mad, you are quite mad . . .'

'Horror!' she murmured falling back against the cushions as though she were losing her senses, exhausted by the effort, deathly pale beneath the flood of bitterness that welled up from the bottom of her heart. But her eyes stayed wide open, fixed as twin crystals, hard as if they had no lashes, staring at him. They prevented him from speaking, from either denying or lessening the impact of the truth they had exposed. After a few seconds they became unbearable. He closed them with his fingers, as one closes the eyes of a corpse. She saw the movement that was infinitely melancholy, felt his fingers touch her eyelids as only love and pity know how to touch. Her bitterness faded, the sharp knot was loosened, her lashes became moist. She stretched out her arm and put it around his neck, then slowly pulled herself up. She seemed to be pulling everything back into herself, becoming light and weak again, full of silent pleading.

'So I must really go then,' she sighed, her voice wet with inner weeping. 'Is there no help for it? Is there no pardon?'

'I love you,' said her beloved.

She freed an arm and stretched her open hand towards the fireplace in supplication. Then she clasped the young man tightly once again. 'Yes, just for a while, a little while! Let me stay with you a while! Then I shall go, I shall go and die far, far away, beneath a tree, on a stone. Let me stay with you a while longer!'

'I love you,' said her beloved.

Blind, indomitable life forces whirled around their heads, around their embrace. Because they sensed them and were afraid, they held each other more tightly, and from that close embrace of their two bodies an agonizing good and evil that were fused together and inseparable were born for

140

their souls. In the silence, the voice of the elements was speaking in an obscure language that was an uncomprehending answer to their mute questioning. Both fire and water, close at hand and from far away, chattered, answered, told tales. Gradually they caught the attention of the Creator, they seduced him, took hold of him, pulled him into the world of countless myths that were born from their eternity. With a sensation that was deep and real, he heard in his ears the sound of the two melodies that were expressing the intimate essence of two elementary Wills, the two marvellous melodies that he had already found and was going to weave in the symphonic structure of his new tragedy. The stabs of pain and vibrations of anxiety ceased abruptly, as in some happy truce, for a period of enchantment in their unhappiness. Even the woman's arms loosened their grip, as though in response to some mysterious command for freedom.

'There is no help for it,' she said to herself, as if repeating the words of a woman condemned to death that she had heard with her own ears in the same way that he had heard the great melodies. She leaned over, rested her chin on her palm and her elbow on her knee. She stayed in that fixed position before the fireplace with a frown on her forehead.

He looked at her, and his pain came back. The truce had been all too brief, but his spirit was reaching towards his work and he was left with an agitation that was like impatience. That pain seemed useless to him now, the woman's anguish seemed almost obtrusive, even though he loved her, even though he desired her and his caresses were passionate and both of them were free and the place where they were living was favourable to their dreams and their pleasures. He would have liked to find a way suddenly to break that iron circle, to sweep away that dismal mist, to lead his beloved back to happiness. He asked his own generosity for some delicate invention that would bring a smile to the grieving woman and sweeten her. But he no longer felt that melancholy abandonment and the trembling pity which had given such a light touch to his fingers as they closed her desperate eyes. Instinct could only provide him with sensual gestures, the caress that dulls the soul, the kiss that confuses thoughts.

He hesitated. He looked at her. She was still in the same position, leaning forward, her chin in her hand, her forehead creased. The fire gleamed on her face and her hair with its bright tongues. Her brow was as lovely as a handsome man's brow, but there was something wild in the natural wave and reddish tint of her thick hair where it sprang from her temples, something crude and proud that reminded him of the wing of a bird of prey.

'What are you looking at?' she asked, sensing his attentiveness. 'Have you found a white hair?'

He bent down, then knelt beside her, yielding, caressingly. 'You are beautiful to me, I keep discovering things in you that I love, Foscarina. I was looking at the way your hair waves, here, so strangely; storms, not combs have made it like that.'

He wound his sensual hands into her thick locks. She closed her eyes, overcome by ice, dominated by a terrible power. She was like a thing he could hold in his fist, like a ring on a finger, like a glove, like a garment, like a word that can be spoken or withheld, a wine that can be drunk or poured away into the soil.

'You are beautiful to me. When you close your eyes like that, I feel you are mine to the very utmost, mine, inside me, like my soul blended into my body. My life and your life are one . . . I don't know how to tell you . . . Your whole face turns pale within me . . . I can feel love rising through your veins and your hair, I can see it overflowing from under your eyelids . . . When you blink those eyelids, I feel them move to the pulsing of my blood and I feel the shadow of your eyelashes touching the deepest part of my heart . . .'

She listened in the darkness, where the vibrating redness of the fire reached her through living tissues. At times she felt that his voice was a long way away and was not talking to her but to someone else and that she was eavesdropping on some lovers' private conversation, and she was wracked

142

with jealousy, struck by bolts of murderous desire, invaded by a bloodthirsty urge for vengeance, but nevertheless she stayed completely still, her hands hung down weighted with lethargy, uselessly, impotently.

'You are all my pleasure and all my awakening. There is an awakening power in you of which you are quite unconscious. The simplest action of yours is enough to show me some reality that I did not know about before. And love is like intelligence, it shines and measures the truths it uncovers. Why are you so bitter? Nothing has been destroyed, nothing is lost. We had to come together as we did so as to ascend to happiness together. It was necessary for me to be free and happy in the truth of your total love so that I could create the work that so many people are waiting for. I need your faith, I need to be happy and to write . . . Your very presence is sufficient to make my mind incredibly fertile. Earlier, when you were holding me in your arms, I heard a rush of music suddenly burst through the silence, a whole river of sound . . .'

Who was he talking to? Who was he asking for happiness? Was not his need for music drawing him towards the woman who could sing and transform the universe with her singing? From whom might he ask happiness and creativity if not from the freshness of youth, the untouched virgin? While she was holding him in her arms, the other woman had been singing within him! And now, who was he talking to now except to that other woman? Only the other woman could give him what he needed for his art and his life. The virgin was a new power, a sealed beauty, a sharp, magnificent weapon that had not yet been wielded in the intoxication of battle. Damnation! Damnation!

Sorrow mixed with rage tormented the woman in the vibrant, broken darkness that she dared not leave. She was suffering as though she were caught up in a nightmare. She felt she was falling into an abyss with the burden she could never shake off, with the life she had lived, with all the years of wretchedness and success, with her tired face and her thousand masks, with her despairing soul and the thou-

143

sand souls that had inhabited her mortal form. The passion that was to have saved her was now pushing her irredeemably towards ruin and death. To reach her, to enjoy her, her lover's desire had to go through the confused entanglement that he thought was made up of countless unknown loves, and it would become contaminated, corrupted, bitter and cruel to the point where his bitterness would turn to disgust, perhaps even to hatred and contempt. He would always see the shadow of other men on his caresses, and that shadow would always arouse the savage, bestial instincts in him that he kept hidden deep within his powerful sensuality. Oh, what had she done? She had armed a raging destroyer and had put him there, between herself and her beloved. There was indeed no escape for her now. On that fiery night she had herself led before him the lovely, young quarry on whom he had cast one of those looks that signify both a choice and a promise. To whom was he speaking now if not to her? From whom was he asking happiness?

'Don't be sad, don't be sad!'

Now she was listening to his words confusedly, more faintly from moment to moment, as though her soul were falling into the depths while the voice went on above her, but she could feel his impatient hands caressing her, tempting her. And in the bloody darkness like the one where madness and delirium are engendered, from her marrow, from her veins, from all her troubled flesh there rose a sudden wild rebellion. 'You want me to take you to her, don't you? You want me to call her, don't you?' she screamed, beside herself, staring straight into his startled face with wide-open eyes, seizing him by the wrists and shaking him with a convulsed strength that showed her nails. 'Go then! She is expecting you. Go on, run! She's waiting!' She stood up, pulled him to his feet, tried to push him towards the door. She was unrecognizable, transformed by violence into a dangerous, threatening thing. The strength in her hands was incredible, the energy that had developed in all her limbs was destructive.

'Who is expecting me? What are you talking about?

What's wrong with you? Come to your senses! Foscarina!'
He was stammering as he called out to her, trembling with
fear because he thought he could discern the shape of madness in her contorted face. She could not hear him, she was
out of her mind.

'Foscarina!' He called her with his very soul, white with
terror, as though he were trying to stop her reason from
leaving her by crying out to her. She gave a great shudder,
then let go and looked around her quite lost, as though
she were awakening and could remember nothing. She was
panting. 'Come, sit down.' He led her back to the cushions
and settled her down gently. She let him soothe her, let
him care for her with pained tenderness. It was as though
she had reawakened after losing consciousness and could
not remember anything. She moaned.

'Who beat me?' She felt her sore arms, touched her cheeks
close to the jaw where it hurt her. She began to shiver with
cold.

'Lie down, lay your head here . . .' He made her lie down,
settled her head, covered her feet with a cushion, gently,
lovingly, and leaned over her as over a beloved invalid,
giving over all his heart to her, still beating hard with terror.

'Yes, yes,' she repeated with a light breath at everything
he did, as though she were trying to make the sweetness of
his caring last a little longer.

'Are you cold?'

'Yes.'

'Shall I cover you?'

'Yes.'

He searched for a cover, and found an old velvet cloth on
a table. He covered her with that. She smiled slightly. 'Is
that comfortable?' She gave the faintest sign of assent with
her eyelids that were already closing. He picked up the
violets which were warm and wilting. He laid the bunch on
the cushion on which she had lain her head. 'All right?' She
gave an even more imperceptible sign of assent with her
eyelashes. He kissed her forehead through the scent, then
he turned to poke the fire, and added more wood, making

145

it blaze up fiercely. 'Is the heat reaching you? Are you feeling warmer?' he enquired in a low voice.

He went back again and bent over the poor soul. He held his breath. She had gone to sleep. The tensions in her face relaxed, the lines of her mouth settled back into the rhythm of sleep, a calm like that of death spread over her pale countenance. 'Sleep! Sleep!' He was so filled with pity and with love that he wished he could fill her sleep with infinite powers of healing and forgetting. 'Sleep! Sleep!'

He stayed there, on the rug, watching over her. For a few seconds he measured her breathing. Those lips had said, 'There is one thing that I can do which love cannot do.' Those lips had shrieked: 'You want me to take you to her, don't you? You want me to call her, don't you?' He could not judge, could not resolve anything, he allowed his thoughts to disperse. Once more he felt the blind, indomitable forces of life whirling above his head, above that sleep, and he felt his terrible will to live.

'The bow is named BIOS and its task is death.'

In the silence, both the fire and the water spoke. The voice of the elements, the woman asleep with her pain, the nearness of fate, the vastness of the future, memory and presentiment, all those signs created a state of musical mystery in his spirit where the unwritten work was emerging and becoming clearer. He heard his own melodies developing without limit. He heard a person in the story say: 'She alone can slake our thirst, and all the thirst that is in us reaches out avidly towards her freshness. If she did not exist, none of us could live here, we should all die of thirst . . .' He saw a landscape through which ran the dry, white bed of an ancient river, where lighted bonfires flared in the extraordinarily calm, pure evening. He saw a funereal gleam of gold, a tomb filled with corpses all covered in gold, the crowned corpse of Cassandra amid the sepulchral urns. A voice was saying: 'How sweet are these ashes! They flow between my fingers like the sands of the sea . . .' A voice was saying: 'She speaks of a shadow that passes over all things and of a damp sponge that wipes out every trace . . .'

Then it was night-time, the stars were shining, there was a smell of myrtle, a virgin was opening a book, reading a lamentation. And a voice was saying: 'Oh, the statue of Niobe! Before she died, Antigone saw a stone statue from which flowed an everlasting stream of tears . . .' The errors of time had vanished, the distance of centuries was abolished. The ancient tragic soul was there in the new soul. With words and with music, the Poet was reshaping the ideal unity of life.

One November afternoon he was coming back from the Lido on the boat, accompanied by Daniele Glauro. They had left the stormy Adriatic behind them, with the roar of green and white waves on the deserted sands, the trees of San Niccolò stripped bare by a rapacious wind, the vortexes of dead leaves, the noble ghosts of departures and arrivals, the memory of bowmen competing for the scarlet prize and of Lord Byron galloping by, devoured by the urge to fulfil his own destiny to the utmost.

'I would have given my kingdom for a horse today too,' said Stelio Effrena, mocking himself, irritated by the mediocrity of life. 'Not a single bowman or a horse out there at San Niccolò, let alone the courage of an oarsman! *Perge audacter*! . . .* And here we are on this ghastly grey wreck that's steaming and boiling like a kettle. Look over there at Venice dancing!'

The sea's anger was spreading to the lagoon as well. The waters were agitated by a spirited trembling and it seemed as though that uneasy movement were being communicated to the foundations of the city and that the palaces, the domes and the bell-towers were heaving like floating vessels. Seaweed torn up from the depths was floating with its whitish roots. Flocks of seagulls wheeled in the wind, and their strange laughter could sometimes be heard above the countless crests of the storm.

* Go forward boldly!

'Richard Wagner!' said Daniele Glauro in a low voice, with sudden emotion, pointing out an old man leaning against the rail at the prow of the boat. 'Over there, with Franz Liszt and Madame Cosima. Do you see him?'

Stelio Effrena's heart began to beat a little faster too, and for him too all the people around him suddenly disappeared, the bitterness of boredom was broken, the oppression of inertia ceased. All that remained was the feeling of super-human power which that name aroused, and the sole reality above all those indistinguishable insects was the ideal world which that name evoked around the little old man leaning over the tumult of the waters.

Victorious genius, fidelity in love, unshakeable friend-ship, the supreme manifestations of the nobility of nature were all there together once again, in the teeth of the storm, in silence. The same dazzling whiteness crowned the three people nearby: their hair was extraordinarily white above their sad thoughts. An uneasy melancholy was revealed in their faces, in their postures, as though the same dark foreboding were weighing down their communicating hearts. The woman had a good strong mouth in her snow-white face, composed of clear, firm lines that revealed her strong soul within, and her pale steely eyes were continu-ously fixed on the one who had chosen her as his companion in the noble fight, constantly worshipping and watching over the one who had conquered all other deadly things, but who could not conquer death, by whom he was perpetually threatened. That fearful caring feminine gaze stood in con-trast to the invisible gaze of the other Woman, and created a vaguely funereal shadow around the man she was pro-tecting.

'He seems to be in pain,' said Daniele Glauro, 'don't you think? It looks as though he is about to faint. Should we approach him?'

Stelio Effrena was watching with inexpressible feelings the way in which the rough wind stirred the white hair on the old man's neck, under the great felt brim, and his almost livid ear with the swollen lobe. That body which had been sustained in the struggle by such a proud instinct of domination now looked like a rag that could be blown away and destroyed by the gale.

'Oh Daniele, what could we do for him?' he said to his friend, seized by some holy need to show his respect and pity for that great oppressed heart with some outward sign.

'What could we do?' his friend repeated, for he had instantly felt an intense desire to offer something of himself to the hero who was suffering the fate of all human beings. They were at one together in that act of thankfulness and enthusiasm, in that unexpected elevation of their profound nobility. But they could offer nothing except that. Nothing could stop the hidden workings of his malady. They both suffered as they looked at his white hair, that weak, half-dead thing stirring at the nape of his neck in the strong wind that was blowing from the open sea, bringing the thundering and foam of that sea to the frightened lagoon.

'Oh proud sea, you must carry me once more! I shall never find the salvation that I seek upon this earth! I shall be faithful to you, oh waves of the mighty sea . . .' The impetuous harmonies of *The Flying Dutchman* came back into Stelio Effrena's mind, along with the desperate refrain that keeps running through them, and he thought he could hear in the wind the wild singing of the crew on the ship with its sails the colour of blood: 'Iohohe! Iohohe! return to earth, oh black captain! Seven years have passed . . .' And in his imagination he saw the figure of Richard Wagner as a young man, living alone and deserted in the living horror of Paris, wretched but unbowed, wracked by a marvellous fever, fixed on his own star and determined to force the world to recognize it. In the myth of the pale seaman, the exile had found an image of his own breathless race, his own passionate struggle, his own supreme hopes. 'But one day the pale man will be free, if only he can meet on earth a woman who will be faithful unto death!'

That woman was there, alongside him, an ever-vigilant guardian. Like Senta, she too knew the supreme law of

149

faithfulness, and that death was about to dissolve their sacred vow.

'Do you think that when he was immersed in the poetry of myth he dreamed of an extraordinary way to die and that every day he prays that Nature will make his end fitting for his dream?' asked Daniele Glauro, thinking of the mysterious will that led the eagle to mistake Aeschylus' forehead for a cliff and caused Petrarch to die alone over the pages of a book. 'What would be a fitting end for him?'

'A new melody, something amazingly powerful that came to him very faintly in his earliest youth and which he could never master, that would suddenly split open his heart like a mighty sword.'

'That's it,' said Daniele Glauro.

Driven by the strong wind, battalions of clouds were fighting in the air, destroying one another; the domes and towers heaving in the background seemed to be changing shape as well, and the shadows of the city and the shadows of the sky, both vast and mobile on the wild waters, blurred together, were changed, as though both were made of substances equally prone to dissolution.

'Look at the Hungarian, Daniele. He is certainly a generous soul, he has served the hero with boundless devotion and boundless faith. That service, even more than his own art, has destined him for fame. But note how he draws an almost histrionic performance from his strong, true feeling, because he constantly needs to give his audiences the illusion of a magnificent image of himself.'

The abbé straightened his thin, bony body that seemed to be clasped in a coat of mail, and standing upright he uncovered his head to pray, to offer up his silent prayer to the God of the Storm. The wind ruffled his long, thick hair, the great leonine mane from which so many flashes and tremors had started that had moved both crowds and women. His magnetic eyes were raised to the clouds, while his unspoken words were shaped by his long, thin lips, spreading an aura of mystery in that face harsh with lines and huge moles.

'What does it matter?' said Daniele Glauro. 'He has the divine power of fervour and he has the taste for all-powerful strength and the passion of domination. His work has aspired to follow Prometheus, Orpheus, Dante and Tasso. He was drawn to Richard Wagner by great natural energy. Perhaps he heard in him that which he was endeavouring to express in one of his own symphonic poems: "What is heard on the mountain-side." '

'Yes,' said Stelio Effrena.

Then they both started as they saw the bent old man suddenly turn with the gesture of a man drowning in the dark and convulsively clutch at his companion, who cried out. They ran. Everyone on the boat was affected by that dreadful cry and rushed to crowd round him. One look from the woman was enough to forbid anyone from daring to go near the body that looked quite lifeless. She was supporting him herself, easing him on to a seat, pressing his pulse, bending over his heart, listening. Her love and her grief made an unbreakable circle around the motionless man. Everyone stepped back, then they stayed there in silence, anxiously, looking at his livid face for signs of a return to consciousness.

His face was quite still, resting helplessly on the woman's knees. Two deep furrows ran down his cheeks to his half-open mouth, deepening near the outer edges of his imperious, hooked nose. The wind stirred the sparse, thin hair on his rounded forehead, the white necklace of beard beneath his square chin, where the strength of his jawbone could be seen through the layers of wrinkles. Sticky sweat was dripping from his temples and there was a slight tremor in one dangling foot. Every slightest detail of that half-dead figure was impressed on the minds of the two young men forever.

How long did his agony last? The play of shadows went on over the dark waters in turmoil, occasionally broken by great bands of sunlight that pierced through the air and sank like arrows. They could hear the steady noise of the engine, the periodic derisive laughter of the seagulls and a dull howling from the Grand Canal, the great groan of the stricken city.

'We will carry him,' whispered Stelio Effrena into his friend's ear, intoxicated by the sadness of things and the gravity of what he was seeing. The unmoving face gave barely a sign of coming back to life.

'Yes, let us offer to do that,' said Daniele Glauro, turning pale. They were watching the woman with the snow-white face. They stepped forward, deathly pale and extended their arms.

How long did that terrible carrying last? The passage from the boat to the shore was very short, but those few steps felt like a long, long journey. The water was rattling against the posts of the landing-stage, the howling was bursting out of the canal as though from the inner regions of a cavern, the bells of St Mark's were ringing vespers, but the confused noise lost all immediate reality and seemed to be infinitely profound and distant, like a lamentation from the Ocean.

They carried the Hero's weight on their arms, they carried the half-dead body of the One who had spread the power of his oceanic soul across the world, the dying flesh of the Revealing One who had transformed into infinite song the essences of the Universe for the religion of men. With an ineffable shudder of fear and joy, like one who sees a river flinging itself down from a cliff, or a volcano break open, or a fire devastate a forest, or a dazzling meteor obscure the starry sky, like a man witnessing the force of nature which suddenly, irresistibly shows its power, beneath his hand that was supporting the torso, holding it under an armpit – as he relaxed a moment to recover the strength that was ebbing from him and looked at that white head next to his chest – Stelio Effrena felt beneath his hand the sacred heart starting to beat again.

'You were strong, Daniele, you who usually can't even snap a straw! That old barbarian's body weighed so much, it was as though his bones were made of bronze. He was well-built, solid, the sort who could stand upright on a shaking deck, a man built to sail over the high seas. Where on earth did that strength of yours come from, Daniele? I was afraid for you. You didn't hesitate! We've carried a hero in our arms! We should mark this day and celebrate it! He opened his eyes and looked straight into my face: his heart started beating again beneath my hand! We were worthy to carry him, Daniele, because of our faith!'

'You were not only worthy of carrying him, you are worthy of taking and preserving some of the best of the promises his works offer to those men who still hope for something.'

'If only I am not overwhelmed by doing too much and if only I can master the anxiety that chokes me, Daniele . . .'

The two friends were walking slowly side by side, intoxicated and confident as though their very friendship had become more significant, as though it had been increased by an ideal treasure. They were walking through the wind and the noise, through the wild evening, spurred on by the fury of the sea.

'The Adriatic seems to have overthrown the Murazzi tonight and wants to defy the ban of the Senate,' said Daniele Glauro, as they paused before the water that was flowing into St Mark's Square and threatening the Procuratie. 'We had best go back.'

'No, let's have ourselves rowed across. Here's a punt now. Just look at St Mark's under water!'

The boatman rowed them across to the Clock Tower. The whole piazza was flooded, resembling a cloistered lake surrounded by porticos, reflecting the sky exposed by the scudding clouds tinged with the greenish-yellow of evening. The golden Basilica was more alive, as though it were a parched forest that the waters had revived, and it gleamed with wings and haloes in the fading daylight, while the crosses on its mitres could be seen at the bottom of the dark mirror, like the pinnacles of another basilica under the water.

'EN VERUS FORTIS QUI FREGIT VINCULA MORTIS,'* Stelio Effrena read on the curve of an arch, under the mosaic of the Resurrection. 'Do you know that it was in Venice that Richard Wagner had his first conversation with death, twenty years ago, when he was composing *Tristan*? Consumed by a desperate passion, he came to Venice to die from it in silence, and he wrote that amazing second act here, which is really a hymn to eternal night. Now his destiny has brought him back to these lagoons. He seems destined to die here, just like Claudio Monteverdi. Venice seems to be filled with immense, indescribable musical desire, doesn't it? Every kind of sound is transformed into expressive voices. Just listen!'

The city of stone and water had become as sonorous as a vast organ in the buffeting wind. The sighing and roaring were changed into a kind of choral imploration which was rising and falling rhythmically.

'Can your ears discern the line of a melody in this chorus of groans? Listen!'

They had left the punt and were walking down the sidestreets, crossing little bridges, lingering by the sides of buildings, wandering haphazardly through the city, but even in the excitement of his pace, Stelio was moving almost instinctively towards a distant house which would appear to him now and then in a flash of lightning, fuelled by the measure of his expectation.

'Listen! I can make out a melodic theme which keeps disappearing and coming back, though it isn't strong enough to develop . . .' Stelio paused, listening with such intense concentration that his friend was astounded and felt as though he were watching him being transformed into the very natural phenomenon he was observing, and slowly being obliterated by a greater, more powerful will that was absorbing him and making him like itself.

'Did you hear that?'

* IN RIGHTNESS IS THE STRENGTH THAT BREAKS THE CHAINS OF DEATH.

'I am not permitted to hear what you hear,' replied the barren aesthete to the brilliant creator. 'I shall wait until you are ready to repeat to me the words that Nature has given you.'

The hearts of both men were trembling within, the one with the utmost clarity, the other quite unaware.

'I don't know,' said the former, 'I don't know now . . . I thought . . .' Now his mind was losing the message that he had received in his fleeting state of unconsciousness. His mind began to labour again, his will was reawakened, toiling with anxious aspirations. 'If I could only restore to melody its natural simplicity, its naïve perfection, its divine innocence! If I could only take it in its living state from the eternal spring, from the mystery of Nature itself, from the very soul of universal things! Have you ever considered the myth about the childhood of Cassandra? One night she was left in the Temple of Apollo, and next morning she was found lying on the marble floor in the coils of a serpent that was licking her ears. From that moment onwards she understood all the voices scattered in the air, she knew all the melodies in the world. The power of divination was simply power over music. A part of that Apollonian virtue entered into poets who co-operated in creating the tragic Chorus. One of those poets boasted that he could understand the speech of birds, another said that he could talk to the winds, and another said that he could even understand the language of the sea. I have dreamed more than once of lying on a marble floor with that serpent coiling round me . . . That myth must be made new, Daniele, so that a new form of art can appear.'

He was becoming more animated with every step he took, following the flow of his thoughts but still feeling that in an obscure part of himself he was in communication with the singing air. 'Have you ever thought what the music was like in that kind of pastoral ode that the Chorus sings in *Oedipus Rex* when Jocasta is fleeing in horror and the son of Laius is still deluded by one last hope? Do you remember it? "Oh, Citheron, let Olympus bear witness, before the time of another full moon . . ." The image of the mountains suddenly breaks into the horror of what is happening for a few moments, a peaceful landscape temporarily brings peace to human terror. Do you remember? Try to think of the verse like a frame within which a series of physical movements are delineated, some expressive dance which melody inspires by the perfection of its life. You would have the spirit of the Earth there before you in the essential design of things, you would have the consoling apparition of the Great Mother along with the tragedy of her stricken, fearful children, and finally a celebration of everything that is divine and eternal over cruel destiny, who drags men down into madness and death. Now try to guess the way in which that song might have helped me find the best and simplest means of expression for my own tragedy . . .'

'Are you going to bring back the Chorus into the theatre?'

'Certainly not! I don't want to revive an ancient form, I want to invent a new one, something that will come from my own instincts and the genius of my race, just as the Greeks did when they created that marvellously beautiful edifice that can never be imitated, which is their theatre. For a long time the three practical arts, music, poetry and dance have been separated and the first two have followed their own development towards a higher form of expressiveness while the third one fell into decay, and because of that I think that it isn't possible to bring them together in a single rhythmic structure without depriving each one of the separate, powerful characteristics they have acquired. If they were competing for a common, total effect, they would lose the particular, superb effect they each have separately, and hence would appear to be less than they are. Of all the materials suited for creating rhythm, the Word is the basis of every work of art that aspires to perfection. Don't you appreciate the fact that in Wagner's works the Word is given its full value? And don't you also think that the musical concept loses its primitive purity if it has to depend on performances that are outside the genius of Music? Certainly Richard Wagner has some sense of this weakness; he admits it when he goes up to some friend in Bayreuth and covers the man's eyes with his hand so that he will give himself utterly to the powers of the pure symphony and so will be open to a greater vision of an even greater joy.'

'Almost everything you are saying is new to me,' said Daniele Glauro, 'and I feel a sort of excitement that I feel when I learn something that has long been predicted or prophesied. So you would not superimpose the three rhythmic arts on one another, you would present them separately though linked by a single idea and raised to the highest level of their energy and meaning?'

'Oh Daniele, how can I give you some idea of the work that is alive inside me?' cried Stelio Effrena. 'The words you use to explain what I am trying to do sound so hard and mechanical . . . No . . . How can I communicate the life and the infinitely fluid mystery that are within me?'

They had reached the foot of the Rialto bridge. Stelio sprang swiftly up the steps and stopped by the balustrade at the top of the arch, waiting for his friend. Like the fringes of a whole army of banners, the wind whipped at his face, the Canal vanished below him in the shadow of the palaces and curved like a river racing towards the distant sound of rapids. There was one clear patch of sky high above amid the agglomerated clouds, as crystalline and clear as the peacefulness that spreads above a glacier.

'We can't stay here,' said Daniele Glauro, leaning against a shop door. 'The wind will blow us away.'

'Go on! I'll catch up with you! Just a minute!' shouted the poet, leaning over the edge of the bridge and covering his eyes with his hands, concentrating his whole body as he listened.

The voice of the whirlwind was tremendous in the stillness of centuries turned to stone. It towered over solitude, as it had when the marble was still slumbering in the womb of the mountains and when wild grasses were growing round birds' nests out on the muddy islands of the lagoon, long before the Doge had his seat on the Rialto, long before the patriarchs led the fugitives to their great destiny. Human

157

life had vanished; there was nothing under the heavens except a vast sepulchre in whose empty spaces that voice, and only that voice echoed again and again. With its song that had no instrument, with its lamentation that had no hope, the voice told of multitudes turned to ashes, of pomp turned to decay, of fallen greatness, of the countless days of birth and death, the nameless, shapeless things of time. All the melancholy of the world blew with the wind through his outstretched soul.

'Ah, now I have it!' the triumphant artist cried out joyfully.

The whole line of the melody had come to him, it was his now, immortalized in his spirit and in the world. Of all things living, nothing seemed more alive to him than that. His very life yielded to the boundless energy of that idea in sound, the generating force of that seed which would be infinitely developed. He imagined it swimming in the symphonic sea and undergoing a thousand changes before it reached perfection.

'Daniele, Daniele I've found it!'

He looked up and saw the first stars in the adamantine sky, intuitively sensing the great silence in which they were sparkling. Images of the sky bending over distant lands flashed through his mind: spinning visions of sands, trees, waters, dust on windswept days, the Libyan desert, the olive grove on the bay of Salona, the Nile at Memphis, the parched Argolides. Other images overtook them. He feared he might lose what he had found. He made an effort to clench his memory shut, as one clenches a fist to hold on to something. He noticed the figure of a man near a pillar, a glimmer at the top of a long pole, he heard the tiny burst of the flame being lighted in a streetlamp. With anxious haste he marked the notes of his theme in a page of his notebook in the light of the lamp; he fixed the language of the elements in five lines.

'This is a day of marvels!' said Daniele Glauro, watching him come down as swiftly and lightly as if he had stolen the quality of elasticity from the air itself. 'May you always be blessed by Nature, brother!'

'Come on, let's go!' said Stelio, taking his arm and pulling him along with childlike enthusiasm. 'I need to run.' He was pulling him through the side streets towards San Giovanni Elemosinario. He repeated to himself the names of the three churches that he would encounter on his way to that distant house which kept appearing to him now and then as though in a flash of lightning, fuelled by the measure of his expectation.

'What you said to me one day is quite true, Daniele: the voice of things is essentially different from their sound,' he said, stopping at the top of the Ruga Vecchia, near the bell-tower, because he could tell that his friend was tired of running. 'Sometimes the sound of the wind resembles the groaning of a terrified crowd, then it sounds like the howling of wild animals, or the roar of a waterfall, or the flapping of unfurled banners. It can be mocking, threatening and despairing. The voice of the wind is the synthesis of all those sounds, it is a voice which sings and tells of the terrible travails of time, the cruelty of human destiny, the war that is being fought everlastingly because of an eternal deception.'

'Have you ever considered that the essence of music might not be in sounds at all?' asked the learned mystic. 'It is in the silence that precedes sound and the silence that follows. Rhythm appears and comes to life in those periods of silence. Every sound and every chord awakens a voice in the silence that can only be heard by our minds. Rhythm is the heart of music, but its beat cannot be heard except during the pauses between sounds.'

The metaphysical rule announced by his contemplative friend confirmed for Stelio the rightness of his own intuition. 'Imagine,' he said, 'the interval between two symphonic movements where all the motifs endeavour to express the inner essence of the characters whose struggle is depicted in the drama, to reveal the intimate source of the action, like for example Beethoven's grand overture in

159

Leonora or in *Coriolanus*. The musical silence throbbing with rhythm is the living, mysterious atmosphere that is the only place where words of pure poetry can appear. So the personages seem to come up out of a symphonic sea as though out of the truth of the hidden being that is working within them. And in that rhythmic silence their spoken language will acquire an amazing resonance and will touch the outer limits of verbal power, because it will be inspired by a continual aspiration to song, that can only be appeased in the melody of the orchestra and rises up again at the end of the tragic episode. Do you understand?'

'You mean you want to locate each episode between two symphonic movements that will prepare for it and round it off, because music is the beginning and the end of human speech.'

'That way I can move the figures in the drama closer to the audience. Do you recall the image that Schiller used in the ode he composed in honour of Goethe's translation of *Mahomet* to signify that only an ideal world can come to life on a stage? The Chariot of Thespis, like Acheron's ferry, is so light that it can only carry the weight of shadows or of images of human beings. On an ordinary stage those images are so distant that any contact with them seems as impossible as contact with mental images. They are strange and distant from us. But by making them appear in the rhythmical silence, having them accompanied by music to the very threshold of the visible world means that I can bring them marvellously close, because I am revealing the most secret depths of the will that produces them. Do you see? Their intimate essence is there, exposed and placed in direct communion with the soul of the public that can sense the profound nature of the musical motifs lying beneath and corresponding to the ideas signified by voices and gestures. What I am showing are the images painted on the veil along with what is happening on the other side of the veil. Do you see? Through music and dance and lyric song I am creating an ideal atmosphere around heroic myths in which the whole of Nature's life is vibrating so that in

160

every one of their actions all the power of their preordained destiny seems to converge, along with the most obscure influences of things around them, of the elemental souls living within the great tragic circle. Because just as Aeschylus' characters contain something of the natural myths whence they derived, so I want my characters to throb with tumultuous savage forces, to feel grief on contact with the earth, to be at one with the air, with water, with fire, with mountains and with clouds in their pathetic struggle against Fate that has to be overcome. I want Nature all around them to be seen as their ancient forefathers saw her, as the passionate actress in an eternal drama.'

They were crossing the deserted Campo di San Cassiano with its ashen canal, and their voices and footsteps echoed above the roar that sounded like a river, coming from the Grand Canal, as though they were in an amphitheatre surrounded by cliffs. Violet shadow seemed to be mounting from the feverish waters and spreading through the air like an exhalation from the river Lethe. Death seemed to have been in possession of that place for a long time. In an upper window a shutter beat in the wind against a wall, creaking on its hinges, a sign of desolation and decay. But all those sights were being miraculously transformed in the poet's mind. He could see once more the wild, lonely place near the tombs of Mycenae, in a valley between the lesser peak of Mount Euboea and the inaccessible flank of the citadel. Myrtles were sprouting vigorously through the harsh stones and the Cyclopic ruins. The water of the Perseian spring that bubbled up through the rocks was falling into a hollow in the shape of a shell, from which it ran down to be lost in a stony ditch. Close to the edge, beneath a bush, lay the dead body of the Victim, stiff, white, motionless. In the mortal silence the rushing water could be heard and the intermittent sighing of the wind through the bending myrtles . . .

'It was in a special place,' he said, 'that I had the first glimpse of my new work: at Mycenae, under the Lion Gate, as I was rereading the *Oresteia* . . . In the Land of Fire, the

161

country of thirst and madness, the home of Clytemnestra and the Hydra, the place made barren forever by the terrible workings of the most tragic destiny that has ever destroyed a human race . . . Have you ever thought about the explorer, the barbarian, who spent most of his existence dealing with drugs behind a counter and then decided to go and look for the tombs of the Atrides in the ruins of Mycenae and who one day (it was the sixth anniversary not long ago) saw the greatest, most astounding sight ever revealed to mortal eyes? Have you ever thought about the mighty Schliemann at the moment when he uncovered the most dazzling treasure that Death had ever hidden in the obscurities of earth for centuries, for millennia? Have you ever thought that someone else might be able to see that terrifying, superhuman spectacle, some young, fervent spirit, some poet, some creator, you, me perhaps? Think of the frenzy, the fever, the madness of it! Just think!'

He was all on fire, trembling, feeling himself suddenly carried away by the storm of his imagination. His visionary eyes reflected the gleam of that funereal treasure. Creative energy flowed through his spirit like blood through his heart. He was an actor in his own drama, his tone and his movements signified transcendental passion and beauty, going beyond the power of the spoken word, the limitations of the letter. His brother hung on his lips, trembling before the sudden splendour that was bringing his divining thoughts into being.

'Just imagine! Imagine the earth you are digging in is evil, it still breathes traces of those ghastly deeds! The curse that weighed upon the House of Atreus was so appalling that there must still be some vestige of it that is to be feared in the dust that was trodden by them. You are stricken by black magic. The dead you are searching for and cannot find come to life again within you violently, and breathe through you with the tremendous breath infused into them by Aeschylus; they are huge and bloodstained as they appeared in the *Oresteia*, forever being stabbed by the sword and branded by the torch that is their Destiny. And so that ideal life

162

which you have nourished yourself takes on the shape and outline of reality! In that land of thirst, at the foot of the bare mountain, locked in the grip of the dead city, you go on digging in the earth, digging in the earth with those terrifying spectres always before your eyes in the fiery dust. Each time your spade strikes, your very bones shake, you are desperate actually to see the face of a member of the House of Atreus still intact, with the marks of the violence and cruel death it suffered still upon it ... And then you really do see it! Gold, gold, bodies, vast quantities of gold, bodies covered in gold ...'

The Princes of the House of Atreus were there in the dark street lying on the cobblestones, summoned in a vision. A shudder flashed through both the summoner and his listener at the same instant.

'A whole series of tombs; fifteen bodies all intact, one after another, on golden beds, their faces covered with gold masks, their brows crowned with gold, their breasts hung with gold, and everywhere, on their bodies, beside them, at their feet, everywhere a profusion of gold things, as uncountable as fallen leaves in a fairy-tale forest ... Do you see it? Do you?' He was choking with anxiety, trying to make that gold palpable, to transform his hallucinatory vision into reality.

'I see it! I do!'

'Just for an instant his soul has spanned hundreds and thousands of years, he has breathed the fearful legend, he has shuddered with the horror of the ancient murders. Just for an instant his soul has lived that ancient, violent life again. There they are, all the ones who were killed: Agamemnon, Eurymedon, Cassandra and the royal escort, there, laid out before your eyes just for a second! And now ... can you see it happening? ... like a wisp of smoke, like a froth of foam, like dust that blows away in the wind, like, I don't know, something incredibly fleeting and tenuous, they all crumble away in silence, swallowed up by the same fatal silence that surrounds their radiant stillness. And there is nothing but a handful of dust and a pile of gold ...'

163

There it was on the stones of the deserted street, the Miracle of Life and Death, just as it had been on the stones of the tombs! In the grip of indescribable emotion, Daniele Glauro was shaking as he grasped his friend's hands, and the poet saw the silent flame of enthusiasm consecrating his masterpiece reflected in those faithful eyes. They stopped again by the dark wall, near a doorway. There was a strange sense of distance in them both, as though their spirits were lost in the depths of time and behind that door there lived an ancient race enslaved by a rigid destiny. Inside the house they could hear a cradle being rocked while a soft lullaby was being sung. A mother was rocking her child to sleep, with a melody that had been handed down from her ancestors, and her soothing voice rose above the menacing roar of the elements. Above them, in the narrow strip of sky, the stars were shining. Far away, the sea was bellowing against the dunes, against the protective walls; somewhere some heroic heart was suffering, waiting for death, while the cradle went on rocking close by, and that maternal voice went on praying for happiness for her wailing baby.

'Life!' said Stelio Effrena, walking on, pulling his friend with him. 'For a single instant, there it is, everything that cries, hopes, yearns or raves in the immensity of life comes together in your mind and is condensed sublimely so fast that you can put it all into a single word. But which one? Do you know? Who could ever speak it?' He was starting to feel anxious and uneasy again, wanting to embrace everything and express everything. 'Have you ever seen the whole Universe before you just for a second like a human head? I have, thousands of times. If I could only cut it off, like the man who cut off the head of the Medusa, and hold it up from the scaffold to the crowd, so that they would never ever forget it! Haven't you ever thought that a great tragedy might be like that deed which Perseus performed? I tell you I would like to take Benvenuto's bronze away from the Orcagna loggia and put it in the entrance hall of my new theatre as a warning. But who would ever give a poet the sword of Hermes or Athene's mirror?'

Daniele Glauro, the man whom Nature had granted the gift of enjoying beauty, though not of creating it, was silent, aware of the turmoil in his brother's mind. He walked silently beside that brother, bending his great, thoughtful brow that seemed pregnant with an unborn world.

'Perseus!' added the poet, after a pause filled with flashes of illumination. 'In the valley below the citadel of Mycenae there is a spring called Perseia. It is the only living thing in that place where everything else is burned dry and dead. Men are drawn to that spring like the fountain of life, in that land where the beds of dried up rivers gleam with painful whiteness late into the evening. All human thirst avidly desires to slake itself in that freshness. The murmuring of that stream will be heard all through my work: the melody of running water . . . I've found it! The Deed of Purity that will round off my new tragedy will be realized through that pure element. The virgin destined to die 'deprived of nuptials' like Antigone will fall asleep in its clear, icy waters. Do you understand? That Deed of Purity will mark the defeat of ancient Destiny. The new soul will burst open the circle of iron that binds it, with a strength of purpose generated by madness, a lucid madness that is like ecstasy, like the most profound of Nature's visions. The last ode by the orchestra will be a hymn to the salvation and freedom of mankind that has won through pain and sacrifice. Hideous Fate will be defeated there, near the tombs in which members of the House of Atreus were laid, before the actual bodies of the victims. Do you understand? The man who will free himself by that Deed of Purity, the brother who kills his sister to save her soul from the horror that is about to take hold of her, has really seen the face of Agamemnon!' He was seized again by the fascination of the gold in the tombs, and the signs of his inner vision made him look almost insane.

'One of those bodies is bigger and more majestic than any of the others, he is wearing a huge gold crown and a breastplate, a cuirass, and gold shoulder-plates, he is surrounded by swords, spears, daggers, cups, covered with

165

dozens of golden discs thrown over him like petals, he is more venerable than a demi-god. The man bends over him, over the body that is about to crumble away in the light, and lifts his heavy mask . . . And then, then he sees the face of Agamemnon! That, surely, is the face of the King of Kings! His mouth is open, his eyes are open . . . Don't you remember what Homer said? 'As I lay dying, I lifted my hand to my sword, but the woman with the eyes of a bitch stepped back and would not close my eyes or my mouth as I descended to the dwelling of Hades . . .' Do you remember that? Now, the mouth of the corpse is still open, his eyes are open . . . He has a wide forehead adorned with a round gold leaf, his nose is long and straight, his chin is rounded . . .'

The poet paused for a second, his eyes dilated and staring. He could see, he was the all-seeing one. Everything around him vanished, only his fiction remained as reality. Daniele Glauro shuddered, because he had seen those eyes.

'Yes, even the white mark on his shoulder! He has taken off the breast-plate . . . There is the mark, the hereditary sign of the race of Pelops "with the ivory shoulders". It must be the King of Kings!'

The poet's words were pouring out in bursts, like a series of lightning flashes that even dazzled him. He was astonished by the sudden apparition, by that unexpected discovery that was coming to light in the darkness of his mind and being expressed and made almost tangible. How had he discovered the mark on Agamemnon's shoulder? From what dark corner of his memory had that strange, yet precise detail emerged that was so important as the means of recognizing the body of a man who had died so long ago?

'You were there!' said Daniele Glauro wildly. 'You took off that mask and that breastplate yourself . . . If you have truly seen what you say, then you are no longer a man . . .'

'I have seen it! I have!'

Again he was transformed into an actor in his own drama, and with a violent shudder he heard the words of the questioner coming from the mouth of a living person, the very

166

words that were to be spoken in the scene. 'If you have truly seen what you say, then you are no longer a man.' At that moment the explorer of the tombs took on the aspect of a great Hero fighting against ancient Destiny that had risen from the very ashes of the House of Atreus to contaminate him and destroy him.

'It cannot be with impunity,' he said, 'that a man opens up tombs and looks on the faces of the dead, and of such dead! He lives alone with his sister, the sweetest woman who has ever lived, all alone with her, in houses full of light and silence, like a prayer, like a vow . . . Now imagine that he drinks something deadly without knowing, poison, something unholy that enters into his blood and contaminates his thoughts. So that all of a sudden, while his soul is peaceful – imagine that terrible curse, the revenge of the dead! – he is suddenly gripped by an incestuous passion, he is at the mercy of a terrifying monster, he fights against it desperately in secret, he never gives up, he keeps fighting it, day and night, every minute, every hour, it grows worse as his poor sister unknowingly takes pity on his suffering . . . How can he ever be freed from it? From the very beginning of the tragedy, from the moment when his innocent companion first speaks, she is doomed to die. And everything that is said and happens in the different episodes, everything that is expressed in music and song and dance in the interludes serves to lead her slowly and inexorably towards death. She is like Antigone. In the brief hour of tragedy she is accompanied by the light of hope and the shadow of foreboding, she is accompanied by singing and by weeping, by the great love that offers joy and the wild love that generates mourning, and she never stops except when she falls asleep in the clear, icy waters of the spring that keeps calling to her all the time with its lonely wailing. As soon as he has killed her, her brother receives the gift of his redemption through death. "Every stain has gone from my soul," he cries. "I am pure now, totally pure! All the sanctity of my first love has returned to my heart in a flood of light . . . If she were to rise up now, she would tread upon

167

my soul as upon new-fallen snow ... If she were to come back to life now, my thoughts of her would be like lilies, lilies ... Now she is perfected, now she can be worshipped like a divine being ... I shall care for her in the deepest of my tombs and place all my treasures around her ..." And so the act of killing that he has been led to commit in the lucidity of his madness is an act of purification and of freedom, which marks the defeat of the ancient curse. As it rises up out of the symphonic sea, the ode sings the praises of man's victory and throws unexpected light on the shadow of disaster, it raises the first word of the renewed drama to the heights of music.'

'The deed performed by Perseus!' cried Daniele Glauro wildly. 'At the end of the tragedy you cut off the Medusa's head and show it to the people who are always young and always new, and end the performance with their great shouts.' They could both see the marble theatre on the Janiculum in their dreams, the crowd ruled by the ideals of beauty and truth, the great starry night over Rome. They saw the impassioned crowd racing down the hillside carrying in their rough hearts that which poetry had revealed to them; they could hear the shouting spreading through the shadows of the immortal city.

'And now goodbye, Daniele,' said the poet, seized again by haste, as though someone were expecting him or calling to him. The eyes of the tragic muse were gazing fixedly at the bottom of his dream, unseeingly, turned to stone in the sacred blindness of statues.

'Where are you going?'

'To Palazzo Capello.'

'Does Foscarina know the plot of your new play?'

'Vaguely.'

'What will her part be?'

'She will be blind, she will already have passed on into another world, already be half living in another life. She will see what others cannot see. Her feet will be in darkness and her face in the light of eternal truth. The contrasts in the tragedy will reverberate in her inner shadow like thunder in

168

the deepest corners of lonely cliffs. Like Tiresias, she will understand everything, that which is permitted and that which is forbidden, heavenly and earthly things, and she will know how "harsh knowing is when knowing is useless". I want to give her marvellous speeches and silences in which infinitely lovely things can come to birth . . .'

'The power she has on stage, when she speaks and when she is silent, is more than human. She can awaken in our hearts both hidden evil and the most secret hope. Through her magic our past becomes present, and through her powers we can see ourselves in the pain suffered by other beings throughout time, as if the soul she reveals to us were our very own.'

They stopped on the Ponte Savio. Stelio was silent, feeling the rush of love and melancholy that so often flowed over him. He could hear her sad voice again: 'To have loved my fleeting glory only because one day it might serve yours!' He heard his own voice again saying: 'I love you and I believe in you. I have given myself completely. You are my beloved. Your hand is whole.' The strength and security of their relationship uplifted his pride, but in the depths of his heart there still trembled indefinable hopes and forebodings that would occasionally thicken and become as heavy as pain.

'I am sorry to leave you tonight, Stelio,' admitted his worthy brother, who was also wreathed in a veil of melancholy. 'When I am with you I can breathe more freely and I feel I am living life at a faster pace.'

Stelio was silent. The wind seemed to be dropping. Intermittent gusts were ripping leaves from the acacia trees in the Campo di San Giacomo and wrapping them around the branches. The brown church and its square bell-tower of bare bricks were silently praying to the stars.

'Have you seen the green column in San Giacomo dall' Orio?' added Daniele, intending to keep his friend for a few minutes longer, for he dreaded saying goodbye. 'Such sublime material! It is like the fossilized condensation of a great green forest. Following its countless veins, one's eye travels in dreams through a woodland mystery. When I looked at it, I saw Sila and Ercinna.'

Stelio knew it well. One day Perdita had leaned against the great precious stem for a long time, looking up at the magical golden frieze that curves out over Bassano's canvas, obscuring it. 'Dreaming, always dreaming!' he sighed, feeling a return of that same bitter impatience that had made him utter words of contempt on the boat from the Lido. 'Living on relics! But think of Dandolus, who overthrew that column and an empire with it, and who chose to remain Doge when he could have been an emperor. He lived more than you do, perhaps, wandering in the forest when you look at his marble trophy. Goodbye, Daniele.'

'Don't lower your aim.'

'I wish I could force it.'

'Thoughts are your weapon.'

'Often my ambition burns my thoughts.'

'You can create things. What more do you want?'

'In another age I might also have conquered an Archipelago.'

'What use would that be to you? Melody is worth more than a province. Wouldn't you give up a dukedom for a new image?'

'I'd like to live a full life and not just be a brain.'

'You can contain the whole world in a brain.'

'Oh, you don't understand! You're an ascetic, you've learned to control desire.'

'And so will you.'

'I don't know if I want to.'

'I'm sure you do.'

'Goodbye, Daniele. You are my conscience. You are dearer to me than anyone.'

They gripped one another's hands firmly.

'I shall call at the Palazzo Vendramin to see if there is any news,' said the poet's good-hearted brother. His words brought back the recollection of the great sick heart, the hero's weight on their arms, that terrible carrying.

'He has conquered. He can die now,' said Stelio Effrena.

He went into Foscarina's house like a ghost. His mental excitement altered the way things seemed. The hall, lit by a galley lamp, seemed immense to him. A small trunk on the floor beside a doorway made him feel that he had come across a coffin.

'Stelio!' cried the actress, leaping up and hurling herself upon him impetuously as soon as she saw him, with all her pent-up expectation in that movement of desire. 'At last!' She stopped abruptly right in front of him, without touching him. Restraining herself so sharply sent a visible quiver right through her from the back of her heels to the nape of her neck; it seemed to throb in her throat with a short gasp. She was like the wind when it suddenly drops. 'Who has taken you from me?' she thought, her heart wracked with doubt, for she had suddenly sensed something in her beloved that made her unable to touch him, and she had seen something strange and distant in his eyes.

But he had seen her leaping from the shadows looking beautiful, fired by a violence not unlike that which fuelled the tempest over the lagoons. Her cry, her gesture, her leap, her sudden stop, the way her muscles quivered under her gown, the way her face faded like a flame falling into ashes, the intensity of her gaze like a gleam of battle, the way her breathing made her lips part, as warmth opens the lips of earth, all those aspects of the real person showed a pathetic life-force that could only be compared to the ferment of natural energies, the action of cosmic forces. The poet recognized a Dionysian creature in her, living material ready to receive the rhythms of art, to be shaped according to the laws of poetry. And because he saw her as varied as the waves of the sea, the blind mask that he wanted to put over her face seemed too stiff, the tragic tale through which she was to move and suffer seemed too confined, while the range of feelings from which she was to derive her expressions seemed too limited, the soul she was meant to reveal almost subterranean. 'Oh, everything that fears, weeps, hopes, yearns, raves in the immensity of life!' His mental images were seized by a kind of panic, a sudden

171

dissolving terror. What could his single work signify faced with the immensity of life? Aeschylus had written more than a hundred tragedies, Sophocles even more. They had shaped a world with colossal fragments lifted by their titanic hands. Their work was as vast as a cosmogony. Aeschylus's figures were still warm from the ethereal fire, shiny with the light of stars, damp from generative clouds. The statue of Oedipus seemed to have been carved from the very stuff of solar myth; that of Prometheus to have been hewn with the primitive tool that the Aryan shepherd had used to make fire on the high plains of Asia. The spirit of the Earth was at work in those creators.

'Hide me, hide me and don't ask me anything, just let me be silent!' he pleaded, unable to conceal his anguish, unable to control the tumult of his distracted thoughts.

The woman's heart throbbed with fear in its ignorance. 'Why? What have you done?'

'I am in pain.'

'With what?'

'With anxiety, with that sickness of mine you know only too well.'

She took him in her arms. He sensed that she had been trembling with doubt. 'Are you still mine? My own?' she asked him, pressing her mouth hard against his shoulder.

'Yes, I am yours forever.'

The same ghastly trembling tormented the woman whenever she saw him leaving her, whenever he came back. When he left, was he going to some unknown bride? and when he came back, was he coming to say a last goodbye to her?

She clasped him in her arms, with the love of a lover, a sister, a mother, with every conceivable human loving. 'What can I do, tell me what I can do for you?' She was constantly troubled by her need to offer something, to serve him, to obey a command that impelled her towards danger and the struggle for some good thing to bring back to him. 'What can I give you.'

He smiled slightly, overcome by tiredness.

172

'What would you like? Ah, I know!'

He was smiling, he allowed himself to be healed by her voice, by her adoring hands.

'Everything, you want everything, don't you?'

He was smiling from sadness, like a sick child whose companion tells him about lively games.

'Oh, if only I could! But no one will ever be able to give you anything of value in this world, dearest love. You can only ask your poetry and your music to give you everything. I remember that poem of yours which began "I was Pan." '

He leaned his head against her faithful heart, filled with beautiful images that were becoming clearer. 'I was Pan!' The splendour of that lyric moment, the wildness of the poem flooded back into his mind.

'Did you go and look at your sea today? Did you see the storm?'

He shook his head without answering.

'Was it a great storm? You once told me that there were lots of sailors among your ancestors. Have you been thinking about your home down there in the dunes? Do you miss the sand? Would you like to go back there? You worked so hard down there, and so well. That house must be blessed. Your mother was there with you, wasn't she, when you were working? You used to hear her tiptoeing through the nearby rooms . . . Did she ever eavesdrop on you?'

He held on to her, in silence. Her voice touched him to the very depths, and seemed almost to be pouring balm on to his closed heart.

'Your sister was there too, wasn't she? You told me her name once. I have never forgotten it. Her name is Sofia. I know that she looks like you. I would love to hear her voice just once, or see her walk along a path . . . You once told me she had lovely hands, didn't you? You once told me that when she is sad, they are painful, "as though they were the very roots of her soul". That's what you said to me, the roots of her soul.' He felt almost blessed as he listened to her. How had she discovered the secret of her cure? From

173

what hidden spring did she draw the melodious flow of those memories?

'Sofia will never know the good she has brought to your poor wandering pilgrim-woman! I know so little about her, but I know that her face is like yours and so I can imagine her. (I can even see her now.) Whenever I have been far, far away in distant lands, among strange, cold people feeling quite lost, she has appeared to me on more than one occasion, she has been there keeping me company. She would suddenly appear, even though I never asked her to or expected her . . . Once I had gone on a long, tiring journey to Mürren to see a dear friend for the last time before she died . . . it was almost dawn, the mountains were that cold, delicate green of beryls, the colour you only see in glaciers, the colour of things that will always be whole and distant and oh, so enviable! Why did she come? We waited together. The sun touched the tip of the mountain peaks, then a dazzling rainbow raced along their rim and lasted just for a second or two before it vanished. And she left with that rainbow, with that miracle . . .'

He felt almost blessed as he listened to her. Surely all the beauty and all the truth that he ever wanted to express were there in a single stone or a single flower from those mountains? Could any more tragic conflict of human passions be worth the sight of that rainbow on the eternal snows?

'Was there another time?' he asked softly, because the silence continued and he was afraid that she would not go on.

She smiled, then became sad. 'Another time, at Alexandria in Egypt, one dreadful, confused day, like the aftermath of a shipwreck . . . the city seemed to be rotting, it was a city of decay . . . I remember a street full of muddy water, a skeletally thin, whitish horse splashing through it, its tail and mane stained with ochre; the turrets of an Arab cemetery; the distant gleam of the Mareotis marshes . . . Feelings of disgust and disintegration!'

'Oh my love, you will never, ever be desperate and alone

174

again!' he said, his heart swelling with brotherly concern for the nomadic woman who was recalling the sadness of her continual travelling. Now his mind, that had been reaching out to the future with such violence, seemed to fall back with a slight shiver towards the past that was being made present by the power of her voice. He felt he was in a state of gentle, imaginative recollection, the kind of feeling aroused when tales are told round the fireside in wintertime. As had happened before, standing outside Radiana's sealed windows, he felt himself caught by the fascination of time.

'Was there another time?'

She smiled, then became sad. 'Another time, in Vienna, in a museum . . . There was a great empty hall, the sound of rain drumming on the windows, countless precious reliquaries in glass cases, signs of death everywhere, things in exile, things no longer prayed to or worshipped . . . We both bent over a case containing a collection of holy arms with their metal hands fixed unmovingly . . . Martyrs' hands, studded with agates, amethysts, topazes, garnets, sickly turquoises . . . You could see scraps of bones through the holes. One of them was holding a golden lily, another had a little city, another a pillar. One was thinner than the others, with a ring on every finger, and it was holding a pot of ointment; it was Mary Magdalene's hand . . . things in exile, that had lost their holiness, things no longer prayed to or worshipped . . . Is Sofia religious? Does she say her prayers?'

He did not answer. He felt he need not speak, he need not give even the slightest sign that he existed in the spell she was weaving of her distant life.

'She used to come into your room sometimes, while you were working, and lay a blade of grass on the page you had just begun.' The enchantress trembled within, for an image that had been wreathed in veils was suddenly exposed and brought other, unspoken words to her mind. 'You know, I began to love that woman who sings, the woman I know you can't have forgotten, I began to love her thinking of

175

your sister. To pour the tenderness my heart wanted to give to your sister, from whom so many cruel things separate me, into another pure soul! Did you know that?' The words were alive, but remained unspoken. Her voice shook with their silent presence.

'Then you would allow yourself a few moments rest. You would go over to the window and look out with her at the sea. A ploughman was driving two young oxen yoked to the plough, he was ploughing the sand to teach the oxen how to make a straight furrow. You used to watch them every day with her, at the same time. When they had been taught, they stopped coming to plough the sand, they went up into the hills . . . Who told me about such things?'

He had told her himself once, in almost the same words, but now the memories returned to him like unexpected visions.

'Then the flocks would go by along the seashore. They came down from the mountains on their way to the plains of Puglia, from one pasture to another. The way those woolly sheep walked was like waves on the sea, though the sea was almost always calm when the flocks and their shepherds passed by. Everything was calm, a golden silence hung over the beach. Sheepdogs would run alongside the flock, shepherds would lean on their crooks, their bells sounding faint in all that emptiness. You used to watch them on their journey as far as the headland. Then later, you and your sister would go and look at the prints left in the damp sand that was studded with holes and golden as a honeycomb . . . Who told me all these things?'

He felt almost blessed as he listened to her. His fever had gone. A slow feeling of peace was descending on him like slumber.

'Then gales would come, the sea would come up over the sand dunes, it would invade the woods, and slaver on juniper and tamarisk bushes, on myrtle and rosemary. Great quantities of seaweed and driftwood would be thrown up on the shore. There had been a shipwreck somewhere out at sea. The sea brought wood for the poor and mourning who

176

knows where! The beach would be crowded with women and old people and children competing with one another to see who could collect the biggest bundle. And your sister would bring another kind of help: bread, wine, vegetables, clothes. Blessings of gratitude would sound louder than the waves. You would be looking out of the window, and you would think that not even one of your lovely images was worth the smell of fresh bread. You would leave your page half-finished and go out to help Sofia. You would talk to the women and children and old people . . . Who told me about all these things?'

Even since that very first night, Stelio had preferred to go to his lover's house through the Gardenigo garden gate, and walk through the trees and shrubs that had returned to the wild. Foscarina had obtained permission to join her garden to that of the abandoned palace by opening a breach in the dividing wall. But some time ago Lady Myrta had come to live in those vast, silent rooms that had welcomed the son of the Empress Josephine, the Viceroy of Italy, as their last guest. The rooms were filled with antique instruments that had no strings and the garden was peopled by beautiful greyhounds that had no prey.

There was nothing that seemed more sad and more delightful to Stelio than the walk towards the woman who was waiting for him, counting the hours that passed so slowly and yet flew by. In the afternoons the embankment of San Simeon Piccolo turned gold like a ridge of fine alabaster. The sun's rays played with the iron of the prows lined up alongside the landing stage, and quivered over the church steps, up the columns of the peristyle, animating the loose, worn stones. A few rotting gondola cabins lay on the pavement in the shade, their black cloth covers spoiled and discoloured by rain, like biers worn away by too many funerals, grown old on the road to the cemetery. The choking smell of hemp seeped out from a decayed palace, reduced to being a rope factory, through barred windows thick with ash-coloured fur like strangled cobwebs. And there at the far end of Campiello della Comare, grassy as a country churchyard, was the garden gate which opened between two pillars crowned by mutilated statues, around whose limbs dry branches of ivy created the impression of raised veins. Nothing could have been sadder or sweeter to the visitor. Smoke rose peacefully from the chimneys of the humble homes around the square towards the green dome. Now and then a flock of pigeons would sweep across the canal, starting from the Scalzi sculptures. The whistle of a train crossing the bridge over the lagoon, the worksong of a rope-maker, the booming of an organ and the chanting of priests could all be heard. A November Indian summer was deceiving the melancholy of love.

'Helion! Sirius! Altair! Donovan! Ali-Nour! Nerissa! Piùchebella!'

Lady Myrta, seated on a bench next to the wall that was embraced by roses, was calling her dogs. Foscarina stood beside her, wearing a tawny dress that seemed to be made of the same proud material described as roan-coloured that was used in Venice in ancient times. The sun surrounded both women and roses in the same golden warmth.

'You are dressed like Donovan today,' said Lady Myrta to the actress, smiling. 'You do know, don't you, that Stelio loves Donovan better than all the others?'

A blush came to Foscarina's cheeks. She turned to look at the tawny greyhound. 'He is the strongest and the most handsome,' she said.

'I think he would like him,' added the old lady with gentle indulgence.

'What would he not like?'

The old woman heard the concealed melancholy in the words of the woman in love. She was silent for a few minutes.

The dogs were close by, serious and sad, heavy with sleep and dreaming, far away from plains, steppes or deserts, crouching on the clover-filled lawn through which marrow plants with their vain, greenish-yellow fruits wound like

178

serpents. The trees were quite still, almost as though they had been cast in the same bronze that covered the three graduated domes of San Simeone. There was the same sense of wildness about the garden and the great stone dwelling, darkened by the tenacious fog of time, streaked with the rust that had dripped from iron railings in countless autumn rains. The crown of a tall pine tree rang with the same twittering that must surely be reaching Radiana too, in her walled garden.

'Does he hurt you?' the old woman would have liked to ask the woman in love, because the silence weighed upon her and she felt the heat of passion in that troubled heart as much as she felt the untimely summer. But she did not dare. She let out a sigh. Her ever-youthful heart throbbed at the sight of desperate passion and beauty under threat. 'You are still so lovely, and your lips still invite kisses, and the man who loves you can still be driven wild by your pale face and your eyes!' she thought, watching the actress who was lost in thought, and to whom the November roses were reaching out. 'But I am a shadow.'

She looked down, at her own twisted hands upon her knees, and she marvelled that they were actually hers, for they seemed so deformed, so dead, miserable things that aroused repugnance from whatever they touched, and that could now only caress drowsy dogs. She felt the lines in her face, her false teeth against her gums, the artificial hair on her head, the ruin of her whole wretched body that had once obeyed the dictates of her sensitive heart, and she marvelled at her own persistence in fighting against the ravages of time, deceiving herself, reconstructing the laughable illusion every morning with waters and oils and lotions and rouge and dyes. Though surely her youth still remained in the unending springtime of her dream? Surely it was only yesterday that she had caressed a beloved face with her perfect fingers, gone fox- and stag-hunting in the northern counties, danced in a park with her affianced husband to an air by John Dowland?

'There are no mirrors in the Countess of Glanegg's house,

and there are far too many in Lady Myrta's!' Foscarina was thinking. 'The one has hidden her decay from herself and from other people, but this woman has watched herself ageing every day, she has counted her wrinkles one by one, has pulled the dead hairs from her comb, felt her teeth loosen in her pale gums, and yet she has tried to repair that unrepairable damage with falsehoods. Poor, gentle soul who would still like to live on smiling and enchanting people! I would vanish, die, sink into the ground!'

She notices the little bunch of violets pinned with a brooch on the hem of Lady Myrta's dress. Fresh flowers were always pinned there, in every season, tucked into a fold, barely visible at all, a sign of her daily illusion of springtime, of the spell that she was forever casting around herself with her memories, with music, with poetry, with all the arts of dream against ageing, sickness and loneliness. 'I would like to live just a single supreme hour of fire and then vanish underground forever, before all my fascination evaporates, before all beauty has died.'

She felt the beauty of her own eyes, the hunger of her lips, the rough strength of her hair blown by the gale, all the power of those rhythms and impulses that lay sleeping in her muscles and in her bones. She heard her lover's words once again, when he had praised her, she saw him again in the full fury of his desire, in the sweetness of languor, in deepest oblivion.

'He will still love me for a while, just for a while I shall seem lovely to him, I will fire his blood. For just a little longer!'

With her feet in the grass and her face in sunlight, wreathed in the scent of fading roses, in that tawny dress that made her resemble the magnificent hunting animal, she burned with passion and expectation, with a sudden rush of life, as though the future that she had renounced by her desire for death were flooding back into her. 'Come! Come!' She was calling her lover inwardly, intoxicatedly, in the certainty of his coming, because she could sense it and had never yet been deceived by her instincts. 'Just for a while longer!' Every second that passed seemed like a cruel theft. Standing motionless, she felt giddy with desire and anguish. The whole wild garden penetrated to its very roots with the heat throbbed to the rhythm of her pulse. She thought she would lose consciousness and fall.

'Ah, here comes Stelio!' cried Lady Myrta, as she saw the young man coming through the laurel bushes.

His lover spun round, blushing. The greyhounds stirred and pricked up their ears. Their eyes met like a flash of lightning. Once again, as always happened in the presence of that marvellous being, her lover experienced the divine sensation of being suddenly in the midst of fiery ether, in a vibrant aura that seemed to cut him off from the ordinary atmosphere and almost ravish him. Once he had associated that miracle of love with a physical image, remembering how he had been walking through a lonely landscape one far-off evening in his childhood and had suddenly found himself surrounded by will o' the wisps and had cried out.

'Everything that lives here in this seclusion was waiting for you,' said Lady Myrta with a smile that concealed the agitation that had seized her poor, youthful heart in the prison of its old, sickly body, at the spectacle of love and desire. 'You have come here in answer to our plea.'

'Absolutely,' said the young man, holding Donovan, who had come up to him mindful of his caresses, by the collar. 'In fact I have come a very long way. Guess where from?'

'From the land of Giorgione!'

'No, from the Santa Apollonia cloisters. Do you know the cloister of Santa Apollonia?'

'Did you make it up just now?'

'Make it up? It's a stone cloister, a real one, with its own little columns and a well.'

'That may be. But all the places that you look at turn into inventions of yours, Stelio.'

'Oh, Lady Myrta, I should love to give you that gem. I should like to transport it here into your garden. Just imagine a tiny secret cloister, that opens on to a row of slender columns that march along in pairs like nuns fasting in the sunlight, terribly delicate, neither black, nor white, nor grey, but the most mysterious colour that the great painter called Time could ever give to stone, and a well right in the middle, and on the edge where the rope has worn the stone away, a bottomless pail. The nuns have long since vanished, but I believe the place is visited by the shades of nymphs . . .'

He broke off abruptly, seeing himself surrounded by greyhounds, and he began making the guttural sounds that the houndsman makes in hunting kennels. The dogs became restless, their sad eyes lit up. Two of them, who were further away, rushed forward with great bounds, leaping over bushes, and came to a stop in front of him, dry and shiny, bundles of nerves covered in silk.

'Ali-Nour! Crissa! Nerissa! Clarissa! Altair! Helion! Hardicanute! Veronese! Hierro!' He knew them all by name, and when he called them they seemed to know he was master. There was a Scottish greyhound, a native of the Highlands, with a rough, thick coat, harsher and furrier around its jowls and nose, grey as new-forged iron; there was a robust, reddish Irish hound that could kill wolves, with mobile brown eyes that showed their whites; there was one from Tartary, spotted in yellow and black, that had come from the immense steppes of Asia where it used to guard a tent at night against hyenas and leopards; there was one from Persia, blond and slender, with ears covered in long, silky hair and a bushy tail, very pale along its ribs and down its legs, more graceful than the antelopes it used to kill; there was a Spanish hound that had migrated with the Moors, the same magnificent beast held on a leash by the dwarf in Diego Velasquez' painting, trained to course and attack on the bare plains of la Mancha or in the scrubland of Murcia and Alicante, thick with brushwood; there was the Arabian sloughi, the famous desert predator, with its dark palate and tongue, with all its tendons clearly visible and all its bone structure discernible beneath its fine skin, a noble, proud animal, elegant and courageous, accustomed to sleep on gorgeous carpets and drink pure milk from spotless vessels.

Quivering, they clustered as though in a pack round the man who knew how to reawaken in their dulled blood those primitive instincts of the chase and the kill.

'Which one of you was Gog's best friend?' he asked, looking into all the beautiful, restless eyes fixed upon him. 'Was it you, Hierro? or you, Altair?' His particular tone excited the sensitive animals who were listening to him with low, intermittent growls. Every movement they made made their different coats stir like waves, and their long tails, which curved like hooks at the ends, were wagging lightly against their muscular haunches.

'All right, I'll tell you what I've kept from you until now. It's about Gog, you know, the one who could kill a rabbit with a single bite. Gog is lame.'

'Really?' cried Lady Myrta, with profound regret. 'How did that happen, Stelio? And how is Magog?'

'Magog is hale and hearty.'

They were the pair of greyhounds that Lady Myrta had given to her young friend and that he had taken with him to his home by the sea.

'However did it happen?'

'Oh, poor Gog! He had already killed thirty-seven hares. He had all the virtues of a great breed: speed, resistance, incredible turning capacity, a constant urge to kill his prey, and the classic technique of seizing it from behind, running in a straight line and almost always angling towards it at the same time. Have you ever seen greyhounds hunt, Foscarina?'

She was so intent that she started at the unexpected sound of her name.

'Never.' She was hanging on his lips, fascinated by their instinctively cruel expression as they spoke of killing.

'Never? So you don't know one of the most amazing spectacles of daring, strength and grace in all the world? Look!' He pulled Donovan towards him, knelt down and began feeling him with expert hands. 'There is no machine in nature that is more powerfully or perfectly suited to its purpose. Its muzzle is sharp enough to cleave the air and long enough for the jaws to snap the prey at first bite. Its

183

skull is wide enough between the ears to hold the greatest courage and skill. Its jowls are dry and muscular, its lips are so small they barely cover the teeth . . .'

He opened the mouth of the unresisting dog with easy assurance. Its gleaming white teeth could be seen, together with the palate marked with long black wavy lines and its thin, pink tongue. 'Look at those teeth! See how its canines are slightly curved at the point so that it can hold on better. No other breed of dog has a mouth built for biting in such a perfect way!' His hands lingered over the examination, and it seemed as though his admiration for that superb specimen had no limits. He was kneeling in the clover, and the dog was breathing right in his face, letting him feel it with unusual docility as though it understood the praise of an expert and was enjoying it. 'Its ears are small and high on its head, they stand up when it is excited but lie flat on its skull when it is resting. They don't get in the way of taking its collar on and off without unbuckling it: like this.'

He took off the collar that fitted exactly around the animal's neck, and put it on again. 'A swan's neck, long and flexible, that enables it to seize its game at maximum speed without loosing its balance. Once I saw Gog bring down a hare in mid-air as it leaped over a ditch . . . But observe the most important points: the length and breadth of its chest made for sustained effort, the oblique line of the shoulders in proportion to the length of its legs, the formidable mass of muscle in its haunches, its short fetlocks, the way its spine curves between two bundles of solid muscle . . . Look! You can see the outline of Helion's vertebrae; the ones here are hidden in a furrow. Its feet are like a cat's, with the claws tucked in, not too much, elastic, sure. And how elegant its ribs are, shaped like a ship's keel, with this line that runs back towards the belly completely hidden. It is constructed entirely for one purpose! Its tail is thick at the root and thin at the tip – look! – almost like a rat's, and it acts as a rudder for the creature, it needs it in order to turn when the hare veers off suddenly. Now, Donovan, let's see if this is perfect in you too.'

He took the tip of the tail, passed it under a thigh, pulled it down towards the bone in its haunch and managed to make it touch the projecting part exactly. 'Perfect! I once saw an Arab from the Arbaa tribe measuring his sloughi like that. Ali-Nour, did you tremble when you caught sight of herds of gazelles? Just think, Foscarina, sloughis tremble when they see their prey, they tremble like reeds, and they turn soft, pleading eyes on their masters to be let loose! I don't know why I like that so much or why I am so moved by it! The urge to kill is terribly strong in them, their whole bodies are ready to leap like arrows, and they tremble! Not with fear or uncertainty, they tremble with desire to kill! Oh Foscarina, if you saw a sloughi at such a moment, you would surely take from it the way it trembles and you would know how to make that trembling human with your tragic skills and you could give mankind a new sensation . . . Up, Ali-Nour, torrent of desert swiftness! Do you remember? Now you're only trembling with cold . . .'

Light-hearted and talkative, he let go of Donovan and took the snake-like head of the gazelle killer between his hands. He stared deep into its pupils through which passed waves of homesickness for the silent, torrid lands, for tents unfolded after a journey that meteors had deceived, for fires lit for the evening meal beneath great stars that seemed alive in the wind that throbbed through the tops of pine trees.

'Eyes full of dreams and sadness, courage and faithfulness! Lady Myrta, have you ever considered that the greyhound with its beautiful eyes is the mortal enemy of other animals with beautiful eyes like gazelles and hares?'

His lover had entered that bodily enchantment of love which makes the confines of the body seem to expand and dissolve into air, so that every word and every movement of the beloved man inspires a quiver sweeter than any caress. The young man had taken Ali-Nour's head between his hands, but she felt the touch of those hands on her own temples. The young man was gazing into Ali-Nour's eyes, but she could feel him gazing into her very soul. And she

185

thought that when he praised those eyes, he was praising her eyes.

She was there, standing on the lawn like one of the proud creatures he loved, dressed like the one he most favoured over and above its companions, filled like them with a confused memory of distant origins, a little stunned by the burning rays reflected off the rose-covered wall, stunned but burning with a faint touch of fever. She could hear him talking about living things, about limbs fitted for the chase and the kill, about strength, skill, natural powers, the vigour of blood; she could see him down on the ground, amid the scent of grass, the warmth of the sun, pliable and strong as he felt the skin and bone, measured the energy of exposed muscles, enjoyed the contact with those generous bodies, almost taking part in that cruel, delicate brutality which he had more than once delighted in depicting in his art. And she too, with her feet on the warm earth, beneath the breath of the sky, in her dress the colour of the tawny predator, could feel a strange sense of primitive brutality rising up out of the roots of her being, the illusion of a slow metamorphosis in which she was losing part of her human consciousness and becoming once again a child of nature, a brief, naïve power, a savage life.

Surely he was touching the deepest mystery of being in her? Was he not making her feel that animal profundity from which the unexpected revelations of her tragic genius had sprung, which had moved crowds and driven them wild, like the spectacle of heaven and earth, like dawn, like tempests? When he had told her about the trembling sloughi, had he not divined the natural analogies from which she derived her powers of expression that so astounded poets and populace? Because she had rediscovered the Dionysian sense of nature, the ancient fervour of instinctive, creative energies, the enthusiasm of the multi-faceted god rising from the ferment of all the juices, she could appear so new and so magnificent on the stage. Sometimes she had felt within herself the imminence of the miracle which used to swell up the breasts of Maenads with holy milk when young panthers desperate for food came near them.

She was there, standing on the grass, slender and tawny as his favourite hound, filled with a confused recollection of distant origins, alive and eager to live completely in the brief hour allotted to her. The soft mists of tears had vanished, the tedious aspirations to be good and to give things up were gone, with all the ashen melancholy of the abandoned garden. The presence of the Creator made space seem wider, altered time, made her blood flow faster, increased her capacity for happiness, created once again the spectre of a magnificent festival. She was once more as he wanted to make her, forgetful of her fears and unhappiness, cured of all her sick sadness, a vibrant creature of flesh in the light, in the heat, in the scent, in the play of appearances, ready to cross the plains and dunes and deserts he described in the wildness of the hunt, to become drunk with his ecstasy, to rejoice at the sight of courage and cunning and bleeding prey. Every instant, by speaking and moving, he was turning her into his own likeness.

'Oh, every time I saw hares torn by a hound's teeth I would feel a flash of regret sear through my exhilaration, on account of those great moist eyes that were being extinguished. Greater than yours, Ali-Nour, or even yours, Donovan, and shining like pools in summer evenings when reeds bend into the water and all the sky is reflected and changed in them. Have you ever seen a hare in the morning, bounding out of a freshly ploughed furrow and running over a patch of silvery frost, then stopping dead in the silence, crouching on its hind legs, pricking up its ears, scanning the horizon? It is as though its gaze could calm the entire universe. A hare, not moving a muscle, studying the steaming fields, pausing in its everlasting anxiety! You couldn't imagine a clearer indication of perfect peace all around you. In that instant, it is a holy animal that deserves to be worshipped . . .'

Lady Myrta broke into a youthful laugh, exposing her

elephantine teeth and shaking the tortoise-like wrinkles beneath her chin.

'Dearest Stelio!' she cried, laughing. 'First you worship it, then you tear it to pieces. Is that your way?'

Foscarina stared at her in amazement, because she had forgotten her. Sitting there on the stone seat, yellowed with lichens, with her twisted hands, with the gleam of gold and ivory between her thin lips, with her little glassy eyes under the baggy eyelids, with her hoarse voice and clear laugh, she gave the impression of being one of those ancient web-footed fairy godmothers that wander through the forest followed by an obedient toad. The words did not touch her in the strange oblivion within which she was lost, but they still sounded as harsh as a shriek. 'It isn't my fault,' replied Stelio, 'if hounds are made to kill hares and not to sleep in a walled garden near the waters of some dead canal.' Again he imitated the guttural sounds that the houndsman makes in hunting kennels.

'Crissa! Nerissa! Altair! Sirius! Piùchebella! Helion!'

The excited dogs stirred, their eyes lit up again, their dry muscles strained beneath their tawny, black, white, grey, spotted, mixed fur; their long haunches curved down to their heels like bows ready to spring and launch into space a bone structure more taut and slender than a bundle of arrows.

'There! Donovan, there!' He was pointing to something greyish or pinkish in the grass at the bottom of the garden, that looked like a hare crouching on its haunches with its ears laid flat. The commanding voice deceived the hesitant hounds. It was marvellous to watch those slim, powerful bodies of living silk trembling and vibrating in the sunlight at the sound of a human voice, like the lightest of pennants on a deck quivering in the breeze at dawn.

'There, Donovan!' The big tawny dog stared back at him, then made a tremendous leap and pounced on its imagined quarry with all the vehemence of its newly aroused instinct. It was there in a second, then stopped, disappointed. Presently, it crouched again, leaning on its front legs, neck outstretched, then pounced again and began to play with the rest of the pack that had followed it in great disorder. It started fighting with Altair, then gave up and with its nose pointing upwards, barked at a flock of sparrows that flew off into the air from the top of the pine tree with a merry rustling.

'It's a marrow! A marrow!' cried the deceiver roaring with laughter.

'Not even a rabbit! Poor old Donovan! Just a mouthful of pumpkin! Oh, poor Donovan, how humiliating! Lady Myrta, mind he doesn't drown himself in the canal for shame . . .'

His merriment was catching, and Foscarina joined in with his laughter. Her tawny dress and the coats of the hounds gleamed in the slanting sunlight against the green of the clover. The whiteness of her teeth and her bright laugh filled her mouth with renewed youth. The tedium of that ancient garden was torn away, like a spider's web when some rough hand throws open a window that has been closed for ages.

'Would you like to have Donovan?' asked Lady Myrta, with a hint of gracious malice that disappeared in her wrinkles like a trickle in a ditch. 'I know, I know what you are doing . . .' Stelio stopped laughing and blushed like a small boy.

A wave of tenderness filled Foscarina's breast at that childish blush, her whole being sparkled with love. A wild urge to take her beloved in her arms made her lips and wrists tremble.

'Would you like him?' asked Lady Myrta again, happy that she could make such a gift and pleased with the man who could receive it with such open, genuine pleasure. 'Then Donovan is yours!'

Before thanking her, he looked for the hound with the lovely eyes almost anxiously. He caught sight of it gleaming, strong, magnificent, with the stamp of quality in all its limbs, as though Pisanello had drawn it on a medallion.

'And what about Gog? What happened to Gog? You

189

haven't told us anything more,' said the giver of gifts. 'See how easy it is for invalids to be forgotten!'

Stelio was looking at Foscarina, who had turned to go over to the greyhounds and was pacing around on the grass with lithe undulating movements like the walk of the ancient Venetians, known as 'the greyhound walk'. Her tawny dress, gilded by the setting sun, seemed to be on fire around her slender body. And it was clear that she was moving towards the dog of the same colour, the dog that the actress resembled so curiously through some profound mimetic instinct, almost to the point of being transfigured.

'It was after a race,' said Stelio. 'I was in the habit of coursing a hare almost every day over the dunes, down by the sea. Peasants would bring me live ones from my own lands, strong and brown and ready to defend themselves, incredibly cunning and well able to bite and scratch. You know, Lady Myrta, there is no place better for the chase than my wild seashore. You know the great Lancashire moorland, the dry Yorkshire soil, the hard plains of Altcar, the marshes of the Scottish lowlands, the sands of southern England, but a gallop along my sand-dunes that are more yellow and more luminous than autumn clouds, over patches of juniper and tamarisk, over the bright little estuaries of tiny streams, over salt-water pools, down beside a sea that is greener than any meadow, within sight of blue, snow-tipped mountains, that would cancel out even your happiest memories, Lady Myrta.'

'Ah, Italy!' sighed the indulgent old fairy godmother. 'The flower of the world!'

'I let my hares out along that beach. I had trained a man to unleash the hounds at exactly the right moment, and I followed the chase on horseback . . . Of course Magog is a fine runner, but I had never seen a dog kill so readily and so keenly as Gog . . .'

'From the Newmarket kennels!' said the giver of gifts, with pride.

'One day I was coming back home along the seashore. It had been a short chase: Gog had caught the hare after only

190

two or three miles. I was coming home at a slow gallop, right on the edge of the calm water. Gog was running alongside Cambyses, and he kept jumping up at the game that was hanging from my saddle and barking. Suddenly, there on the shore was a carcass, and the horse flung itself to the right and its shoe hit the dog, who started to howl and held up his left front leg. It appeared to be broken at the fetlock. I managed to rein in the terrified horse and went back. But when Cambyses saw the carcass again he spun round and bolted. Then we made a mad dash through the dunes. I cannot tell you the emotion I felt when a few seconds later I heard Gog panting along behind the horse's tail. He was following me, you see. With his broken leg, driven by the goodness in his blood and forgetting his own pain, he caught up with me, he followed me, he even went on in front! I looked into his dear, soft eyes and while I tried to control the frenzied horse my heart was breaking each time I saw his poor, wounded paw touch the sand. I adored him, I simply adored him . . . Do you think me able to weep?'

'Yes,' said Lady Myrta, 'I do.'

'Well, when my sister Sofia started to clean the wound with those lovely hands of her, and the tears dripping down, I believe I . . .'

Foscarina was there, holding Donovan by the collar, and she had turned pale again, almost faded, as though the evening chill were starting to enter into her. The shadow of the bronze dome was extending over the grass, over the laurel bushes, over the hornbeams. A violet dampness, in which the last atoms of solar gold were floating, was spreading between the stems and the branches that quivered in the intermittent wind. Once again their ears caught the twittering that was filling the topmost branches of the pine tree with its empty cones.

'See, we belong to you,' the woman seemed to be saying, holding the dog that was starting to shiver as it pressed against her knees. 'We belong to you for ever. We are here to serve you.'

'There is nothing in the world that perturbs me or excites

191

me so much as such unexpected examples of the quality of blood,' the young man went on, roused by the memory of that hour of emotion.

The long whistle of a train crossing the bridge over the lagoon was heard. A gust of wind stripped off all the petals of a great white rose, leaving nothing but its centre at the end of a stick. The dogs felt cold, and came closer, bunching together, pressing against one another. Their slender bones shivered under their thin skin, and their sad eyes glittered in their long, flat, reptilian heads.

'Stelio, did I ever tell you how a lady from one of the best families in France died during a great hunting party when I was present?' Lady Myrta asked him, for that tragic, pitiful image had been reawakened in her as she caught sight of the expression on Foscarina's white face.

'No, never. Who was she?'

'Jeanne d'Elbeuf. She was hurt, perhaps because of her own foolish inexperience, or because of the man who was riding with her – nobody ever knew who was to blame – together with the hare that was caught up under her horse. She was seen to fall, and we all ran to her, and found her lying there on the grass covered in blood, next to the hare which was in agony. In the silence and dismay, as we all stood there petrified, nobody daring to speak or move, the poor woman raised her hand ever so slightly and pointed to the wounded animal (I shall never forget the sound of her voice) and said: *"Tuez-le, tuez-le, mes amis . . . Ça fait si mal."* Then next moment she died.'

The agonizing sweetness of that late November, smiling like an invalid who believes he is recovering and feels so well in himself that he does not know he is close to death!

'What is the matter with you today, Fosca? What's happening? Why are you so distant with me? Tell me! Say something!'

Stelio had gone to St Mark's by chance, and had seen her beside the door of the chapel that leads to the baptistery.

She was standing there all alone, not moving at all, with her face devoured by fever and darkness, her eyes filled with terror, staring at the terrible figures in the mosaics that burned with a yellow flame. A choir was practising on the other side of the door, the singing would stop, then start again with the same cadence.

'Please, please leave me alone! I need to be alone! I beg you!' The sound of her voice betrayed the dryness of her convulsed mouth. She made as if to turn and run away. He caught hold of her.

'Speak to me! At least tell me something to help me understand.'

Again she made as if to break free, and her gesture revealed her unspeakable suffering. She looked like a creature lacerated by torture, crippled by an executioner. She was more wretched than a body lashed to the rack or branded by red-hot irons.

'I beg you! If you feel any pity for me, there is just one thing you can do for me: let me go . . .' She was speaking quietly, and the fact that she did not cry out or that screams and sobs did not come from her throat seemed quite inhuman, for the horror that wracked her soul was so evident.

'Just one word, anything, to help me understand!'

A flash of rage passed over her ravaged face. 'No. I want to be left alone.' Her voice was as hard as her eyes. She turned, took a few steps as though she were about to faint, and moved quickly to support herself.

'Foscarina!' But he did not dare to hold her back. He watched the desperate woman walk through the patch of sunlight that flooded into the Basilica like a rushing stream through the door that an unknown hand had opened. The deep, golden cavern with its apostles, its martyrs and its sacred beasts sparkled behind her as though a thousand torches of day were in it. The singing stopped, then started again.

'I am drowning in sadness . . . such an urge to rebel against my destiny and just go away somewhere, looking for . . .

193

Who can rescue my hope? From whom will light come to me? . . . Singing, singing! I would like to sing a hymn to life . . . Can you tell me where the Lord of Fire is these days?' The words of Donatella Arvale's letter were printed on her eyes, printed on her soul, with all the particularities of her handwriting, all the different signs, as alive as the very hand that had penned them, beating like her impatient pulse. She saw the words carved in stone, traced in clouds, reflected in the water, as indelible and unavoidable as decrees of fate.

'Where can I go? Where?' Through her agitation and despair the gentleness of things reached her, the warmth of golden marble, the smell of the calm air, the languor of human idleness. She watched a woman of the people, wrapped in a brown shawl sitting on the steps of the Basilica, who was neither young nor old, neither pretty nor ugly, but who was simply enjoying the sunshine and eating a great wedge of bread, tearing off mouthfuls with her teeth, then chewing them slowly, savouring her enjoyment, her eyes half closed and her blond lashes shining against her cheeks. 'If I could only become you, take on your destiny, be content with bread and sunshine and not think or suffer any more!' The poor woman sitting there seemed like unbounded happiness to her.

She turned away with a start, fearful yet hopeful that her lover had followed her. She could not see him. She would have fled had she caught sight of him, but her heart was failing her as though he had sent her to her death without a reprieve. 'It is all over.' She was losing all sense of proportion and all certainty. Confused thoughts raced though her dragged along fragmentedly by her pain, as plants and stones are swept along by a river in flood. In all the things around her, her distracted eyes saw confirmation of her own doom or the dark threat of new harms or a reflection of her state of mind or signs of hidden truths that were about to wreak cruel havoc on her very existence. In a corner of St Mark's Square, by the Porta della Carta, she felt the four kings come alive as though dark blood flowed through them, those porphyry kings who seal their pact each with one arm round his companion in an embrace, while their free, strong hands grip a sword-hilt that tapers down into a hawk's beak. The countless veins of different marbles with which the side of the temple was encrusted, those indistinct threads of diverse colours, those intertwined paths and labyrinths, seemed almost to make her own inner differences visible, to reveal the confusion of her thoughts. She felt in turn that things were remote, distant, nonexistent and then familiar, close, part of her intimate life. Sometimes she thought she was in unfamiliar places, surrounded by shapes that appeared as though she had devised them from her own substance. Like a dying woman, she was at intervals illuminated by images from her most distant childhood, by memories of far-off events, by the swift, sharp apparition of a face or a gesture or a room or a landscape. And through all those phantoms, from some shadowy background, her mother's eyes were watching her, kindly, firmly, no larger than her human eyes had been in earthly life, but yet as infinite as the horizon that had summoned her. 'Shall I come to you? Are you really calling me for the last time?'

She had gone through the Porta della Carta, she had crossed the entrance hall. The delirium of pain led her to the place where their three paths had crossed on that glorious night. She looked for the well that had been their meeting place. Around its bronze rim, all the life of those few seconds was revived with the evidence and outline of reality. That was where she had smiled and, turning to her companion, had said: 'Donatella, here is the Lord of Fire!' The great shout from the crowd had drowned her voice and the sky over their heads had been lit with a thousand flaming doves.

She went over to the well. When she looked at it, every detail was impressed upon her mind and acquired the strange force of living fatality: the furrow made in the metal by the rope, the green rust that streaked the base stones, the breasts of the caryatids worn away by the knees of countless women who had leaned on them in the effort of drawing water, and the deep mirror within that was no longer disturbed by the impact of a bucket, that small subterranean circle that could reflect the divine sky. She leaned over the edge and saw her own face, she saw her fear and her ruin, she saw the motionless Medusa that she carried in the centre of her soul. Unknowingly, she was repeating the action of the man she loved. And she also saw his face and Donatella's, as she had seen them just for a second close together, on that night, illuminated by the heavenly flashes as though they were leaning over a furnace or a crater. 'Love one another! Love one another! I shall go away, I shall disappear! Farewell!' She closed her eyes at such thoughts of death, and in the darkness those gentle, firm eyes returned, infinite as the peaceful horizon. 'You are in peace and waiting for me, you who lived and died passionately.' She stood up. There was an extraordinary silence in the deserted courtyard. The richness of the high, carved walls lay half in shadow, half in light. The five mitres of the Basilica rose up over the cloisters as lightly as the snowy clouds that made the sky seem even more blue, just as jasmine flowers make leaves appear even greener. 'Life could still be so sweet!'

She went out on to the quay, stepped into a gondola and was rowed out to the Giudecca. The harbour, the Salute, the Riva degli Schiavoni, all that stone and all that water were a miracle of opal and gold. She scanned the Piazzetta anxiously to see if someone might appear. The image of dead Summer dressed in gold and sealed in her coffin of opalescent crystal flashed into her mind. She imagined herself at the bottom of the lagoon, laid on a bed of seaweed. But the memory of the promise made on those very waters and kept on that delirious night stabbed through her heart like a knife, making her writhe convulsively once again. 'Never again? Never?' All her senses could remember his caresses. The young man's lips, his hands, his strength, his passion flowed in her blood as though they had melted into her. The poison burned through every fibre of her being. With him at the furthest point of pleasure, she had experienced a spasm that was not quite death but yet was beyond life. 'Never again? Never again?'

She came to the Rio della Croce. Green leaves were growing over the red wall. The gondola stopped at a closed gate. She stepped out, looked for a tiny key, opened the gate and went into the garden. It was her refuge, her secret hiding place, guarded by the steadfastness of her melancholy thoughts as though by silent custodians. They all came forward to meet her, both old and new ones; they surrounded her and walked with her.

With its long arbours, its cypresses, its fruit trees, with its borders of lavender, its oleanders, its carnations, its rose-bushes, crimson and crocus yellow, miraculously soft and tired in the colours of its decline, it was as though the garden were lost on the furthest edge of the lagoon on an island that men had forgotten, like Mazzorbo, Torcello, San Francesco del Deserto. The sun embraced it and penetrated every part of it, so that the shadows were so slight they barely existed at all. The air was so still that the dry vine leaves still hung on to the vine. Not a single leaf fell, even though they were all dying.

'Never again?' She walked under the arbours, she went down to the water, stopped on a grassy knoll, felt tired and sat down on a stone. She clutched her temples between her hands, made an effort to pull herself together, to regain control of herself, to think, to deliberate. 'He is still here, he is close by, I can see him again. Perhaps I shall soon meet him on my own doorstep. He will take me in his arms, he will kiss my eyes and my lips, he will tell me again that he loves me, that he loves everything about me. He does not know, he does not understand. Nothing irreparable has happened. So what is the fact that has distressed me, has crushed me like this? I have received a letter from a woman who is a long way away, imprisoned in a lonely villa with her demented father, and who is complaining about her lot and would like to change it. That is the fact. There is nothing else. Just a letter.' She took it out and opened it, to read it again. Her fingers were shaking, she thought she could smell Donatella, as though she were there next to her on the self-same stone.

'Is she lovely? Really? What is she like?' At the very beginning the lines of her image had been blurred. She had tried to recollect them, yet they escaped her. One detail above all others fixed itself, coming sharply into evidence: her big heavy hands. 'Did he notice that, that night? He is so sensitive to beautiful hands. He always looks at them when he meets a woman. He adores Sofia's hands, doesn't he?' She let such childish considerations occupy her for a few seconds, then smiled bitterly. All of a sudden the image fleshed itself out and came to life, shining with strength and youthfulness, and overwhelmed her, dazzled her. 'She is beautiful. And she is beautiful as he would wish her to be.'

She stayed there transfixed beside the silent splendour of the water, with the letter on her lap, nailed down by the inflexible truth. Across her disheartened passivity there flashed involuntary thoughts of destruction: Donatella's face burnt in a fire, her body deformed by a fall, her voice ruined by illness. She felt revulsion against herself, and then pity for herself and for the other woman. 'Doesn't she have the right to live too? Let her live, let her love, let her have her own joy!' She imagined a marvellous love story for her, a happy romance, an adorable husband, wealth, luxury, pleasure. 'Surely there must be some man on this earth that she could love?' She might even meet the man who would steal her heart away tomorrow. Destiny might suddenly direct her towards another place, take her far away, lead her down an unknown path, separate her from us forever. Does she have to be loved by the man that I love? They may never meet again . . .' So she endeavoured to escape from her own presentiments, but an unkind spirit kept saying: 'They met once, they will seek each other out, they will meet again. She is not an obscure soul who can be lost in a crowd or down some hidden path. She carries within herself a gift as radiant as any star, that will always make her stand out from a distance: her singing. The miracle of

198

her voice will be like a beacon. She will make that power of hers known in the world, she too will move amongst men and leave a trail of glory behind her. She has beauty, and she will have glory too: two great lights that will call him to her with ease. They met once, they will meet again.'

Pain pressed down on the woman like a yoke. At her feet the blades of grass were soaking up the rays of sunlight and seemed to he holding on to them, breathing in a green light that they were tinting with their quiet transparency. She felt tears behind her eyelashes. She looked out through that veil at the lagoon which quivered with the tremble of tears. A pearly clarity gleamed over the water. The islands of La Follia, San Clemente and San Servillo were wreathed in the palest of mists. Now and then faint cries came from them, as of shipwrecked sailors lost in the calm, and were answered by the wailing of a siren or the hoarse laughter of scattered seagulls. The silence became terrifying, then turned gentler.

She found her deep goodness again. She recovered her tenderness for the lovely woman in whom she had once satisfied her illusion of loving Sofia, his kindly sister. She thought again about the hours spent in the lonely villa on the hill at Settignano, where Lorenzo Arvale used to create his statues in the fullness of strength and inspiration, oblivious to the lightning bolt that was about to strike him down. She lived again through that time, saw those places again: she was posing for the famous sculptor who was modelling her in clay, and Donatella was singing an old song, and the spirit of the song animated the model and the effigy; her thoughts and that pure voice and the mystery of art combined to make divine life appear in that great studio, open on all sides to daylight, from which Florence and its river could be seen down the spring-like valley.

What else, apart from the reflection of Sofia, had drawn her to the girl who had never known the love of her mother, who had departed this life in bringing her into being? She saw her again, beside her father, serious and steady, a comfort to his great work, a guardian of the sacred flame and of her own secret will that had to be kept sharp and cutting like a sword in its scabbard.

'She is sure of herself, she is mistress of her own strength. When she feels free, she will dominate. She is made to enslave men, to arouse their curiosity and inspire their dreams. Her bold, cautious instinct is already leading her...' And she thought of how she had behaved towards the young man that night, with her almost contemptuous silence, her brief, dry words, the way she had risen from the table and gone out of the supper room, vanishing forever yet leaving her image framed in the circle of an unforgettable melody. 'Yes, she knows the art of disquieting a dreaming soul! Of course he has not forgotten her! Of course he must be waiting for the allotted time to meet her again, and he is impatient, as she is, asking me his whereabouts.'

She took the letter and began glancing through it, but her memory moved more swiftly than her eyes. The enigmatic question was there at the foot of the page like a postscript, almost ingenuously. As she saw the handwriting again, she felt the same savage laceration that she had felt before. Again, everything in her heart was in turmoil, as though the danger were imminent, as though her passion and her hope were already irreparably lost. 'What will she do? What is she thinking? Did she perhaps expect him to seek her out immediately, and is now trying to tempt him because she is disappointed? What will she do? She was wrestling now with that uncertainty as though it were an iron door, on the other side of which there might be the light that could revive her life. 'Shall I reply to her? What if I reply in such a way that enables her to understand the truth? Would my love be sufficient prohibition against hers?' Revulsion, shame and pride surged through her soul. 'She shall never hear from me about my wound, never, not even if she were to ask.' She could feel all the horror of open rivalry between a lover who is no longer young and a girl with the strength of her intact youth. She felt the humiliation and the cruelty of that unequal struggle. 'But,' said an unfriendly spirit, 'if it were not her, surely it would be some other woman? Do you really think you can hold a man like that with your melancholy passion? You could only love him and offer him your faithful love until death on one condition: and that was the prohibition which you have broken.'

'That's true!' she murmured, as though answering a precise voice, a clear sentence pronounced by invisible Destiny in the silence.

'There is only one condition on which he can now accept your love and recognize it, the condition that you allow him to be free, that you renounce possession, that you always give everything and never ask anything in return: the condition of your sacrifice. Do you understand that?'

'That's true! That's true!' she repeated, looking up, for all her moral beauty was again flashing from the summit of her soul.

But the poison gnawed at her. Once again all her senses remembered his caresses. The young man's lips, his hands, his strength, his passion flowed in her blood as though they had melted into her. She sat there, rigid with pain, silent with fever, consumed in her flesh and her spirit, like those red, spotted vine leaves that seem to burn round the edges as papers do when thrown on to a fire.

Then distant singing quavered through the unmoving air, vibrating through the immense stupor: the sound of women's voices that seemed to be coming from broken bosoms, from throats snapped like fragile canes, similar to the sounds that the broken strings of ancient spinets might make if a hand were to touch their worn keys, a faint, yet shrill sound, with a cheerful, vulgar rhythm that was as sad as the saddest things of life in all that light and stillness.

'Who is singing?' With obscure emotion, she rose to her feet, crossed over to the water's edge and leaned out to listen.

'It's the mad women in San Clemente.'

From the island of La Follia, from that desolate, clear asylum, from the barred windows of the huge prison there rose a cheerful, yet lugubrious chorus. It quivered, hesitated in the ecstatic immensity, became almost childlike, grew

201

fainter, seemed about to die away. Then it rose up again, gaining strength, turned into an almost piercing shriek, then it stopped abruptly, as though all the vocal chords had snapped simultaneously, rose up once more like a cry of agony, like the cry of doomed shipwrecked sailors who see a ship on the far horizon, like the screams of the dying; then it dwindled, stopped and did not start again.

The agonizing sweetness of that late November, smiling like an invalid who experiences a lull in his suffering and knows that it is for the last time and savours life which, with exquisite grace, shows him its most delicate flavours even as it is about to leave him, and his daily nap is like a little child's, who falls asleep full of warm milk in the very lap of death!

'Just look at the Euganean Hills, Foscarina. When the wind rises, they will float through the air like veils, over our heads. I have never seen them so transparent . . . Some day, I would like to go to Arqua with you. The villages down there are rose-pink like the shells that you can find in myriads all over the ground. When we get there, the first drops of a sudden shower of rain will steal a few petals from the peach trees in flower. We shall take shelter beneath a Palladian arch. Then we shall look for Petrarch's spring, without asking anyone the way. We shall take the little Misserini edition of his *Rime* with us, that tiny book which you keep by your bedside and which can no longer close because it is so full of dried flowers, like a doll's herbarium. Should you like us to go to Arqua, one day in spring?'

She did not answer, but she watched the lips that were speaking such delightful things, and hopelessly, fleetingly, she enjoyed the sound and the movement and nothing else. She derived the same enchantment from those images of springtime as from one of Petrarch's stanzas. But in the latter she could put some sign that would help her find it again, while the images were lost with the hours. 'I shall never drink from that spring,' she wanted to say, but she remained silent so that she might continue being caressed without a pause. 'Oh yes, give me illusions, deceive me, play your game, do with me what you will.'

'Here is San Giorgio in Alga. We shall soon be at Fusina.'

The little walled island went by, with its marble madonna forever reflected in the water like a nymph.

'Why are you so gentle, beloved? I have never felt you like this before. You are quite bottomless today. I don't know how to tell you what infinitely melodious feelings I find today, being with you. You are here next to me, I can hold your hand, and yet you are diffused into the horizon, you are the horizon and the water, with its islands and the hills I want to climb. When I was speaking, I thought that every syllable was creating circles within you that were widening out into infinity, like the ones over there around that leaf which has fallen from that golden tree. Is that true? Tell me it is! Look at me!'

He felt that the woman's love flowed round him like light and air. He breathed in her soul, as though it were elemental, and received such ineffable fullness of life in return that it was as though a melodious river of mysterious things were rising out of her and out of the depths of the day and pouring into his overflowing heart. The need to return the happiness he was being given raised him to an almost holy level of gratitude, and prompted words of thanks and praise in him that he would have spoken if he had been kneeling before her in the shadows. But the splendour of the sky and the water had become so immense around them that he, like her, was silent. It was a miraculous moment of communion in the light for both of them, a brief, yet tremendous journey on which they traversed the giddy distances that lay within them.

The boat touched the shore at Fusina. Startled, they gazed at each other with dazzled eyes, and both experienced a sense of loss rather like disillusion when they stepped on to dry land, when they saw that dreary shore with its pale, sparse grass. The first steps they took were onerous to them, because they could feel the weight of their flesh that had seemed to become lighter during their watery journey.

'Does he really love me?' Pain together with hope stirred once more within the woman's heart. She did not doubt the sincerity of her lover's ecstasy, nor that his words derived from an inner fire. She knew how completely he abandoned himself to every wave of feeling and how he was incapable of dissimulation or falsehood. More than once, she had heard him speak cruel truths with that same flexible, feline grace that some men skilled in the arts of seduction reveal when they are lying. She knew his clear, direct gaze well, and how it could become icy and cutting though never anything but straight. But she also knew the marvellous speed and diversity of feeling and thinking that made his mind so impossible to grasp. There was always something voluble, fluctuating and powerful in him that suggested the double, yet diverse images of fire and water. And she wanted to hold him, keep him, possess him! There was always a boundless desire to live in him, so that every moment seemed almost to be the last, as if he were about to take leave of the joy and pain of existence, of the caresses and tears of a lovers' farewell. And she wanted to offer such an insatiable appetite nothing to feed on but herself!

What then was she for him if not an aspect of that 'Life of the thousand, thousand faces' towards which his desire, expressed in an image from one of his poems, constantly brandished 'its bundle of wands'? She was for him a source of inspiration for visions and images, like hills and woods and rain. He drank mystery and beauty from her as he did from everything else in the universe. And already he had moved on, he was in search of something new, his open, seeing eyes were looking round at the miracle to wonder at and to adore.

She looked at him, though he did not turn his face towards her, so intent was he on gazing at the damp, misty fields through which their vehicle was slowly moving, She was there, deprived of all strength, no longer able to live in or for herself, to breath with her own breath, to pursue any thought apart from that of her love, even hesitating to enjoy any natural things that he did not point out to her, anxiously waiting for him to tell her about his feelings and his dreams before she could reach out her aching heart to that landscape.

Her life seemed alternately to be dissolving and condensing itself. One instant of intensity had happened, and she was waiting for the next. In between, she had nothing but the feeling that time was flying, the lamp was burning low, her body was ageing, an infinite number of things were decaying and passing away.

'My darling, my darling,' said Stelio suddenly, turning round and taking her hand, overwhelmed by emotion that had been gradually increasing until it threatened to choke him. 'Why have we come to this place? It is so gentle and yet so terrifying.'

He was gazing at her with the look that would sometimes flash into his eyes like a tear, the look that touched the very secret of another existence down to the farthest depths of the unconscious, a look as all-knowing as an old man's, as wise as a child's. She trembled at it as though her soul were a tear upon his eyelashes.

'Are you in pain?' he asked, with such anguished pity that the woman turned pale. 'Do you sense the terror?'

She looked around her with the anxiety of a fugitive, and she thought she saw a thousand dismal phantoms rising out of the fields.

'Those statues!' said Stelio, in a tone of voice that turned them in her eyes into witnesses of her own decay.

The countryside stretched out silently around them, as though its inhabitants had deserted it centuries ago or were all sleeping in graves dug only yesterday.

'Shall we go back? The boat is still there.'

She did not seem to hear him.

'Foscarina, answer me!'

'Let's go on,' she replied. 'Wherever we go, destiny does not alter.'

Her body was following the slow, rolling movements of

the wheels, and she was afraid of interrupting it. She shrank from even the slightest effort, the smallest exertion, overcome by the weight of inertia. Her face was like the delicate veil of ashes that forms around lighted coals and conceals their consumption.

'Dearest, dearest soul,' said her lover, bending towards her and brushing her deathly cheek with his lips, 'Hold on to me, trust me and abandon yourself to me. I shall never fail you, and you will never fail me. Together we shall find the secret truth on which our love will rest unchangingly forever. Do not shut me out from you, do not suffer alone, do not hide your suffering from me! Tell me when your heart swells with pain. Let me at least hope that I can comfort you. Let nothing be kept silent between us and nothing be hidden! I dare remind you of a pact that you yourself have made. Tell me and I shall always answer you without telling a lie. Let me help you, because so much that is good comes to me from you. Tell me you aren't afraid to suffer . . . I believe your soul is able to suffer all the pain in the world. Don't let me lose faith in this strength of passion in you that has made you seem divine to me on more than one occasion. Tell me you are not afraid to suffer . . . I don't know, perhaps I am mistaken . . . But I have felt a shadow in you, like some desperate urge to go away, to hold back, to find a way of ending . . . Why? Why? Before, when I was looking at the terrible desolation smiling on us here, a great fear suddenly gripped my heart because I thought that even your love could change like everything else, it could pass away into dissolution. "You will lose me." Oh, those were your words, Foscarina, words spoken by your lips.'

She did not reply. And for the first time since she had loved him, his words seemed empty, useless noises that stirred in the air and were quite powerless. For the first time, he himself seemed like a weak, anxious being controlled by unbreakable laws. She felt pity for him and for herself. So he was imposing upon her too the condition of being heroic, a condition of pain and violence. While he was trying to comfort and uplift her, he was imposing hard tests, preparing her for torture. What purpose did courage serve? What use was effort? What worth did wretched human distress have? Why had they ever thought about the future, about the uncertainty of tomorrow? The Past alone reigned over them, and they were nothing, everything was nothing. 'We are dying, you and I are both dying. Let us dream and then die.'

'Hush,' she said in a light whisper, as though she were walking through a graveyard. The slightest hint of a smile appeared around her mouth, like the smile that was spreading through the fields, and stayed there, motionless, as though painted on the lips of a portrait.

The wheels rolled on over the white road, beside the banks of the Brenta. The river, magnificent and glorified in the sonnets of gallant *abbés* in the days when barges filled with music and pleasure sailed down its length, now had the humble aspect of a canal on which flocks of blue-green ducks sported. Across the low, well-watered plain the fields were steaming, trees were losing their foliage, leaves were rotting in the dampness of the turf. The slow golden steam floated over a mound of decomposing compost that seemed to touch stones, walls and houses and untwine them like leaves. From the Foscara to the Barbariga, patrician villas – where a life of pale veins, delicately poisoned by cosmetics and perfumes, had faded into languid games around a beauty spot, around a little dog, around a dessert – were falling into decay in the silence and desolation. Some had the appearance of a human ruin, with their empty apertures like blind eye-sockets or toothless mouths. At first sight some of them seemed about to disintegrate and crumble into dust like the hair of dead women when tombs are unearthed, or like ancient garments gnawed by moths when wardrobes that have long been closed are opened. The surrounding walls had fallen down, the pillars were broken, the gates were twisted, the gardens were overgrown with weeds. But here and there, close by and a long way away, everywhere, in orchards, vineyards, between rows of silvery cabbages, amid the vegetables, in the middle of meadows, on mounds of manure and refuse from the wine-press, under haystacks, on the threshold of hovels, everywhere throughout the countryside by the river there rose those surviving statues. There were countless numbers of them; they were like dispersed people, still white or grey or yellowed with lichen or green with moss or spotted, in every posture, expressing every gesture; of Gods, Heroes, Nymphs, Seasons, Hours, with their bows, their arrows, their garlands, with horns of plenty, with torches, with all the emblems of power, wealth and voluptuousness, exiled from the fountains, the grottoes, the labyrinths, the arbours, the porticoes, friends of the evergreen box tree and the myrtle, protectresses of fleeting loves, witnesses to eternal pledges, figures from a dream more ancient than the hands that shaped them and the eyes that had looked on them in those decaying gardens. In the gentle sunlight of that Indian summer their shadows stretching out across the countryside were like the shadows of the irrevocable past, of all that no longer loves, no longer laughs, no longer weeps, will never live again, will never ever return. And the silent word on their stony lips was the same that the unchanging smile of the worn-out woman was saying: NOTHING.

They encountered other fears that day, other shadows. The tragic sense of life filled them both, and they tried in vain to overcome that bodily sadness within which their minds were becoming increasingly clear and uneasy. They held hands as though they were walking in the dark, but from time to time they would look into each other's eyes and the look of one would pour a confused wave of overwhelming love and horror into the other. But their hearts remained heavy.

'Shall we go on?'

'Yes.'

They were gripping one another's hands, as though they were undergoing some strange test, determined to experiment and test the depths to which the forces of their combined melancholy would descend. At Dolo, the chestnut leaves lying in the road creaked under the wheels, and the great trees that were changing colour flamed over their heads like crimson draperies on fire. Further on, the Villa Barbariga was lonely and desolate, with traces of ancient paints on the cracks in the façade, like the remains of rouge in the wrinkles of a worldly-wise old woman. Everywhere they looked the open spaces of the countryside were becoming fainter and more blue, like things that are slowly sinking under water.

'There is Strà.'

They stepped out in front of the Pisani villa. They went in and, accompanied by the custodian, passed through the deserted apartments. They could hear the sound of their footsteps on the resounding marble, the sound of an echo under painted ceilings, the groan of doors as they were opened and shut, the droning voice that was awakening memories. The rooms were enormous, hung with faded materials, furnished in the style of the first Empire, with Napoleonic emblems. In one of them, the walls were covered with paintings of the Pisani as procurators of St Mark's; in another there were marble medallions of all the Doges, in another a series of water-colours of flowers mounted in delicate frames, pale as those dried flowers that are preserved under glass in memory of a love-affair or a death.

Foscarina went into yet another room and said: 'In time! Even here!'

There on a bracket was a marble version of Francesco Torbido's figure, made even more horrible in relief by the subtle cunning of the sculptor, who had chiselled every wrinkle, every vein, every furrow, one by one. At the doors leading out of the room appeared phantoms of crowned women who had concealed their misfortune and their decay in that spacious dwelling that was like a palace and yet like a monastery.

'Maria Luisa di Parma, in 1817,' the monotonous voice continued.

Stelio said: 'Oh yes, the Queen of Spain, wife of Charles IV, mistress of Manuel Godoi! She appeals to me more than all the others. She came to this place during her exile. Do you know if she stayed here with the king and her favourite?'

The custodian knew only the name and the date.

'Why does she appeal to you?' asked Foscarina. 'I don't know anything about her.'

'The way she died and the last years of her life in exile after so much passion and struggle are quite astonishingly poetic.' And he told her about that violent, strong-willed woman, and the weak, credulous king, about the handsome adventurer who shared the queen's bed and who was dragged through the streets by the furious mob; he told her of the tumult of those three lives that fate had bound together and then driven like twigs in a whirlwind before the will of Napoleon, of the riot at Aranjuez, of the abdication and their exile.

'So Godoi, the Prince of Peace as the king called him, faithfully followed his sovereigns into exile. He was true to his royal mistress and she was true to him. They always lived together under the same roof, and Charles never suspected Maria Luisa of unfaithfulness, lavishing kindness on both lovers until he died. Imagine their stay in this place, imagine such a love here that had escaped intact from such a frightful hurricane. Everything was wrecked, broken, reduced to dust by the might of the destroyer. Bonaparte had passed by and yet their love, which was already white-haired, had not been crushed to death beneath the ruins. I feel as moved by the devotion of those two violent people as by the credulity of the gentle king! That is how they grew old. Just think! First the queen died, then the king and then the favourite, who was younger than they were, he lived on for a few more years and travelled . . .'

'This is the Emperor's room!' said the custodian solemnly, throwing open a door.

The great shade seemed to be everywhere in Doge Alvise's villa. The imperial eagles, sign of his power, dominated from on high all those pale relics. In the yellow room it occupied the great bed, it stretched out beneath the canopy, between the four columns tipped with gold flames. The formidable sign between the crown of laurels gleamed on the head of the bed. And that kind of funeral couch was reflected endlessly in the dim mirror between two Victories holding candelabra.

'Did the Emperor sleep in this bed?' the young man asked the custodian, who was showing him the figure of the warlord, wearing an ermine cloak, a crown of laurels and holding a sceptre laughingly, as he had appeared in the consecration blessed by Pius VII. 'Is that certain?'

He was surprised that he did not feel the agitation, that energetic throb he knew so well that is aroused in ambitious hearts by traces of a hero. Perhaps his spirit was numbed by the smell of closed rooms, the musty odour of old materials and mattresses, the deafness of the silence in which the great name did not even echo, while the gnawing of a woodworm could be heard so distinctly he thought it was actually in his ear.

He lifted the edge of the yellow counterpane, then let it drop as quickly as though the pillow underneath had been full of worms.

'Let's go! Let's go out!' begged Foscarina, who had been looking at the park through the window, where tawny bands of slanting sunlight alternated with blue-green patches of shadow. 'One cannot breathe in here.'

In fact, the air was as close as in a crypt.

'Now we are in the room belonging to Maximilian of Austria,' the boring voice went on, 'who placed his bed in the dressing room of Amalia Beauharnais.'

They crossed the room in a glare of vermilion. The sun was beating on a crimson sofa, arousing rainbow tints in a gracious chandelier with crystal drops hanging from the ceiling, lighting up the perpendicular red stripes on the walls. Stelio paused on the threshold and turned back to the resplendent blood-red, recalling the pitiful figure of the young archduke with his blue eyes, the handsome flower of

211

the Habsburgs fallen on barbarian soil one summer morning.

'Let's go!' begged Foscarina again, as she saw him lingering.

She fled through the great hall painted by Tiepolo, while behind her the Corinthian bronze gate, as it swung shut, resounded with a sharp ringing noise that spread itself in long vibrations through the emptiness. She fled in terror, almost as though everything were about to collapse around her and the light were about to go out and she was afraid of finding herself alone in the shadows with those phantoms of misfortune and death. As he walked through the air set in motion by her flight, past those walls weighed down with ghosts and relics, behind the famous actress who had represented the fury of all mortal passions, all the desperate struggles of will and of desire, the violent conflict of proud destinies on all the stages of the world, Stelio Effrena felt the heat in his veins draining away as though he were walking in an icy blast, he felt his heart start to freeze, his strength to fail, his reason for living lose all its will, his links with people and things start to loosen, and the magnificent illusions that he had given to his own soul so as to inspire it to go beyond its own limits and beyond its own destiny start to waver and fade away.

'Are we still alive?' he said, when they were out in the open, in the part away from the grim odour. He took the woman's hands and shook her slightly, then gazed deep into her eyes and tried to smile. Finally he pulled her over to the sunlight, on the grassy meadow. 'How warm it is! Can you feel it! How lovely the grass is!' He closed his eyes so that the rays would fall on his eyelids, instantly seized again with the pleasure of living. She followed his example, seduced by her beloved's pleasure, and from between her lashes she watched his fresh, sensual mouth. They stayed like that for an instant in the sun's embrace, with their feet on the grass, holding hands, feeling their veins throb in the silence like streams that flow faster when the ice melts in springtime. She thought again about the Euganean Hills,

212

the pink villages like fossilized shells, the first drops of rain on new leaves, Petrarch's spring, all those lovely things.

'Life could still be so sweet!' she sighed, in a voice that revealed the miracle of hope about to be reborn.

Her lover's heart was like a fruit which suddenly ripens and melts in a miraculous ray of sunlight. Happiness and pleasure spread through his spirit and his flesh. Once more he enjoyed the moment like one who is about to depart. Love was raised to a higher place than destiny.

'Do you love me? Tell me!'

The woman did not reply, but she opened her eyes wide and the vastness of the universe was contained in the circles of her pupils. The immensity of love was never more powerfully signified by any earthly creature.

'Life is so sweet with you, sweet for you, yesterday and tomorrow!' He seemed intoxicated by her, by the sun and the grass and the divine sky, as though he had never seen or known them before. The prisoner who comes out of a suffocating gaol at dawn, the convalescent who sees the sea after having seen the face of death were not so intoxicated as he. 'Shall we go away? Shall we leave all sadness behind us? Shall we go to lands where there is no autumn?'

'Autumn is within me, I carry it with me wherever I go!' she thought, but she smiled her slight, concealing smile. 'I shall go away, I shall disappear, I shall go far away and die, my dearest love!' She had not succeeded in overcoming her sadness and recovering hope during that pause, but nevertheless her pain had softened, she had lost all trace of bitterness and rancour.

'Shall we go away?'

'Always leaving, wandering round the world, travelling great distances!' thought the nomadic woman. 'No peace ever, no respite! The anxiety of the race is still not over, and yet already the truce has expired. You would like to comfort me, my darling, and to comfort me you suggest yet more travelling, when I returned home only yesterday!' Suddenly her eyes changed to watery springs. 'Let me stay at home a while longer! And you stay too, if you can. You will be free later on, you will be happy . . . You have so much time ahead of you. You are young. You will have all you deserve. The one who waits for you will not lose you.' Her eyes wore twin crystal visors that sparkled almost fixedly in the sunlight in her feverish face.

'Oh, that same ghost again!' cried Stelio regretfully, with an impatience that he could not manage to contain. 'What are you thinking? What are you afraid of? Why don't you tell me what it is that hurts you? Let's talk then. Who is waiting for me?'

She trembled with fear at that interrogation which came so suddenly and unexpectedly, even though her own words were repeated in it. She trembled at finding herself so close to danger, as though a precipice had suddenly opened up beneath her feet even as she walked on that rich grass.

'Who is waiting for me?'

Suddenly, there in that unfamiliar place, in that lovely meadow, at close of day, after the apparition of so many blood-stained and bloodless spectres, a shape alive with will and desire rose up that filled her with even greater terror. Suddenly, over all those shapes from the past there rose a shape from the future; what she had thought was life was transformed again, all the benefits of that brief pause were already lost, and the soft grass beneath her feet lost all its value.

'Yes, let us talk, if you want to . . . But not now . . .' Her throat was so tight that her voice could barely escape, and she was holding her head slightly raised so that her eyelashes might keep back her tears.

'Don't be sad, please don't be sad!' begged the young man, his soul suspended from her lashes like the tears that did not fall. 'You hold my heart in your very hands. I shall never fail you. Don't torment yourself! I am yours!'

Donatella was there for him too, tall, with her broad back and her strong, supple body like a wingless Victory, armed with her virginity, enticing yet hostile, ready both to fight and surrender herself. But his soul hung there from those

214

eyelashes that veiled the pupils in which he had glimpsed the immensity of love.

'Foscarina!'

The warm drops fell at last, but she did not let them flow down her cheeks. With one of those movements that often sprang from her pain, with the unexpected grace of an unfolding wing, she brushed them away, wetting her fingers and spreading the dampness across her temples. And as she so marked herself with her own tears, she tried to smile.

'Forgive me, Stelio, I am so weak.'

Then he loved the delicate signs that ran from the corners of her eyes to her dampened temples quite desperately, and the tiny dark veins that made her eyelids look like violets, and the curve of her cheeks, and her tired chin, and everything about her that was tinged with autumn, all the shadows in her impassioned face.

'Oh, those dear fingers, as precious as Sofia's fingers! Let me kiss them while they are still wet, like this.'

He led her in his embrace across the meadow to a patch of green gold. Very lightly, holding his arm beneath hers, he kissed each one of her fingertips that were more delicate than unopened buds. She shuddered. He could feel her shudder at every touch of his lips.

'They taste salty.'

'Come, Stelio, someone will see us.'

'There is nobody here.'

'Over there, in the greenhouses.'

'There isn't a sound. Listen.'

'Such strange silence. Like ecstasy!'

'You could hear a leaf fall.'

'What about the guide?'

'He must have gone to meet the next visitors.'

'Whoever comes here?'

'I know that Richard Wagner came here the other day with Daniela von Bulow.'

'Ah, she is the niece of the Countess of Agoult and Daniel Stern.'

215

'I wonder with which of those phantoms the great, sick heart conversed?'

'Who knows!'

'Perhaps he only conversed with himself.'

'Perhaps.'

'Look how the glass in the greenhouses gleams. It looks like crystal. Rain and sun and time make it like that. Doesn't it seem to you that there is some distant twilight reflected in it? You must have stood sometimes on the Fondamenta Pesaro and looked at the beautiful five-paned window with the Evangelists. If you looked up, you could see the windows of the palace with marvellous designs formed by the weather.'

'You know all the secrets of Venice, don't you?'

'Not yet, not all of them.'

'How hot it is here! Look how tall those cedars are! There is a swallow's nest up there, hanging from a branch.'

'The swallows were late leaving this year.'

'Will you really take me to the Euganean Hills in spring?'

'Yes, Fosca, I should like to.'

'Spring is so far away!'

'Life can still be so sweet.'

'One dreams that.'

'Think of Orpheus with his lyre, all dressed in lichens.'

'Oh, what a highway of dreams! Nobody ever passes us. Grass, just grass . . . Not even a footprint.'

'Think of Deucalion with the stones, Ganymede with the eagle, Diana with the stag, all of mythology.'

'So many statues! But at least these are not in exile. Those old hornbeam hedges are holding them in.'

'Maria Luisa of Parma used to walk here, with the king and her lover. She would stop sometimes and listen to the clicking of the shears that were trimming the hornbeams into arches. She would let her jasmine-scented handkerchief drop, and Don Manuel Godoi would pick it up so gracefully that he would manage to conceal the pain in his hip when he bent down, a memento of the agony he had endured in the streets of Aranjuez at the hands of the mob. And since the sun was warm and the tobacco in his enamelled box was excellent, the king who had lost his crown would smile and say: "Indeed, our dear Bonaparte is certainly not so well off on Saint Helena." But the demon of power, struggle and passion would stir once more in the queen's heart . . . Look at those red roses!'

'It is as though they were on fire. They seem to have a live coal in their hearts. They really are on fire.'

'The sun is turning crimson. This is the time when one can see the Chioggia sails out on the lagoon.'

'Pluck a rose for me.'

'Here it is!'

'Oh, it's withering!'

'Then here's another!'

'That is withering too!'

'They are all dying. No, maybe this one isn't.'

'Don't pick it!'

'Look. They are turning even redder. Bonifazio's velvet . . . do you remember? The same shade.'

'The inner flower of the flame!'

'What a memory!'

'Listen. They are closing the greenhouse doors.'

'It's time to go back.'

'The air is already turning chilly.'

'Are you cold?'

'No, not yet.'

'Did you leave your wrap in the carriage?'

'Yes.'

'We shall wait for a train at Dolo. We can go back to Venice by train.'

'Yes.'

'There's plenty of time.'

'What's that? Look.'

'I don't know . . .'

'What a bitter smell! A little wood of box and hornbeam hedges . . .'

'Oh yes, it must be the maze.'

It was entered through a rusty iron gate, between two

217

pillars on which were two Cupids riding stone dolphins. Nothing could be seen on the other side of the gate except the start of a path and a sort of hard, intricate thicket, dense and mysterious. A tower rose out of the centre of the maze, and on its summit the statue of a warrior seemed to be keeping a lookout.

'Have you ever been in a maze?' Stelio asked his lover.

'Never,' she replied.

They lingered to look at the game of deception devised by an ingenious gardener for the delight of ladies and their gallants in the days of tiny high-heeled shoes and panniered skirts. But neglect and age had turned it wild and desolate, had removed every trace of lightheartedness and regularity, transforming it into an enclosed brownish-yellow patch of undergrowth, full of inextricable circumlocutions, where the slanting rays of the setting sun so reddened bushes here and there that they were like bonfires that burned without smoke.

'It is open,' said Stelio, feeling the gate yield as he leaned against it. 'Look.'

He pushed open the rusty iron that creaked on its loose hinges, then stepped forward over the threshold.

'What are you doing?' said his companion, instinctively afraid, reaching out a hand to hold him back.

'Don't you want to go in?'

She was perplexed. But the maze drew them towards it with its mysteriousness, lit as it was by that deep flame.

'What if we get lost?'

'Look, it's only small. We shall easily find our way out again.'

'And what if we don't?'

He laughed at her childish fear. 'We shall wander through it forever!'

'But there is nobody else about. No, let's go.' She tried to hold him back. He defended himself, stepped back towards the path and immediately disappeared, laughing.

'Stelio! Stelio!' She could not see him, but she could hear

218

his laughter ringing down the wild deceiving paths. 'Come back!'

'Come and find me!'

'Stelio, please come back! You will get lost!'

'I shall find Ariadne.'

She felt her heart leap at the sound of that name, then contract in confused yet terrible pain. Was that not the name he had called Donatella on that first night? Had he not called her Ariadne, out there on the water, sitting beside her knee? She could even remember his words: 'Ariadne has a divine talent and so her power can accomplish miracles . . .' She could recall the way he spoke, how he was sitting, the look in his eyes.

She was shaken by a great wave of anguish that obscured her reason, prevented her from considering the chance spontaneity of what had been said, or from recognizing that her beloved had been quite unaware of it. The terror concealed within her desperate love rose up and took control, blinding her wretchedly. That small, insignificant incident took on the appearance of cruelty and contempt. She could still hear his laughter ringing through the wild deceiving paths.

'Stelio!' She cried out as though in some frenzied hallucination she had actually seen him in the other woman's arms, forever torn from her embrace. 'Stelio!'

'Come and find me!' he answered laughingly, still nowhere to be seen. She darted into the labyrinth to find him. She went straight towards the sound of his voice and his laughter, driven by impulse. But the path twisted; a blind impenetrable box hedge appeared in front of her and stopped her. She followed the deceptive winding way, and one turn followed another and they all looked the same and the circle seemed to have no end.

'Come and find me!' repeated the voice a long way away, from behind the living hedges.

'Where are you? Where are you? Can you see me?'

She was looking here and there for thinner patches in the hedge through which to see. All she could make out was the thick web of branches and the redness of evening that

219

was lighting up everything on one side while the shadows darkened everything on the other. The box and hornbeam bushes were intertwined, their evergreen leaves entangled with leaves that were dying, darker foliage with lighter, in a contrast of strength and feebleness, an ambiguity that grew together with the distress of the breathless woman.

'I am lost. Come towards me.'

Again his youthful laughter pealed through the undergrowth. 'Ariadne, oh Ariadne, your thread!' Now the sound was coming from the opposite direction, and hit her between the shoulder-blades like a staff. 'Ariadne!'

She turned and ran, spun round, tried to get through the hedge, tore at the branches, snapped one off. She could see nothing but the intricate, identical pathways. Then she heard a footstep so close by that she thought he was standing behind her and she started. But she was deceived. Once again she explored the unsolvable leafy prison that hemmed her in. She listened, waited. She could hear her own breathing and the beat of her own heart. The silence had become intense. She looked at the vast, pure sky that curved over the two leafy walls that held her prisoner. There seemed to be nothing else in the world except that vastness and that narrow space below. Her thoughts could not distinguish between the reality of the place and the image of her own inner torment, between the natural appearance of things and the kind of living allegory created by her own anguish.

'Stelio, where are you?' There was no answer. She listened. She waited, but in vain. Minutes went by like hours. 'Where are you? I'm frightened.' There was no answer. Where could he have gone? Had he found the way out? Had he left her there alone? Was he going to continue this cruel game?

A terrible desire to scream, to sob, to throw herself to the ground, to struggle, to hurt herself, to die came over the frenzied woman. Once again she looked up at the silent sky. The tops of the great hedges were becoming as red as vine prunings that had ceased to burn and were turning to ashes.

220

'I can see you,' said the laughing voice suddenly out of the shadows, very close at hand.

She jumped and bent down into the shadow. 'Where are you?'

He laughed from between the leaves, without showing himself, like a faun in hiding. The game was exciting to him, all his limbs were warm and stretched with that exercise of skill, and the mysterious wildness, the contact with the earth, the smell of autumn, the unusual nature of that unexpected adventure, the woman's terror, the very presence of those stone deities all combined with his physical pleasure to create an illusion of ancient poetry.

'Where are you? Please stop this game! Don't laugh like that! Stop it!'

He had crept under the bushes on all fours, with his head uncovered. He could feel the rotting leaves and soft moss under his knees. And as he breathed and his heart beat among the branches, all his senses were filled with the pleasure of it, the communion between his life and the life of the trees deepened, and in that entanglement of doubtful paths the spell of his imagination renewed the task of the first maker of wings, the myth of the monster conceived by Pasiphae and the bull, the ancient fable of Theseus in Crete. All that world became real to him. In the purple autumn evening he was transfigured, following the instincts of his blood and the memories stored in his mind, into one of those ambiguous beings, half-beast, half-god, one of those woodland creatures whose throats were swollen with the same glands that hang from the neck of goats. A sense of jovial lasciviousness aroused strange actions and gestures in him, and surprises and tricks, making him imagine the joy of a chase, of capture, of a rapid coupling on the mossy ground or up against the wild box-hedge. And then he desired a being like himself, a fresh breast to whom he could communicate his laughter, two swift legs, two arms ready to fight him, a prey to carry off, a virginity to be forced, a rape to accomplish. Donatella with her broad back reappeared before him.

'Stop it! I cannot go on Stelio! . . . I am going to fall.'

Foscarina let out a scream as she felt a hand reach through the hedge and tug at the hem of her gown. She bent down, and in the shadows she saw the face of a laughing faun through the branches. His laughter flashed across her soul without touching it, without breaking the terrible distress that had encased it. She even suffered more acutely from the contrast between his enjoyment and her own sadness, between his ever-renewable joy and her perpetual uneasiness, between his light-hearted forgetfulness and the weight of her burden. She recognized her mistake more clearly, together with the cruelty of life that was bringing the image of the other woman into the very place where she was suffering. As she bent down and saw his youthful face, she saw with the same clarity the face of the singer bending down behind her, imitating her action as a shadow repeats an action on a lighted wall. Everything in her mind grew confused, and her thoughts were not able to put a space between reality and fantasy. The other woman was upon her, oppressing her, forcing her down.

'Let me go! Let me go! You are not looking for me . . .' Her voice was so changed that Stelio stopped laughing and stopped the game. He withdrew his arm and stood up. She could no longer see him. The leafy wall rose impenetrably between them.

'Take me out of this! I cannot bear it any longer, I am exhausted . . . I am in pain!'

He could find no words to calm her down and comfort her. The coincidence of his own recent desire and her instant divination of it had struck home. 'Wait, just wait a little! I shall try and find the way out. I shall call someone . . .'

'You're not going, are you?'

'Don't be afraid, please don't. There is absolutely no danger.' And while he was talking like that to reassure her, he could feel the inanity of what he was saying, the disparity between his entertaining adventure and her dark disturbance that was due to an entirely different cause. Now he too could feel the strange ambiguity within himself that

222

made such a slight incident seem to be two different things, for beneath his solicitude he was holding back an urge to laugh, and her suffering was as new to him as those disturbances that are born from extravagant dreams.

'Please don't go!' she begged, in the grip of her hallucination.

'Perhaps we shall meet there at the next turning. Let us try. Take my hands.' He gripped her hands through a space in the hedge and started as he touched them, they were so cold. 'Foscarina! What is the matter? Are you really ill? Wait. I shall try to break through the hedge.' He wrestled with the thicket and snapped off a few branches, but the dense hedge was powerful enough to resist him. He hurt himself to no purpose. 'It can't be done.'

'Shout, call someone.'

He shouted through the silence. The tops of the hedges had died out, but a redness was spreading over the sky above like the reflection of woods on fire on the horizon. A flock of wild ducks flew over in an orderly black triangle, their long necks stretched out.

'Let me go! I can easily find the tower, and I can shout from there. Someone will hear me.'

'No! No!'

She heard him running away, followed the sound of his footsteps, was ensnared again by the maze, and found herself alone and abandoned once more. She stopped. She waited. She listened. She looked up at the sky and saw the triangular flock disappearing into the distance. She lost all sense of time. Minutes seemed liked hours.

'Stelio! Stelio!' She was no longer able to control in any way the agitation of her nerves that were stretched to the limit. She could feel an extreme attack of manic depression coming on, just as one can feel a whirlwind approaching. 'Stelio!'

He heard the anguished voice and desperately tried to find the tower that kept coming nearer and then moving further away along the curving paths. His laughter had frozen in his heart. His soul trembled to its very roots each time his ears caught the sound of his own name spoken in such accents of invisible agony. And the failing light gave him the impression of blood dripping away, of life that is fading.

'I have reached it. I'm there!'

Finally one of the paths opened on to the little space from which the tower emerged. He raced wildly up the winding stairs; he felt dizzy when he reached the summit and closed his eyes, holding on to the railings. He opened them again and saw a long strip of fire across the horizon, the disc of the rayless moon, the plain like a grey marsh, the labyrinth beneath him black with box hedges and spotted with hornbeams, quite narrow in its interminable windings, looking like a dismantled building invaded by undergrowth, like a ruin in a wild, dismal wood.

'Stop! Stop! Don't run like that! Someone has heard me. A man is coming. I can see him coming. Wait! Stop!' He was watching the woman running through the blind, uncertain paths like a mad thing, like a creature condemned to some pointless torment, some useless but eternal torture, the sister of mythical martyrs. 'Stop!' It was as though she had not heard him or else she could not stop her fatal agitation, and he could not help her but was forced to witness her terrible punishment.

'Here he is!' One of the custodians had heard the shouting and had come to them. He was just coming through the gate. Stelio met him at the foot of the tower. Together they went to look for the lost woman. The man knew the secret of the labyrinth. Stelio stopped him chattering and making remarks by astounding him with generosity.

'Has she lost her senses? Has she fallen?' The shadows and the silence seemed sinister to him now, and frightened him. He called her, but she did not answer, nor could they hear her footsteps. The place was already in darkness, and dampness was falling from the peacock-coloured sky.

'Has she fainted, shall I find her on the ground?' He started, as round a bend in the path there suddenly appeared before him a mysterious figure, whose pale face caught all the twilight and was shining like a pearl, with great staring eyes and tightly sealed lips.

They went back towards the Dolo and took the same road back beside the Brenta. She did not speak, she never opened her mouth, she never answered him, as though she could not unclench her teeth. She lay stretched out on the floor of the carriage, her cloak pulled up to her chin, occasionally overcome by violent shuddering that was like sobbing, her colour as ghastly as if she had malaria. Her lover took her fingers and held them in his own to warm them, but in vain. They were quite stiff, almost lifeless. And the statues kept going past them.

The river was flowing between its banks, under the violet, silvery sky in which the full moon was rising. A black barge was sailing downstream, pulled by two grey horses treading heavily on the grassy towpath, led by a man who was whistling placidly as he walked, and the funnel was smoking on the deck, like a chimney-pot on the roof of a hovel, and a lantern gave off a yellow light in the hold and the smell of the evening meal was spreading through the air. Again and again, in that watery landscape, the statues kept going past them.

It was like a Stygian plain, like a vision of Hades: a land of shadows, vapours and water. Everything was going misty and disappearing like spirits. The moon was enchanting and pulling at the plain just as she enchants and pulls at the sea, drinking all that vast earthly dampness from the horizon with her silent, insatiable throat. Solitary pools glistened everywhere; tiny silvery canals could be seen, gleaming in the indefinable distance between rows of bending willows. The earth seemed to be loosing its solidity by degrees and becoming liquid, the sky seemed to be watching its own melancholy reflected in countless silent mirrors. And along the shore that had lost all colour, like the spectres of a vanished people, every now and again the statues passed by.

* * *

225

'Do you often think about Donatella Arvale, Stelio?' Foscarina asked suddenly, after a long interval during which neither of them had heard anything except the sound of their own footsteps on the Glassmakers' Quay, lit up by the manifold gleam of the fragile pieces filling the windows of the neighbouring shops.

Her voice sounded like breaking glass. Stelio stopped, in the attitude of someone who finds themselves in unexpected difficulty. His spirit was spread across the red and green island of Murano, studded with flowers, depressing in its poverty that was causing it to lose even the memory of that joyful time when poets called it 'the place of nymphs and demigods'. He was thinking of the famous gardens where Andrea Navagero, Pietro Bembo, Aretino, Aldo and the learned throng had competed with one another in the elegance of their Platonic dialogues *lauri sub umbra*. He was imagining the convents luxurious as brothels, where nuns dressed in white camel-hair cloth and lace used to dwell, their foreheads ornamented with curls and their breasts uncovered like honest courtesans, given to secret loves, greatly favoured by licentious noblemen, called by lovely names such as Ancilla Soranzo, Cipriana Morosini, Zanetta Balbi, Beatrice Falier, Eugenia Muschiera, pious mistresses of pleasure. His drifting dream was accompanied by a little tune he had heard in the museum, that had wailed slowly in units of sound from a small metal contraption which the turn of a key set in motion, concealed beneath a glass garden where lovers ornamented with tiny pearls danced around an agate fountain. It was an unexceptional melody, a forgotten dance tune, from which some of the notes were missing because of broken keys or dust, but yet so haunting that he could not shake it from his ears. Now everything around him possessed the same fragile, distant melancholy of those figures dancing to sounds slower than falling drops. The faint soul of Murano had idly spoken through that old pastime.

At the sudden question, the little song stopped abruptly, his imaginings vanished, as did the spell of that distant life.

His wandering mind came back regretfully and shrank a little. Beside him, Stelio felt the beating of a living heart that he must inevitably wound. He looked at his beloved.

She was walking beside the canal, between the green of that sickly water and the iridescence of the delicate vases, not at all agitated, almost calm. Her chin, that had become slightly thinner, quivered just a little between the edge of her veil and her sable collar.

'Yes, sometimes,' he replied, after a moment's hesitation, refusing to lie, feeling the need to raise their love above common deception and demands so that it might remain a source of strength for him and not of weakness: a free bond between them, not a burdensome chain.

The woman went on walking ahead without wavering, but she had lost all feeling in her limbs in the terrible beating of her heart that was pounding like a single thread from the back of her neck down to her heels. She could no longer see, though she could feel the fascinating presence of the water close at hand.

'One cannot forget her voice,' he added after a pause, having plucked up his courage. 'It has such extraordinary power. From that very first evening I thought she might make a marvellous instrument for my play. I would like her to sing the lyric parts of my tragedy, the odes that arise from the symphonies and eventually come together in a dance movement between each episode. La Tanagra has agreed to dance. I trust in your good offices, my dearest, to obtain Donatella's agreement. That way the Dionysian Trinity would be reconstituted perfectly in my new theatre for everyone to enjoy . . .'

As he was speaking, he realized that his words rang false, that his casualness contrasted too sharply with the mortal shadow that had spread across the veiled face of his mistress. In spite of himself, he had exaggerated his frankness in considering the singer as a mere artistic instrument, as a pure, ideal force to be drawn into the circle of his magnificent undertaking. In spite of himself, perturbed by the suffering of the woman walking beside him, he had inclined

227

slightly towards deception. Certainly, what he had said was true, but his mistress had asked him for a different truth. He broke off abruptly, unable any longer to bear the sound of his own voice. He felt that at that moment, between himself and the actress, art had no meaning at all, no living value. Another, more imperious, more turgid force was in control of them. The world created by the intellect was as dead as the old stones over which they were walking. The only true, strong power was the poison that was running through human veins. The woman's will was saying: 'I love you and I want you all for me, body and soul.' The man's will was saying: 'I want you to love me and serve me, but cannot give up anything in life that arouses my desire.' The struggle was unevenly matched and atrocious.

Since the woman was silent, though she involuntarily quickened her pace, he prepared to confront the other truth. 'I understand that this is not what you wanted to know . . .'

'No, it is not. So?'

She turned to him with a kind of spasm of violence that reminded him of her fury one distant evening and her wild cry: 'Go on, run! She's waiting!' On that peaceful towpath, between the sluggish water and slender glassware, on that weary island, the face of danger flashed before him. But an importunate stranger crossed their path, offering to show them round a nearby glass factory.

'Let's go in,' said the woman, following the man, entering the passage as though she were seeking shelter, to escape from the shame of the street, and the bare light of day that could see her ruin.

The place was damp and stained with seasalt, smelling of salt like a sea-cave. They went through a courtyard full of firewood, through a decrepit door and came to the place where the furnace was. Its fiery breath surrounded them, and they found themselves before a great incandescent altar that dazzled their eyes as though their very eyelashes were about to burst into flame.

'Disappear, be swallowed up, leave not a trace behind!' roared the woman's heart, drunk with destruction. 'That fire could devour me in a instant, like chaff, like a piece of straw.' And she moved closer to the open mouths through which the liquid flames could be seen, more splendid than noonday in summer, licking around the earthen pots in which the shapeless mineral was being melted. The craftsmen standing round were approaching with iron tubes to shape it with the breath from their mouths and the skill of their craft.

'The power of fire!' thought the Creator, his anxiety quite gone as he looked at the marvellous beauty of the element that was as familiar to him as a brother ever since the day when he had discovered its secret music. 'Oh, if I could only give the forms of perfection that I long for to the life of those beings who love me! If only I could melt all their weaknesses in the hottest furnace and turn them into obedient matter and impress the commandments of my heroic will and the images of my purest poetry in them! Why, why, why, my darling, do you not want to be the divinely mobile statue of my spirit, the work of faith and sacrifice that would allow our life to be greater than our art? Why are we on the point of resembling those petty lovers who curse one another and complain? I really believed you could give me more than just love, when I heard your own lips utter the miraculous words: "One thing I can do, which even love cannot." You must always do everything you can, and everything that love cannot in order to match my insatiable nature.'

The work around the furnaces intensified. The molten glass at the end of the iron tubes was swelling, twisting, turning silvery like a cloud, shining like the moon, bursting, fragmenting into a thousand delicate sparkling, crackling threads, finer than the webs which hang between the branches in the forest in early morning. The craftsmen were fashioning harmonious goblets, each one as he worked following his own rhythm, determined by the quality of the material and the habitual pattern of movements necessary to control it. The apprentices would put a tiny pear of burning paste where the masters told them to, and that pear would grow longer, would twist, change into a handle, a lip, a spout, a stem, a base. The redness gradually died away under the tools, and the half-formed goblet was again placed in the fire fixed on the end of the tube, then taken out again, softened, malleable, sensitive to the most delicate finishing touches that completed it, making it conform to the pattern handed down through generations, or follow the free invention of a new creator. The movements of the human beings around the elegant creatures of fire, breath and iron were extraordinarily light and agile, like the movements of a silent dance. The image of La Tanagra appeared to the Creator in the perpetual wavering of the flames, like a salamander. Donatella's voice sung the powerful melody to him.

'Yet again, today, I have given her to you as a companion!' Foscarina was thinking. 'I have summoned her here between us. I have recalled her while you were perhaps thinking of something quite different. I have led her to you unexpectedly as I did on that delirious night!'

It was true. It was true. From the moment that the singer's name had echoed against the side of the warship, spoken for the first time by her lover's lips in the shadow cast by the hull of the armed colossus out on the twilit water, from that very moment she had been unconsciously fostering that new image in his mind, feeding it with her own jealousy and her own fears, strengthening it and magnifying it every day until she had at last illuminated it with certainty. More than once she had repeated to the man who had perhaps forgotten: 'She is waiting for you.' More than once she had presented that far-off, mysterious waiting to his perhaps careless imagination. Just as on that Dionysian evening, Venice ablaze had lit up their two youthful faces with the same glow, so now it lit up their passion and they were only burning because she had wanted them to burn. 'Of course,' she thought, 'now he possesses that image and is possessed by it. My very suffering arouses his desire. He rejoices in loving her before the very eyes of my despair . . .' And her torment was nameless, for she could see that the love that was killing her was being fed by her own love, she could feel that her own passion provided the necessary atmosphere outside of which it would not have been able to survive.

'As soon as it is formed, the vase is put in the furnace chamber to be tempered,' one of the master-craftsmen was telling Stelio who had asked him a question. 'It would shatter into thousands of pieces if it were suddenly exposed to the air.' In fact they could see through an opening in the receptacle that was an extension of the furnace, the gleaming vases, still slaves of the fire and under its control, all placed together. 'They have been in there for ten hours now,' said the glass-maker, indicating the graceful family.

Then the lovely, delicate creatures left their father, they were separated from him forever. They turned cold, became icy jewels, lived their own new lives in the world, were subordinated to pleasure-seeking men, went out to meet danger, followed the variations of the light, receiving cut flowers or intoxicating beverages.

'Is that our great Foscarina?' the little man with the red eyes asked Stelio in a low voice. He had recognized the actress when she had lifted her veil, feeling suffocated.

Trembling with naïve emotion, the master glassmaker took a step towards her and bowed respectfully. 'One evening, Madam, you made me shake and cry like a babby. In memory of that evening, which I shall never forget as long as I live, allow me to offer you a small token that has been made by the hands of your humble servant Seguso.'

'Seguso?' cried Stelio Effrena, bending down swiftly to look the little man in the face. 'One of the great families of glassmakers! Are you really? From the true line?'

'I am that, sir.'

'So you're a prince.'

'Yes, a clown-prince.'

'And you know all the secrets, don't you?'

The man from Murano made a mysterious gesture that conjured up all the ancient, ancestral knowledge of which he declared himself to be the last heir. The other glassmakers smiled as they stood around the furnaces, having stopped work while the glass at the end of their tubes changed colour.

'Well, Madam, would you accept it?'

It was as if he had stepped out of a panel by Bartolomeo Vivarini, brother of one of the faithful kneeling beneath the cloak of the Virgin in Santa Maria Formosa. He was bent, skinny, dried up, as though the fire had refined him, fragile as though his skin were covering a skeleton made of glass, with sparse, grey wisps of hair, a thin, sharp nose, a pointed chin, two narrow lips from the corners of which ran wrinkles of concentration and quick-wittedness, with two careful, mobile, flexible hands, reddened with scars from burns, expressive of his skill and precision, used to the movements that shaped beautiful lines in sensitive matter, true instruments of that delicate art, made perfect by the inheritance of the uninterrupted practice of the craft by so many working generations.

'Yes, you are a Seguso,' said Stelio Effrena, looking at him. 'The proof of your nobility is in your hands.'

The glassmaker looked at them, smiling, and held them out flat.

'Leave them in your will to the Murano Museum, along with your blowing pipe.'

'Yes, so they can pickle them like Canova's heart or fruit from Padua.'

The frank laughter of the workmen rang through the air, and the half-formed goblets trembled at the end of iron tubes half-rosy, half-blueish like clusters of hydrangeas about to change colour.

'But the decisive proof will be your glass. Let's see it.' Foscarina had not spoken, afraid of the unsteadiness of her voice, but all her gracious sweetness suddenly blossomed again through her sadness, accepting the gift and thanking the giver. 'Let's see it, Seguso.' The little man scratched his sweaty forehead with an air of perplexity, recognizing an expert.

'Perhaps I can guess,' added Stelio Effrena, going over to

the crucible chamber and looking enthusiastically at the collection of vases. 'If it's that one . . .'

His presence had brought an unusual animation into the midst of daily toil, the bright ardour of the game that he pursued perpetually in his life. All those simple souls, after first smiling, became passionately involved in the test. They waited for him to make his choice with the same curious anxiety with which one waits for the result of a wager, soliciting a confrontation between the subtlety of the master-craftsman and that of the judge. And the young, unknown man who moved through the workshop with such familiarity, relating equally to men and things with such swift, spontaneous sympathy was no longer an outsider to them.

'It it's that one . . .'

Foscarina could feel herself drawn into the game and almost compelled to unbend, quickly emptied of her previous bitterness and rancour in the face of her lover's happiness. There too, without any effort, he had lit up fleeting moments with passion and beauty and had contagiously communicated the strength of his own vitality to those around him, raising their spirits to a superior sphere, arousing once more in those degenerate artisans the ancient pride in their own craft. The harmony of a pure line had become for a few moments the centre of their world. And the Creator bent over the collection of vases as though the fortune of the hesitant little glassmaker depended on the choice he would make.

'Yes, it is true, only you know how to live,' she said to him as she watched him tenderly. 'You must have everything. I shall be content to see you live, to see you happy. Do with me as you will.' She smiled as she annihilated herself. She belonged to him like something he could hold in his hand, like a ring on his finger, like a glove, like a coat, like a word that can be spoken or not spoken, a wine that can either be drunk or poured away on to the ground.

'Well, Seguso?' cried Stelio Effrena, impatient with the prolonged hesitation.

The man looked him in the eyes, then, having become quite frank, trusted in his own native instinct. Five vases, among a great many others, had been made by his hands; They were as distinctive as though they belonged to a different species. But which of the five was the best? The craftsmen all turned towards him, while they held the goblets fixed to the end of their tubes in the flames lest they should become cold. And the flames, clear as those which flare up from a crisp wreath of laurels, quavered inside the furnace, seeming to hold the men chained by the instruments of their craft.

'Yes!' cried Stelio Effrena, as he saw the master glassmaker carefully take out the chosen piece. 'Blood cannot lie! This gift is worthy of the Dogaressa Foscarina, Seguso.'

The man from Murano held the stem of the goblet between finger and thumb and smiled at the woman, cheered by the warm praise. His sharp, penetrating look brought to mind the little golden fox that is chasing the cockerel's tail in the Murano coat-of-arms. His eyelids, reddened by the violent glare of the furnace, flicked across his gaze that was directed at the fragile piece which was still glistening in his hands before leaving them, and in his almost caressing fingers and his whole appearance the hereditary ability to feel the difficult beauty of simple lines and delicate tonalities could be seen. The goblet which the bent man was holding, which he had made, was like one of those miraculous flowers that blossom on scraggy, twisted bushes.

It was indeed beautiful, and like all natural things it was mysterious, holding within its concave shape the breath of human life, its transparency reflecting water and sky, its violet rim recalling floating creatures of the oceans, simple, pure, with no other decoration except that sea-coloured rim, no other limbs but its foot, its stem and its lip. No one would have been able to explain why it was so beautiful, not with one word or with a thousand words. Its worth was either nothing or incalculable, according to the quality of the eyes that looked on it.

'It will break,' said Stelio.

Foscarina had wanted to take her gift with her unwrapped, as one carries a flower. 'I shall take off my glove.' She stood the goblet on the edge of the well that stood in the middle of the churchyard. The rusty pulley, the worn façade of the basilica with its Byzantine remains, the red brick of the bell-tower, the gold of the haystacks on the other side of the wall and the bronze of the tall laurel trees, the faces of the women who were threading glass beads on their door-steps, and the grass and the clouds and everything around her altered the sensitive tones of the luminous glass. All colours were blended in its colour. And it seemed to live a manifold life in its very frailty, like the animated rainbow in which the universe is reflected.

'Just imagine the wealth of experience that has gone into the making of this lovely thing!' said Stelio in wonderment. 'All the generations of Segusos throughout the centuries contributed with their breath and their touch to the birth of this object in that happy moment when the unknowing little glassmaker was able to follow some distant impulse and transmit it precisely into the glass. The fire was the same, the paste was rich, the air was temperate, everything was favourable and so the miracle took place.'

Foscarina took the stem of the goblet in her fingers. 'If it were to break, we should raise a mausoleum to it as Nero did to the shades of his broken cup! Oh, such love for an object! Another despot, Xerxes, preceded you, my darling, and hung necklaces on a gorgeous tree.' On her lips, just where the edge of her veil touched, was a very slight but continuous smile. He knew that smile, and had suffered from it on the banks of the Brenta, in the countryside haunted by statues.

'Gardens, there are gardens everywhere! Once they were the loveliest gardens in the world, earthly paradises as Andrea Calmo described them, dedicated to poetry and music and love-making. Perhaps one of these old laurel trees heard Aldo Manuzio speaking Greek with Navagero or

235

Madonna Gasparina sighing as she followed the Count of Collalto . . .'

They were walking along a road hemmed in by desolate walled gardens. On top of the walls, in the gaps between the blood-coloured bricks, a few strange grasses blew, as long and stiff as fingers. The tops of the bronze laurels were gilded by the setting sun. The air was shining with a thick golden dust like quartz.

'What a romantic, poignant fate Gaspara Stampa had! Do you know her poems? Yes, you do, I once saw them on your table. Such a mixture of ice and fire! Occasionally her mortal passion, through Cardinal Bembo's version of Petrarchism, lets out a great cry. I know a wonderful line of hers:

> To live on fire and not to feel the pain!

'Stelio,' said Foscarina with that inextinguishable smile which gave her the appearance of a sleepwalker. 'Do you recall the sonnet that begins:

> My lord, I know I in myself no longer live
> And see that I in you am now quite dead . . . ?'

'No, I don't recall it, Fosca.'

'You remember your delightful image of dead Summer? Summer was lying in her funeral barge, dressed all in gold like a Dogaressa, and the funeral cortège brought her out to the island of Murano where a Master of Fire was to seal her in an opalescent crystal coffin, so that after she had sunk into the lagoon she could at least see the floating fronds of seaweed . . . Do you remember all that?'

'It was one evening in September.'

'It was the last evening in September, the night of the Allegory. There was such light over the water . . . You were slightly intoxicated, you kept talking and talking . . . You said so many things! You had come back from isolation, you were full to overflowing. You poured a whole river of poetry over your beloved. A barge went by loaded with pomegranates... I was called Perdita then... Do you remember?'

As she walked, she could feel the extreme lightness of her step and sense that in herself something was disappearing, as though her whole body were about to change into a wraith. The sensations of her physical body seemed to depend on the glass that she was carrying, to exist simply in the anxiety created in her by the fragility of the object and by her fear of dropping it, while her ungloved hand was gradually becoming colder and her veins were assuming the same hue as the sea-coloured rim that ran round the edge of the goblet.

'I was still called Perdita... Stelio, can you call to mind another of Gaspara's sonnets that begins:

> I would that Love should tell me
> How to follow him...

And the madrigal that begins:

> If you think to please my Lord...?'

'I didn't know you were so familiar with poor Anasilla, my darling.'

'Then I shall tell you... I was just fourteen years old when I performed in an old romantic tragedy entitled *Gaspara Stampa*. I played the lead... It was at Dolo, which we passed through the other day on our way to Strà, in a little country theatre, a sort of tent... It was the year before my mother died... I remember it well... I remember some things as though they happened yesterday. And yet twenty years have gone by! I remember the sound of my voice which was still feeble when I forced it in big speeches, because someone behind the scenes hissed at me that I should shout louder, louder... Gaspara was in despair, in great pain, deliriously in pursuit of her cruel count... There were so many things that my young, inexperienced soul

237

did not know or understand, and I do not know what painful instinct led me to find the tone of voice or the shrieks that were to move the wretched audience who provided our daily bread. Ten hungry people were torturing me because I was a means of livelihood. Brutal necessity cut off and uprooted all the flowers of my dreams that my early timidity had cultivated ... It was a time of sobs, of feelings being suffocated, of terror, of appalling tiredness, of frank horror! The people who tortured me did not know what they were doing, they were poor people whose senses had been dulled by poverty and exhaustion. May God forgive them, let them rest in peace! Only my mother, Stelio, and she too

> From greatly loving and being little loved
> Died, as she lived, unhappy,

only my mother took pity on me, and suffered the same torment with me and knew how to hold me in her arms and stop my ghastly trembling and weep with me, comforting me. Oh, that blessed, blessed woman!'

Her voice changed. Her mother's eyes reopened within her, kind and firm and infinite as a peaceful horizon. 'Tell me, you tell me what I have to do! Show me, teach me, you know how!' All her soul could feel again the clasp of those arms, and the hurt flowed back towards her through the years in all its fullness, but almost gently now, with all the bitterness gone. Memories of what she had suffered and how she had struggled seemed to fill her with a warm wave, comforting her again and raising her spirits. On what anvils had the iron of her will been forged, in what waters had it been tempered? The trial had been so very hard for her, victory had been difficult, and had been won at the cost of hard work and perseverance against brutal, hostile forces. She had witnessed the most atrocious poverty and the most sombre deaths, she had experienced heroic effort, pity, horror and the threshold of mortality.

'I know what hunger is, Stelio and what it means to see night approaching when shelter is uncertain,' she said gently, stopping between the two walls. Lifting her veil to her forehead, she looked at her lover with uncovered eyes.

He turned pale under that gaze, so sudden was his agitation, so great his dismay at the sight of that unexpected look. He felt confused as though in some incoherent dream, unable to connect this extraordinary apparition with what had just happened in life, unable to attach the meaning of those words to the figure of the woman who was smiling at him and still holding the delicate glass in her ungloved hand. And yet he had heard her, and she was there in her beautiful sable coat, with all the softness of her lovely eyes that lengthened out under her moist lashes as though tears were continually rising and dissolving again without falling, there on the lonely pathway between the two walls.

'And I know more.'

It was unusually good for her to talk like that. Humility seemed to strengthen her heart as much as the greatest act of pride could do. She had never felt her awareness of the power and the glory she enjoyed in the world raise her higher in the opinion of the man she loved, but now the memory of her distant martyrdom, of her poverty and her hunger created a feeling of real superiority in her over the man she had believed invincible. Just as his words had seemed pointless to her for the first time as they walked beside the Brenta, so now for the first time she felt superior to him in her experience of life, for fortune had smiled on him from his very cradle and all that troubled him was the fury of his desire and his burning ambition. She imagined him faced with real need, compelled to work like a slave, oppressed my material limitations, subjected to vile discomforts.

'Would he have found the energy to resist or the patience to endure it?' She pictured him weak and lost in the sharp claws of necessity, humiliated and broken. 'Ah yes, you must have everything joyous and noble around you, as long as you live!' She could not bear the sadness of that image, and so pushed it away with an impulse of defensiveness and almost motherly protectiveness. Then, involuntarily, she

239

put her hand on his shoulder; drew it back as she realized, then placed it there again. She smiled like a woman who knew what he should never know, like a woman who had conquered what he could never conquer. She heard once more within herself the words heavy with terrible promise: 'Tell me you are not afraid to suffer . . . I believe your soul is able to bear all the pain in the world.' Her eyelids that were like violets were lowered over that secret shame, but an infinitely subtle, complex beauty appeared in the lines of her face, deriving from a new concordance of her inner forces, from a mysterious direction of her reawakened will. In the shadow that the folds of her lifted veil cast over her eyebrows, her paleness was animated by inimitable life.

'I am not afraid of suffering,' she said, answering the man who had spoken to her on the banks of the distant river. And lifting her hand from his shoulder, she stroked her beloved's cheek very slightly, and then he understood that she was answering his distant words.

He was silent, intoxicated, as though she had given him the very essence of her heart pressed like a bunch of grapes in the goblet. Of all the forms of nature around him in that tenuous light, none could equal for him the mystery or the beauty of that human face which was allowing him to see beyond its features a glimpse of sacred profundity where doubtless some great thing was taking place in silence. He trembled, waiting for her to continue.

They walked for a while side by side between the walls. The pathway was unpaved, soft and dull beneath their feet, but the gleaming clouds hung over it. They reached a crossroads, where there was a wretched, half-ruined hovel. Foscarina stopped to look at it. The worm-eaten, broken shutters were held open by a stick propped up diagonally. The low sunlight shining in fell on a smoky wall, exposing the furnishings: a table, a bench and a cradle.

'Stelio,' she said, 'do you remember the inn we went into at Dolo to wait for a train? Vampa's inn: there was a big fire blazing in the chimney, gleaming pans on the walls, slices of polenta cooking on the grill. It was exactly the

240

same twenty years ago: the same fire, the same pans, the same polenta. My mother and I would go in there after the performance, and we would sit down on a bench at a table. I would have wept and screamed and raved and died from poison or by the sword in the theatre. The lines would still be ringing in my head, in a voice that was not my own, and in my heart there would be a strange will that I could not shake off, as though someone were trying to go through the steps and the movements again despite my tiredness . . . The simulation of life was still there in the muscles of my face, and some nights I could not control them . . . A mask, that feeling of a living mask that was already growing . . . I used to open my eyes terribly wide . . . There would be a cold chill in the roots of my hair . . . I could not regain full consciousness of myself and of what was going on around me . . . The smell from the kitchen would make me feel nauseous, the food on my plate seemed too coarse and heavy as stones, impossible to swallow. My repugnance rose from something indefinably delicate and precious that I could feel in the depths of my exhaustion, from some confused nobility that I could feel in the depths of my humiliation . . . I can't explain . . . Perhaps it was the obscure presence of the strength that was to develop in me later, that difference and special quality that Nature had bestowed on me . . . Sometimes my awareness of that difference became so strong that it almost separated me from my mother – May God forgive me! – and almost alienated me from her . . . There was such tremendous loneliness in me, nothing could touch me, nothing that was around me. I was alone with my fate . . . My mother, who was beside me, was retreating into infinite distance. Yes, she would die soon and was already preparing to depart, and perhaps those were the signs! She would try to persuade me to eat, with the words only she could say. And I would answer: "Wait! wait!" All I could do was drink, I was so thirsty for cold water. Sometimes, when I was even more tired and more shaky, I would smile for hours. And even that blessed woman with her understanding heart could not understand where that

241

smile came from . . . Hours that have never been repeated, when it seemed as though my soul actually broke through the prison of my body and wandered out to the farthest limits of life! What must your adolescence have been like, Stelio? Who could imagine it? We have all experienced the weight of sleep that suddenly makes our bodies heavy as lead after exertion or ecstasy, and comes as swiftly and soundly as a hammer blow and seems to annihilate us completely. But sometimes the power of dreams takes control of us when we are awake with the same violence and holds us fast, and our will cannot resist. It seems as though the very fabric of our existence is coming unravelled and that our hopes are using the thread to weave another stranger, brighter one . . . I remember some of the lovely things you said about Venice that night, when you described her wonderful hands bent on shaping her own light and shadow into one continuous work of beauty. You alone know how to describe the indescribable . . . There, on that bench, sitting at that rough table in Vampa's inn at Dolo, where fate led me again just the other day with you, I had the most extraordinary visions that dreams have ever awakened in my soul. I saw things I can never forget: I saw images from my own thoughts and instincts superimpose themselves on the real forms of things that were around me. There, before my staring eyes that had been burned by the red, smoky glare of the make-shift paraffin footlights, I saw the world of my own expressiveness begin to take shape . . . The first lines of my art were developed in that state of agitation, exhaustion, feverishness and revulsion, when my senses had become what I might describe as malleable, like the incandescent material that the glassmakers were holding at the end of their tubes. There was a natural desire in me to shape that material, to breathe life into it, to fill the hollow of a mould . . . Some nights I used to see myself reflected as though in a mirror on that wall where the pans were hanging, caught in a moment of rage or pain, with a face I could not recognize. And I would blink very rapidly to escape that hallucinatory sight or to interrupt the way I was

242

staring. My mother used to say over and over again: "Eat, child, at least eat this!" But what was bread and wine and meat and fruit and anything else that was real, purchased by hard labour, compared to what I had within myself? I used to say: "Wait!" And when we stood up to go, I used to take a big piece of bread with me. I liked to eat it next morning, out in the fields, under a tree or beside the Brenta, sitting on a rock or on the grass . . . Oh, those statues!'

Foscarina stopped again, at the end of a new walled pathway that led to a deserted field, the Campo di San Bernardo, where the ancient monastery used to be. The bell-tower of the Angeli could be seen across the field, while a beautiful cloud hung over it, like a rose at the end of a stem. The grass was soft, quiet and bright green, like the grass in the Pisani park at Strà.

'Those statues!' the actress repeated, with such an intent look that it seemed almost as though there were great numbers of them standing in front of her, barring her path. 'They did not recognize me the other day, Stelio, but I recognized them.'

The distant hours, the damp, misty landscape, the bare trees, the ruined villa, the silent river, the remains of queens and empresses, the crystal visor over her feverish face, the overgrown maze, his vain pursuit, her terror and agony, her splendid, terrible pallor, her ice-cold body on the cushions in the carriage, her lifeless hands, all those sad things appeared in a different light in her lover's mind. He looked at the marvellous being, panting with surprise and dismay, as though he were seeing her for the first time, as if her features, her step, her voice, her garments were extraordinarily loaded with manifold meanings that he could not grasp because they flashed past him in such numbers and with such rapidity. She was there, a creature of perishable flesh, subject to the sorry laws of time, and yet a great mass of real and ideal life was pressing down upon her, spreading out around her, throbbing with the rhythm of her breathing. The desperate, nomadic woman had touched the limits of human experience; she knew things he could never know. He, the man of joy, felt drawn to so much accumulated pain, to such pride and humility, such struggle and such conquests. He would like to have lived such a life. He felt envious of her fate. Astonished, he watched how the delicate violet veins in the back of her hand stood out as though there were no skin to cover them, and how her slender nails gleamed as she gripped the stem of the goblet. He thought of a drop of that blood circulating through her substance, limited by her basic bodily form and yet as immeasurable as the universe. It seemed to him that only one temple existed in the whole world: the human body. He felt a desperate urge to stop the woman, to stand in front of her, to examine her completely, to discover everything about her, to ask her endless questions.

Strange questions came into his mind: 'When you were a girl, did you ride down the highways on a cart loaded with props and scenery, lying on a bundle of leaves, followed by a company of travelling actors, past vineyards, and did some harvester offer you a basket of grapes? Did the man who possessed you for the first time have the appearance of a satyr, and in your terror did you hear the wind roaring over the plain, carrying away that part of you which you will always search for and never find again? How many tears had you drunk, the day I heard you, for the voice of Antigone speaking through you to sound so pure? Did you conquer nations, one after another, as battles are won to acquire an empire? Do you recognize them by their different scents, as one can do with wild animals? One nation rebelled, but you fought back and in the conquest you came to love it more than those who adored you at first sight. Another, on the other side of the ocean, to which you revealed a new way of feeling, can never forget you and sends you messages asking you to return . . . What unexpected beauty will I see arising out of your love and your pain?'

In that lonely field on the forgotten island, beneath the clear winter sky, she appeared to him once again as she had appeared on that Dionysian night amid the praise of the

244

poets sitting around her dinner-table. The same life-giving, revelatory power flowed from the woman who had raised her veil and said: 'I know what hunger is . . .'

'It was in March, I remember,' went on Foscarina softly. 'I went out early into the fields with my bread. I was going to seek my fortune. My destination was the statues. I would go from one to another and stay a while as though I were paying a visit. Some of them seemed quite beautiful to me, and I would try to imitate their gestures. But I always stayed longest with the mutilated ones, as though I were instinctively trying to comfort them. In the evening, on stage, as I performed I would remember one or other of them and I used to have such powerful feelings about how far away and lonely they were out in the peaceful countryside under the stars, that I could hardly speak. The crowd used to lose patience with those over-long pauses of mine . . . Sometimes, when I had to wait for the end of an actor's big speech, I would take up the position of one of the most familiar statues and stay motionless as if I too had been made of stone. I was already starting to shape myself . . .' She smiled. The grace of her melancholy surpassed the grace of the declining day.

'I really loved one statue that had lost the arms that used to support a basket of fruit on its head. But its hands were still there fastened to the basket, and I used to feel such pity. It stood on its pedestal in a field of flax; there was a stagnant little canal nearby, where the reflected sky continued the blue of the flowers. When I close my eyes, I can see its stone face and the sun changing colour as it shone through the stalks of flax as though through green glass . . . From that time onwards, in the most impassioned moments of my work on stage, images from remembered landscapes have always come to me, especially when I succeed in communicating a great shudder to the spectators through the pure power of silence . . .'

The tops of her cheekbones were slightly flushed, and as the setting sun shone around her, glinting off her sable coat and her goblet, so her animation seemed like an increase of light.

'What a spring that was! For the first time in my wandering life I saw a great river. It suddenly appeared, swollen and racing along between its wild banks in the midst of a plain that was blazing like stubble in the horizontal rays of the sun which was just scraping over its surface like a red wheel. It was then that I felt how much of the divine there is in a great river flowing over the earth. It was the Adige, coming down from Verona, from the city of Juliet . . .'

An ambiguous turmoil was taking place secretly within her as she recalled the poverty and the poetry of her adolescence. She was impelled to go on by a kind of fascination, and yet she did not understand how she had come to be admitting so much when she had wanted to talk to her beloved about another young life that was not past but present. What trickery of love had brought her by an unexpected tightening of her will, a resolute determination to confront painful reality, and a summoning of her lost energy to linger in memories of distant times and to conceal another very different image with a virginal image of herself?

'We entered Verona one evening in May, through the gates of the Palio. I was choked with anxiety. I was clutching to my breast the notebook in which I had copied out Juliet's lines in my own hand, and I kept saying to myself the words she says when she first enters: "How now! Who calls? I am here. What is your will?" My imagination had been fired by a strange coincidence: I was fourteen years old on that very day, the same age as Juliet! I could hear the gossip of the Nurse ringing in my ears, and gradually my fate was becoming intertwined with that of the girl from Verona. On every street corner I expected to see a procession coming towards me following a coffin covered with white roses. When I saw the Arche degli Scaligeri studded with iron nails, I shrieked at my mother: "It's Juliet's tomb!" – and I burst into tears; I wanted so desperately to die for love. "Oh you, too early seen unknown, and known too late!" '

The voice with which she repeated the immortal words pierced her lover's heart like an agonizing melody. She paused a moment, then said again: 'Too late!'

They were the same terrible words that her beloved himself had spoken and which she herself had repeated in the garden at night, where the hidden stars of jasmine gave off their strong scent and the fruits too smelled as strongly as in gardens out on the islands, when they were both about to yield to cruel desire. 'It is late, it is too late!' There on the soft grass, the woman who was no longer young was now confronted with an old image of herself, with her virginity trembling in the garments of Juliet and with her first dreams of love. She had reached the limit of her experience, and yet had she not kept that dream intact, over men and over time? Though what was it worth? She was recalling her earliest lost youth merely in order to tread it under foot as she led her lover towards the other woman who was alive and waiting. With her inimitable suffering smile, she said: 'I was Juliet.'

The air around them was so still that the smoke from the furnaces was lazily contaminating it. Gold seemed to tremble everywhere like quartz. The cloud over the bell-tower of the Angeli was turning purple at the edges. The water could not be seen, but its softness flowed over everything around.

'I was Juliet one Sunday in May, in the huge Arena, the ancient amphitheatre, in the open air, before an audience of working people who had breathed in the legend of love and death. No applause from the most enthusiastic public, no cheers, no triumphal success ever meant more to me than the fullness and the intoxication of my great hour then. Truly, when I heard Romeo say . . . "Ah, she doth teach the torches to burn bright!", truly my whole being turned to flame. I had bought with my savings a great bunch of roses in the Piazza delle Erbe, under the statue of Madonna Verona. Those roses were my only prop. I mingled them with my words and my gestures, with every pose I struck. I let one fall at Romeo's feet when we met, I plucked the petals from another and dropped them on his head from the balcony, and at the end I completely covered his body with them in the tomb. I was carried away by their scent, and by the light and the air. The words flowed with strange ease, almost spontaneously, as though I were delirious, and I could hear them through the constant drumming of my heartbeat. I could see the great bowl of the amphitheatre half in sunlight and half in shade, and in the lighted part there was a glitter as of thousands and thousands of eyes. The day was as still as it is today. Not one breath of wind stirred the folds of my gown or my hair, which shivered all down my bare neck. The sky was so far away, nevertheless it seemed to me that even the faintest words might echo through its distance like thunder, or that its blueness was becoming so dark that I would be imbued with it as though I were drowning in seawater. And I kept looking at the long grasses that were growing on the tops of the walls and it seemed that they were sending me some kind of encouragement of what I was saying and doing, and when I saw them sway in the first puff of breeze that was rising in the hills, I could feel my energy rising and the strength of my breathing. Oh, how I spoke of the lark and the nightingale! I had heard them both in the countryside thousands of times, I knew all their songs in woods, meadows and clouds, I could hear them wild and alive in my ears. Before I uttered it, every word seemed to go right through the heat of my blood. There was not a fibre in me that did not contribute to the harmony. Oh, grace, it was a state of grace! Every time I have ever managed to touch the heights in my work, I have felt again that indescribable sense of abandonment. I was Juliet. "It is day, it is day," I shrieked in my terror. The wind blew through my hair. I could feel the extraordinary silence in which my speech of lamentation fell. The crowd seemed to have vanished underground, they were sitting in silence on the curved benches that were now completely in the shade. At the top, the tips of the walls were still on fire. I spoke of the terror of day, but I did truly feel the "mask of night" on my face. Romeo had come down. We were dead

248

already, we had gone into the darkness. Do you remember? "Now you are there, you appear as a dead man within a sepulchre. Either my eyes deceive me, or you are very pale . . ." I was ice cold when I said such things. My eyes were searching for the gleam at the top of the wall, but it had gone out. The crowd was stirring in the Arena, demanding death; they no longer wanted to listen to the Mother or the Nurse or the Friar. The quiver of its impatience made my heart beat intolerably fast. The tragedy rushed to its conclusion. I remember a great sky white as pearl, and that almost sea-sound which quietened when I appeared, and the smell of resin in the torch and the roses covering me wilting from my body-heat, and a distant sound of bells that made the sky come nearer, and that sky which was gradually losing its light just as life was ebbing away from me, and a star, the first star which sparkled in my eyes with my tears . . . When I fell on Romeo's body, the crowd let out such a great roar that I was terrified. Someone lifted me up, and pulled me towards the roaring. They held the torch close to my tear-stained face; it was crackling very loudly, it smelled of resin and was red and black with flames and smoke. I shall never forget that either, like the star. I must have looked like death myself . . . And that, Stelio, was how I came to be presented to the people of Verona one May evening as the reincarnation of Juliet.' She paused again, and closed her eyes as though overcome by giddiness, but her aching lips smiled on at her beloved.

'And then? Well, we had to move on, to go somewhere else, to journey through space and to breathe in the wind . . . My mother followed me in silence. We crossed a bridge, we walked along the Adige, then we went over another bridge, down a narrow road, lost our way in dark alleys, found a square with a little church, and so we kept on moving. My mother would sometimes ask me: "Where are we going?" I wanted to find the Capuchin monastery where Juliet's tomb was hidden, since to my great grief they had not buried her in one of those lovely tombs with the splendid gates. But I did not want to say that, and I could not say it. I was as incapable of opening my mouth or of uttering a single word as of taking a star down from the sky. My voice had vanished with the last words of the dying girl. My lips had been sealed by a silence as necessary as death. And my whole body seemed only half alive, alternately on fire and freezing and then sometimes, I don't know, as though only my joints were burning hot and the rest of me was ice. "Where are we going?" my kind, worried mother asked again. And Juliet's last words answered within me! We were beside the water again, next to the Adige, about to cross a bridge. I think I started to run, because soon after that I felt my mother's arms around me and I stayed there, crushed against the parapet of the bridge, sobbing my heart out. "Let us throw ourselves into the river in this embrace!" I wanted to say, but I could not. The river was carrying the night with all its stars away in it, and I knew that the desire to disappear was not just in me . . . Oh, that blessed woman!'

She turned very pale, and her very soul could feel those encircling arms once again, the kiss of those lips, the tears of all that tenderness, the depth of that grief. But she glanced at her lover, and instantly a living wave of blood spread across her cheeks, rising to her forehead, as though stirred by her secret shame.

'Whatever I am saying? Why am I telling you all these things? One talks and talks without really knowing why!'

She lowered her eyes in her confusion. At the memory of that mysterious terror that had preceded the signs of puberty, the memory of her mother's love and concern, the original instinct of her sex reawakened in her sterile womb. Her female eagerness that rebelled against the heroic proposition of total abnegation was strangely disturbed, and ready to be deceived. From the very roots of her being there rose an unformed desire that she dared not contemplate. The possibility of divine compensation flashed across the sadness of her inevitable renunciation. She could feel her heart shake, but she was like someone who dares not look up at an unknown face for fear of reading there a sentence of life or death. She feared she might suddenly see that thing dissolve which was not a hope and yet seemed so like hope, springing from her body and her soul in such a new way. She resented the great light that illuminated the sky, and the place through which she was walking and the steps she was compelled to take, even her lover's presence. She thought of slow half-waking, the lingering slumber of dawn when some veiled will lightly guides delightful dreams. She wanted solitude, peace, a distant, closed room, the shade from heavy curtains. Suddenly, in a rush of anxiety that came from her impatience, as though with an effort of will she wanted to hold back a phantom that was about to disappear, she formed these words that rose to her lips but were not uttered: 'A child, by you!'

She turned to her lover and looked into his eyes, trembling all over. The secret thought floated in her gaze, beseeching and yet despairing. She seemed to be searching anxiously for some unrevealed sign from him, for some unknown aspect, almost for some other man. She said quietly: 'Stelio!'

Her voice was so changed that the young man started within himself, and turned towards her as if to help her.

'My darling, my darling!'

Surprised and fearful, he watched those great waves of life flowing through her, those extraordinary expressions, that alternating light and shadow, and he did not dare to speak, he did not dare to interrupt the hidden travails in which the powers of her great, unhappy soul were embroiled. He could feel the beauty and sadness of inexpressible things in her words, but confusedly, and whilst he was sure that some difficult good would result from such feverishness, he did not know to what end her love might be led by the desire to perfect itself or perish. His spirit was taut in miraculous expectation, and he could feel himself live in those forgotten places, on that humble grass, that silent road with such passion. He had never experienced in himself a more profound awareness of the incalculable strength of which the heart of man is possessed. And as he listened to his own heartbeat and sensed the violent throbbing of her heart, it seemed to him that he could hear the blows of a hammer on the hard anvil upon which all human destiny is forged.

'Tell me more!' he said. 'Let me come close to you again, my dearest. Since I first loved you, no other moment has ever been as important as this walk of ours today together.'

She was still walking ahead, looking down, wrapped in her illusion. 'Could it be?' She could feel her barrenness around her thighs like an iron band; she thought of the inexorable obstinacy of illness rooted in brute flesh. But the strength of her passion and her desire, reinforced by an idea of justice, appeared to be about to accomplish a miracle. And everything superstitious in her nature rose up to blind her lucidity and encourage her rising hope. 'Have I ever loved until now? Have I not been waiting all my life for this great love that will either save me or destroy me? From which of all those men who have only increased my sadness have I ever desired to have a child? It is only fair that new life should come from my body, since I have given my master the gift of myself. Have I not just given him my untouched virginal dream, Juliet's dream? Surely my whole life from that spring evening to that autumn night has been abolished?' She saw the universe transfigured by her illusion. Memories of her mother turned maternal love into something sublime. Those kind, firm eyes were opened again within her, and she prayed: 'Oh, tell me that I shall be what you were to me to a creature of my flesh and my soul! Tell me I shall, you who know!' The loneliness of her past seemed frightful to her. All she could see in the future was death or that one way of salvation. She thought she would have undergone anything to be worthy; she saw it as a grace to beseech, she was overwhelmed by a religious desire to sacrifice herself. The feverish throbbing of the far-off adolescence she had summoned up was renewed in her agitation, and she was walking as she did then, moved by an almost mystical power.

She was going towards the figure of Donatella Arvale, which was taking shape on the fiery horizon at the end of

252

a path that opened out on to the water. And her earlier, sudden question re-echoed within her: 'Do you often think about Donatella Arvale, Stelio?'

The short road led on to the Fondamenta degli Angeli, with the canal crowded with fishing boats, from which the great, calm, radiant lagoon could be seen.

She said: 'Such light! Just like that evening when I was still called Perdita, Stelio!' She was touching a note that she had already touched in an unfinished prelude. 'The last evening in September,' she added. 'Do you remember?'

Her heart was so exalted that occasionally she thought she had lost it, that she was no longer in control of the strength of her feelings, and that they might escape from her between one moment and the next, leaving her prey to the savage furies to whose sudden impulse she had yielded on more than one occasion. She wished that her voice did not shake when she spoke the name that had to be heard in the silence between herself and her lover.

'Do you remember the warship anchored near the Gardens? It fired a salute when the flag was lowered on the deck. Our gondola scraped its side as we passed it.' She paused for a moment. Her paleness was animated by inimitable life. 'And in its shadow you spoke Donatella's name.' She made a renewed effort, like a swimmer submerged by a new wave who shakes her head free of the spray. 'She began to be yours.'

She felt herself stiffening from head to foot, as though stabbed by a poisoned dart. She fixed her staring eyes on the sparkling water. 'She must be yours,' she said, with the harshness of necessity in her voice, as though with that second shock she were resisting the terrible things that were trying to struggle out of the depths of her passion.

Seized by violent anguish, unable to speak or interrupt those lightning apparitions of her tragic soul with empty words, Stelio Effrena stopped. He laid his hand on his companion's arm so that she would stop too.

'It is true, isn't it?' she asked, with almost tranquil gentleness, as though her tension had suddenly relaxed and her love had accepted the yoke that will had placed upon it. 'Tell me. I am not afraid to suffer. Let us sit down here. I am a little tired.'

They rested on a low wall, overlooking the water. The lagoon was so calm and still in the solstice that the shape of clouds and shores reflected in it seemed to take on an ideal quality as though imitated by art. Things near and distant, the red palace of the Da Mula on the canal and the leafy Forte di Tessara further off had the same distinctness when reflected. The black boats with lowered sails and nets hung from the masts seemed to carry in their keels a feeling of infinite rest that came from far horizons. No words of human suffering could affect any of those shapes, and they were all teaching the meaning of silence and promising peace to mankind in time.

'What can I say?' said the young man, in a choking voice, almost as though he were talking to himself rather than answering the woman, unable to overcome the agitation created in him by the certainty of his present love and awareness of his desire that was inexorable as fate. 'Perhaps what you have imagined is true; perhaps it is nothing but a thought in your mind. What I know for certain today is that I love you and I perceive everything that is noble in you. I know something else as well: I have a work to finish writing and a life to live according to Nature's plan. Even you should remember that! On that evening last September I talked to you at length about my life and about the impulse that drives it towards its destiny. You know I can give up nothing . . .' He was shaking, as though he were holding a sharpened weapon in his hands and could not help wounding the unarmed woman if he so much as moved.

'Nothing! Especially not your love which raises my strength and my hopes every day. But did you not yourself promise to give me more than love? Are you not able to give me that which love cannot give? Do you not want to be a constant source of inspiration for my life and for my work?'

She was sitting quite still, listening to him, without even

254

blinking an eyelid. She was like an invalid, deprived of voluntary movement, who assists at some horrific spectacle like a spirit inside a statue.

'It is true,' he went on, after an anxious pause, recovering his courage, overcoming his compassion, feeling that the fate of their free alliance depended on his sincerity at that moment, for he wanted it to be increased and not diminished. 'It is true. When I saw you coming down the staircase that night, in the midst of the crowd, accompanied by the woman who had been singing, I thought that some secret thought was guiding you not to come alone towards me . . .'

She felt a subtle thread of ice run through the roots of her hair, and her eyes dimmed although they were still quite dry. Her fingers around the stem of the goblet trembled, and the colours of the sky and the water tinted the glass that quivered in her aching hand.

'I believed that you yourself had chosen her . . . You had the appearance of one who knows and can foretell . . . I was disturbed by it.'

Through her agonizing torture, she could feel how sweet it would have been if he had lied to her. She wished he would either tell her lies or be silent. She measured the distance between herself and the canal, from the water that swallows and soothes.

'There was something hostile in her towards me . . . I found her obscure, impenetrable . . . Do you recall the way she disappeared? Her image faded, all that was left was the desire of her song. You who led her to me have more than once revived her image. You saw her shadow where it did not exist.'

She saw the face of death. No other thrust had pierced her more deeply, had wounded her more horribly. 'With my own hand! With my own hand!' she repeated. And she heard again the cry of her own damnation: 'She is waiting for you!' With every second that passed her knees gave way a little more, her worn-out body was on the point of obeying the wild desire that was impelling her towards the water. But one lucid point still remained that made her consider

255

that it was neither the time nor the place. The sandbanks uncovered by the low tide out in the lagoon were beginning to darken. Suddenly, her inner tempest seemed to disappear behind an apparition. She felt she had ceased to exist; she was amazed to see the glass sparkling in her hand; she lost all sense of her own body. Everything was happening in her imagination. Her name was Perdita. Dead Summer was lying in the depths of the lagoon. Words were merely words.

'Could I love her?'

One more breath and darkness would fall. As a candle flame bends in the wind and seems to be splitting away from the wick, though still attached to it by a thin blueish thread, almost a pale spark that will flare up again and burn brightly if the wind drops, so the unhappy woman's reason seemed about to be extinguished. An aura of madness stirred around her. Terror whitened and convulsed her face.

He was not looking at her, but staring fixedly at the stones. 'If I were to meet her again, would I want to turn her fate towards me?' He saw once more the youthful figure with her strong, curved back rising out of the forest of instruments, amid the alternating movement of the bows that seemed to be drawing their notes from the secret music within her.

'Possibly.'

He saw once more that hermetic, almost adamantine face, preoccupied by an intensely secret thought, and the way she knotted her brow and became hostile. 'But what does all this matter? And what do all the vicissitudes of life and all its necessities matter compared to the faith that binds us together? Could we ever be like meaner lovers who spend their days fighting and weeping and cursing each other?'

She gritted her teeth. A wild instinct to defend herself and attack him in a desperate struggle rushed over her. The flash of a murderous will exploded through her vacillating thoughts. 'No, you shall not have her!' The crudeness of her master seemed monstrous to her. She felt she was bleeding from his repeated, well-aimed blows, like the man she had once seen on a white road in a mining town. The ghastly scene returned to her memory: the man had been felled by a blow from a club, but he stood up again and tried to throw himself on his adversary, and then the club hit him again, blows were struck one after another by a cold, steady hand, resounding dully against a human head; he obstinately tried again to get up, clinging on to life, his face reduced to red pulp. The images of that dreadful memory mingled with the reality of her own torment in her mental incoherence. She leapt to her feet, terrified by the savage force that was invading her veins. The glass shattered in her convulsed hand, wounding her, and fell at her feet in splinters.

The man started, for he had been deceived by the woman's motionless silence. He looked at her and saw her, and he saw again, as he had on that evening when the logs were crackling, he saw the image of madness in her distorted face. He stammered painfully, but impatience was boiling beneath his dismay.

'Ah!' said the woman, overcoming her trembling with a bitterness that twisted her mouth. 'How strong I am! Next time, my darling, you should wound me less slowly, since I resist so feebly.' She realized that blood was dripping down her fingers. She wrapped her handkerchief around them, and it turned crimson. She looked at the scattered splinters of glass glistening on the ground. 'The goblet is broken! You must have praised it too highly! Shall we raise a mausoleum to it here?' She was so bitter, she was almost mocking, her lips set in a sharp, soundless laugh. He was silent, disappointed, full of resentment at seeing something as beautiful as the goblet destroyed when it had cost so much to make.

'We could follow Nero's example, since we have already followed Xerxes'!' She could feel the stridency of her sarcasm more acutely than her lover, and the falsity of her voice, the malignity of her smile which was more like a muscular spasm. But she could not regain control of her soul and she saw it slipping relentlessly away from her will, like sailors on a ship who have let go of the handle and stand helplessly watching the windlass spinning wildly

257

round unreeling the ropes and chains. She felt a sharp, irresistible desire to jeer, to despise, to tread everything under foot as though some evil demon had entered into her. Every trace of tenderness and kindness had vanished, along with every hope and every illusion. Dull hatred that lies in wait beneath the love of passionate women took control. She noticed the same shadow that passed over her own gaze in the man's expression.

'Am I annoying you? Would you like to go back to Venice on your own? Would you like to leave dead Summer here behind you? The water may be low, but there is still enough for one who has no intention of returning to the surface. Would you like me to show you? Could I be any more obliging?' She was saying all these insensate things with a hiss in her voice, and she had become almost livid, suddenly consumed by corrosive poison. And he remembered seeing that same mask on her face one far-off day of pleasure, fury and sadness. His heart contracted, then relaxed.

'Oh, forgive me if I have hurt you!' he said, trying to take her hand and calm her down with a tender gesture. 'But did we not start out together towards this point? Was it not you . . .'

She interrupted him, irritated by his gentleness, by his habitual caring. 'Hurt me? What does that matter? Don't feel pity for me! Don't shed any tears for a crippled hare with lovely eyes . . .' She was walking along the quay, beside the violet-coloured canal, in front of the doorways in which women were still sitting in the fading light with their baskets full of glass beads. Words broke between her teeth. Her tight lips changed into wild, convulsive laughter that sounded like heart-rending sobs. Her companion shuddered, and, appalled, he spoke to her under his breath, followed by the curious gaze of the onlookers.

'Do stop this, Foscarina, I beg you! Stop it! Don't behave like this! Please! We shall be at the landing stage very shortly, then home again . . . I shall tell you . . . you'll understand then . . . We are in public . . . Are you listening to me?' On one of the doorsteps she had seen a pregnant woman with a huge belly, swollen like a barrel, filling the space between the doorposts, and eating a piece of bread with a dreamy look in her eyes. 'Are you listening to me? Foscarina, please! Pull yourself together! Lean on me!'

He was afraid she might collapse in her dreadful convulsion, and held himself ready to support her. But she quickened her pace, unable to answer, choking back her laughter with her bandaged hand, and in her agony she thought she could feel the skin peeling off her face.

'What is the matter? What have you seen?'

The man would never forget the change in her eyes. They were staring sightlessly, deadly still, in spite of her relentless shuddering, as though the eyelids were missing, and yet they could still see. They could see something that was not there, they were filled with an unknown vision, occupied by a monstrous image that must be causing that laughter full of pain and madness.

'Would you like us to stop? Would you like a sip of water?'

They were back on the Glassmakers Quay, where the shops were closed, where their footsteps echoed, where the bursts of her ghastly hilarity seemed to continue as though echoing under a portico. How much time had passed since they had walked beside that dead canal? How much of their life had passed away in the meantime? What shadows were they leaving behind them?

She stepped into the gondola, huddled into her coat, more white-faced than on the road to Dolo, and tried to control her spasms by holding her jaws together with both hands. But the malignant laughter kept escaping, shattering the sleepy silence and breaking the rhythm of the oars. She pressed against her mouth even harder, as though she were trying to suffocate herself. Between the veil raised above her eyebrows and her blood-stained handkerchief her eyes were still wide and staring at the vastness of twilight.

The lagoon and the gathering darkness were swallowing all shapes and colours. All that interrupted that monotony of greyness were the rows of posts, like a procession of monks on a path of ashes. In the distance Venice was

259

smoking like the remains of a vast pillage. When the sound of the bells reached her, her soul remembered, her tears began to fall, her horror was conquered.

The woman let her hands fall, leaned slightly on her beloved's shoulder and recovered her voice to say, 'Forgive me!'

She humbled herself, she was ashamed of herself. From that day onwards every gesture she made silently begged him to forget and forgive her.

A new grace seemed then to be born in her. She became lighter, she spoke quietly, she moved about the room with delicacy, she wore softer colours, she let her lashes veil her lovely eyes that did not dare to look at her beloved. Fear of oppressing him, of irritating him, of becoming tedious to him gave wings to her instinct. Her alert sensitivity watched and listened at the inaccessible doorway to his thoughts. At certain times she reached the point of being able to feel another life throbbing beneath his heartbeat.

Her soul, intent on creating a new feeling that could overcome the violence of instinct, revealed in her face with amazing singularity the difficulty of her secret task. Never had her theatrical arts discovered such singular expressions, nor had such profound meanings come to light in the shadow of her features. One day, as her lover looked at her, he told her about the infinite power accumulated in the shadow made by the helmet over the face of Il Pensieroso.

'Michelangelo,' he said, 'concentrated all the efforts of human thought into a tiny dent in the marble. And just as a river fills up a hollowed palm, so the eternal mystery that surrounds us all filled up that little space which the Titanic sculptor chiselled into the marble taken from the mountains, and it has stayed there and become more powerful through the centuries. The only thing I have ever seen that equals and even surpasses that intensity, Fosca, is the changing pattern of shadow in your face.'

She reached out to the Creator, eager for poetry and

knowledge. For him, she was the ideal figure of a listening, understanding woman. The strong, wild waves of her hair reminded him of impatient wings around her lovely forehead. Words of beauty would instantly bring tears to her eyes, like drops that fall into a brimming vase and cause it to overflow.

She read him pages from the greatest poets. The august form of the Book seemed to be magnified by the way she held it, by her movements as she turned the pages, by the religious seriousness of her concentration, by the harmony of her lips that changed the signs imprinted in it into vocal figures. When she read Dante, she was as noble and severe as the Sibylls on the ceiling of the Sistine Chapel, who bear the weight of sacred volumes with all the heroism of their bodies stirred by the breath of prophecy. The lines of her pose, down to the slightest folds of her garment spoke the divine text together with her modulations.

When the last word had been read, she watched her beloved jump to his feet, trembling as though with fever, and pace about the room, agitated by the divinity, breathing heavily with the anxiety that the confused turmoil of his creative energy produced in him. Then she saw him come towards her, his eyes shining, transfigured by a sudden blessedness, illuminated by an inner flame, as though some supreme hope had unexpectedly appeared in him or some immortal truth been revealed to him. With a shudder that abolished from her blood the memory of every caress, she saw him come towards her and lean across her knees, overcome by the terrible upheaval of the world he was carrying within himself, by the shock that accompanies a hidden metamorphosis. She suffered and was glad, not knowing whether he was suffering or rejoicing; she felt pity and respect, feeling his sensuous body so profoundly gripped by the genesis of an idea. She stayed silent, waiting. She worshipped the unknown thoughts in the head that was resting on her knees. But she understood his great struggle better one day, after she had been reading, when he told her about the Exile.

'Just imagine, Fosca, if you can do so without being astounded, the wildness and the passion that measureless soul must have had to be able to mingle himself with the energy of the elements in order to create those worlds of his! Imagine Dante Alighieri, already filled with his visions, on the road into exile, a restless pilgrim, driven by anger and poverty from place to place, from shelter to shelter, across fields and mountains, over rivers and seas, in every season of the year, smothered by the sweetness of spring, stricken by the harshness of winter, always alert, always watchful, his eager eyes always open, troubled by the inner struggle that would result in his gigantic work. Imagine the fullness of his soul in the contrast between his everyday needs and the flaming apparitions that would suddenly come to meet him at the turning of a road, or on some river-bank, in the hollow of a rock, on the slope of a hillside, in the depths of a wood, or in a meadow where larks were singing. Through his senses, multifaceted life in its many forms poured into his mind and transfigured the abstract ideas crowded in there into living images. Everywhere he went, unexpected sources of poetry flowed from beneath his aching feet. The voices, forms and essence of the elements entered that secret toil and increased it with countless sounds, colours, movements and mysteries. Fire, Air, Water and Earth all contributed to the divine poem, they pervaded all its doctrine, they gave it warmth, they soothed it, watered it, covered it with flowers and leaves . . . Just open this Christian book and imagine the statue of a Greek god on the other side of it. Can't you see clouds and light, lightning and winds from heaven bursting out of both of them?'

Then she began to feel that her own life depended on that all-absorbing work, as though drop by drop her soul were entering into the character in his drama, and her features, her stance, her gestures, the tone of her voice were combining to create the figure of the heroine 'living beyond life'. She became the quarry of those voracious eyes which would stare at her sometimes with unbearable violence. Thus she encountered another way to be possessed. It seemed to her that she was being broken down into her essential elements in the fire of his intellect and then being reconstituted more perfectly through his heroic need to dominate destiny. Her secret task concorded with the power of his ideal being, and she did not want to be discordant from the image that was to be like her. Art fostered the appearance of the new feeling for which she had prepared.

Nevertheless, she suffered from that image which cast its shadow over the reality of her pain and sacrifice. A strange ambiguity arose from the resemblance between fiction and her real existence. Sometimes it seemed to her that her hidden efforts were preparing her for success in the theatre and not for the victory of her conscience over the darkness of instinct. Sometimes she felt she was losing her human sincerity and was back again in that state of excitement for the fictitious into which she used to enter whenever she was learning the role of the tragic character she was to represent. And so she learned another form of pain. She retreated into herself, contracted herself, under his enquiring gaze, as though to prevent him penetrating her and stealing away her secret life. She was afraid of the Watching Man. 'He will read the silent words in my soul that he will put in the mouth of his creation, and I shall only be able to speak them on a stage, behind a mask!' She felt her spontaneity being blocked. She experienced strange sensations of loss and discouragement, from which she sometimes emerged with a wild desire to break the spell, to become different, to detach herself from the image that was supposed to resemble her, to break the lines of beauty that held her in and were forcing her towards a predetermined sacrifice.

Was there not also in his tragedy a young virgin thirsting for love and yearning for joy, in whom another mind could recognize the living apparition of his lightest dream, the Victory he so often invoked who was to crown his life? And was there not also a loving woman who was no longer young, who had already put one foot in the shadows and who would only move when she took a small step towards oblivion? More than once she was tempted to fight against her resignation with some violent act.

Then she would shudder at the prospect of falling once again into horror, of being in the grip of that dreadful fury, of being in the jaws of the cunning beast that was still not dead but lived on, waiting and watching in the darkness for the moment to pounce. Like a penitent, she redoubled her struggle against danger, she inflicted yet harsher discipline upon herself, intensified her vigilance. In a kind of intoxication she would repeat the act of supreme devotion that had emerged from the depths of her unhappiness at the sight of the purifying flame: 'You must have everything. I shall be content to see you live, to see you happy. Do with me what you will.'

Then he loved her for the unexpected visions that she aroused in him, for the mysterious sense of inner happenings that she communicated to him with the changes in her appearance. He was astonished that the lines of a face, the movements of a human body could so touch and fertilize the mind. One day he shuddered and turned pale as he watched her step silently into the room, her face composed in such extraordinarily calm agony, as sure of herself as if she were coming from the depths of Wisdom, from the place where all human turmoil seems like a game played by the wind in the dust of an endless road.

'Ah, I have created you! I have created you!' he cried, deceived by the intensity of his hallucination, believing that he was seeing his heroine standing there on the threshold of the distant room full of treasure taken from the tombs of the Atrides. 'Stand still a moment! Don't even blink! Keep your eyes quite still, like two stones! You are blind. You can see things that other people cannot see. And no one can hide anything from you. And here, in this very room, the man you love has just revealed his love for the other woman who is still shocked by it. And they are both here; they have only just let go of each other's hands and their passion is still in the air. The room is full of treasure from the graves; all the wealth that adorned the corpses of

264

Agamemnon and Cassandra is laid out on two tables, and there are the chests full of coins and there are the urns filled with ashes. The window is open; it looks out over the plain of Argos and the distant mountains. It is sunset and all this terrible gold is gleaming in the shadows. Do you understand? You are there, on the threshold, your nurse had led you there. You are blind, but you know everything. Stand still a moment!' He was talking in the sudden heat of inspiration. The scene kept appearing and vanishing again, as though a torrent of poetry were rushing over it.

'What will you do? What will you say?'

The actress could feel ice in the roots of her hair. Her soul was pulsing like a force of sound to the very limits of her body. She was becoming blind, she was acquiring second sight. The cloud of tragedy descended and stayed above her head.

'What will you say? You will call them, you will call both of them by name in the silence where the great royal remains are lying.'

The actress could hear the sound of her own blood in her ears. Her voice would have to ring through thousands of years of silence, from distant times, it would have to reawaken ancient griefs of men and heroes.

'You take them by the hand, and you can feel their two lives reaching out to each other with all their strength, gazing at one another through your unmoving sorrow as though they were looking through crystal that is about to shatter.'

The blindness of immortal statues was in her eyes. She saw herself sculpted in the vast silence, and she felt the quivering of the silent crowd, as their heartstrings were gripped by the sublime power of her appearance. 'And then?'

The Creator bounded towards her as though he wanted to strike sparks from her. 'You must call Cassandra out of her sleep, you must feel her ashes coming alive in your hands, you must see her in your vision. Will you do that? You do understand! Your living soul must touch her ancient soul and blend with it and make one single soul and one single misfortune, so that the errors of time seem to be wiped out and the unifying process of life which is the whole basis of my work will be seen. Cassandra is in you and you are in her. Have you not loved, do you not love the daughter of Priam? Who, if they ever heard you, could ever forget the sound of your voice and the way your lips convulsed with that first cry of prophetic fury: "Oh, Earth! Oh, Apollo!" I can see you again on your chariot, deaf and dumb, like a newly captured wild beast. And among all those terrible cries there were also some infinitely sad, gentle whispers. The Old Men compared you to the "tawny nightingale". What words did you say when you were remembering your lovely river? What did you say? And what did you say when the Old Men asked you about the love of the god? Do you remember?'

The Tragic Actress was trembling, as though she were once again invaded by the breath of the god. She had become hot, pliant matter, subject to all the animations of the Poet.

'Do you remember?'

'Oh, wedding feast of Paris, death-bringing to your dear ones! Oh ye paternal waters of Scamandros! There, beside your banks, my youth was fed from you . . .'

'Oh, you divine creature, your voice does not let one forget Aeschylus' words! I remember. The soul of the crowd, gripped by the lament "in discordant sounds", relaxed and was blessed by that melodious sigh, and each one of us saw again your own distant past and our innocent happiness. You can say: "I was Cassandra!". When you speak about her, you are remembering a former life . . . Her golden mask is in your hands . . .'

He gripped her hands and, without realizing, he hurt her. She did not feel the pain. They were both intent on the sparks generated by their joint energies. The same electric vibration was racing along their heightened nerves.

'You are there, beside the remains of the enslaved princess, and you are touching her mask . . . What will you say?'

In the pause that followed they seemed to be waiting for a flash of lightning in order to see. The actress's eyes became fixed once more, the blindness filled them again. Her whole face turned to marble.

Instinctively, the Creator let her hands drop and they made the gesture of touching the sepulchral gold.

In a voice that created a tangible form, she said: 'How large her mouth is!'

He shivered with almost fearful suspense. 'Can you see her then?'

She stood there, her eyes fixed and unseeing. 'I can see her too. It is large. The ghastly task of divination has made it expand. She screamed and cursed and grieved endlessly. Just imagine her mouth in silence?'

Almost ecstatically, not changing her position, she said slowly: 'How astounding it is when she is silent!'

It was as though she were speaking words prompted by some mysterious power, whilst it seemed to the Poet as he listened that he himself had been about to suggest them to her. A profound shudder went through him, as though he were participating in a miracle. 'What about her eyes?' he asked, shaking. 'What colour do you think her eyes must have been?'

She did not answer. The marble lines of her face changed as though a slight wave of pain had passed over her. A furrow appeared between her eyebrows.

'Black, perhaps!' he added softly.

She spoke. 'No, they were not black, but they seemed to be because in her prophetic fury her pupils would become so dilated that her irises would disappear . . .'

She stopped, as though the breath had suddenly failed her. A light veil of sweat was spreading over her forehead. Deathly pale now, Stelio watched her in silence. The pause was filled with the rapid beating of his agitated heart.

'In between those fits,' the Far-sighted Woman went on, with painful slowness, 'when she dried the foam from her white lips, her eyes were soft and sad as twin violets.' She stopped again, exhausted, looking like someone who is dreaming and suffering in her dream. Her mouth was dry again. Her temples were wet. 'That is what they must have been like before they were closed forever.'

Then he was completely caught up in a whirlwind of lyricism; he breathed only the fiery ether of his poetry. The musical sentiment that inspired the drama was determined in the forms of the Prelude that he was composing. On that pivot of sound, the tragedy found its perfect balance between the two forces that would give it life, the power of the stage and the power of the orchestra. The appearance of ancient Destiny was marked by an extraordinarily powerful motif in the symphonic ocean.

'You will perform *Agamemnon*, *Antigone* and finally *The Triumph of Man* in the new theatre. My tragedy is a battleground: it celebrates the renewal of the drama with the defeat of the monstrous Will that dragged down the race of Labdacus and of Atreus. It opens with the groans of an ancient victim and ends with a "cry of light".'

Revitalized by melody, the Fates lived in visible form before him, just as they must have appeared to the savage eyes of Coephorae beside the mound of the butchered king.

'Do you remember,' he said to the actress, to bring that violent presence to her attention, 'do you remember the severed head of Marcus Crassus in that story of Plutarch's? I told myself that one day I would use it in the theatre. The Armenian Artavasdes was entertaining the king of the Parthians, Orodes, at a great banquet in his royal tent. Their captains were sitting around, drinking, and the spirit of Dionysus entered into those barbarians who were not insensible to the power of rhythm, because at the table there was a performer of tragedies called Jason Trallianus, who was reciting the tale of Agave in the *Bacchae* of Euripides. They had still not risen from the table when Sillaces came in carrying the head of Crassus and, after saluting the King, he flung it down bleeding into their midst. The Parthians raised a great shout of rejoicing. Then Jason gave the garments of

Pentheus to one of the Chorus, who snatched up the head and, filled with Dionysian fury, sang these lines:

> Let us bring home from the hills
> some freshly cut ivy,
> a worthy trophy . . .

'And the Chorus leaps with joy, and when Agave says she has caught the lion cub without a net, the Chorus asks who wounded it first, and Agave answers:

> Mine is the honour . . .

'But Pomaxoethres who had still not finished dining, leaped to his feet and tore the head from the frenzied actor, shouting that he was more worthy than Jason to say those words, since he was the man who killed the Roman. Can't you feel the portentous beauty of such a scene? The fierce face of Life suddenly flashing beside the Mask of wax and metal, the scent of human blood arousing the rhythmic frenzy of the Chorus, an arm that has inflicted death tearing the veils of tragic fiction. I feel so inspired by that unexpected ending to the expedition of Crassus. Well, the way the Fates suddenly burst into my modern tragedy is like the unexpected arrival of Sillaces at the Armenian's banquet. At the beginning, the virgin is standing on the balcony that looks out over the Cyclopic Walls and the Lion Gate, and she is holding a book of Greek tragedies, reading Antigone's lament. Fatal divinity is enclosed in that book, dominating images of suffering and crime. But those images are created by living words, and next to the pure homespun of the Theban martyr glows the insidious crimson spread by Clytemnestra, and the heroes of the *Oresteia* seem to come to life again as the man explores their tombs in the Agora. They move in shadow at the back of the stage like Ghosts, leaning forward to listen to what is being said, poisoning the air with their breathing. Suddenly shouts are heard announcing the great event. On comes the man who has uncovered the tombs and has looked upon the faces of the members of the House of Atreus, and he is still lit up by the marvels of death and gold! He is here, like one delirious. The souls are trembling. Will the legend rise again out of the earth to deceive men still? The souls watch and tremble. Suddenly, the power of the curse and destruction rushes over them, dragging them towards evil deeds. The desperate struggle begins. Tragedy is no longer wearing a fixed mask, it is showing its naked face. And the book which the unconscious virgin was reading can no longer be opened without a shudder, because the souls know that the distant horror has come back and is alive around them, and they are breathing and raving in its unavoidable reality. The Past is in action. The illusion of Time has been destroyed. There is only one Life.'

The enormity of his creation filled him with dismay. Sometimes he would look anxiously around himself, scrutinizing the horizon, examining voiceless things as though looking for help, as though waiting for some message. He would lie in silence for long periods, with his eyes closed, waiting.

'I have to, don't you see? I have to raise this huge mass at one stroke before the eyes of the audience. That is why my Prelude is so difficult. This first effort is the hardest part of my entire work. I have at the same time both to create my world out of nowhere and place their countless souls in the most suitable musical state ready to receive my unexpected revelations. The orchestra has to perform that miracle. "Art, like magic, is practical metaphysics," Daniele Glauro says, and he is right.'

Sometimes he would arrive at his lover's house panting and agitated as though tormented by one of the Furies. She never asked him anything, but her whole being became a comfort to the afflicted man.

'I was afraid,' he said one day, smiling at her. 'Afraid of being suffocated . . . You think me slightly mad, don't you? Do you remember that stormy evening when you came back from the Lido? You were so gentle, Fosca. Just before that, on the Rialto Bridge, I had found a Motif, I had translated the language of the Elements into music . . . Do you know what a Motif is? It is a tiny spring that is capable of giving birth to a great flock of rivers, a little spark that can produce an endless chain of fires, a productive nucleus of infinite power. In the world of ideal origins, there is no more powerful thing, no reproductive organ of greater virtuosity. And there is no greater delight for an active brain than watching how such energy develops . . . Delight, yes, and sometimes terror too, my darling!'

He laughed his ingenuous laugh. The manner with which he talked about such things was an indication of the extraordinary faculty that caused his spirit to resemble that of those primitive men who had transfigured Nature. There was a profound analogy between the spontaneous formation of myths and his instinctive need to animate everything that came into contact with his senses.

'A while ago I had started to develop the Motif from that stormy evening, which I want to call "Aeolus' Wine-skin". Here it is. Listen to this.' He went over to the keyboard and touched a few keys with one hand. 'That is all it is! But you can't imagine the creative potential of these few notes. A whole whirlwind of music has been generated by them and I have not yet managed to control it . . . I have been overwhelmed, suffocated, compelled to flee . . . !' He laughed again, but his soul was swaying like the sea. 'The wine-skin of Prince Aeolus, which the companions of Odysseus opened! Do you remember? The winds imprisoned in it burst out and forced the ship back again. Men trembled with fear.'

But his soul could find no rest, and nothing could free it from its burden. He kissed his beloved's hands and moved away from her; he wandered about the room, pausing in front of the harpsichord that Donatella had played while singing Claudio Monteverdi's melody. He crossed relentlessly over to the window and saw the leafless garden, the lovely, solitary clouds, the sacred towers. His aspirations went out to the musical being, to the woman who should sing the hymns at the height of the tragic symphonies.

271

In a low, clear voice, the woman said: 'If only Donatella were here with us now!'

He turned, took a few steps towards her and stared at her fixedly without saying a word. She smiled her slight, concealing smile, seeing him at once so close and yet so far away. She felt that in that moment he did not love anyone, not her, not Donatella, and that he considered both of them to be simple instruments of his art, energies to be used, 'bows to be drawn'. He was burning in his own poetry, and she was there with her poor, wounded heart, with her secret torment, with her silent pleading, thinking of nothing except the preparation of her sacrifice, ready to go beyond love and beyond life, like the heroine of his future drama.

'Oh, what could bring you closer to me, throw you upon my faithful heart, make you tremble with another kind of passion?' she thought, as she saw him so distant, lost in his dreaming. 'Some great sorrow, perhaps, some sudden blow, a cruel disappointment, some irreparable harm.'

The line of Gaspara Stampa's that he had praised came back into her mind:

To live on fire and not to feel the pain!

She saw again his sudden pallor when she had stopped on the path between the walls and had declared her first titles of nobility in the struggle to survive. 'If only one day you could truly feel the worth of a devotion such as mine and servitude such as this I am offering you! If only some day you really needed me and could restore your lost faith through me and find new energy in me when you had none!'

She was reduced to invoking sorrow in order to assist her hopes, and whilst she kept saying 'if only . . .' to herself, the awareness of time preoccupied her again, an awareness of time passing, of the flame that was burning down, of her ageing body, of all the many things that decay and perish. Henceforth every day would leave its mark on her face, discolouring her lips, thinning her hair; henceforth every day would be in the service of old age, would hasten the destruction of her wretched flesh. 'What then?'

She realized again that desire, unconquerable desire, was the forger of all her illusions and all those hopes that seemed to help her to accomplish 'that which love cannot do . . .' She could see that all her attempts to root it out would be in vain, and, discouraged, she saw the artifice that her will had imposed upon her soul disappear in an instant. With secret shame, she acknowledged then how poorly she resembled the actress who can lay aside her character when she leaves the stage. In speaking those words which had broken the silence, expressing false regret in tones of sincerity, had she not been like a woman acting out a part? But she had suffered, she had wrung her heart, she had extracted that sweetness from the greatest bitterness in her blood. 'What then?'

She recognized that the torturing constraint of those days had not served to create even the slightest trace in her of the new sentiment by which their love was to be made sublime. She was like those gardeners who with their shears give an artificial shape to tenacious bushes, which nevertheless still keep their strong trunks and all their roots intact so as to blossom out wildly and rapidly through the design, unless the work of the metal shears on their branches is maintained assiduously. All her efforts were therefore not only painful, but useless, because all they had was some outward efficacy, while the base remained unchanged; in fact the pain was even more intense through trying to hold it back. Was her secret task then to be reduced to continual dissembling? Was it worthwhile living for this?

She could not and did not want to go on living except on condition that she would eventually find her own harmony. But the experience of those days had done nothing except make the discord between her goodness and her desire seem even greater, nothing except to intensify her anxiety and her sadness or make her lose herself completely in the whirl of the creative mind that was pulling her towards him to shape her like some pliable substance. And she was so far

273

away from the harmony she longed for, that at a certain point she had felt her spontaneity ceasing and her sincerity becoming clouded, and a dull ferment of revolt began to swell in her heart and the fearful aura of madness began to return.

Was she not the same woman who, sitting on the cushions of her divan one October evening, gnawed at by poison, had said to her lover: 'Must I die?' Was she not the same woman who had leaped up in rage and flung herself at him as though to devour him?

If the young man's turgid desire had caused her to suffer so cruelly then, was she not suffering even more cruelly now, realizing that his passion had calmed and that her lover had become more reserved, sometimes even impatient of her slightest caress? She was ashamed at her regret, seeing him possessed by his ideals and concentrating intently all his energies on the effort taking place in his mind. But a dark rancour would come over her on certain evenings when he took his leave, and blind suspicions tormented her sleepless soul at night.

She gave in to that nocturnal evil. Breathing heavily, feverish in the darkness of a gondola cabin, she drifted down the canals. She hesitated before giving the oarsman the name of a distant canal; she wanted to go back; she sobbed choking on her wounds; she felt her agony becoming unbearable; she leaned over towards the lethal fascination of the water; she spoke with death; then she gave in to her misery. She spied on her lover's house. She stayed long hours in fearful, pointless waiting.

That was the worst pain of all, in that profoundly sad Rio della Panada which ends in a bridge under which the funeral island of San Michele can be seen out in the open lagoon. The old Gothic palace on the corner of San Canciano was like a suspended ruin that might all at once crash down upon her and bury her alive. Black boats were rotting beside corroded walls uncovered by the low tide, giving off the stench of decay. And once at dawn she heard the little birds awakening in the garden of the Poor Clares.

'To go away!' The need to do that came upon her with sudden urgency. She had already said to her lover one memorable day: 'Now I feel that there is only one thing for me to do: to go away, disappear, leave you free with your destiny. This I can do, which love cannot.' Now she could no longer delay. She had to break through every hesitation, she had to come out at last from that kind of fatal paralysis of events in which she had for so long wavered between life and death, as though she had fallen into the silent, sluggish waters out there by the funereal island and was struggling desperately, feeling the soft mud giving way beneath her feet, thinking she was about to be swallowed up and always seeing before her eyes the level stretch of that great calm and never drowning.

Nothing had in fact happened, nothing was happening. Since that October dawn their outward life had continued unchanged. No word had been uttered that might establish an end, might hint at an interruption. It almost seemed as though the delightful promise of the visit to the Euganean Hills were about to be kept, as the flowering of the peach trees drew nearer! Yet nevertheless she felt at that point the absolute impossibility of continuing to live like that, as she was living, close to her beloved. It was a definite, undeniable feeling, like the sensation of someone who finds himself in a burning house or who stands on a mountainside at the edge of an abyss, or someone in the desert who has drunk the last drop of water from his bottle. There was in her something fully realized, like a tree that has born all its fruit, like a field that has been harvested, like a river that has reached the sea. Her inner need was like the needs of natural events, like tides, seasons, heavenly transformations. She accepted it, without question.

Her courage returned, her soul grew stronger, her energies reawakened, her manly qualities of leadership rose up in her. In a short time, she established her itinerary, called together her company, fixed their departure date. 'You will go and work over there, among the Barbarians on the other side of the ocean,' she told herself harshly. 'You will go on wandering from city to city, from hotel to hotel, from theatre to theatre, and every night you will make the crowds who pay to see you roar their approval. You will earn a great deal of money. You will come back laden with money and with wisdom, unless you happen to be crushed beneath a wheel at a crossroads, one foggy day . . .'

'Who knows!' she reflected. 'Who gave you the order to leave? Someone who is inside you, deep inside you, who can see what you cannot see, like the blind woman in his tragedy. Who knows if maybe over there, beside one of those great placid rivers, your soul may not find its harmony and your lips may not learn the smile they have so often tried in vain to shape! Perhaps you will find that smile at the very moment that you find a white hair when you look in your mirror. Go in peace!'

She was preparing her *viaticum*.

From time to time a premature breath of the coming season seemed to be passing through the February sky.

'Can you feel the spring?' said Stelio to his lover, and his nostrils quivered.

She leaned back slightly, feeling that her heart was breaking. She lifted her face to a sky strewn with scattered vapours like drifting feathers. The hoarse wail of a siren lingered round the pale estuary, gradually becoming as soft as the sound of a flute. It seemed to the woman that something was escaping from her inmost heart and fading away into the distance with that sound, like grief that is gradually changing into memory.

She replied: 'It has arrived at Tre Porti.'

They were wandering at random across the lagoon again, over those waters which were as familiar to their dreams as cloth is to a weaver.

'Did you say Tre Porti?' cried the young man joyously, as though some spirit were awakening in him. 'When the moon was setting, close to the flat beach, that is where the sailors took the Breeze prisoner and carried it in chains to

276

Dardi Seguso . . . I will tell you the story of the Archorgan some day.'

She smiled at the mysterious way in which he had referred to what the sailors had done. 'What story is that?' she asked, yielding to the enchantment. 'And how does Seguso come into it? Do you mean the master glassmaker?'

'Yes, but an ancient one, who knew Latin and Greek, music and architecture, who had been admitted to the Accademia dei Pellegrini whose gardens are on Murano, a man who was frequently invited to dine with Vecellio in his country house at Biri, and who was the friend of Bernardo Cappello, Iacopo Zane and other noble Petrarchans . . . It was in Caterina Zeno's house that he saw the famous organ which had been made for Mattias Corvinus, King of the Hungarians, and his wonderful idea came to him during a dispute with Agostino Amadi, the man who had managed to acquire a genuine Greek lyre in his collection of musical instruments, a great heptachord from Lesbos, ornamented with gold and ivory . . . Oh, just imagine that relic of the school of Mitylene brought here to Venice by a galley that sailed through the waters of Santa Maura, dragging the dead body of Sappho like a bundle of dry grass! But that is another story.'

Once again the nomadic woman seemed to recover her youth to smile with the surprise of a young girl who is being shown a picture book. How many marvellous stories, how many delightful fantasies had the Poet found for her out on the water in the slowness of the hour! How many enchantments had he created for her to the rhythm of the oars, with those words of his that could make everything visible! How many times had she sat beside him in the slender boat, delighting in that kind of clear-thinking slumber in which all troubles ceased and nothing but poetic visions hovered around her!

'Tell me!' she begged, and would have liked to add: 'For this will be the last time,' but she did not, because she was concealing her resolution from her beloved.

He laughed. 'You are as greedy for stories as Sofia is!'

277

At the sound of that name, she felt her heart breaking as it had done at the mention of spring, and the cruelty of her fate swept through her soul and her whole being reached out to the good things she had lost.

'Look,' he said, pointing to the silent surface of the lagoon, rippling here and there as the breeze blew over it, 'aren't those infinite lines of silence trying to become music?'

In the calm of the afternoon the islands were resting as lightly on the pale lagoon as the softest clouds in the sky. The long thin strips of the Lido and the mainland were as vain as the blackish scraps that float in patches on kindly waves. In the distance, Torcello, Burano, Mazzorbo, San Francesco del Deserto did not seem like real landing-places, but rather like submerged lands, the summits of which were protruding through the skin of the water like the masts of sunken vessels. Traces of mankind were indeed faint in that lonely flatness, like letters corroded by time in ancient headstones.

'Well, then, when the master glassmaker was in the house of the Zenos and heard the famous organ of Mattias Corvinus being praised, he cried in his wonderful Venetian dialect: "By the body of Bacchus! Wait and see what kind of an organ I shall make with my blow-tube, my singing fluid Muse! I shall make the Lord of all organs! *Dant sonitum glaucae per stagna loquacia cannae . . .** I want the waters of the lagoon to give me their voice, and the posts and the stones and all things to sing as well! *Multisonum silentium . . .*** Body of Diana, just wait and see!" All those present laughed, except Giulia da Ponte because she had blackened teeth. And then Sansovino gave a dissertation on hydraulic organs. But before he took his leave, the boastful man invited the company to hear his new music on the day of the Sensa, and promised that the Doge in his galley would come to a halt in the middle of the lagoon to listen too. That night word spread through Venice that Dardi Seguso

* The sea-green reeds raise their voice over the motionless waters.
** A silence with many voices!

278

had lost his reason, and the Council, who treated their glassmakers with the utmost consideration, sent a messenger to Murano for news. The messenger found the craftsman with his courtesan, Perdilanza del Mido, who was anxiously caressing him in some dismay, since she thought he was raving. The master looked at him with flaming eyes, then burst into mighty laughter which gave more assurance of his sanity than any words could have done, and calmly ordered him to tell the Council that Venice was to have another marvel by the day of the Sensa, to rank with St Mark's, the Canalazzo and the Doge's Palace. Next day he asked permission to be granted one of the five little islands that lie around Murano like moons around a planet, and which have long since disappeared or turned into sandbanks. Having explored the waters around Temodia, Trencore, Galbaia, Mortesina and La Folega, he chose Temodia as one might chose a bride. And Perdilanza del Mido began to suffer greatly . . . Look, Fosca! Perhaps we are sailing over the memory of Temodia now! The organ pipes are buried in the mud, but they cannot decay. There were seven thousand of them. We are sailing over the ruins of a forest of musical glass. How delicate the seeweed is here!'

He leaned out over the beautiful water, and she did the same on the other side. The ribbons, feathers, velvet and other dainty materials that through serious, skilful workmanship had gone into the making of Foscarina's hat, her eyes and the seablue shadows around them, the very smile with which she made her fading beauty seem so enchantingly graceful, the bunch of daffodils that was fixed in the prow where the lantern hung, the wide-ranging imaginings of the poet, the dream-like names of the vanished islands, the blue that came and went in the grey mist, the faint cries from a flock of invisible birds that came and went again, all those most delicate things were conquered by the play of those fleeting appearances, by the colours of that salt hair which lived in the movements of the tide, twisting and turning as though occasionally caressed by it. Green as the corn that springs out of the furrow, tawny as a leaf dying

279

on a young oak tree, green and tawny in the endless variations of plant-life that comes to life and dies, they created the image of an ambiguous season that belongs to the lagoon in its bed. The day was growing lighter and its clarity did not diminish but rather increased its powers of mystery, so that in its softness there lingered a memory of their obedience to the changes of the moon.

'But why did Perdilanza suffer?' asked the woman, still leaning out over the delightful waters.

'Because her name had been overtaken by the name of Temodia in her lover's mouth, which he pronounced with such passion, and because the island was the one place where she was not allowed to follow him. He had built a new workshop there, and he stayed there most of the day and almost every night, assisted by his workmen, who were bound to him by swearing a secret oath before the altar. The Council gave orders that the master should have everything he required for his terrifying task, and condemned him to be beheaded if the result should be inferior to his pride. So then Dardi wore a scarlet thread around his bare neck.'

Foscarina straightened herself as though in a dream, and settled herself more comfortably. She was losing herself as in a labyrinth between the things she could see at the bottom of the lagoon and things in his story, and she began to feel the same anxiety, confusing reality with fantasy in her mind. He seemed to be talking about himself in those strange images, like the time he had told her the myth of the pomegranate on that last evening in September, and the name of the woman in his story actually began with the first two syllables of the name that he used to call her then! 'Was he trying to signify something under the veil of his story! What could it be? And why, so close to the place where she had been overwhelmed with that ghastly laughter, did he enjoy recalling a fantasy that seemed to be inspired by the memory of the broken goblet?'

The spell was broken, oblivion vanished. Trying to understand, she herself fashioned an instrument of torture with

the material of dream. She appeared to have forgotten that
her beloved was unaware of her coming farewell. She looked
at him, and saw in his face that intellectual happiness which
always shone in him like something sharp and hard as ada-
mant. Instinctively, she said to herself: 'I am leaving. Do
not hurt me.'

'Zorzi, what's that white thing floating there beside the
wall?' he asked the oarsman in the stern.

They were sailing close to Murano. The garden walls were
appearing, and the tops of the laurel trees. The black smoke
of the furnaces was floating like mourning clothes hanging
in the silvery air.

Then, with sudden horror, the actress had a vision of the
distant port where the great, throbbing ship was waiting for
her. She saw once more the perpetual cloud over the brutal
city of thousands and thousands of streets, the mountains
of coal, the forests of masts, the monstrous arms. She could
hear once more the thud of sledge-hammers, the creaking
of winches, the pounding of machines, the great groaning
of iron in the blazing darkness.

'It's a dead dog,' said the oarsman. A swollen, yellowish
corpse was floating near the red brick wall, in the cracks of
which grasses and flowers were trembling, children of decay
and of the wind.

'Row!' cried Stelio, filled with horror.

The woman closed her eyes. The boat sped along with
the force of the oars, gliding over the milky water. The sky
was turning white. A similar splendour was spreading across
the estuary. Sailors' voices could be heard from a barge
laden with vegetables. A twittering of sparrows was coming
from San Giacomo di Palude. A siren wailed in the distance.

'And so the man with his scarlet thread . . .' said Foscarina, eager to hear what followed, for she wanted to understand.

'He felt his head shake on his shoulders more than once!'
Stelio continued, laughing. 'He had to blow tubes that were
as thick as tree-trunks, and do that with the skill of a living
mouth, not with the power of a bellows, and he had to do

it in one breath, with no pauses! Just imagine! The lungs of a cyclops would not have been adequate! Oh, some day I shall write about the passion of such a life, balanced between the executioner's axe and the need to produce a miracle, in communion with the elements! He had Fire, Earth and Water; what he needed was Air, the movement of Air! Meanwhile the Council of Ten sent a red-haired man to him every morning to bid him good-day; you know, the red-haired man with the hood down over his eyes who is embracing the column in the *Adoration of the Magi* by Boniface the Younger. After endless attempts, Dardi had a brilliant idea. One day he was talking to Priscian beneath the laurel trees, about the home of Aeolus and his twelve sons and the arrival of the Laertian on the island of the west. He reread Homer, Virgil and Ovid in Aldo's beautiful type-face. Then he went to find a wizard who was renowned for being able to cast a spell on the winds in favour of long journeys by sea. 'What I'd like is a little wind that's neither too strong nor too feeble, a gentle wind that I could handle as I please, a little wind that would help me blow some glass that I have in my head . . . *Lenius aspirans aura secunda venit* . . .* Know what I mean, mate?' The story-teller burst out laughing loudly, because he could see the scene in all its detail in a house in the Calle de la Testa at San Zenepolo, where the wizard lived with his daughter, the renowned courtesan Cornelia Sciavonetta (at the house of her father, two crowns).

'What's up with him? Is he daft?' thought the two oarsmen, hearing him speak in a mixture of dialect and unknown words. Foscarina tried to second his gaiety, but his youthful laughter hurt her as it had done when she was caught in the maze.

'It's a long story,' he went on. 'I shall do something with it some day. I'm keeping it for a time when I am idle . . . Just imagine! The wizard casts his spell. Every night Dardi sends sailors to the Tre Porti to try and catch the Breeze.

* A breath of wind that's softer than a sigh!

Finally, one night just before dawn, as the moon is setting, they find it sleeping on a sandbank surrounded by a flock of tired swallows that it has brought with it . . . It is there, resting, breathing as lightly as a child in the salty air, almost covered by countless fishes' tails. The tide lets it sleep; the black and white travellers are fluttering around it, exhausted by their long flight . . .'

'How lovely!' exclaimed the woman at the delightful image. 'Where did you see that?'

'This is where the charm of the story begins. They capture it, bind it with willows, take it on board and sail to Temodia. The ship is invaded by swallows who refuse to abandon the leader of their flight . . .' Stelio paused, because the details of the story were flooding into his imagination in such numbers that he did not know how to choose between them. His ears caught the sound of singing in the air coming from San Francesco del Deserto. He could see the slightly tilted bell-tower of Burano and, beyond the island of lace, the bell-towers of Torcello in their isolated magnificence.

'And then?' urged his companion.

'I can't tell you anything else, Fosca. I know too much . . . Imagine that Dardi falls in love with his captive! . . . His name is Ornitio, because he is the leader of the migrating birds. Swallows always twitter around Temodia, their nests are hanging from the hewn fir trees and the posts of the fences that surround his work. Sometimes a wing is burned in the furnace when Ornitio blows into the iron, making a light, luminous column with the incandescent paste. And what trouble he went through before taming it and teaching it its work! The Master of the Fire began to speak Latin and recite some lines of Virgil to him, believing he was understood. But blue-haired Ornitio spoke Greek, naturally, with a slightly sibyllant accent . . . He knew two of Sappho's odes by heart that none of the Humanists knew, which he brought one spring day from Mitylene to Chios, and as he breathed into the unequal tubes he recalled the pipes of Pan . . . One day, I shall tell you about all these things . . .'

'What did he live on?'

283

'Pollen and salt.'

'What was he searching for?'

'Nothing. He was glad enough to breathe the pollen and the salt in the air around him.'

'Didn't he try to escape?'

'All the time. But Dardi took infinite precautions, like the lover that he truly was.'

'Did Ornitio love him too?'

'Yes, he began to love him, especially because he loved that scarlet thread which the master always wore around his bare neck.'

'What about Perdilanza?'

'She grew pale from neglect and grief. I'll tell you one day . . . One summer I shall go to the beach at Palestrina to compose this story for you in the golden sands.'

'How does it end?'

'The miracle happened. The Archorgan was built on Temodia, with its seven thousand glass pipes, like one of those frozen forests that Ornitio – who always exaggerated his travels – said he had seen in the land of the Hyperboreans. The day of the Sensa arrived. The Most Serene Doge flanked by the Patriarch and the Archbishop of Spalatro sailed across the harbour of St Mark in their galley. So great was the splendour that Ornitio thought it was Cronos returning in triumph. The weir was opened around Temodia, and in the eternal silence of the lagoon the gigantic instrument touched by the fingers of the new musician spread such a great wave of harmony that it reached the mainland and drifted down the Adriatic Sea. The galley stopped, for its forty oars were lowered at its sides like exhausted wings, abandoned in the rowlocks by the terrified crew. Then suddenly, the wave broke, it splintered into a mass of discordant noise, faded away and ceased. Dardi suddenly felt the instrument growing dumb beneath his hands, as though his soul were failing him, as though a strange power were devastating the miraculous instrument from within. What had happened? All he could hear was a great scream of mockery resounding through the silenced pipes, and the

284

noise of gunfire and the cries of the mob. A small boat left the galley, bearing the red-headed man with his axe and his block. The blow aimed at the scarlet thread and did not miss. The head fell, and was thrown into the water where it floated like the head of Orpheus . . .'

'What had happened?'

'Perdilanza had thrown herself into the weir! The water had dragged her down into the depths of the organ. Her body and all her famous hair had drifted into the great, delicate machinery, and had blocked the very heart of the music . . .'

'What about Ornitio?'

'Ornitio plucked the bleeding head from the water and flew away with it towards the sea. The swallows sensed his flight and followed him. Within seconds they had formed a black and white cloud behind the fugitive. Throughout Venice and the islands, all the nests were abandoned as a result of that intemperate flight. There were no flights in summer. In September, there were none of the farewells that used to bring such sadness and such joy . . .'

'What happened to Dardi's head?'

'No one knows where it went,' the story-teller concluded, laughing. Once again he listened to the aerial song in which he was beginning to distinguish a rhythm. 'Do you hear that?' he asked. He signalled to the oarsmen to stop. The oars were lifted on to the rowlocks. The silence was so intense that the distant song could be heard as sharply as the drip from nearby palings.

'It's the woodlarks,' said Zorzi quietly. 'Poor things, they're still singing the praises of Saint Francis.'

'Row!'

The gondola slid over the milky quiet.

'Fosca, would you like us to go out as far as San Francesco?'

The woman's head was bent in thought. 'Perhaps there is a hidden meaning in your story,' she said, after a pause. 'Perhaps I understand.'

'Good heavens, yes, maybe there is some resemblance between my daring and that of the man from Murano! I think perhaps I should wear a scarlet thread around my neck too, as a warning.'

'You will have your fine destiny. I am not afraid for you.'

He stopped laughing. 'Yes, my darling, I have to win. And you will help me do it. Every morning I too have a visit from something that threatens me – the expectations of those who love me and those who hate me, my friends and my enemies. Expectation should wear the clothes of an executioner, because there is nothing so pitiless on earth.'

'But that is the measure of your power!'

He felt the vulture's beak pluck at his liver. Instinctively he stood up, seized by blind impatience that made the slowness of their pace infuriating.

Why was he so idle? He should be experimenting every hour, every moment, fighting, growing stronger, asserting himself against the forces that destroy, diminish, spoil and contaminate. Every hour, every minute he should keep his eye trained on the target, and focus all his energies on that goal, ceaselessly, relentlessly. His need for glory always seemed to awaken the instinct of war in him, the fury of combat and revenge.

'Do you know Heraclitus' famous saying? "The bow is called Bios and its task is death." That phrase excites our minds even before communicating its precise meaning. I kept hearing it in my head all the time sitting at your dinner-table, that night last autumn on the Epiphany of Fire. I experienced an hour of truly Dionysian life, an hour of delirium that was restrained, but was still as terrible as though I were containing within myself the blazing mountain where the Thyades howled and burst their chains. Every so often I really did seem to be hearing shouts and songs and cries from some distant massacre. I was amazed that I could sit so still, and my awareness of the stillness of my own body increased my profound frenzy. All I could see was your image, and you had suddenly become amazingly beautiful, and the power of all your souls was in you, and behind it I could see other countries and crowds of people. If only I could tell you how I perceived you then! In

286

the confusion, while those marvellous images were passing through my mind accompanied by waves of music, I was talking to you as though we were in battle, I called out to you and perhaps you heard me, not only for love but also for glory, not for one thirst, but for our twin thirsts, and I did not know which was the most desperate. And then I saw the face of my play, just as I saw your face. I saw it! Do you realize! With incredible speed, the words, the songs, the movements, the music of my work took shape and lived so totally, that if I could only have managed to turn one bit of it into the forms that I want to express, I should truly have been able to set the whole world on fire.'

He was controlling his voice as he spoke, and the smothered impulse of his words was strangely reflected in the still water, in that white glare that prolonged the regular cadence of the oars.

'To express myself! That was what I had to do! Even the most lofty visions are worthless if they cannot be demonstrated and condensed into living forms. I have everything to create. I am not pouring my essence into inherited moulds. My work is completely new. I can't and won't obey anything except my own instinct and the genius of my race. And yet, just as Dardi saw the famous organ in the house of the Zenos, so I have another work before my spirit, created by an extraordinary being, a giant amongst men.'

The image of the creative barbarian came back to him, the blue eyes blazing under his great forehead, his lips sealed tightly over the strong chin armed with sensuality, pride and disdain. Then he saw the white hair again, blown by the rough wind against his old neck, under the wide brim of his felt hat, and the almost livid ear with its swollen lobe. He saw once more the motionless body laid across the knees of the woman with the snow-white face, and the slight tremor in one dangling foot. He thought once more of his own ineffable shudder of fear and joy when he had felt the sacred heart beating again against his hand.

'No, I should have said round my spirit, not before it. Sometimes it is like a storm-tossed ocean that threatens to

287

overwhelm me and swallow me up. My Temodia is a granite rock out at sea, and I am like a craftsman who is building a perfect Doric temple on it amid the violence of the waves, against which he has to defend the order of his columns, while his spirit is ceaselessly straining through all that noise to keep hearing the intimate rhythm that is the only thing which will regulate the gaps between his lines and his spaces. In this sense too, my tragedy is a battle.'

He saw once more the patrician palace as it had appeared to him in that early October dawn, with its eagles and its horses, its amphorae and its roses, closed and silent as a great tomb, while above it the breath of dawn was turning the sky to flame. 'That was the dawn,' he added, 'after our delirious night, and as I sailed down the canal, alongside a garden wall, I plucked some purple flowers from gaps in the brickwork, and I had the gondola stop at Palazzo Vendramin, so that I could throw them before his door. It was too slight an offering, and I thought of laurel and myrtle and cypress. But that spontaneous gesture served as an expression of my gratitude to the Man who made my spirit feel the necessity of being heroic in its struggle for freedom and creativity.' With a burst of sudden laughter, he turned to the oarsman in the stern. 'Zorzi, do you remember our race that morning to reach the fishing boat?'

'I certainly do, sir! What a row that was! My arms are still aching from it! And that rascally hunger of yours, sir, where did you put it all? Whenever I see the captain of that boat, he always asks me about the stranger who ate such a load of bread, along with a basket of figs and grapes . . . He says he'll never forget that day, because he had the best catch of his life! He caught mackerel, the like of which he'd never seen before . . .' The oarsman went on chattering until he realized that his master was no longer listening to him, and he would be better advised to hold his tongue, maybe even to hold his breath.

'Do you hear that singing?' said Stelio to his beloved, gently taking her hand, because it distressed him to have revived a memory that caused her pain.

She looked up, and said: 'Where is it? Is it in heaven, or on earth?' An infinite melody was spreading through the peaceful whiteness.

She said: 'How it rises!' She felt a tremor in her lover's hand.

'When Alexander enters the luminous room where the Virgin has been reading Antigone's lament,' he said, bringing into his consciousness a sign of the hidden labour that had been going on in the secret depths of his mind, 'he tells her how he has ridden over the plain of Argos, and has crossed the Inachus, the river with the dried-up willows. The countryside was covered with tiny wild flowers, all dying, and the sky was filled with larks singing . . . Thousands of larks, countless numbers of them . . . He tells her how one of them suddenly fell under his horse's hooves, heavy as any stone, and lay there dumbstruck by its own wild music, because it had sung with too much joyfulness. He had picked it up. "Here it is!" Then you reach out your hand, you take it and you whisper: "Oh, it is still warm." As you speak, the Virgin trembles. You can feel her trembling . . .'

The Tragic Actress felt ice again in the roots of her hair, as though the soul of the blind woman were entering her again.

'At the end of the Prelude, the impetus of chromatic movements expresses that rising joy, that urge for happiness. Listen! Just listen! . . . Isn't it marvellous? I was working this morning, Fosca . . . And now my own melody is taking shape up there in the sky . . . We must surely be blessed!'

A spirit of life was flowing through the loneliness, powerful hopes were disturbing the silence. It was as though some natural desire to rise upwards were passing like an awakening or like the announcement of some great return over the unmoving lines, the empty horizon, the watery flatness and the low-lying land. The woman gave up her whole soul to it, like a leaf in a whirlwind, and she was swept towards the heights of love and faithfulness. But the young man was seized by a feverish impatience to act, by his haste to go on writing, by his need to complete his task. His capacity to work seemed to be increasing. He thought of the fullness of the hours to come. He saw the concrete details of his work, the heap of pages, the size of the musical score, the variety of things needing to be done, the wealth of material able to receive rhythm. Likewise, he saw the Roman hillside, the rising construction, the harmony of cut stones, the builders intent on laying bricks, the watchful task-master in charge of the building, the great walls of the Vatican against the Theatre of Apollo, the Holy City below. Smilingly, he recalled the image of the little man in charge of the work in papal magnificence; he greeted the bloodless, hook-nosed image of the Roman prince who, not betraying his ancient name, was raising an harmonious Temple to the Rebirth of the Arts that had illuminated the strong lives of his ancestors with beauty, using gold accumulated through centuries of nepotism and plunder.

'In one week's time, Fosca, my Prelude will be finished, if grace stays with me! Then I shall try it out with the orchestra straight away. I shall probably go to Rome for that. Antimo della Bella is even more impatient than I am. There is a letter from him practically every morning. I think my presence in Rome is necessary for a few days, to ensure there are no mistakes in building the Theatre, too. Antimo says that they are talking about demolishing the ancient stone steps that go up to the Janiculum from the Corsini gardens! I don't know if you can recall the place. The road that leads to the theatre runs under the Arch of Septimus, bends round the side of the Corsini Palace, through the gardens and on to the foot of the hill. The hill itself – do you remember it? – is all green, covered with tiny fields, canes, cypresses, plane trees, laurels and holm-oaks; it looks like a sacred woodland, crowned by tall Italian pines. On the slopes there is a veritable forest of holm-oaks watered by underground streams. There is a wealth of living waters all over the hill. To the left is the huge Paoline fountain, and below is the dark patch of the Parrasian wood, the ancient home of the Arcadians. There is a flight of stone steps, divided into two branches by a series of large, overflowing basins, which goes up to a flat piece of ground opening on to two avenues of laurels which are truly worthy of leading men to poetry and positively Apollonian. Could anyone imagine a more magnificent entrance? Centuries have shrouded it in mystery. The stone of the steps, the balustrades, the basins and the statues compete in roughness with the bark of the ancient plane trees that old age has made hollow. All you can hear is bird-song, the splashing of fountains and the murmuring of leaves. Yes, and I believe that poets and simple hearts can hear the pulse of the Hamadryads there, and the breath of Pan . . .'

The heavenly chorus was tirelessly rising and rising, never wavering or pausing, filling every space with itself, like an immense desert, like infinite light. In the sleepy lagoon, the impetuous melody was creating an illusion of a universal desire to follow the ascension, rising out of the water, the sand, the grass, the mist and all things of nature. All those things that had seemed to be lifeless were now breathing deeply, possessed of a feeling soul and a desire to speak.

'Listen!'

The images of Life evoked by the Poet, and the ancient names of immortal energies circulating in the Universe, and the desire of mankind to transcend the circle of their daily torment to seek comfort in the splendour of Idealism, and the wishes and hopes and daring and effort in that place of prayer and forgetfulness, within sight of the humble island on which the Bridegroom of Poverty had left his footprints, were freed from the shadow of Death by the power of that melody alone.

'Doesn't it seem like the frenzied joy of an attack?'

The squalid shores, the crumbling stones, the putrefying roots, the traces of works destroyed, the smell of decay, the funereal cypress trees, the black crosses, all reminded him in vain of the same words spoken by the statues with their stone mouths beside the river. Stronger than all those signs, only that song of freedom and victory could touch the heart of the man who wanted to create with joy. 'Forward! Higher, ever higher!'

And Perdita's heart, purified from all cowardice, ready for any trial, seconded the rising hymn and promised itself again to life. As she had done in that distant hour of nocturnal passion, the woman repeated the words: 'Let me serve! Let me serve!'

The boat went into a canal enclosed between two green banks, which reached the line of sight so perfectly that the countless numbers of reeds could be seen, and the new ones could be distinguished by their lighter colour.

Praised be, my Lord, for our sister, Mother Earth,
who nourishes and governs us
and brings forth divers fruits with coloured flowers,
and grass.

From the fullness of her soul, the woman considered the love of the Poor Friar for all things in creation. Such was her abundance, that she was looking round at every living thing to worship it. She was beginning to see again with the eyes of a.child, and all those things were reflected in her gaze as though in calm waters; some even seemed to have returned from her most distant past, so that she would recognize them again, and were appearing to her in unexpected apparitions. When the wood touched the landing stage, she was astonished that they had arrived so soon.

'Do you want to disembark, or would you rather go back?' asked Stelio, coming to himself again. She hesitated at first, because her hand was in his, and the separation might seem like a lessening of the sweetness. 'Yes,' she answered, smiling. 'Let us walk a little on this grass too.' They landed on the island of San Francesco. A few young cypress trees timidly welcomed them. No human face appeared. The invisible throng was filling the wastes with its song of praise. The mist was breaking up and condensing into clouds as the sun went down.

'We have walked on so much grass, have we not, Stelio?'

He said: 'But now we have to climb the rock face.'

She said: 'It can be climbed, however hard it may be.'

He was surprised by the unusual joyfulness in her voice. He looked at her, and saw intoxication in her lovely eyes. 'Why,' he said, 'do we feel so happy and so free on this desolate island?'

'Do you know?'

'This is a sad pilgrimage for most people. Those who come here, leave with the taste of death in their mouths.'

She said: 'We are in a state of grace.'

He said: 'Those who have most hope, live most.'

She said: 'Those who love most, hope most.' The rhythm of the heavenly song was still pulling their ideal essences towards it.

He said: 'How beautiful you are!'

A sudden blush coloured her passionate face. She stopped, breathing heavily. She closed her eyes. She said, in a choked voice: 'There is a gust of warm air. Didn't you feel a rush of heat out there on the water at times?' She breathed in the air. 'It is like the scent of new-mown hay. Can you smell it?'

'It's the smell of the banks of seaweed that are being uncovered by the tide.'

'Look at those beautiful fields!'

'That is Vignole. And over there is the Lido. And that is the island of Sant' Erasmo.'

The sun had cast off its veils and was now embracing the estuary. The dampness of the emerging banks was like the brightness of flowers. The shadows of the little cypress trees were lengthening and turning blue.

'I am sure,' she said, 'that somewhere close by there are almond trees in blossom. Let us go along the shore.' She threw her head back, with one of those spontaneous gestures of hers that seemed to be breaking some bond or freeing her of some burden. 'Wait!' And hastily pulling out the two long pins that kept her hat in place, she uncovered her head. She went back to the landing stage and threw the

shining object into the gondola. She returned lightly to her
beloved, running her fingers through her mass of hair, to let
the air flow through it and the sun shine on it. She seemed
to feel a great sense of relief, as though her breathing were
easier.

'Were your wings restricted?' said Stelio, laughing. And
he looked at the rough waves that had been made not by
any comb but by the storm.

'Yes, even the slightest weight troubles me. If I were
not afraid of being thought bizarre, I should always go out
bareheaded. But when I see the trees, I simply can't resist.
My hair remembers that it descends from a savage species
and wants to breathe in its own way, especially in lonely
places . . .' She was talking cheerfully and openly, walking
across the grass with a swift, undulating movement. Stelio
remembered the day in the Gradenigo Gardens when she
had seemed like a lovely, tawny greyhound.

'Oh look, there's a monk.' The friar in charge was coming
to meet them, and greeted them affably. He offered to show
the man round the monastery, but pointed out that the rules
of his order forbade his female companion from entering.

'Shall I go in?' said Stelio, looking at his beloved, who
smiled at him.

'Yes, do!'

'You'll be here on your own.'

'Then I shall stay on my own.'

'I shall bring you a splinter from a sacred pine tree.' He
followed the Franciscan under the little portico with its
beamed ceiling, from which swallows' empty nests were
hanging. Before he crossed the threshold, he turned to wave
to his beloved. The door closed.

OH BLESSED SOLITUDE!
OH SOLITARY BLESSEDNESS!

Then the woman's thoughts were suddenly transformed,
just as the change of stops immediately alters all the notes
in an organ. The horror of absence, the worst of all evils,

294

struck that soul in love. Her beloved was no longer there, she could no longer hear his voice or feel his breathing, she could no longer touch his firm, soft hands. She could no longer see him living, could no longer see light, shadow, air and the life of the world in harmony with his life. 'What if he never comes back, what if that door never opens again!' It could not happen. Of course he would come back through the door in a few minutes, and she would take him back into her eyes and into her blood. But in a few days, he would disappear just like that, just like that, and first the plain, then the mountain, then more plains and mountains and rivers, and then the straits and the ocean, an infinite space that cries and weeping could never overcome would lie between her and his forehead, his eyebrows, his lips. The image of the brutal city, black with coal and bristling with arms filled the gentle island; the thud of sledge-hammers, the creaking of winches, the pounding of machines, the great groaning of iron obliterated the melody of springtime. In contrast to each of those simple things, the grass, the sand, the water, the seaweed, the lightest feather that was falling from above, perhaps from some tiny singing throat, were those streets flooded with people, the houses with thousands of deformed eyes, full of fevers that destroy sleep, the theatres filled with men breathing, who are surprised enough to relax for just an hour their desires that are so fiercely aimed at fighting for gain. She saw once more her face and her name on walls defiled by the leprosy of advertising, on placards carried by stupefied bearers, on great factory bridges, on the sides of swift-moving vehicles, high up, low down, everywhere.

'Here you are! Look! A sprig of almond! The almond tree in the monastery garden is in flower, it's in the second cloister near the grotto of the holy pine. And you knew that!'

Her beloved was running towards her, as happy as a small child, followed by the smiling monk who was carrying a bunch of thyme. 'Here you are! What a marvel!'

She was trembling as she took the branch, and tears veiled her sight.

'You knew that!'

He noticed the sudden brightness between her eyelashes, something soft and silvery, a glistening, moving wetness that made the whites of her eyes look like the petals of a flower. Then, above all things in that beloved person, he loved to distraction the delicate signs that ran from the corners of her eyes towards her temples, and the dark little veins that made her eyelids look like violets, and the curve of her cheeks, and her tired chin and everything that would never blossom again, all the shadows in her passionate face.

'Oh, Father,' she said with an air of gaiety that concealed her anguish. 'Won't Christ's Poor Friar in paradise shed tears for this torn-off branch?'

The monk smiled with witty indulgence. 'When he saw the tree,' he answered, 'this good gentleman did not even give me time enough to open my mouth. He already had the branch in his hand, and all I could say was Amen. But the almond tree is wealthy enough.' He was cheerful and placid, with a crown of hair that was still almost all black around his tonsure, a refined olive face and two great hazel eyes that sparkled as brightly as topazes. 'Here is some sweet-smelling thyme,' he added, offering her the bunch of herbs. A choir of youthful voices singing a Response could be heard. 'Those are novices. We have fifteen of them.'

He walked with the visitors to the meadow that extended behind the monastery. Standing on the shore, at the foot of a cypress tree that had been struck by lightning, the kindly friar showed them the fertile islands, praising their abundance, listing the varieties of fruit that grew there, praising the best ones in their different seasons and pointing out the boats sailing towards the Rialto with fresh produce.

'Praise be, my Lord, for our sister, Mother Earth!' said the woman with the flowering branch. The monk was sensitive to the beauty of that female voice and was silent.

Tall cypresses surrounded the pious meadow, and four of the most ancient ones were marked by lightning, leafless and quite hollow. Their tops were completely still, the only shapes to rise up out of the supine flatness of the land and the water that ran on the same level out to the far horizon. Not even the slightest breath of wind ruffled the endless mirror. The depths full of seaweed were transparent as though filled with treasures, the marsh reeds shone like amber rods, the exposed sandbanks imitated the changing colours of mother-of-pearl, the mud was like the opaline softness of jellyfish. Enchantment, as profound as any ecstasy, was making the waste land blessed. The song of the winged creatures was still going on in invisible places, but it seemed to be finally sounding fainter in that holy silence.

'In the hills in Umbria, at this time of year,' said the man who had injured the almond tree in the monastery, 'a bundle of cut branches is placed like spoils at the foot of every olive tree, and they seem even more gentle because the bundle hides the strength of their twisted roots. Saint Francis floats past in mid-air and with his finger he soothes the wounds made by the shears.'

The monk crossed himself and took his leave. 'Praise be to Jesus Christ!'

The visitors watched him walk away through the shadows cast across the little meadow by the cypress trees. 'He is at peace,' said the woman. 'Don't you think so, Stelio? There was such great peacefulness in his face and in his voice. Just look at the way he walks.' A band of sun and a band of shadow touched the monk's robe and tonsure alternately.

'He gave me a splinter of the pine tree,' said Stelio. 'I shall send it to Sofia who has such devotion for Saint Francis. Here it is. It no longer smells of resin. Smell it.'

For Sofia's sake, she kissed the relic. His good sister's lips would touch the place her own lips had touched. 'Send it to her.'

They walked on for a while in silence, their heads bent, in the direction the man at peace had taken, beside the cypress trees laden with berries, towards the landing stage.

'Don't you want to see her again?' Foscarina asked her lover, with a timid shiver.

'Yes, very much.'

'And your mother . . .'

'Yes. My heart goes out to her, waiting for me every day.'

'Don't you want to go home?'

'Yes, perhaps I shall go back.'

'When?'

'I don't know yet. But I do want to see my mother and Sofia again. I want that very much, Foscarina.'

'Then why don't you go? What is keeping you here?'

He took her hand, which was hanging loosely by her side. They walked on like that. As the slanting rays of the sun shone on their right cheeks, they saw their linked shadows moving together over the grass.

'When you were describing the hills of Umbria just now,' said the woman, 'perhaps you were thinking of the hills of your own lands. That image of olive trees after pruning was not new to me. I remember you telling me about the pruning one day . . . In no other labour can the man of the soil find such a profound sense of the silent life of the tree. When he stands before a pear tree or an apple tree or a peach with his pruning knife or his shears, which are meant to strengthen the tree's forces but which could cause its death, then the genial spirit of divination rises up in him, from all the wisdom he has acquired in his communion with the earth and the sky. The tree is at its most delicate time, when its sensitivity is returning to life, flowing into the buds that are swelling and about to open. The man with his crude metal must regulate the balance of the mysterious rising of the sap! The tree is there, still untouched, knowing nothing of Hesiod or Virgil, in labour to bring forth its blossom and its fruit; every branch in the air is as much alive as an artery in the arm of the man about to prune it. Where will the cut fall? Will the sap heal the wound? . . . That was how you talked to me one day, about your orchard. I remember. You told me that all the cuts had to face north, so that the sun would not find them . . .' She was speaking as she had on that distant November evening, when the

298

young man had come to her breathless from the great gale, after he had borne his hero.

He smiled. And he let himself be led by her dear hand. He could smell the scent of the flowering branch, which was like slightly sour milk. 'That's true!' he said. 'And Laimo used to prepare San Fiacre's ointment, pounding it in a mortar, and Sofia would bring him stronger bandages to bind up the larger wounds, after they were dressed...' He could see the peasant on his knees, mixing cow dung, clay and barley husks in a stone mortar, following the rules of ancient knowledge. 'But in ten days' time,' he added, 'the hill that you can see from the sea will be like a fresh, pink cloud. Sofia has written to remind me of that... Has she appeared to you again?'

'She is with us now.'

'She is leaning out of the window now, looking at the sea which is turning purple, and Mother is with her beside the sill, saying: "I wonder if Stelio is on that boat out there in the mouth of the estuary, waiting for a wind? He promised me he would come back by sea on a fishing boat when we least expected him." And her heart is aching.'

'Why disappoint her so?'

'You're right, Fosca. I can live away from her for months and months and feel that my life is complete. But then, well, there comes a time when nothing in the world matters to me as much as her eyes, and there is a part of me that can never be consoled. I've heard the sailors from the Tyrrhenian Sea call the Gulf of Venice the Adriatic. This evening I feel that my home is in the Gulf and it seems nearer to me.'

They had reached the landing stage. They turned to look back at the island of prayer which was lifting up its cypress trees beseechingly.

'That is the canal of the Tre Porti over there, which leads out to the open sea!' said the homesick man, who could see himself on the deck of a fishing boat within sight of his tamarisk groves and myrtles.

They went on board. They were silent for a long time.

299

In the meantime the melody descended faintly over the archipelago. Just as the light in the sky was impregnated by the water, so the melody from the skies rested upon the earth. But Burano and Torcello were like two beached galleons against the brightness in the west. Clouds were forming into battalions over towards the Dolomites.

'Now that the shape of your work is complete, what you need is peace for your writing,' said the woman, gently continuing her persuasion, while her soul trembled in her breast. 'Haven't you always been able to write at home? You will never be able to quieten the anxiety that chokes you anywhere else. I know that.'

He said: 'That's true. When the wild urge for glory comes over us, we believe that the conquest of art is like laying siege to a city with mighty ramparts, and that shouts and trumpet blasts accompany the bravery of an attack. Instead, what really matters is for the work to develop in austere silence, what counts is slow, indomitable tenaciousness, hard, pure solitude and the absolute devotion of flesh and spirit to the Ideal that we want to bring to life amongst men forever as a conquering force.'

'Yes, you know that!' The woman's eyes filled with tears at those insensitive words, in which she could feel the depth of male passion, the heroic need of moral domination, the firm resolve to go beyond himself and force his destiny onwards relentlessly. 'You know that!'

She felt the shudder that the spectacle of cruelty produces, and before that living will everything else seemed futile; the tears that had veiled her sight when he offered her the blossom seemed weak and feminine in comparison to the ones that now rose to her lashes and which alone were worthy of being tasted by her lover.

'Then go home to your own sea and your own land! Light your lamp again with oil from your own olive trees!'

His lips were tightly clenched, and there was a frown between his brows.

'Your kind sister will come once again to lay a blade of grass on a difficult page.'

He bowed his head, troubled by thought.

'You will find rest as you speak to Sofia at her window, and perhaps you will see the flocks go by again, on their way to the mountains from the plain.'

The sun was about to touch the gigantic acropolis of the Dolomites. The battalion of clouds was in disarray, as though it were in the thick of battle, pierced by countless gleaming darts and steeped in glorious blood. The water was extending the vast battle that was raging around the impregnable towers. The melody had dissolved in the shadows of those islands that were already a long way off. The whole estuary was mantled in a dark warlike magnificence as though dozens of banners were flying over it. The silence was waiting for the blare of imperial trumpets.

He said, softly, after a long pause: 'What if she asks me about the fate of the Virgin who was reading Antigone's lament?'

The woman started.

'What if she asks me about the love of the brother who is searching the tombs?'

The woman was afraid of that phantom.

'And what if the page on which she places her blade of grass is the one in which the fearful soul tells of his desperate, hidden struggle against the ghastly evil?'

The woman could find no words in her sudden dismay. They were both silent, and they stared at the sharp points of the distant chain that were flaming as though they had just emerged from primeval fire. The sight of that eternal, desolate grandeur stirred in their two spirits a sentiment of mysterious fatality, an almost indefinable terror which they could neither overcome nor understand. Venice was overshadowed by that mass of blazing porphyry; she lay on the waters wreathed in a violet veil, from which her marble stems rose up, shaped by man to hold the bells that give the sign for daily prayer. But the daily tasks and prayers of men, the ancient city tired from having lived too long, the ravaged marble and worn-out bells, all those things oppressed by the weight of memories, all those perishable things were rendered humble in comparison with the tremendous blazing Alps that tore at the sky with their thousand unyielding spikes, a vast, solitary city that was waiting, perhaps, for a new race of Titans.

After a long silence, Stelio Effrena asked abruptly: 'What about you?' She did not answer.

The bells of St Mark's rang out the angelic Salutation, and their powerful tolling faded into drawn-out waves over the still crimson lagoon which they were leaving in the power of shadow and death. Bronze voices replied from San Giorgio Maggiore, San Giorgio dei Greci, San Giorgio degli Schiavoni, San Giovanni in Bragora, San Moisè, the Salute, the Redentore and all the rest, through the entire domain of the Evangelist, from the farthest towers of the Madonna dell'Orto, San Giobbe, Sant'Andrea, and blended into a single great chorus, spreading a single vast invisible dome of metal over the silent collection of stones and water, that seemed to be in communication by its vibrations with the twinkling of the first stars.

They both shivered when the gondola slid into the dampness of the dark canal, sailing under the bridge that overlooks the island of San Michele, brushing past the black gondola cabins putrefying beside the decaying walls. Other voices replied from nearby bell-towers, from San Lazzaro, San Canciano, San Giovanni e Paolo, Santa Maria dei Miracoli, Santa Maria del Pianto, and the rumbling above their heads was so strong that they thought they could feel it down to the roots of their hair, like a shiver through their own flesh.

'Is that you, Daniele?'

It seemed to Stelio that he could see Daniele Glauro standing by the door to his house, on the Fondamenta Sanudo.

'Yes, Stelio, I was waiting for you!' cried the agitated voice through the whirlwind of sound. 'Richard Wagner is dead!'

* * *

Something important had gone from the world.

The nomadic woman armed herself with courage and prepared her *viaticum* for the journey. Great inspiration for noble hearts was derived from the hero, lying in his coffin. She was able to receive it and transform it into action and into thoughts of life.

Now it happened that her lover came upon her as she was gathering together her favourite books, the special little things from which she could not bear to be parted, the pictures that had the powers of dream and consolation for her.

'What are you doing?' he asked her.

'I am preparing to leave.' She saw his face change, but she did not falter.

'Where are you going?'

'A long way away. I am crossing the Atlantic.'

He turned a little pale. Then at once he doubted her; he thought that she was not telling the truth, that she was only testing him, or that her decision was not final and she was expecting him to change her mind. The unexpected disappointment on the shore at Murano had left its traces in his heart.

'Did you take this decision all of a sudden?'

She was straightforward, sure and ready. 'No, it was not sudden,' she answered. 'My idleness has lasted a long time, and I have the responsibility for my company upon my shoulders. While I wait for the Theatre of Apollo to open, and for *The Triumph of Man* to be finished, I shall go and take my leave of the Barbarians. I shall work for our marvellous undertaking. A lot of gold will be needed to bring the treasures of Mycenae back again! And everything must be exceptionally splendid in your work. I don't want the mask of Cassandra to be made of some base metal . . . I particularly want to find a way to realize your wish that for the first three days the people shall have free access to the Theatre, and that this practice will continue one day a week permanently. That belief is helping me to go away from you. Time flies. We must all be in our places, with our energy at the ready, when the time comes. I shall not fail you. I hope you will be pleased with your beloved. I am going to work and, naturally, that is somewhat harder for me to do this time than on previous occasions. But you, my poor, darling child, what a burden you have to bear! We are asking so much of you! We are expecting such great things from you! Oh, you know that . . .'

She had started bravely, in a tone that had at times seemed almost cheerful, trying to appear as she most wanted to be above all else: a good, faithful instrument at the service of a genius, a virile, enthusiastic companion. But occasional waves of repressed emotion kept escaping, and would rise up into her throat and her voice. Her pauses became longer, her hands that were wandering over books and relics became uncertain. 'May everything, always, be beneficial to your work! That is all that matters, and the rest is nothing! May our hearts look upwards!' She shook back her head, with its two wild wings, and reached out both hands to her lover. He gripped them, looking pale and serious. In her dear eyes, that were like turbulent water, he saw the same flash of beauty that had dazzled him one evening in that room, when the logs crackled and two great melodies had begun to unfold.

'I love you, and I believe in you,' he said. 'I shall never fail you, and you will never fail me. Something will be born from us that will be stronger than life itself.'

She said: 'Melancholy!'

On the table in front of her were her familiar books, some with corners of pages turned down, others with notes in the margins, some containing leaves or flowers or blades of grass between the pages, tokens of grief that had asked for and been granted the consolation of enlightenment or forgetfulness. All her favourite little things were laid out before her, strange, various, nearly all quite valueless: a doll's foot, a sacred silver heart, a little ivory compass, a watch with no face, a tiny iron lantern, an odd earring, a flint, a key, a seal, other trivia; but they were all made holy by revered memories, animated by some superstitious belief, touched by the finger of love or death, relics that spoke just to one soul, telling her about tenderness and cruelty, war and truce, hope and despair. In front of her were images that aroused thoughts and inspired reflection, pictures to whom the artists had confided some secret confession, complex networks of signs in which they had concealed some enigma, simple lines that imparted peace just like the sight of a horizon, arcane allegories that veiled some truth that, like the sun, could not be gazed on by human eyes.

'Look,' she said to her beloved, showing him an old print. 'You know this well.' They both knew it well, but they leaned over it together to look at it again, and it seemed as new as music that always gives a different answer whenever questioned. It was by Albrecht Dürer.

The great earthly Angel with the eagle's wings, the sleepless Spirit, crowned by patience, was sitting on bare stone, with his elbow resting on his knee, his fist supporting his chin, with a book on his knee and a compass in his other hand. At his feet, coiled like a serpent, lay his faithful greyhound, the dog that had hunted alongside man since the dawn of time. By his side, crouching almost like a bird on the edge of a mill-stone, slept a sorrowful child, clutching the stylus and the tablet on which the first words of science were to be written. Around him were spread the tools of human endeavour, and over his watchful head, near the tip of a wing, the silent sands of Time ran through an hourglass. In the background was the sea, with its bays and its ports and its lighthouses, calm and indomitable, and across the sun, setting with all the glory of a rainbow, flew a twilight bat with words of revelation written on its wings. The sleepless Spirit, crowned with patience, had constructed those ports and lighthouses and cities. He had cut the stones for those towers, chopped down pine trees for the ships, tempered the iron for every battle. He himself had imposed upon Time the instrument that measures it. Seated, not to rest but to contemplate another task, he was gazing at Life with his powerful eyes, shining with the light of a free soul. Silence rose up to him from all the forms around him,

305

except one. Only the voice of the roaring fire could be heard in the furnace, under the crucible where sublime matter was about to generate some new power to destroy evil or produce a law. And thus did the great earthly Angel with the eagle's wings, by whose steel-clad side hung the keys that open and close, answer those who questioned him: 'The sun is setting. Light, which is born in heaven, is dying in the sky. Each day is ignorant of the light of other days. But night is one, and its shadow is on all faces and its blindness is in all eyes, except on the face and in the eyes of the man who keeps his own fire blazing to strengthen his own force. I know that the living are as the dead, the awakened are as the sleeping, the young are as the old, because the one changes into the other, and every change has as its equal companions both pain and joy. I know that the harmony of the Universe is made of discord, as in the lyre and the bow. I know that I am, and I am not; and that there is only one way, high or low. I know the stench of putrefaction and the countless diseases that are linked to human nature. And yet, beyond my knowledge, I continue to carry out my tasks, both manifest and secret. I see some perish while I endure, I see others that must remain eternally lovely and immune to all ills, no longer mine, although born from my worst evils. I see all things changing before the fire like fortunes before gold. One thing alone is constant: my courage. I never sit down, except to rise again.'

The young man put his arm around his beloved's waist. They went across to the window like that, without saying a word. They saw the distant skies, the trees, the domes, the towers, the far-off lagoon across which the face of twilight was bending, the peaceful, blue Euganean Hills like the wings of the earth folded to rest in the evening. They turned towards each other. They looked into the depths of one another's eyes. Then they kissed, as though to seal an unspoken pact. Something important had gone from the world.

*   *   *

306

Stelio Effrena asked the widow of Richard Wagner if the two young Italians who had carried the unconscious hero one November evening from a boat to the shore, together with four of their companions, might be granted the honour of carrying the bier from the chamber of death to the boat and from the boat to the hearse. That much had been granted.

It was the sixteenth of February. It was one hour past midday. Stelio Effrena, Daniele Glauro, Francesco de Lizo, Baldassare Stampa, Fabio Molza and Antimo della Bella were waiting in the hall of the palace. The latter had come from Rome, having managed to bring with him two artisans, who were working on the Theatre of Apollo, so that they could bring to the funeral bunches of laurels gathered on the Janiculum.

They were waiting without speaking, not looking at one another, each one overwhelmed by the beating of his own heart. All that could be heard was the gentle slapping of water on the steps beside that great door, where on the candelabra of the doorposts were carved the two words: DOMUS PACIS. The oarsman, who had been dear to the hero, came down to call them. His eyes were burning with tears in his faithful manly face. Stelio Effrena went first and his companions followed him. They went up the stairs and into a low, poorly lit room where there was a sorrowful smell of flowers and ointments. They waited a few minutes. The other door opened. They went into the next room one by one. They all turned pale, one after the other.

The corpse was there, sealed in its crystal coffin, and standing beside it was the woman with the snow-white face. The mouth of the second coffin, made of polished metal, gleamed on the floor beside it. The six bearers stood around the body, waiting for the signal. The silence was intense, and they did not stir, but sudden grief assailed their souls like a storm and shook them to the very roots.

They were all staring at the One, chosen by Life and Death. An infinite smile lit up the face of the prostrate hero, as infinite and as distant as a rainbow in a glacier, as

307

the gleam of the sea, as a halo around a star. Their eyes could not bear it, but their hearts, with wonder and fear that made them holy, believed they were being granted the revelation of a divine secret. The woman with the snow-white face made a slight gesture, standing rigidly as any statue in the same position. Then the six companions moved towards the body; they held out their arms and summoned up their strength. Stelio Effrena took his place at the front, with Daniele Glauro at the rear, as they had done before. They lifted the weight together, at a low command from their leader. Their eyes were dazzled, as though suddenly a patch of sunlight were passing through a crystal. Baldassare Stampa burst into sobs. The same knot tightened in all their throats. The coffin wavered, then descended; it went into the metal container as though into a suit of armour. The six companions remained prostrate around it. They hesitated before lowering the cover, fascinated by the infinite smile. Hearing a slight rustle, Stelio Effrena looked up: he saw the snow-white face bending over the corpse, a superhuman image of love and grief. The moment seemed to last forever. The woman disappeared.

The cover was lowered, and now they took up the increased burden. They carried it out of the room and down the stairs, very slowly. Swept by sublime anguish, they could see their fraternal faces reflected in the metal of the coffin.

The funeral barge was waiting outside the door. The pall was spread over the coffin. The six companions waited, bareheaded, for the family to come out. They came out close together. The widow went by veiled, but the splendour of her appearance stayed in their memory forever. The procession was a short one. The funeral barge went on ahead, then came the widow with his closest relations, and then the boat with the young men. The sky above the great pathway of water and stone was overcast. The profound silence was worthy of the Man who had transformed the powers of the Universe into infinite song for the benefit of men. A flock of doves flew down from the Scalzi marbles with lightning speed, over the bier and across the canal, wreathing the green dome of San Simeone.

A silent crowd of devoted admirers was waiting at the landing stage. Great wreaths scented the ashen air. They could hear the water slapping against the curved prows.

The six companions removed the coffin from the barge and carried it on their shoulders to the carriage that was waiting on the iron road. The admirers came forward and laid their wreaths on the bier. No one said a word. Then the two artisans with their bundles of laurels gathered on the Janiculum stepped forward. They were powerful, well-built men, chosen from the strongest and the finest, and seemed to be shaped in the ancient mould of the Roman race. They were calm and serious, with the wild freedom of the Campagna in their bloodshot eyes. Their experienced features, their low foreheads, their short, curly hair, their strong jaws, their bull-like necks recalled the profiles of consuls of old. Their attitude, free from any servile obsequiousness, made them worthy of their task. The six companions in turn, equal in their enthusiasm, took branches from the bundles and spread them over the hero's coffin.

Those Latin laurel branches were the most noble of all, and had been cut in the wood on the hill where in ancient times the eagles had been wont to fly down bringing omens, and where in more recent, yet marvellous times, the legionaries of the Liberator had shed rivers of blood for the glory of Italy. The branches were strong, brown and straight, the leaves were hard, strongly veined, with sharp edges, green as the bronze in the fountains, rich with the scent of triumph. And they travelled towards the Bavarian hillside still slumbering in the frost, while in the light of Rome their noble trunks were already sprouting new buds to the murmur of hidden springs.

Settignano di Desiderio
the XIII of February MDCCCC